**Who is fal**



I watched the last ma

recognize him at an angle, but dead on, there was no mistaking it. The man from the key party, Nathan, was the last man to walk into the room. I gasped, dropping everything in my hands out of pure horror.

I'd recognize my mystery man anywhere. I'd scanned almost everywhere I've been for months, hoping to see him amongst the other strangers. I knew his first name, how sexy he sounded when he came, what his cum tasted like, and now that he worked for the New Jersey office of the same company I worked at for the last six years. I stared in disbelief as he walked back into my life, waving at the room of his co-workers with a beaming smile I wish I saw every day.

He was devastatingly handsome in daylight, wearing a three-piece suit, and his brown eyes were actually a striking amber shade. I missed seeing him clearly the last time around. His dark brown hair was up in spikes again, and his skin looked pale against the dark gray suit.

It didn't matter how pale he looked. My desire for a man I barely knew seized my body and stopped me dead in my tracks.

# Falling for Two

*Falling Book One*

by

Melanie Hoffer

This is a work of fiction. Names, characters, places, and incidents are either the product of the author's imagination or are used fictitiously, and any resemblance to actual persons living or dead, business establishments, events, or locales, is entirely coincidental.

**Falling for Two**



Contact Information: info@thewildrosepress.com

Cover Art by *Diana Carlile*

The Wild Rose Press, Inc.
PO Box 708
Adams Basin, NY 14410-0708

Visit us at www.thewildrosepress.com

Publishing History
First Scarlet Rose Edition, 2019
Print ISBN 978-1-5092-2708-2
Digital ISBN 978-1-5092-2709-9

Published in the United States of America

**Dedication**

To my husband, Craig. Love you always.

# Prologue

The knock on the door startled me, but only at first. I knew someone would come into the room. I knew what was supposed to happen next.

My hands were lightly bound behind my chair and a masquerade mask concealed the top of my face. I sat naked under the short skirt and my breasts were a few buttons away from being bared. It was all part of the game. A shortcut to getting laid.

The anticipation hiked up my arousal a few notches a second. I didn't doubt you could see my perked up nipples through my white button down shirt. I was ready for the next couple minutes and needed them desperately.

I didn't know what made me finally surrender to be a part of Lucy's swinger poly games, especially her infamous key party game. It sounded simple enough. Grab a numbered key from a chosen fantasy bowl, then open the same numbered door and make whatever you want of it.

My gut told me I'd never muster the nerve to open a door, therefore, I chose to be the fantasy.

There was supposed to be some secrecy to this game, but you could only keep your identity unknown for so long with Lucy's latest crew of "friends." Lucky for me, I'd met them all several times and managed to remain under the radar. No one remembered me. I sighed at my self-inflicted stab to my bruised confidence. I actually worried who was going to walk through that door.

*Why did he knock?* He knew I wouldn't be decent. *He, crap, who will he be?* Hopefully, it wasn't the master of ceremonies Kelsey or Tom. I hated Tom. He was always extra prick-like every time he introduced himself and shook my hand. I truly hated something specific about every man in the crew.

*Fuck, I'm going to psych myself out of this mess.*

The door opened and a man I'd never seen before appeared in the light. He neglected to wear the cheap black mask assigned to the men. I gasped which probably gave away that I could see him. I hope he knew this wasn't going to be a full stranger fantasy.

He was tall, about six feet, with dark brown hair spiked haphazardly in the front. I couldn't tell his eye color, but fuck, he was hot. The dark room enhanced his chiseled jaw and natural contours in his cheeks. He wore an open dress shirt over a black T-shirt and jeans. He was so gorgeous I swallowed my spit at least three times over.

This guy wasn't in the normal crew. *I know all of them even if they didn't know me.* He seemed hesitant as he inspected the room. There wasn't much in here. Only me, two chairs including the one I sat on, and a desk in the corner with candles to create the ambiance of the scene. It was sparse for what could possibly happen.

*Please don't get cold feet, Bri,* I thought. *You can do this. He's someone new.*

The mystery man shut the door and gazed over at me. He licked his lips and took a long breath out. *Was he nervous? Did I not look sexy enough for him?* A million thoughts raced through my head as he walked over to me.

"Hi, welcome to door sixteen. I'm yours," I said Lucy's scripted words.

"Wow!" His voice came out as a high squeak. He cleared his throat and whispered, "You're here for me?"

"I think you have one of my dear friend's keys so yes, I'm here for you. You can come closer. I won't bite, I promise." I flirted. I cursed myself for sounding cheesy. After the first line, it was up to me to finish it. My nerves were getting to me and the courage I built up was bolting for the door.

"This is fucking crazy. I've never done anything like this before." He tilted his head to the side, peeking behind me. "Are your hands tied behind the chair?"

"Yes. I'm tied up, waiting to play."

"Don't tempt me here. There are too many things I'd want to do to you." He shrugged off his button down and draped it over the empty chair.

"You don't have to whisper. No one can hear us," I confirmed.

"I think my voice sounds sexier when I whisper. Can you see me?" He waved his hand in front of me.

"Yes, sorry. I couldn't do this without being able to see. Please don't let it change the fantasy."

He sat down on the chair opposite me. His inquisitive eyes were a deep brown and they roamed over the room again settling on me. "I wouldn't want you to be uncomfortable. Um…So…I'm not quite sure what to do. Do I tell you my name?"

"Only if you want to tell me. We can do whatever we want here," I said. He hadn't moved from the chair or said anything else so I continued. "You should take your pants off. Would you like me to put my mouth on your cock?"

I shocked myself. I had no idea where this brazen, sexually independent woman was coming from. Part of why my last relationship fell south was because we couldn't get our sex life to sync up. I kept telling myself it wasn't my fault. This woman always dwelled inside.

*Easier said than done.*

The gears of doubt turned in his gaze. He was thinking too much. I knew that feeling all too well.

"So, mystery man. Why don't you come over here and untie my hands to start with, okay?" I tried.

"I kind of liked you tied up, but all right. Can I touch you?" Finally, he spoke. His lips curled up in a side smile.

"You can do anything you'd like," I admitted. If anyone else had walked through that door, I would have quit already. This man, whoever he was, could be the right amount of perfect for this game.

He got up from the chair and adjusted the front of his jeans. *So he's attracted to me enough to get hard. Good boy, check one done.*

He walked around me and undid the simple knot around my hands. Relief and control washed over me. I had liked being tied up, but it wasn't what I wanted now. He returned to standing directly in front of me.

"Whisper me your name, please."

He answered when I sucked one of his fingers into my mouth. "Nathan."

I opened my legs wide on the chair and held back a moan at the feeling of being spread apart. I was still wet from the anticipation. Nathan stepped into the open space my legs created.

He lifted up his shirt, so I could get to his jeans. I undid the top button and pulled down his zipper. The outline of his cock strained against his blue boxers. I feathered my hand over his length and smiled at the audible shudder I earned from him. I smoothed my other hand under his shirt over the soft trail of hair on his flat stomach.

His jeans dropped around his ankles and his belt buckle cracked to the floor. I could smell his musk mixed with his cologne. He smelled so fucking good. There was no turning back now.

I glided my hands over the thin hair on his thighs to the top of his boxers and pulled them down. His cock flopped forward jutting out from between his legs. I was right. He was hard already. Nathan drew in a shaky breath as I slid my hand over the soft skin of the tip of his cock and twisted my wrist to the right.

"What's your name?" he asked, whispering again.

"Brianna," I answered quietly, peeking up at him. He placed his hand over mine and looked down with half-lidded eyes.

He moved his thumb over the top of my hand like a caress and guided my hand down his length. His cock was smooth all the way down to his buzzed happy trail. I had to taste him. I craved the feel of his hard flesh in my mouth.

When our hands reached his pelvis, I licked the head of his cock and his moan spurred me on more. I took him into my mouth, swirling my tongue under the rim of the tip. Our hands rested at his end, but I broke the connection and dragged my hand up his cock to meet my mouth.

I didn't take him down my throat, yet. I wanted to play with him. I wanted to make him feel good. I put my lips over my teeth and moved faster up and down, swirling my tongue each time. After a couple times, I sucked half of his cock into my mouth. He groaned and murmured yes repeatedly.

Nathan stepped closer and grabbed my hair. "Is this okay?"

I popped off his cock and dragged my lips up and down the sides. "You can pull my hair if you want. I like it. If it's too much I'll say stop."

Nathan threaded his hand through my hair, testing his grip. He gently pumped in and out of my mouth. A tremor of pleasure rolled through my body. I'd always loved going down on a man's cock, hearing him moan above me. It wasn't the power play, no; it was something else. Sucking Nathan's cock was making me wet. The pressure built and mini flares throughout my pussy turned me on more. I needed to relieve some of the buildup.

I stole a glance up at Nathan and was surprised to see him staring down at me. He watched me fuck his cock with my mouth. His mouth was slack, and his eyes glazed over. It caught me off guard to see such an enduring look from a stranger. My ex never gave me that look. Not even at three years in.

"Are you going to touch yourself? I want to see," Nathan said out of breath.

My hand left his cock and I just moved my mouth and tongue to keep fucking him. I scrunched my skirt to the side of my waist and bared my pussy to Nathan's gaze. I massaged my clit as he watched. He moaned and pumped faster into my mouth.

When he slowed down, I hollowed my cheeks, sucking on his tip.

"Please do that again! Yes!" Nathan shouted.

I teased him with a few flicks of my tongue then did it again. The back of his other hand caressed the side of my face. I stole another glance up at him. I saw exactly what I needed. Reassurance. He liked that. I was doing it right.

I could come any minute. It was such a hot blend of lust-filled fantasy I craved. I was sucking a stranger's cock and he actually liked it. I was so wet I moved from my clit down to my pussy and thrust my fingers inside. I moaned around his cock. I wished he was fucking me. I'd love to have this long smooth cock fuck me hard. I bet he would fill me up to the brim, and then I'd grind it out in his lap.

*Would we take it that far?*

I moved my skirt under my thigh, so Nathan could continue watching me finger myself and I returned to jerking him off.

I smoothed my fingers over his balls. He groaned, jerking hard into my mouth hitting the back of my throat. I almost gagged but he recouped fast moving back to his shallow thrusts in my mouth. His cock was completely bathed in my salvia from the tip to his pelvis. My hand moved down him so easily. With each stroke, Nathan's body trembled.

"Fuck. Please don't stop. You're going to make me come," Nathan pleaded. He thrust his hand into my shirt and gripped my breast hard. It was my turn to shout around him. I loved having my breasts squeezed and plumped. I sucked harder and that was all he needed to let go.

He thrust haphazardly, spurting his cum into my awaiting mouth. He tasted salty and sweet at the same time. I licked around his head trying to reach every drop.

His moans were the sexiest sound I had ever heard. He continued to taunt my breast too, prolonging the onslaught. He slowly pulled his cock from my mouth, dragging a whimper from him.

I looked up and his head was thrown back. I stroked my lasting saliva down his softening cock. He gripped my hand. "You're going to kill me if you keep that up. I'm too sensitive after I come. I'm sorry. I need a minute."

I smiled. At least he was being honest, and I had successfully made him come. Nathan staggered down to the empty chair. He slumped forward, forearms on his knees and took a few large breaths.

I stopped fingering myself when he came. I was almost there, but it wasn't enough. I pulled my skirt from under me letting it fall over my aching lap. I wasn't mad that I didn't finish. I was used to it. I wiped my hand with only my saliva on the side of my skirt.

I stood up and ruffled Nathan's hair. His gelled up spikes were softer than they looked. He didn't look up.

I walked over to the box of tissues. I grabbed two and wiped at my wetness lingering on my fingers. The chair moved behind me, and I heard the sound of rustling clothes. *Was he going to leave? Was that it?* I forgot what Lucy said to do after.

Nathan's hands slid over my hips and jerked me against him. The back of my head hit against his chest. At my five feet five inches, he had to be at least six feet tall. I reached behind me and gasped, grabbing a naked thigh.

Fuck, he hadn't pulled up his jeans; he took them off.

"Did you come, Brianna?" Nathan whispered into my ear, kissing down my neck. Each kiss sent a shiver down my spine.

I almost lied. I had faked so many orgasms in my life; an unfortunate skill I refined to an art. I pushed that urge aside as Nathan unzipped my tiny skirt. It fell to my feet and I stepped out of it without a thought. He kicked it against the wall. Nathan pushed gently at my back bending my body over the desk. My breath caught when my pussy met his naked hardening cock. Nathan slid the tip of his cock between the wetness clinging to my pussy.

"Oh yeah, baby. Answer me. Did you make yourself come before?" Nathan asked again.

He stopped moving, creating a small gap between us, as if my answer would be his motivation.

"No. I didn't come," I confessed. I dropped my forehead to the desk.

Nathan kissed the back of my neck. "I want to make you come. Can I fuck you?"

I didn't have to think twice. "Please."

Nathan retrieved a condom from his jean's pocket. He rolled the condom onto his cock faster than I thought possible. I was so wet Nathan slid inside me with a single thrust. We both cried out at the intensity of the feeling. This was way farther than I thought we'd go, but fuck, it felt amazing. He held onto my hips and began to thrust. I grabbed the edge of the desk to hold on as he picked up the pace, fucking me into the unrelenting desk.

"Shit. This isn't how I want to take you." He groaned, pulling out of me. I straightened up immediately, panicked, and turned around.

"I'm sorry I swear I've never done anything like this before. I under…" I didn't get a chance to finish my sentence because Nathan kissed me, banishing any doubt that he wanted to stop. His kiss hit me with the perfect amount of breathless pressure.

Without breaking the kiss, he pushed me back until my ass hit the desk. Our lips came apart with a loud pop. "Sit on the desk. Spread those long legs for me. I only wanted to be able to see you when I fuck you," Nathan explained.

*Where the fuck had this man been all my life?*

Nathan lifted me effortlessly onto the top of the desk. His cock perfectly aligned to my awaiting pussy. "Is your hot pussy still wet for me?" Nathan asked.

Words escaped me. I nodded my head fast up and down. Nathan found his nerve in this game and mine ran out the door.

"Fuck yeah, you're wet." He caressed and fingered me, finding his answer. I glanced down at his fingers glistening from me.

Nathan took his cock in his hand and speared it into my pussy. My back instantly bowed. Nathan's hands were there to keep me upright. He kissed me again and pounded into me fast and steady. His pelvis smacked my clit each time he thrust to the hilt. I tore my mouth away from his to breathe, moaning each pant.

We were cheek to cheek now. He trailed his tongue up my neck and I screamed into his ear. The lacey scrap of fabric threatened to fall from my face, but I didn't care. I grabbed onto the back of his shirt. We never finished undressing. I wished I could touch him skin to skin. He would feel perfect for fucking me into oblivion.

He reached down to rub my clit and I was done. My orgasm shot through me, radiating deep within my inner core. "I'm coming," I moaned. Nathan thrust faster, and I slammed my eyes shut. I couldn't stop moaning as my orgasm claimed me.

Nathan burrowed his face in my neck and shouted, "I'm coming too, baby."

His whole body shuddered, riding out his orgasm. Nathan slumped against me, wrapping both of his arms around my lower back, holding me close.

"That was fucking amazing," he said, removing his face from my neck.

I nodded unable to respond. My mouthy start was finished, and I was back down on earth. Nathan kissed me and pulled out of me slowly. He tried to end the kiss, but I kept it going. I planted a deep kiss goodbye on his irresistible lips.

"Thank you for everything, Nathan," I said, hopping off the desk. I picked up my discarded skirt. Somehow, my white button down shirt miraculously remained covering my boobs. I stepped into the skirt, zippered it up, and walked out the door.

# Chapter One

*Six months later.*

"Yes, I'll be there around seven-ish. I'm driving in this morning. The traffic is terrible on the Cross Bronx right now." The other New York City drivers were extra feisty this morning

"There's traffic everywhere today. I only got here a few minutes ago. I appreciate you driving in this morning, Bri. This is going to be a busy day," Paul said, energetic as if it were six at night, not six in the morning.

"No worries, Paul!" A car honked for no reason. I hated driving into the city. Today was going to be stressful enough and I had road rage as icebreaker. I should've woken up at four a.m. and taken the train.

"Thanks again. I don't fully understand how this whole limo thing got messed up. We use them every week. How could they forget our reservation?" Paul vented.

"Trust me, I know! Marcia triple confirmed the reservation. At least the back-up service came through last minute. The majority of the New Jersey branch will arrive at eleven a.m. The analysts will be in the second car, which might be delayed a few minutes. They wrote the opening presentation so I'm sure it'll be fine if they miss a little bit."

"Great. You really saved the day! Have you talked

to Lucy? Her flight should be landing soon, right?"

"Yup! Lucy's heading in straight from the airport. She landed about twenty minutes ago and is going to take the train into Penn."

"Good. That takes care of her. By the way, another email came over late last night with some budget changes."

Paul discussed our morning checklist. I'm not his secretary, but technically, he was my boss. We're both analysts and are always assigned to the same teams for new accounts. We got shit done and gave credit where it was due.

We are a print and deliver vendor, which aids startup companies in marketing and social media. Our lucrative client list doubled last year. I agreed to come in early to set up for the meeting of the New Jersey branch to butt heads with the New York City branch on the biggest project proposal we ever had.

"Did you have your coffee yet?" Paul asked.

"Only one cup. I'm okay for now, adrenaline works just as fine." A taxi this time beeped at me as I hit another wall of traffic.

*Ugh, remember duty calls and brownie points are the best. This will all add up to something one day.*

"That's unacceptable! I'll make sure you have your usual coffee when you get in. Thanks a bunch, Bri!"

"No worries. See you soon," I responded and ended the call.

Hopefully, he'll be thanking me when we land this huge account.

****

I arrived at work closer to seven thirty a.m. than seven o'clock. Paul kept his promise. There was a caramel mocha cappuccino from the café downstairs waiting at my desk with an extra cozy on it. I needed the extra shot of caffeine after that horrific drive in.

I sipped my amazing coffee and ran through my final checks. The information packets I assembled were ready to go for the meeting. I connected my laptop to the charger underneath my desk. Hopefully, I wouldn't have to speak at the meeting, but damn, if I got stuck on a question… I wanted to be fully prepared to impress and take my rightful place next to Paul on the project manager board.

"He only got one coffee? Ugh, I swear he likes you!" Lucy shouted behind me.

She startled the fucking shit out of me, and I nearly spilled my coffee all over my favorite dress. No cleavage, A-line cerulean perfection, and it hit right above the knee. A thirty-dollar dry cleaning bill would have been right out the window.

"Shit, Lucy! You scared me," I scolded.

"Come on, Bri! You have to be used to it by now. I scare you about three times a day. Aww, I missed you, scaredy cat! Come here!" Lucy hugged me.

"I missed you too. What the hell is going on? You choose the most inconvenient time to go on vacation? And you're blonde now?" I said sarcastically. She was my best friend, and I'd been in the dark for a week. One small text that she was going to Cancun and that was it. *I needed answers here!*

"I'm sorry, Bri. I meant to call you and explain, but I couldn't be here for Diane's bridal shower. I needed to get away," Lucy said. Even though, her makeup was flawless, her expression couldn't hide her sorrow.

"Lucy, no one expected you to go. I would never

have let you torture yourself into suffering through it."

"Did anyone ask about me?"

"Yeah, and I showed them the pictures you posted."

"Good. I hope Kelsey saw them. I used the miles he raked up on my credit card."

"For the trip?"

"Yup, I used all of them. We had our official final fight. It's over. We're done."

"Over? Like, finished done? I thought he said he loved you?"

"Yeah, he said it, but of course he didn't mean it "that" way and there is no way in hell I'm going near that fucking wedding. Men suck." Lucy stuck her finger in her mouth, mimicking a gag.

"Hasn't Kelsey always been a douchebag? What about Diane? I'm confused where she fits into all of this. They can't both throw away what you all had," I said.

Lucy continued, "I don't know. I'm still fucking pissed. A few months ago, Kelsey called me almost every day, needing a fix, and now, with their wedding coming up, he doesn't want to know me. I figured it would naturally fade out once they got married, but this is harsh."

Lucy's face fell. Her mask of usual indifference cracked. She blinked hard and looked up. Her eyes pooled with tears.

"Men are rats. They're fleas on rats," I said.

Lucy chuckled at my *Grease* reference. "Okay, Frenchie."

"See, I made you laugh. You're able to smile and laugh. There's proof life will go on."

"I just want a primary in my life. Why is that so hard to find?"

For the past few years, I had been trying to follow my best friend's polyamory ways, but lately it only brought her sadness. Her last relationship with Kelsey and Diane lasted almost two years. She had been their third, but their impending wedding ruined everything. I wish I had the magic words to comfort her or even a spare man to go around. We were both hurting in the love department.

"What about going to a yenta? Aren't there mixers with tons of available men at your temple?"

"I wish. It's the same people my parents have been insisting I date since I was twelve. Back to the meet-ups I go. At least I got a new tan on Kelsey's free miles." Lucy wiped under her eyes.

"Hey, let's have a girls' night soon. Isn't there a speakeasy place you've wanted to try? I think your friend Brady is the new bartender. I think they're having a Grand Opening party soon." I handed her a tissue.

Lucy shrugged. "Kelsey might be there."

"I'll call Diane and check for you. If not, pencil it in."

"All right. You be my wing woman, and I'll be yours."

"Deal." It was settled. We were going. Her friend Brady was a dick, but he made great drinks. I got a bit of a thrill at these new plans. I kept saying I needed to do more in the city and get out there. *This was perfect.*

My phone buzzed with reminders for the meeting pep talk. "Hey, we're going to be late to the scrimmage upstairs."

“That’s all you, girlie. I’m handling the new shopping center in Brooklyn. I got the update a few minutes ago.” Lucy poked at her phone.

“Ah, that sucks. Does Paul know? He thought we’d be together.”

“I caught Paul when I came in. He seemed disappointed. Something’s up with him. He’s like really off. He isn’t his chipper self this morning.”

“He’s extra panicky today. The car service got messed up, and I have to finish setting up the conference room because someone overbooked it. I like Marcia, but she’s fucking up so much lately. I covered for her big this time.”

“I heard she might be pregnant. Maybe she has baby brain. Don’t worry; it’ll work out great. I got to go. I need caffeine. I barely slept on the plane. Good luck today, Bri.”

Lucy gave me a long hug. She gripped me extra tightly.

“Thank you. I missed you. We’ll get through this, okay?” I told her.

She pulled back and smiled. “Thanks, hun. You always cheer me up!” She squeezed my shoulder and walked out of my cubicle. Her expensive shoes pounded away, the sound disappearing softly.

I texted Paul. *—Just talked to Lucy...She’s not going to be part of the project proposal? Did a lot change?—*

He answered immediately. *—Yes. Come upstairs. A few things have been rearranged. Trying to get more details.—*

So this was going to be a typical Monday morning after all, scrambling everywhere last minute for the right information. I took a big swig of my coffee. I welcomed the burning sensation down my throat. Gratefully, it woke me up a little bit more.

# Chapter Two

The eleven o'clock meeting started out boring as planned. My colleagues gave the usual opening speeches outlining the company's progress. The New Jersey employees sat around the long round table along with the newly assigned team members. I chose to stand in case I had to run to my desk for anything. They skipped the first questions part, which hopefully didn't fluster Paul too much. My laptop buzzed behind me for the next round.

I checked my watch several times looking for the last limo of guests. At a quarter after eleven, the analyst team walked into the conference room. Paul and I sighed with relief. I grabbed six more information packets from the back table.

"Finally, I can stop bullshitting up here. Everyone get settled, and we'll start up again in a few minutes," James, one of the number crunchers in Accounting, shouted. The conference room filled with monotone laugher.

I watched the last man walk into the room. I didn't recognize him at an angle, but dead on, there was no mistaking it. The man from the key party, Nathan, was the last man to walk into the room. I gasped, dropping everything in my hands out of pure horror.

I'd recognize my mystery man anywhere. I'd scanned almost everywhere I'd been for months hoping to see him amongst the other strangers. I knew his first name, how sexy he sounded when he came, what his cum tasted like, and now that he worked for the New Jersey office of the same company I worked at for the last six years. I stared in disbelief as he walked back into my life waving at the room of his co-workers with a beaming smile I wished I saw every day.

He was devastatingly handsome in daylight, wearing a three-piece suit, and his brown eyes were actually a striking amber shade. I missed seeing him clearly the last time around. His dark brown hair was up in spikes again, and his skin looked pale against the dark gray suit.

It didn't matter how pale he looked. My desire for a man I barely knew seized my body and stopped me dead in my tracks.

"Bri, keep it together," Paul muttered, coming to stand in front of me. He blocked my view of Nathan with his encouraging smile. I snapped out of my swarming anxious thoughts. Paul knelt down and picked up the papers I'd dropped. I kneeled next to him. At least, the bindings held on the packets. One disaster averted.

"Are you okay? We're almost done," Paul whispered.

"Yes, sorry. It's been a long morning. I'm happy he finally got here."

"He? No, that's the whole team. Come on. We only have a little bit more to go."

I stood back up and locked eyes with Nathan, who had moved right behind Paul. Paul turned around to greet him. Nathan was a few inches taller than Paul and younger. Right, he was tall, but Nathan's cock fit perfectly inside me if he leaned forward. *Shit.*

"Mr. Richards! It's great to meet you. I'm Paul. I'm sorry again for the limo mishap." Paul said, adding more info to my brain about Nathan. Nathan Richards? *God, even his name was sexy.*

"Please call me Nathan and don't worry. It happens. We had extra time to look over the initial stats. It's been a crazy few days." The two men shook hands and a thousand watt smile crossed Nathan's face. Even his teeth were a perfect shade of white. Another thing I had missed.

"I can imagine it being nuts over there. I'd like you to meet one of the members of your new team. This is..." Paul said, but Mr. Grant, the owner of the company, strolled over to us. At eighty-nine, he still barged his way into any conversation without anyone blinking.

"Anna! Please show our guests to their seats and hand out the information packets." Mr. Grant interjected. Something everyone learned fast about Mr. Grant was that he sucked at names. He remembered faces, but he never quite got anyone's name right.

"Pleased to meet you, Anna. I'm Nathan." I didn't dare correct him. His voice, not only in a whisper, was deep, melodious even, and oozed charisma. He could narrate the fucking phonebook and I would sit here patiently listening, growing wetter by the minute.

He held out his hand, and I took it. His palm was sweaty and warm as hell. *Was he nervous?* Outwardly, you'd never know it.

He dropped my hand, and I felt the loss. Fuck, I wanted him to touch me again. I missed the flash of contact already. I'll never forget the feeling when he buried his face in my neck as he fucked me into the desk. I had a bruise on my hip for a week from his hands digging into my waist. *I'd do anything to feel that wanted again.*

It suddenly dawned on me I was staring at him imagining him fucking me again in a conference room full of people. Shit, he talked to me. *What did he say?* Oh yeah, got it. He furrowed his brow.

"Likewise," I answered.

"Have we met before?" he asked.

My eyes shot up to his face. From one word, he could tell it was me? What the fuck? No, this couldn't be happening. Men as gorgeous as him probably had tons of one-night stands. There was no way he'd remember me instantly. I had on a mask and the room only had candlelight. My waking wet dream was free falling into a pit of anxiety. My chest pinched, and heat flared up my body as hot as his sweaty palm. Panic gurgled in my stomach, rising up to my throat.

*Please don't catch me. Not here, not now.*

"I don't think so. Here's a copy of the presentation," I said it so fast I barely heard myself. There was my chance and I blew it.

Nathan took the packet and turned around to the rest of the room. He waved again, and I jumped at the opportunity to touch him. I placed my hand against his back ushering him to his seat. His suit jacket stuck to him and he felt hot like a sauna. I was having a full-blown panic attack and he was secretly sweating to death. A match made in misery heaven.

I wish I could smooth my hand over his back. I definitely didn't touch him enough that night. *Was he still as jacked? Did he have dimples over his ass?* I never found out. *Fuck, I have to keep it together.*

Reluctantly, I let him go. He sat down and looked up at me. "Thank you, Anna." Ah shit, I really should have corrected him on my name. This was bad, so bad. *How could this spiral out this bad so fast?*

"You're welcome!" The words sounded like a schoolgirl who got caught by her crush drawing little hearts all over her notebook. I pretended to clear my throat. He flashed me another odd glance and swiveled around to look at the packet.

The only man I had been with in months was right in front of me, a world out of reach, and I was acting like a fucking weirdo. And on top of it, he was calling me by the wrong name. *Great. Just fucking great.*

"Hey, Bri, can I use your computer? I need to check the G drive for something," James asked me. *Right, I'm Bri and I'm hovering creepily over the last man I've had sex with, but no one knows that except me.* Real life crept back into focus. I'd worked for this company for six years and everyone came to me with their problems. This was the biggest project of my career and I went insane three minutes ago.

I nodded at James and pried myself away from Nathan. I went to the back of the room, grabbed a small cookie, jammed it in my mouth, and reached for a bottle of water. Marcia, the troublemaker, gave me the side eye of *what the fuck is wrong with you?* and with a mouthful of cookie, I said, "Low blood sugar." Marcia made a big silent O with her mouth and touched my hand.

I rolled my eyes when she turned away. She'll believe anything. I peeked at her stomach. Still flat. If she was pregnant, she was newly pregnant. But she had been messing up for at least four months now.

The meeting turned into French or Indonesian. I couldn't hear a thing except the blood rushing through my ears. Like I'd done a thousand times in the past six months, I went over every erotic detail down to how his cock felt on my tongue, how his lips kissed my sensitive neck, and how he pushed me over the edge. I had never come that hard from sex alone. It was a first. You never forget your first.

A few times during the meeting, Nathan perked up his head, glancing at different people. Every time he scrolled my way, I became overly interested in Paul's speech. He should be at the last of it by now and then I could get the fuck out of here. If there was any hope of Nathan not finding me odd, I had to leave immediately or hang out back here until the coast was clear.

Everyone clapped when Paul said the final statements. On a delay, I did too. Whew. I was almost in the clear.

"Thank you for your patience. There is one more thing to discuss. Every project needs a leader to represent the pitch. Analyst Nathan Richards will officially head the pitch for Traill Associates. His second in command will be our Brianna Owens."

I heard my name before the applause started and the wrong name before it. *What the fuck?* Paul was supposed to lead the project.

The gorgeous man of my fantasies swiveled in his chair, smiling at the room. I would be reporting to him for everything.

*Fuck.*

Nathan said thank you to everyone congratulating him. Marcia started the line to congratulate me too. She talked in my face, patted my shoulder, but I didn't hear her. My focus latched onto Paul and Nathan. This completely blindsided me. *How the hell did I miss this?*

"Congratulations, Nathan. I hope you've been briefed about your relocation for the duration of the project. We have an empty office ready for you," Paul added. He walked up to Nathan, bypassing me. *How could Paul not tell me? What happened when I left the meeting prep to set up the conference room?*

"Thank you, Paul. I got the call this morning. I'll have to move some things around, but I'd be happy to switch here for the project. I might be late the first few days." Nathan laughed. It didn't sound like I thought it would. The fake laugh was strained and forced. This was definitely unexpected for him.

"Wonderful. We'll work out the specifics later. Come officially meet your partner in crime."

My other co-workers left the large conference room, congratulating me on the way out. Apart from my full-blown anxiety attack, the praise made me feel vindicated that I belonged here. Every late night and dedicated effort was not a waste. If only I could keep this boost of confidence all the time.

I turned back to Paul and Nathan. *You can do this, Bri. Hold steady.*

"Bri, sorry we got interrupted before. Nathan Richards, please meet Bri," Paul said.

"Hello again. I'm sorry I called you the wrong name before." Nathan waved. His shirt's top button was now undone. He was going to need to do a lot more to cool off with all this pressure.

I smiled, only pursing my lips together. "It's fine. Mr. Grant is bad with names." *Small sentences seem to be working. I'm not stuttering or staring at him blankly.*

"Me too," he said.

"I'm sure you two will get along great. Bri is our top analyst in this branch. You're lucky to have her on your side, Nathan. I will also be part of the team. I'm the new chief revenue manager, but you both will support the main duties with the other team members," Paul continued on.

Nathan could hide his nervousness before, but now it visibly boiled over. He scratched his neck underneath his shirt collar leaving a red streak up his skin. He looked how I felt during a panic attack. I got them too often not to recognize the signs.

"Awesome, Paul. Where is the men's room?" Nathan stammered.

"Down the hall and then the first right turn in the hallway." Paul pointed to the left.

"Cool. I'll be right back." Nathan slammed his brief case down on the large table and ran for the door. Peeking through my lustful thoughts, I remembered hearing his last name in the meeting prep. He was supposed to be the best analyst from the New Jersey branch. Ivy league, the whole nine yards…he was smart and praised for several other projects. *What's got him in such a dire state?*

"He seems nice!" Paul said, shutting off the slideshow.

"I guess so. Um, Paul, when the hell were you going to tell me that it wouldn't be us leading the team?" I inquired.

"I'm so sorry, Bri. I knew you'd be mad. I got promoted this morning. The reorganization happened fast."

"Really? Wow, that's great, Paul! Why didn't you say anything at the prep meeting?"

"Thank you. I didn't think I'd get the position. I'm not supposed to say anything until the next press release. There isn't a lot that's going to change. I'm not losing my other daily stuff with you."

"Ah, I see. Congratulations. I feel so blindsided this morning. I thought we were actually prepared for this one," I admitted. I leaned against the table next to Nathan's briefcase. I wondered what was in there. A wave of tiredness flooded over me. I hated actual rollercoasters and mental ones were ten times worse. With Nathan out of the room, I calmed down.

"I know. We pulled it off. Nathan will be a great fit here. He's been with the company two years, and he compiled the initial demographics for the project. He's the NR signature over everything."

The pieces were falling into place. I never go to the other branch, so I would never have seen him. The Christmas parties became client only and sales reps so again I wouldn't have passed him in the hall. *It made sense, I guess.*

"Sorry about that, guys. My team is getting a tour before the shuttle. I'm going to join them," Nathan said from the doorway.

Paul lit up again around Nathan. I froze on the spot. I got sidetracked and didn't plan out my escape. His top button was buttoned up again. The reserved façade back in place.

"No worries, Nathan! Is it possible for you to stay the afternoon? We are having a three o'clock team consultation to review the preliminary setup. I'm sure we can arrange transportation back to the office for you."

"Today? Sure, whatever you need. Should I go on the tour or wait here?" Nathan asked.

"Go on the tour. I'll meet you back here. Don't forget your briefcase," Paul said.

Nathan walked back into the conference room and headed right for me. I beat Paul to the punch and picked up Nathan's briefcase. It was oddly heavy for a regular leather briefcase. The closer he got to me; he became more handsome and untouchable. I couldn't help looking him up and down.

I lifted the briefcase to him. He took it, grazing my fingers with his own. "Thank you," Nathan said. "See you after the tour." He smiled. His hand was cool now; the heat subsided for him at least. I was still burning up. He lingered failing miserably on concealing his once over glance on me.

*Yes, Nathan, get a good look at me. You've fucked me before, and I hope to God you don't remember.*

# Chapter Three

I ran back to my cubicle and texted Lucy. Did she know about Nathan? Did she forget to tell me? It was definitely him.

Lucy quickly responded—*Who? Be there in ten.*—

Did he recognize me? Was he pretending not to know me? Was that why his hand was dripping with sweat? *Shit, he's going to be my project manager on the most important account of my career.* "*Fuck!*"

"What happened?" Paul peered over my cubicle wall.

I jumped. I really needed lower cubicle walls. I was high strung, but fuck, everyone sneaking up on me was getting on my nerves. Paul looked happy as a clam in his damn ignorance.

"Don't be upset, Bri. Everything worked out fine. I'm going to be part of it too. I'll conduct the final audit on the project."

"I know. We're good." I mustered up the fakest smile ever.

"Great. I'll need you after Nathan finishes the tour. Can you set up a car for him to go back home at five? No wait make it four p.m. Maybe he can beat some of the traffic back to Jersey. I'm going to get the empty office ready for him." With that, Paul bounced off.

Nathan was getting the empty office down the hall? What the fuck? Yes, he was the top analyst, but I'd been here six frigging years. I don't get the red carpet treatment on anything. This wasn't fair. The anger was calming down my panic button.

All the prep work I'd done seemed like a waste of time. Everything had changed. I grabbed a few of the preliminary sheets, and low and behold, an *NR* with the date was in the footer. Paul was right. Nathan was good at what he did, even at making me come.

"Ugh, brain, work with me here," I whispered.

"Geez, you look like shit. What happened in there?" Lucy rounded the corner.

"You're never going to believe this, Lucy." I dropped my voice down to a whisper and pulled her into my cubicle space. "You know the guy Nathan that I wound up with at the key party?"

"The sensitive guy?" Lucy said.

"Seriously?" I rolled my eyes. "That's the first thing that comes to your mind?" Lucy shrugged. "Well, he's now the fucking leader for the Traill Associates' proposal. I'm his second in command, and he's getting the empty office down the hall."

Lucy's mouth dropped open. "No way, are you fucking kidding me?"

"Look at me, Lucy. I could cure a drought with my sweat right now." I fanned myself with the sturdy info packet.

"Are you sure it's him?"

I stared her down. "It's him, Lucy. He even squinted at me like he was trying to figure out if he knew me."

"Yikes. It *was* good sex. Why not tell him and have a throw down in the parking lot?"

"God, I froze up. I could barely get out two words

without spazzing out. I have no clue what happened in the meeting. I stared at the back of his head the whole time!"

"Did he turn around? Did he feel you lusting for him?" Lucy said, puckering up her lips.

"Really? You're not helping here! I don't know what the fuck to do!" I waved my hands frantically.

"So, he knows you guys fooled around. It's not the end of the world." Lucy pulled my arms to my sides. She was pissing me off more than helping.

"I don't want him to know! This is the biggest opportunity for me since I started here. I can't blow my chance on some stupid fucking night."

"Okay, okay…Bri, stop. You're going to hyperventilate or your favorite, have a panic attack. Are you one hundred percent sure it's really him? Did he say anything about the party?" Lucy grabbed my shoulders, forcing me to face her.

"He didn't mention the party, but trust me, it's him. He even asked me if we knew each other."

"What did you say?"

"No. I chickened out. What the fuck is wrong with me? I messed up so bad. What am I going to do now? Tell him I lied?" My heart was yelling at me to slow down.

"All right, first take a deep breath and drink some water. Then figure out what you want to do. You just said you didn't want him to know you and now you're trying to find a way to tell him." Lucy thrust my water bottle into my hand. I wanted to pour it over my head. "I can't wait to meet this guy. He must be hot to get you all worked up like this."

Nathan was hot, but normal hot-guy hot. My last

boyfriend was a musician with no work ethic, a sea of tattoos and piercings, and always dressed for a show. The other guys I dated before him were an array of hipsters, each with a gimmick I stupidly fell for every time. My dating history was weak. I deserved to meet a guy who could actually make me come and hold down a steady job.

"Honestly, I don't have a fucking clue what I want right now." I sat down in my chair. My frustration blossomed into a nice headache.

"Okay. He'll be gone in a few hours and you can go home and really think about it. I'm not apologizing for letting you be part of that game. I know deep down you had fun and you're entitled to it. Nathan could be the nicest guy in the world, and you'll never know it if you keep this up. Why don't you keep it in the dark unless he full out says something? This way you can have a plan of action and see if he's someone you actually like." This is why we're friends. Lucy always had my back and gave phenomenal advice.

"Ever get déjà vu, Lucy?" Less than four hours ago, I was doing this for her.

"Maybe all men aren't rats?" She kidded.

"I hope so. Thank you for the advice."

"Hey, Bri, are you ready for us?" Paul rounded the corner. "Hi, Lucy, I hope there are no hard feelings about bumping you from this project."

"Nah, I'm just peachy! I wish I could have been a fly on the wall in that meeting. I heard Nathan from the Jersey branch is heading the project, not you?" Lucy set up the bait.

"It's a long story. Yes, Nathan Richards will be handling it with Bri. You'll like him. Everyone does."

Paul was taking it.

"Is he devilishly handsome or married with three kids?" Lucy asked.

"Uhh, I'm not sure if he's married. He comes highly recommended."

"I do?" Now Nathan was standing in my cubicle. I jolted up from my chair. *Fuck, how much did he hear?*

"Yes, Nathan. Mr. Grant picked you personally for the top position. Nathan, please meet Lucy Davis. She is one of our media planners for the NYC territory."

Lucy launched out her hand. "Nice to meet you, Nathan."

"Nice to meet you too, Lucy. Are you on this floor? I thought the media department was down two floors?

"I'm always around. If you need anything, Bri is always available to help. She's our go-to gal." She smiled, forcing her ruby red lips up past a normal limit and poked me in the arm. She had to add her two cents in and bring attention to me.

Nathan switched his gaze to me. His smile and his laugh were more natural and warmer than before. "Please don't hate me, then. I'm going to be bugging you a lot these first few days. This place is huge."

"She won't mind! Will you, Bri?" Lucy urged me forward.

"Nope. Not at all," I told Nathan.

"Whew." He wiped imaginary sweat off his brow. It was so cute I almost melted.

"Are you ladies busy or can I steal Bri?" Paul asked.

"Steal her away!" Lucy nudged my shoulder.

"Great. This way, Nathan." Paul motioned for

Nathan to follow him down the hall toward the office I had been eyeing for months. When their backs were turned, Lucy pushed me forward encouraging me to follow. She glanced in their direction, fanned herself, and mouthed, "He's hot." I laughed silently.

I followed behind Paul and Nathan, grateful for the shift in emotion. I could replace dread with anger. I'm the queen of resting bitch face.

Paul entered the office and flipped the light on. There was a desk, two chairs, and a standard bookcase in the corner. Minus the bookcase, it looked exactly like the room where Nathan and I fucked. I hoped this wouldn't help his shitty memory out.

"Home sweet home," Paul sang out.

"Um, Paul? This is a big office for just me. I only have a cubicle like Bri in my building."

"At the moment, we're short on space, so think of this as a mini promotion."

Nathan was sweating profusely again. His calm, joyful demeanor was gone, switching back to something else. I guess he didn't know he was going to be the leader of the pack on this one.

Nathan placed his briefcase on his newly assigned desk. "This is nuts. I feel so unprepared," he said barely above a whisper. His gaze scanned the empty room, and he placed his hands on his hips. Against my better judgment, I felt bad for the guy. He looked like he was in over his head.

I surprised myself by asking, "Hey, what do you need? I have all the prep work for the meeting at my desk." Paul sighed, and his brow furrowed. Sometimes Paul needed to lighten up. He basically threw an unexpected man into a shark tank with filets strapped to his belt. *Give the man a break.*

"Thank you, Bri. That'll be helpful. Do you have any extra legal pads and a pen too?" Nathan said.

He was flustered to the max. He had a pen in his suit jacket pocket. I coughed and pointed at his lapel. He looked down and sighed. He half smiled at me. "I'm blowing first impressions with you, aren't I?"

In that moment, I wanted to come clean. I wished I could ease his discomfort. It was even hard to tear myself away from him. There were so many things I missed seeing about him in that dark, shameless room. He had a slight cleft in his chin, a small line in his ear that indicated he once had a piercing and he had a small scar marring the perfection of his left eyebrow. He was every adjective you could possibly dream of to describe the most handsome man I'd ever met.

"I'll be right back." *Fuck. Seriously, that was all I managed to say?*

"Please hurry back. You're my life line right now."

I held back the urge to keep running down the hall. Lucy hadn't waited at my desk, but I'd call her later.

I grabbed a clean information packet and my copy of the presentation. In the file cabinets over my desk, I snatched a box of pens, a Wite-out glider, and a steno pad. Then a binder, some index tabs, a mechanical pencil, two highlighters, and box of mints.

It didn't dawn on me how much more crap I piled into the post office bin until I placed it on Nathan's desk. He might think I'm a crazy hoarder now, but when he peeked into the contraband carrier, his megawatt smile returned, making it all worth it. "Girl after my own heart. I owe you one."

"I think he's good for the next year and half, Bri.

Thank you," Paul said, giving me a puzzled look.

"Anytime," I stated.

"Nathan and I have to go see HR to file some paperwork, but can you meet us around two p.m. in the small conference room?"

"Sure." I walked back to my desk. *Well, that wasn't too bad.*

# Chapter Four

When I got home, I collapsed onto my bed. I was so fucking tired; I missed eating dinner.

I had no luck on Lucy recognizing Nathan. We went back to our earlier conclusion that he was a friend of Kelsey's.

Sure enough with his last name and knowing that he lived in New Jersey, I found Nathan online. His profile photo gave nothing away, only a silhouette of him dunking a basketball into a net. The only other non-private detail was that he liked the band, Sublime. No relationship status, no work place, only a Rutgers "R" for groups. Nothing revealed too much about him.

I escaped him the rest of the day. HR and Paul kept him busy and they canceled the team meeting. I didn't think he remembered me from the party, because he didn't even say goodbye at the end of the day. I wondered if he was exhausted like me. Stress takes a toll, and he was definitely riding his own hurricane today.

This was going to royally suck if I had to come down off an anxiety peak each day. I should have said something, but alas, I didn't. I missed my chance.

Even though, I slept like the dead, I took my time getting into work the next day. I missed my express train and got to the office close to nine a.m. My lateness gave me more time to think, and I decided to leave

Nathan alone. File it away and move the fuck on.

I peeked over the tops of the cubicles to spy on Nathan's office. The light was still off. Would he say good morning? *Ugh, I've been here ten minutes and I'm forgetting my plan. Great. In an hour, I'll want him to marry me. Gulp.*

I focused on my daily tasks and missed when Nathan arrived. No hello from him, only an email asking for the team to assemble after lunch. Somehow, I dodged this catastrophe. *Thank you, guardian angel, wherever you are.*

However, my luck ran out, when a small computer glitch in our servers threw the entire office into a panic. Our emails were down, and our client access portals were locked.

"Can you have a heart attack at thirty-seven?" Paul came over to my desk.

"Do you really want me to answer that question?" I was desperately calling our employees to log out of the system. "Come on, sit down, pull yourself together, and start calling people. Take the bottom of the list. I've already called one through twelve."

"You're really good in a panic. You're doing a great job," Paul remarked, patting me on the back.

"Thank me later. Can you tell Nathan to log off? He wasn't in his office before." The Nathan avoidance plan had failed again as I took the long way back to my desk after I got coffee.

"Sure. Yet again, I don't know how this happened. We back up our work all the time. Shouldn't IT noticc when we run out of space?"

"Paul, it's a lot more involved than the usual system crash. The faster we get everyone out of the system, the quicker we can be up and running. I gave Marcia some of the list and Tracey. You only need to call the bottom five and Nathan."

"Okay. I'll tell Nathan." Paul stormed away.

Paul came back. "Hey, Nathan isn't in his office. I know he's here, but I haven't seen him in at least an hour. His computer is still up, and his phone is going off like crazy."

"Maybe he went to get coffee."

"Can you check? I don't want to shut down his computer without his permission."

"Come on, Paul, I'm making calls. Sue in California won't pick up her phone, but she's been logged in since nine a.m."

I had to act normal. The last thing I needed was for Paul to realize I had been avoiding Nathan. He should know something was up if he didn't already. I always got excited for new projects. This time I was off my game.

"I'll take over the calls. Can you also go into the storage closet and get an external drive in case the reboot screws up?" Paul added.

With a huff, I left my cubicle and walked down the side of the building toward accounting. I avoided the talkers and pulled the storage key from the main board.

I opened the backdoor and jumped because someone sat on the floor. Nathan, wearing another immaculate three-piece suit sat Indian style on the floor, his head thrown back against the wall.

"Nathan? Shit, did you get locked out?" I asked. Nathan slowly opened his eyes and looked up. He puffed out a breath and rolled his eyes.

"A little bit."

"I'm sorry. Didn't someone give you a box key yet?

"No, and I forgot my phone and the code sheet. Did you fuck up this much on your first day?" Nathan looked defeated. I reached out a hand without thinking and he took it, pulling himself up from the floor. His hand was cool to the touch today.

"I kept forgetting to hit nine first for every fax Paul gave me for the first month. Nothing went out and we missed several client deadlines."

He chuckled. "Damn, that's pretty bad. He must have been pissed?"

"I'm shocked I didn't get fired."

"He runs a tight ship."

"You can say that again. So you got locked out. It's not a big deal. If you hit 1515, the stair door opens for every floor."

"Thanks, Bri. I appreciate it."

The two of us stood in the hallway less than an arms width apart. My hand tingled where we touched. I zoned out on the pattern of his tie and imagined his chest underneath his suit. I wished I had ripped his black shirt off that night.

Nathan cleared his throat. I jerked my gaze up. "Shit. Sorry. Our system crashed. Everyone's going crazy in there. It's nice and quiet back here," I said.

"That sucks. I wouldn't mind hiding out here for a few more minutes. We should get a couch for over there by the window. It's a perfect place to take a nap and chill." He pointed over his shoulder to the large floor to ceiling windows. There was a perfect little nook I definitely took for granted. I wish I could chill out all cozy with him on the imaginary couch.

*Ugh, seriously, why does he have to be likeable?*

"A secret hideaway would be nice. Unfortunately, we need you to log out of the system. IT has to reboot the servers, and everyone has to be out. Sorry to the kill the moment."

"It's okay. Party's over," Nathan declared, his lips turning up for half a smile. He still seemed slightly ruffled over his mishap.

I hit the door code for Nathan, and as I opened it, he placed his hand on the door above my head, letting me go first. I walked back into the office, but then remembered why I went out there in the first place.

"Damn, I forgot. I need to get something." When I turned back around, Nathan's head was tilted to the side and his gaze was unmistakably on my ass. He barely caught himself from stumbling into me.

"Um, sorry. Let me get the door." Nathan stopped it right before it closed. His lips pursed together like he got caught doing something he shouldn't.

If I were Lucy, I would have called him out on it. But I'm not her. I said thanks fast and walked back out into the hallway. He left before the door shut.

"What the fuck?" I said to myself. I discounted it and went to the closet to get the external hard drive. Guys as good looking as Nathan are probably so focused on work, his buddies, and his one-night-stand bed notches. However, this was the second time I'd seen him check me out. *I'm probably so hard up that I'm imaging things. I need to fucking hold it together.*

The project was only three months long. *I can do this...*

****

At the afternoon meeting, Nathan was completely

reset and any heartfelt moment I thought we shared obliterated. Even his voice changed into business mode. It was still hot to watch.

He jotted down notes, getting familiar with everyone's specialties. I scribbled a few things until we got to my part.

"I arranged for the mapping department to provide us the key demographic categories—average income, households with children, women, ethnicity, and a few others. I think it's too many. We need to cut it down to at least top five options so we don't overload Traill with pages of numbers."

"That's a great idea, Bri, but isn't that a lot of unnecessary work if we are only going to take a few of them? We should brainstorm more before we waste time."

*Strike one against his pretty face*. Before I could offer a rebuttal, Paul chimed in. "Nathan, it's not extra work if we miss one making a key area look better. Trust Bri. She knows what she's doing."

"I'm sorry, Bri. I didn't mean to undermine your suggestion." Nathan looked up, his robot ego deflating.

"None taken," I lied. I remembered in the back of my mind thinking anger would replace my anxiety over him. That would be a great idea to resume right away.

"Bri, why don't you take over from here? I'll take my cues from you until I learn the ropes. The New Jersey office is handled slightly different from here." He smiled.

"No, it's all right. We should try to make this pitch as efficient as possible. Go on." I couldn't be a total bitch, not with Paul, Marcia, and James in the room.

"Okay. Paul and James, can you maybe make a pie

chart reflecting estimates of how much money we can use for each part?"

"I'm already running the numbers now." Paul confirmed.

"Great. If you can send it to Bri and I by tomorrow, that would work out nicely."

As we got back on track, I noticed more cracks in Nathan's façade. He rubbed his ear with the tiny scar when someone spoke longer than a minute, and he was big on eye contact. James drowned on about expenses and he even lost me too. Nathan held strong. It made me remember how he looked down at me when I worked his cock with my mouth. His stare read intense and mesmerized.

He caught me looking at him and turned toward me. He had no idea what I was thinking. "Bri, does that work for you?"

I agreed to whatever it was I missed.

# Chapter Five

For the next week, I avoided being alone with Nathan and to my agony he followed me every step of the way. He used me as a liaison for everything. If I got coffee, he followed me into the kitchen. If I headed to accounting, he used it as an excuse to meet new people. I was trapped in hell.

Nathan was completely oblivious to my standoffish attitude. I even kept my earphones around my neck ready to put them back on—a clue to leave me alone.

None of it worked.

I walked into the copy room and there he stood. The right machine had every red light blinking for help.

"I got it." This machine broke down at least once a week. I read the symbol for paper jam and quickly pulled out the drawers to reset the damn thing. I smelled Nathan's cologne and my chest tightened. He wore the same cologne from the night he fucked me into a desk.

Nathan stepped back, but I was already done. His copies came out again.

"Where's a white flag when you need one? Thanks for the save."

"No problem. You have to reset every drawer after the paper jam has been cleared." I scooted past him.

"Ah, don't teach me how to fix it. I'll have no reason to bug you now." Nathan chuckled. I looked back at him and he was smiling. I felt my eyes go wide. *Ugh, was he trying to flirt with me again?* It had been a while. I dismissed the thought and headed toward the door.

"Did you need something?" Nathan yelled back.

"What?"

"You came in here, helped me, but didn't do anything else. I can use the other copier if you need this one."

*Fuck.*

"You know I completely forgot why I came in here. Don't worry about it." I lied.

I didn't wait for him to respond. I ran out of the little room, hitting the side of my arm against the door. It stung, reminding me how foolish I was acting around him. He was just a simple man, who I had sex with one crazy night.

I sat down in my cubicle waiting until he left the area. A few moments later, he shuffled by my cubicle. A small knock made me look up from my internal nightmare.

"Hey, Bri, you got a minute?" Nathan asked.

"Yeah, what's up?"

"This might sound nuts, but did I do something to offend you? Or I don't know. It seems we got off on the wrong foot the last couple of days," Nathan said.

When he stared down at me with a bewildered look, my insides twisted hard. I gulped. Too many times, I imagined him this close to me again and here I was being awkward as fuck.

"No, you did nothing wrong. I drink too much coffee. It makes me jittery and high strung," I bullshitted.

"Is that it? I feel like I make you nervous." He took another step toward me. My cubicle was spacious for one, but two was a crowd. I resisted the urge to pull away from him. *Don't act nervous. Don't look at his crotch, which was less than a foot from my face.*

"You just don't know me well enough yet. You're reading me wrong."

"Do you always wear glasses?" Nathan prodded.

"Yes. Contacts freak me out."

He squinted. He was trying again to activate that lost bit of his memory. *Shit.* "Have you ever visited the New Jersey office before?"

"Once about two years ago for a conference prep. It's nice out there. Isn't there a great Hibachi place near it? Mount Something?"

"Fuji. Mount Fuji. It's really good. You only came to the office once?"

"Yes. I use the chat when I need something. Why?"

"Hmm…I guess I saw you then. You look familiar." He half-smiled and glanced at the pictures on my desk.

"What's with the questions, Nate? Why are you grilling my employee? Let our little Anna get back to her work. Bring her some coffee too, my boy," Mr. Grant shouted.

Nathan stepped back so fast he knocked one of my maps from its pushpin as Mr. Grant entered my cubicle too. Usually, he sang his way over, but every now and again, a sneaky attack of kindness surprised us. Even though, he still got my name and Nathan's name wrong.

Before Nathan could respond, I stood up and jutted in. "Nathan is only learning the ropes here. Can I get you both some coffee? Nathan, please put the map on my desk. I'll fix it. How do you take your coffee?" I reached out and touched Nathan's arm. He was too cute when surprised. Yes, the muscles were still there.

"Such a good kid," Mr. Grant remarked. "Stay on her good side, buddy." He lulled a tune lost with time and meandered back to his corner office.

Nathan bent down to pick up my map. "Shit, he scared the fuck out of me."

"Yeah, he pops up at random times. You get used to it. So how do you like your coffee?"

"You don't have to get me coffee. I'm a one cup in the morning guy. Do you want coffee? I can get it for you. I have to work on getting on your good side." He winked. *Flirting or non-flirting...that is the question.*

"No, it's okay. I'll get my own. Maybe we can get Marcia and go over the new demos later?"

He nodded. "Sounds great. Email me." He flashed me a smile. I returned it as best as I could, then he was gone.

I didn't need any more coffee so I sat back down staring aimlessly. *I think I'm going to have to tell him who I am. He's going to figure it out. Or execute Plan B...stay away from him completely.* This was getting ridiculous. It'd been almost a week of trying to avoid him. Obviously, I sucked at it because he caught on.

I was shocked our paths hadn't crossed at any of Lucy's other functions, but I guess he really was Kelsey's friend. He was damn cute though...

****

Two days later, staying away from him completely wasn't working either.

"I'm starting to think you're purposely screwing with this printer," I accused Nathan.

"I swear, I'm not. It's not a complete day unless I have at least two fights with something without a pulse." He held up two fingers and placed his other hand over his heart.

"Ha-ha. Okay." I leaned down to pull out the drawers.

"What were you listening to?"

"One of my playlists. I make a new one every day."

"You're a music girl aren't you?"

"I'm a queen of all trades, Mr. Richards. How about you?" I slammed the last drawer shut and the printer started up again, spitting out his copies.

Nathan leaned against the island in the room, arms crossed, and took in the view of me. His head cocked to the side and his eyes glistened in the harsh lighting. *Did I flash him or something?*

"Nathan?" I said.

"Hmm? Sorry my brain wandered. My roommate is a total music guy. He's in a band. If you want some music, let me know. I'll share mine if you share yours?"

"I have a lot of Sublime already on my phone. I'm good."

"How did you know I like Sublime?"

This is why I was trying my hardest to stay away from him. He'll know I snooped on him.

"Every guy likes Sublime." *If that's true, I'll be ever so grateful.*

"Best band ever. I also like 311 a lot too." Of course he did. I love 311 and went to their concerts whenever they were in town. This silly conviction of mine to stay hidden was stupider and stupider. *I fucking like this guy.*

"Me too. Tickets for their new tour go on sale soon."

"Yeah! My roommate already got us presale tickets."

*I would give anything to go to that concert with him.* "Awesome."

"I'm pretty stoked. Thanks for the help, Bri." He looked at his watch and grimaced. "Sorry, I have a conference call to take for one of my other accounts."

I shooed him off and cursed myself. I made this whole ordeal worse for nothing.

# Chapter Six

After two weeks of non-stop work, Lucy and I planned our night in the city. The speakeasy's opening perfectly matched up with Halloween weekend. She persuaded me to wear a flapper dress too. Her dress was white and mine was black.

We walked down the steep stone steps to the fast food restaurant. The setting confused me. I thought it was going to be a bar or at least look like one. The small space had picnic style tables and a marquee sign of all-you-can-eat hot dog entrees. There were large electrical outlet holes at each table.

"It's a dive, isn't it?" Lucy said with a mischievous grin.

"This is it?" I asked.

"Yup! Isn't it homey?" Lucy responded.

"I bet they have the best hot dogs ever. What happens now?"

"I thought Brady was going to be out here. He's probably already in the back. Come on." Lucy grabbed my hand and we entered the small space.

Near the entrance was an old sit down, wooden phone booth. A large "Occupied" sign hung next to it.

Lucy giddily walked up to the phone booth and played the part of an unknowing bystander. "I'll be right back. I have to make a call." I rolled my eyes at her cheesiness. She knew I loved it.

She opened the foldable door, sat down on the little seat, and closed the door. She pointed up at something and then picked up the phone. The inside turned so all you could see was wood.

*All right, this was kind of cool.* The wooden plank snapped back, and the phone booth returned without my best friend. I entered the tiny space and sat down, pulling the door closed. The sign Lucy pointed to read, "Dial 1-8-4 and wait. One ride per customer."

I picked up the phone, dialed the number, and low and behold someone picked up on the other line. "Number thirty-seven, now being served." The line went dead and the booth swiveled around.

Without a frame of reference, I didn't know what to expect. The glitz and glam never faded from these secret walls. The room was painted gold, even the tin paneled ceilings were gold tinted, and the room snaked around the whole restaurant. The electrical outlets on the outside were peepholes and each table was lined up accordingly to spy on unsuspecting bystanders.

Lucy twirled her arms around the room. "I told you this was worth seeing!" I agreed, and she put her hand through the crook of my arm. Along the wall was a large bar with men dressed like the 1920s and the waitresses wore chandelier dresses with all the frills. At the end of the long bar, we spotted her friend Brady, tipping his zoot suit hat our way.

Brady said something to the waitress closest to him and she immediately rushed toward us.

"Lucy and guest, party of two?"

Lucy said yes, and the woman showed us to a small high-top table against the wall with a reserved sign on it. I ignored the "guest" assignment for me. Same old shit from these guys. These guys couldn'tt retain my name.

We gave our drink order to the waitress after she insisted we order this raspberry moxie twist thing. As long as the drink was sweet, I'll try anything once.

"I wish I lived in the twenties. These flapper dresses are super cute and that short haircut! I miss my short hair," Lucy added. I definitely loved the fashion, but no thank you on living in the twenties. I liked my modern luxuries very much.

"Maybe if I could go to one of Gatsby's parties than come back to my right time," I remarked.

"What an adventure that would be?" Lucy beamed.

A different waitress handed us our drinks a few moments later. I needed this liquid eraser. It was sweet as fuck, but it went down deliciously smooth.

"Don't forget to peep through the holes. Who knows what you might see?" The woman reminded before she disappeared into the madness.

I unhooked the latch and peeked inside. I gasped at who sat at the table on the other side of the wall. Fucking Nathan and another guy.

"Holy shit, Lucy! Nathan is here!"

"Really? Did you mention we were coming here tonight?"

"Hell, no! I told Marcia, but Nathan definitely wasn't around when we talked. I can't even drink in peace."

"This is one of the hottest new places." Lucy shrugged.

"I guess. Why did I have to do your damn party? This is making me miserable."

"Come on, Bri. You needed to get laid, and I

helped. Admit it, you had fun with him."

"Of course I had fun, but I'm trying to avoid him, you know!"

"Why avoid him? He seems like a decent guy and he's fucking gorgeous. Don't be so embarrassed about your sex life!"

"I'm not embarrassed," I whispered.

From her look, I knew she saw right through me. It wasn't embarrassment exactly. I just didn't know how to handle the situation, and I walked out before we talked. It was a one-night stand, and I wanted to keep it that way.

"I'll finish scolding you in a minute. I have to pee. Don't stare at him too hard, he might see you," Lucy chastised.

I rolled my eyes and resumed my voyeurism. The two men ate their hot dogs and French fries chatting and laughing. It was loud in this part of the speakeasy. The place was packed and swing dance music blared through the overhead speakers. Nathan and the guy's conversation was lost to me. I placed my ear by the holes, but it was no use. I settled for watching them.

Then Nathan leaned over and kissed the man across from him.

The kiss wasn't deep, but it wasn't a peck on the cheek either. No tongue, only lingering lips. Both sets of eyes closed to the feeling. I knew that type of a kiss. I craved it every day.

When it hit me exactly what I just witnessed, I gasped and knocked over the last remnants of my very pink cocktail.

"Fuck…" I muttered under my breath. I didn't tear my eyes away from them while my drink dripped to the floor. I mindlessly dabbed at the mess with a napkin while I watched them.

The two men ended the kiss and Nathan looked shy with downcast eyes. He looked up and smiled at the other man. The other guy, wearing a fedora, scooted his chair closer to the table and rubbed his neck, saying something hidden from me.

"They have the weirdest bathrooms here. There's two toilets next to each other in one room!" Lucy sat back down, shouting about her adventure. "Bri? Hello? What are you doing?"

My hand still made circles to clean up the drink long gone, and I dragged my gaze away from my disappointment.

"I'm sorry. I'm…I think I'm in shock right now," I stammered the words out. I stopped wiping the table. I scrunched up the cloth napkin and threw it at the wall.

"Shock? Did he peek back at you?" Lucy was still feeling the lightheartedness of a silly night in a speakeasy behind a hot dog stand. My night had severely changed.

"Look through the peephole, Lucy. See for yourself. Nathan is on a fucking date."

"Nathan? Really? We can take her." Lucy hoisted up her fists.

"Really and not really. *Look through the fucking hole!*" My anger boiled up and over. The cheap, strong drink went straight to my head.

"Damn, I thought he was hot in a suit. He's cuter in regular clothes. Bri, he's with a friend now, there's no girl. Calm down he's probably with a group of friends."

"Lucy, that's the date! The guy is the date! He kissed him! Full on the mouth, smashed noses, a fucking swapping spit kiss!" I screamed. Luckily, the loud bar masked my outburst.

"Was it hot?" Lucy asked, leaning toward me.

"Seriously? That's your response. I could have sworn he's been hitting on me. Just my luck, he's gay. You or one of the other guys didn't set this joke up for me did you?" I wagged my finger at her.

"I swear on my life I never met Nathan before you introduced us in the office. I would never do that to you. I'm still confused how he got your room. A lot of planning goes into my parties. You were supposed to be with Tom."

"Tom? You got to be fucking kidding me?" I almost threw up my raspberry moxie concoction.

"I heard he's jacked. Boring, but he can fuck for hours. He said he thought you were pretty, so I hoped you'd take a chance."

One of the best parts of our friendship was her honesty. She wouldn't lie about something this serious. I'm far from being a virgin, but not as sexually adventurous as she claimed to be. She knew I put myself out of my comfort zone that night. She wouldn't make it a sham.

"I know it had been forever since Matt, but if Tom walked through that door I would've walked out. Something about him irks me and he marinates in cheap cologne. I have a coughing fit every time I'm near him."

"Ha-ha, yeah, I remember now. He thinks you're allergic to dogs or something." Lucy sipped her untouched cocktail.

"Your friends don't know me at all. We don't know anyone who even has a dog!" I peered back through peepholes.

Nathan looked cute as hell and his equally hot date laughed and picked at the same basket of fries. My anger cyclone slowly subsided. Sadness inched in. The night with Nathan was far beyond any casual sexual encounters I'd ever had. Now, he wasn't available at all.

"Maybe he's bisexual, Bri? Didn't you make him come twice?"

"Shh for fuck's sake." I hunched over the table. "What if he can hear us?"

"Hey, ladies!" Brady came over with two shots for us. "There's sound proofing in the walls. The outside can't hear or see you! And who came twice?"

"Hey, Brady. This place is wild!" Lucy said, ignoring his follow-up question.

"It's not too shabby. I have to get back behind the bar. My shift doesn't end for another two hours. Do you ladies need anything else?"

"Nah, we're good. Thanks for the invite!"

"Of course! Lucy, you better save a dance for me later."

"Perhaps." Lucy turned up her charm and I swear she batted her fake eyelashes at Brady. He ate it up. His eyes dipped to her exposed cleavage. She oozed sex appeal like it was her second job. All she had to do was sit there and men just flocked around. I lacked that special gift.

"All right, ladies. See you in a bit." Brady disappeared back into the crowd.

I looked once more through the peephole. Nathan was gone. I turned quickly to the speakeasy entrance. *Was he going to come in here? How the fuck was I going to weasel out of this one?*

After a ten minute panic attack, this hidden gem wasn't their final destination.

"Come on, Bri; don't let him ruin your night. So you saw them kiss, okay, but you have no idea what you really saw. There could be a million reasons why they kissed. Maybe he's poly?"

"The whole world isn't poly, Lucy."

"I know! I'm just trying to make you feel better. He seems like a nice guy. Don't shut the door on him yet."

"The door isn't even open!"

"It could be if you let it," Lucy reminded me.

Lucy tried relentlessly to alleviate my angst the rest of the night, but I was stuck in my head on this one.

# Chapter Seven

After Saturday night's reveal, it became easier to avoid Nathan. Lucy tried repeatedly to convince me to talk to him, but the ship had sailed. Our small interactions diminished to only good mornings and emails. He got the hint.

In our weekly recap meeting, I purposely sat away from him. The more distance between us the clearer I could think. When we were leaving the meeting, Nathan asked me out to lunch, smiling all the way. I almost said yes. My answer remained a firm no. His contagious smile deflated. A fake smile of pursed lips replaced it, and he pointed at me promising next time I'd join them. I lied, taking the infinite rain check, and flipped my earphones back on.

It killed me to be abrupt and rude. That wasn't in my nature. But the week continued with a busy ease and I welcomed every bit of work stress.

By late Friday night, I had a healthy handle on the project. The perfectly quiet office helped. Since Nathan set up station here, I barely thought past my log-in password. I even had to physically type it out to remember it. This was bad. I couldn't afford to mess up this project.

The project should be done right before the Christmas party. I'm not in the right pay grade or executive enough to be invited, even though my hard work earned the praise. Nathan was invited. *Ugh, fuck Nathan.*

I should've told him who I was when he tried to recognize me. Now, he probably thought I was this introverted weirdo, who was only good for printer problems. *How could I screw this up so badly? Why the fuck did he have to be such a nice guy?*

I shook my head to clear my thoughts and shut down my computer. I turned off the lights in my cubicle and my solar-powered dancer toys slowly stopped. Monday would be a new day to tackle more.

I shut off the printers and the few lights I left on. In the distance, an office phone rang. It was past midnight…No one else had clearance to be in the building. Even the cleaning crew packed up at nine.

On second thought, a few of the customer service girls worked the graveyard shift on this floor…Dismissing it, I finished shutting everything off in my wing.

Then the voice I tried my fucking hardest to forget blared from down the hall.

"Fuck, man, I fell asleep. I would never stand you up. *Shit! The train!* Why didn't you call earlier, Clark?"

*Turn around and walk to your car. It's not your problem. Keep walking; he won't hear your boots. Sneak out. He doesn't know you're here too.*

"When I didn't show up for your set, you should've called! Fuck, I'm not going to make it. *Shit!*"

I was almost at the door when my conscience bit back hard. He rode the train into the city and the last one would probably be about now to New Jersey. I drove in today because I knew I'd be staying late. *I could give him a ride.*

"Man, you suck. What the fuck am I supposed to do now? Take out a small loan and grab a hotel room in Manhattan, or I'll take the subway to Brooklyn and rent an Air BnB ready to go in the middle of the night."

I felt terrible as my feet dictated my actions. I reached the outside door and stopped. I wasn't that person. He was stuck, and I couldn't let him stay here.

Dreading my decision, I walked past my cubicle to the row of offices. Nathan's light was on and I heard him rustling stuff around.

"Yes, dear, I have a couch, a lovely side bathroom for quick touch-ups, and I can't forget the turn down service with a chocolate on my pillow on the fifteenth floor." He said sarcastically on the phone. "I'm not going to pay an arm and leg for a taxi when you can come get me."

I peered into the office. Nathan attempted to straighten a stack of my handouts I printed out this morning. I knocked, trying not to scare him. It didn't work and all the papers fell out of his hand.

"Shit, you scared me, Bri." Nathan's eyes bulged, and he clutched his heaving chest. "Why are you still here?"

He ran a hand mindlessly through his hair and a male voice shouted something inaudible on the phone. "Clark, I'll call you back." Nathan hung up the office phone, pissed.

"So, why are you still here?" His voice held a rough edge to it.

"This office is never quiet, as I'm sure you've learned. Sometimes, I stay late on Friday nights when no one can catch me." I leaned down to pick up the papers that spilled over the desk.

"Ah, now I know why your work is so good. Your ears must ring like crazy from the music you blast. That blonde woman near your desk doesn't shut up."

I laughed and peeked up over the top of the desk. I dragged my gaze up to his tired eyes. His handsome face was creased from sleeping on the plotter and his right eye was bloodshot. He looked like hell and utterly adorable.

"Yeah, she drives me nuts. Are you okay? Did you fall asleep?"

Nathan brought his finger up to his kissable mouth and whispered, "Shh. This shit is fucking boring, especially when you're catching a five thirty a.m. train into the city every day. I won't tell your secret if you keep mine."

"Secret's safe with me. You do sound sexy when you whisper…" The words escaped my mouth before I registered what I even said. I shuffled the papers into some semblance of order when it hit me. That's what he told me before he obliterated any sexual experience I had before him. I still kneeled on the floor and clasped my hand over my mouth. My hands shook and anxiety flipped my stomach. *Shit. Fuck. Please tell me I stuttered those simple words and he didn't hear them. Fuck why isn't he talking?* I glanced at him sideways.

Nathan cocked his head to the side, and his fading bloodshot eyes squinted. "Why did you say that?"

"Sorry, long night. Are you stuck here?" I said as I stood up.

"Don't change the subject. Bri…Anna…Brianna… Tell me why you said that." He dragged out my name slowly as if he heard himself say it for the first time. Looking down at me on the floor in a position we'd been in before, recognition finally gripped him.

"It was you," he said, quietly.

Game over. *Do I weasel out of it? No. He doesn't deserve this crap. I'm so tired of going over this in my head.* I had to give it up.

I looked up and he looked pissed. "What do you want me to say?" I asked.

"Admit it! Oh my God, I've been going crazy trying to figure out where I knew you. It's been driving me fucking nuts!" Nathan placed his hands on the desk and leaned forward.

"Nathan, look, I'm sorry. I wanted to tell you, but I think I felt ashamed. I don't know. That night was so crazy." The worst feeling ever worked up my spine.

"You wanted to tell me? You think that makes it okay? You've been the nicest one here, a little weird, but you knew the whole damn time! That's fucking mean, Bri. Duh, Bri is short for Brianna. Am I still dreaming?"

"I'm sorry, okay?"

Nathan threw down the papers and yanked his tie up off his head. "You're sorry? That's not going to cut it. What the serious fuck? I didn't think it was you, but I knew it. You've been like a freaking magnet, attracting me to you. I knew I had seen you somewhere." He continued glaring down at me. He moved out of sight and plopped down onto his chair. From where I was on the floor, I couldn't see him. The palpable heat from his anger suffocated the room. *Why didn't I just go the fuck home?*

I stood up fast, pushing my skirt down like it mattered. Nathan had his head down on the desk resting on his hands. He breathed heavily.

"I debated telling you a couple times. I froze up."

Nathan picked up his head; frustration stamped over his face. "Anytime would have been a great fucking time." His voice was oddly calm. "Do you have any idea how shitty I felt after you just walked out?"

"It doesn't matter. You didn't even try to follow me."

"Like hell I did. You just fucking walked out. I stared at the door with my dick still wet from you by the way and was paralyzed by rejection. I didn't expect to cuddle, but you just left! Kelsey explained some of the stupid rules to me, but he didn't say it ended immediately after. I felt like a fucking fool. When I went after you, I walked into a huge fight between Kelsey and some girl he was fucking around with behind Diane's back. Actually, I haven't seen Kelsey since that stupid night. Regardless, the last thing I needed that night was for you to bail on me seconds after we fucked."

It took a few moments, but his anger subsided and insecurity took hold of him. "Did you go to another room? Was I bad? The whole thing was rushed, but I didn't hurt you or do something wrong?"

"Nathan, I'm so sorry. I never thought you'd feel that way. I'm so embarrassed. You were fucking amazing. I've never had an experience like that in my entire life. Seriously, that was my first and only time playing their silly game, and I don't know what came over me. I lost my nerve." I felt terrible. The last thing I wanted for him was to feel inadequate.

"Where did you go?"

"I walked down the hall to Lucy's room, got changed, and left. I was sort of in a daze. I never would have thought you'd come after me. I missed the big fight between Lucy and Kelsey. She called me after and we met at a diner. I asked about you, but she didn't know who you were. She was confused like me."

"Lucy? Wait *the* Lucy, the woman I met the first day? Holy shit, it *was* her. I thought she was a redhead?" The gears worked in his brain again. He pieced it all together.

"Yeah, she changes her hair color a lot."

Nathan tipped his chin up. He wiped at his eyes like a tired child and slumped back in the chair. His cell phone rang, and he swiped it on, hitting the speaker button. "Clark?"

"Did you figure out a ride home or am I coming to get you when I sober up?" Clark asked.

"I'll take you home. I drove today," I interjected.

"You have a car?" Nathan sighed.

"Who's that?" Clark said.

"You know the girl I work with that I thought I knew?"

"The cute brunette with the nice ass?"

Nathan winced at Clark's words. I didn't dwell on it long, but my heart skipped a beat in hopes that I didn't fuck up royally. He thought I was cute? But he's dating a guy though? *I'm so confused.*

"Yup and you're on speaker phone, Clark. She owes me, so she'll drive me home."

"Sorry, Nate. Hey, that's fine. I won't have to pay the damn GW toll. I'm going to crash."

"Okay. Tell me about your set tomorrow. Later."

"Have fun. Bye."

I felt glued to the floor. My feet were killing me from a week's worth of heels and my anxiety seized up my body. I made this whole mess myself. *Why didn't I stay in the room? Why did I run? What was I really scared of?* Nathan gave me the best orgasm of my life and I ran. He fucked me exactly how I'd always wanted to be taken. It was a fucking terrible thing to just walk out.

"I'll go get the car," I offered.

"Are you crazy? It's almost one in the morning in New York City. We'll walk together. Give me a second."

Nathan grabbed his phone and locked the top desk drawer. He got up from his chair and grabbed his jacket off the wall hook.

"Are you ready to go?" he asked.

"Yeah, I was ready before. I overheard you on the phone and came back."

He nodded and shrugged on his coat. I willed myself to move out of his office before he shut the lights. We were uncomfortably silent the whole way down to the garage. *Were we done with the cross-examination?* In the elevator, I glanced up at him and he was staring down at me. He half-smiled and I just blinked a lot.

"What?" I said.

"You look different with your hair up and glasses. It's a shame I couldn't see your eyes that night. They're very pretty."

"Thank you. You're still sexy."

"Ha-ha, thank you back. How old are you?"

"I turned thirty-one back in August. You?"

"I'm thirty-two."

The silence resumed until we were driving. "Can you put your address into my phone?" I asked, breaking the silence.

"It says forty minutes. Is that okay?"

"It's fine. I wasn't going to leave you to find a hotel in the middle of the night."

"Clark was giving me a hard time."

"Is that your roommate?" I wondered if he was the guy at the speakeasy? I hoped he wasn't the boyfriend. *How fucking awkward would that be because I've seen them kiss before?*

"He's my roommate. He knows Kelsey too."

"The world knows that fucking guy."

"I met Kelsey in college."

"I thought I knew all of Kelsey's friends. I was relieved it was you, not one of his other friends."

"Why? He hangs with some good guys."

"To other guys, yeah, I guess they're good. To me, they're all assholes. It really bothers me when people don't remember me, and I'm constantly getting reintroduced."

"I tried to recognize you, but you wouldn't let me," Nathan proclaimed, sucking in air to make his lips pop.

"That's different. I didn't want you to know me."

Nathan turned in his seat toward me. "I'm sorry for yelling before. I know it was a game, but I was really disappointed it ended so fast. I didn't try hard enough to find you either. I was afraid I was too rough or something."

"Nathan, I'm sorry too. That was the craziest thing I'd ever done. I had just gotten out of a bad relationship, and I wasn't thinking about you or your feelings. You were the best sex I've ever had. I came so hard I barely remember walking to the other room. I hope you can forgive me. I wouldn't want it done to me." I cried.

He didn't look angry. He intently listened and mulled over what I said. I pulled up to a traffic light.

"Bri, it's okay. Please don't cry. I understand." As I turned to him, he kissed me. The same little zap I felt the first time we kissed rushed back. His cold hand cupped the side of my face. Someone's car horn jolted me back to reality. The light was green and the moment was over.

He swiped his hand over the tears on my cheek.

"Let's put some music on. Use my phone," I said.

"Good idea," he agreed.

# Chapter Eight

The drive to New Jersey wasn't as bad as I thought it would be. I was exhausted and it began to snow by the time we got to the George Washington Bridge. A few scattered flurries peppered my windshield.

"I didn't know it was supposed to snow. I've been buried in this project. Do you live far from here?" Nathan asked.

"I live in Westchester."

"Shit, that's far. Now, I feel like a dick."

"Hey, I offered to take you home. It's the least I can do."

Nathan crossed his arm over his chest and dragged his other hand through his hair.

"Aren't you tired? You're not going to get home until three a.m. and it's snowing. Can you turn on the radio?"

"Of course, I'm tired, but I didn't want to leave you in the office."

"Thank you."

As soon as we hit New Jersey, the snow steadily increased. The flurries stuck to the sides of the road and the grass. The radio said we were getting two to three inches. It wouldn't be a bad storm, but we were smack dab in the middle of it. I hated driving in the snow. Luckily, the GPS stated only fifteen more minutes until Nathan's apartment.

Nathan lived in a large apartment building a couple blocks from a hospital. An ambulance sped by us, sirens blaring. "Isn't that annoying to hear all time?"

He shrugged. "It makes rent cheaper. You get used to it." We were back to simple questions and short curt responses. *I wanted the fuck out of my car.*

I parked in the large parking lot in an unmarked spot already covered with snow. He told me to hold on and I stayed in the car until he opened my door for me, reaching out his hand. I stared at him perplexed.

"See you on Monday," I said.

"Hell, no. You're coming up with me. It's too bad out." Nathan opened my door wider.

"Nathan, thank you, but I got it. It's only snow. I'll use second gear, and take my foot off the brake if I swerve," I said.

"I don't care. I'm not letting you drive home. Come on."

"Fine," I acquiesced. I shut off the car and unbuckled my seat belt. I stepped out and Nathan took my hand. His hand was fucking freezing. I took my hand back from him, but he grabbed it again.

"It gets icy," Nathan said.

"Thanks."

"Yup!"

*Oh yes, we were doing great in the healing period. We're fighting over snow.*

We walked up the wet stairs into the lobby. The old man behind the desk waved and Nathan returned the sentiment.

"Goodnight, Bobby."

"Goodnight, Mr. Richards! Check your emails for the snow removal schedule."

"Will do."

So, everybody generally liked Nathan and I was the asshole on his shit list. *Great. Just fucking great.*

We entered the elevator, and he hit the fifth floor button. He had stopped holding my hand when we entered the building. The tension was thick and frankly I couldn't tell if he was still pissed off or tired.

"Nathan, it's not that bad out there. I can make it home. There's barely anyone on the road now," I said.

"I would never let you drive home in this mess. Let's get some sleep and talk in the morning, okay?"

"All right. I'm sorry. I feel like I'm making things worse by staying the night."

"The whole thing is already fucked up, Bri."

The elevator dinged for his floor and Nathan stormed out. I followed reluctantly. I missed lighthearted Nathan, forever tormented by a silly printer. I wanted to see the smile he gave me every time I gave him good work. Pissed off Nathan sucked.

We headed down the hallway past a few doors decorated with pretty wreaths for the upcoming holidays. His door had a "Rock On" welcome mat, generations different from the others.

He opened the door and waited for me to go first into the darkness.

The apartment opened into a kitchen nook. Clark had left the overhead light on. The rest of the apartment was quiet and dark. There was one large, long room, with enough space for a dinette, a desk, and two large couches.

"Please be quiet. Clark is probably asleep," Nathan whispered close to my face. I took my high heels off, so I didn't make noise on the hardwood floors.

"Okay."

"Come with me."

I followed him to the right side of the apartment down the hallway. There were three doors and a bathroom at the end of the hallway. Nathan opened the second door on the right, parallel with another door on the left side.

Nathan ushered me inside and closed the door. He flipped on the light and took off his coat and blazer. "What size T-shirt do you wear?" He walked toward the closet. The thought dawned on me that all I had to do to get him to leave me alone was tell the truth. It would have been so easy.

"I can sleep in my clothes."

Nathan's shoulders slumped down. "Bri, stop being a pain in the ass. You're staying here, and you don't have to sleep in a skirt. Let me do something nice for you. I have tons of clothes; tell me what size you wear." I needed to stop talking. He was letting me sleep in his apartment; I could at least be forthcoming.

"Okay. Anything will work. I'm a medium/large in shirts, and an XL in pants."

"Thank you." No smile yet, but his brisk tone was fading.

Nathan opened a set of drawers that lined the bottom of his closet. He pulled out a pair of black sweat pants and took a shirt off a hanger. He held it up to me and then threw it over his shoulder.

"Take the bed. I'll take the couch," Nathan offered.

"Absolutely not. I'll take the clothes, but I'm not putting you out of your own bed."

"Fine, take the couch." He handed me the shirt and sweats.

"The door at the end of the hallway is the bathroom. There should be a new toothbrush under the sink. I'll get you a blanket." Nathan reached over to his bed and picked up one of the two pillows.

"Thank you, Nathan. I appreciate your hospitality," I said.

"Bri, you've helped me enough in the last three weeks. We're good. Don't worry about it." For the first time since he kissed me in the car he smiled at me. I leaned up and gave him a kiss on the cheek.

Nathan glided his hand up my arm to my shoulder and moved up to cup my right cheek. This was the most he'd touched me since we'd met again. He looked down at me, his gaze scanning my face. "What?" I asked.

"Nothing," Nathan said, swallowing. "See you in the morning, Bri." It took him a few moments to walk away and leave the room. I stood there, staring ahead.

*Maybe Lucy was right. I had absolutely no fucking clue what I saw in that bar.*

# Chapter Nine

"Why the hell is she on our couch, Nathan? Why are you not fucking her in your room?" A deep voice shouted. I woke up instantly.

"Keep it down. I'm sorry for taking your feelings into consideration. I'm still pissed at her, too," Nathan scolded. Light shined from the kitchen area.

"Dude you've been talking about her for the past three weeks *and* two months after that night. Don't worry about us. If you want to kiss her or whatever, I'm not going to stop you because I can tell it's what you really want."

"I kissed her already in the car. Are you mad?"

"No, you prick. Listen to me. Make it right with her now. She's fine, told you everything, and turns out she's a good person. I told you it wasn't you and now she's saying you did nothing wrong. Don't get cold feet now."

"She'll probably just leave right after."

"That's seriously not funny. You have no idea what she'd do. You barely know her. From what you said a hundred times she enjoyed it as much as you. Give her the benefit of the doubt."

"I do like her, but if she leaves again it would crush me."

"You're lucky that the snow will keep her here."

"Ha. Ha." I heard footsteps and then a few heavier

ones followed.

"Don't you dare go jerk off while she's on our couch," Clark said.

"You know way too much."

"Sorry, that was harsh. All I'm saying is that if you like her and want a repeat fantasy at least talk to her. She's right here, Nathan, in our apartment. Don't let the opportunity pass. Monday is going to be fucking crazy awkward if something doesn't get cleaned up between you two."

"Fuck, the damn office."

"Here, make it simple. Either you're attracted to each other and want to work something out or not. So then nothing happens, you finish your project together, and you go back to your office when it's done. No harm no foul and you are just an asshole for caring about her safety in the snow.

"But you might see her at Kelsey's wedding if they're still close…"

A door shut and silence followed.

*He liked me before he knew I was the girl that night? How?* I'd been so standoffish, yet he tried to spend any minute with me. *God, did my ex mess me up so bad I can't even recognize when a guy likes me?*

He had gotten me a few coffees and came to me for every little thing on the project, so I hadn't felt like he took over. But he did check me out twice that I was aware of.

"Bri, are you awake?" Nathan whispered near my ear. I jolted and opened my eyes. He stood over me. I must have dozed off in my thoughts.

"Yeah. I'm a light sleeper," I lied.

"Can we talk?"

"Please." It was now or never.

Nathan sat next to me on the sofa. He cracked his knuckles and turned on the lamp on the side table. He looked so sexy in his white undershirt and pajama pants. A tattoo wrapped around his right bicep. I traced the thorny pattern with my fingers. Goosebumps arose on his warm flesh.

"I have two more tattoos on my back." I arched my eyebrows up. "Surprised?" he asked.

"Yes. You seem so conservative at the office and focused. I don't think I've caught you bullshitting longer than a minute."

"I take Adderall. It's time release for the whole day."

"Ah, that makes sense. So are we going to small talk more or are you going to talk to me?" Watching him beat around the bush was painful.

"I'm sorry. My life is complicated and meeting you, like really meeting you, messed it up for me a little more." Nathan stopped. He stood up and paced through the small living room.

"I get it. I appreciate the gesture letting me sleep here tonight with the snow and all. Tomorrow morning I'll go home and we will just finish the project for the next few weeks. Then I'll see you at the check-in meetings okay? No drama needed." I laid out the fire escape for both of us to use.

He stopped pacing. "I'm not okay with that. Are you?"

"Not really…" I fidgeted under his gaze. I glanced at the marquee poster on the wall. I wondered briefly if the hot guy posed with the guitar was Clark the roommate.

"That's not what I want either. I can't stop replaying that night in my head. You were so hot in that outfit. When I watched you sucking me off, and saw you finger yourself, shit, I almost busted my load. You were turning me on like crazy." Nathan walked over to me. With me on the couch and him standing over me we mimicked our previous scandalous positions. He caressed my cheek with the back of his hand.

It was different when I stared up into his eyes. I had no cheap lace blindfold to hide behind. We were both out in the open.

"Why is your life complicated?" I asked.

"Clark and I…we're not just roommates. We've been having a sexual relationship for the past few months. He…Um…Wow…I've never said that out loud to anyone. I'm a little unsure of everything right now, but I know I'm going to regret it if I let you walk out that door in the morning without feeling you against me again. I'm…"

A door down the hallway opened up quickly and the man in the poster walked out with a Rancid T-shirt on and pajama shorts. He was a bleached blond with messed up short-cropped hair, shaved sides, and piercing blue eyes behind glasses. He looked pissed. His slightly taller frame glared at Nathan.

Oh and yeah, he was also the guy from the speakeasy…

"Hi, Bri, I'm Clark, it's a pleasure to meet you. I'm Nathan's live-in sort of boyfriend. I'm fine with whatever you two do tonight. So there you have it. This is the disclaimer for tonight's festivities. Now seriously, will you two go in his room and figure out if it was one night of lust-filled fuckery or something else? It's three a.m. and I have to be at the recording studio at ten a.m. Goodnight all." Clark smiled baring all his teeth in a fake smile. I had to laugh at the outburst. His message was loud and clear.

Clark kissed Nathan on the cheek. "You're welcome." He bowed his head at me and retreated back to his room like a freaking cuckoo clock bird.

"Did that really just happen?" I asked Nathan, who was still staring at the direction of the hallway.

"Yup, um yeah that's Clark. So…" I stopped him with a kiss. I was done talking. Nathan immediately kissed me harder. His tongue plunged into my mouth and my core tugged deep inside. Nathan thrust his hand under my shirt to grab my breast and my body remembered the last time he did that to me. I moaned as the memory crashed over me.

"I want you so fucking badly," Nathan whispered into my mouth. He resumed his devastating kiss. He pulled at my waist making us flush against each other. His hard cock nudged my stomach.

I pulled back from the kiss. "Nathan, can we go to your bedroom?"

He nodded and linked our fingers together leading me to the other side of the apartment. I was so happy I practically skipped after him.

Nathan barely opened his door fast enough. We stumbled into his bedroom all mouths, tongues, and fumbling fingers. My back hit against the door and Nathan lifted off the shirt I borrowed from him. With my breasts bared Nathan leaned down and took my left nipple into his mouth. He flicked his tongue over and over and sucked it hard. My legs quivered. I sank deeper into the feeling when Nathan plumped my other breast in his hand. A small moan escaped my mouth.

I fumbled my hands over the head of his cock through his pajama bottoms. He bit down on my breast and the sharp tug made me yearn for more. Nathan's mouth popped off my breast. He stared at my wet nipple and blew warm air on it, making me shiver.

I needed more. All those months wasted remembering him. I clasped both hands on his cheeks and brought him back up for another kiss. I tiptoed forward and pushed him lightly onto the bed when his legs hit the bottom. I straddled him and grinded onto his lap. He groaned and pulled me down onto the bed with him. We scooted up to the top and Nathan fingered the hem of his pants that I wore. "I don't think you need these anymore."

He slid the pajama pants and my panties off and kissed the side of my knee. He traveled up my body with a few kisses on my thighs, stomach, and back up to my breasts. His hand moved between my legs and thrust his fingers into my pussy. "I want to watch you fuck yourself again."

"Will you stroke your cock for me?" I moaned out.

"Uh-huh."

Nathan took off his pants and boxers, letting his cock spring free. The tip glistened from our foreplay. I slid my hand over the head of his cock and brought my hand up to lick at the precum I took from him. His lust-filled stare was back. I stretched my hand down, parted my folds, and massaged my clit. Nathan's fingers continued to thrust into my pussy. His other hand stroked his cock.

"You're so beautiful. I can't believe you're in my bed."

He added another finger into my pussy. My body clenched around it, craving more than just his fingers.

"Nathan, I want you so bad."

Nathan leaned over me and grabbed a condom from the bedside table. I was on the pill, but I appreciated his need for safe sex. We definitely needed to have that conversation later. I wanted to be filled up with his bare cock inside me. He would feel so fucking good.

When he was ready, I practically panted with need. I pulled at his waist, impatient to fuck. He eased inside inch by delicious inch and, we both groaned when his stomach fell against me, his mouth seeking mine.

"I wanted to do this again for so long," Nathan murmured against my mouth. "Fuck, Bri."

I couldn't see his slow thrusts, but I felt him. Dear God, he was so deep. His cock filled up my pussy and waves of pleasure cascaded through me. It had been so long since I had sex. Too much time had passed since Nathan was inside me. The joyous feeling of being fucked, infused my every thought. I lifted up my hips so he could reach deeper inside me.

"Oh, Bri, I wanted you so badly," he whispered. If I started talking, I wouldn't stop. I grunted his name and he lifted his body off mine. Now I could see our bodies and peer down at his cock fucking me into his bed. Nathan held my hips and jerked my body onto his cock. Still slow, but fuck, it was hitting me inside perfectly.

"Nathan!" I screamed his name when he thumbed my clit, staring down at our lovemaking. The edges of my orgasm ignited.

"Fuck! I want to come so bad. Come with me."

I dragged my hand up his smooth chest and pulled his head down. I needed more of him. He kissed me and squeezed my breast, tugging at my nipple. He fucked me harder and took my nipple into his mouth sucking it and letting it go after each thrust. He switched to the other breast pulling away and sucking then pulling away and I just lost it. My pussy twitched around his cock, my orgasm flared out, squeezing shiver after shiver from me.

I arched my body up and unraveled around him. I moaned, I whimpered, I grabbed a fist of his hair keeping him from releasing my breast. He moaned against my nipple and pumped faster in me.

His gaze flicked upward, and he let my breast go. “You’re going to make me come, baby.”

“Come, Nathan,” I ordered. Nathan closed the gap between us, and fucked me hard into the mattress. He buried his face into the crook of my neck and didn’t let me go until he was shouting and coming inside me.

I caressed him everywhere my hands reached. He lost his rhythm and stayed inside me panting against my neck.

# Chapter Ten

"How did you get that scar?" Nathan traced a line from my half-moon scar outlining my areola up to my budded nipple.

"I had a fibroid tumor removed. It hurt like a bitch, but I can't complain. I was grateful I didn't have breast cancer." I answered.

"Wow, that's scary. Is that like a lump?"

"Yeah, it's like having a golf ball in your boob." Nathan inspected my breast over with his fingertips. I had to squirm. His finger traveled down further.

"What about that scar?" Under my breasts a few inches above my naval I had three little white lines.

"Gall Bladder removal. Trust me, Nathan, the other scars get more boring as you go down my body," I said. I was doing it again. I was trying to steer the focus off my imperfections.

"There is nothing boring about you," Nathan said.

Nathan kissed me, reigniting my fire, which had cooled to a low simmer. I straddled his toned body and inspected him in the dim light. He pulled me forward, but I stayed up strong undulating on his softened cock. His chest was smooth to the touch with just a few hairs around his nipples and a short happy trail.

"Do you shave your chest?" I asked my new lover.

"You're going to laugh." Nathan shifted my hips to grind a little harder against him.

"Tell me, Nathan. You pointed out every one of my flaws." He stared at where our bodies were smashed together. "Nathan?" He rubbed my clit where it massaged his hardening cock. "Nathan, are you listening?"

"How can I possibly listen when I have you again?" He leaned up to take the nipple of my right breast into his mouth. He flicked his tongue around the little scar. I didn't have the heart to tell him my skin was numb over the scar because the visual was enough to light me on fire.

"Come on. Tell me," I persisted.

"All right. Hair just doesn't grow on my chest. I can't grow a mustache either."

"Whew, that's not terrible."

"Tell that to the bullies in high school."

"Aww, Nathan, I'm sorry. At least you grew up hot?"

"Gee thanks."

I scooted back onto his thighs and stroked his hardened cock with my wetness. "Do you like that or am I being too rough?"

"It's perfect," he said.

Nathan flipped me onto my back and brought my arms over my head. He bent down to nibble my neck. "I felt terrible I couldn't fuck you on a bed that night. I wanted to do this the second I walked into the room."

He released my hands to hold his cock steady. He felt up my pussy for just the right place. His cock nudged inside me and I lifted my hips up. He gasped and sat back on his heels. "Shit, hold on."

Nathan reached over to his side table again. He almost fell over trying to open the drawer.

"Nathan, it's okay. I'm on the pill and I don't have any STDs. You can fuck me bare."

"For real?" His eyes widened.

"Well, do you have anything?"

"No, Clark and I are clean. Yes!" Nathan smiled and kissed me and rolled me back on top of him. "Fuck me, baby. I want to feel your wet pussy."

I grabbed his cock and sank down onto him slowly. He was so fucking long and deep. Nathan flipped his head back against the headboard and groaned the loudest I'd heard him so far. Hopefully, Clark was asleep by now.

Nathan's cock stretched me completely and I spread my legs wider over his hips until there was no more left to go.

"Fuck! You feel so good, Bri," Nathan moaned.

I leaned up on my knees dragging his cock inside me. His hard grip on my hips jerked me back down, drawing helpless moans from my throat each time. He watched my pussy fuck his cock until I grinded down on him and his breath hitched into a gasp.

"Come here, baby," Nathan whispered. His hand left my hip and he pulled my neck toward him. Our kiss made me shiver and it left him grunting with each thrust of his hips. My breasts jiggled against his chest, rubbing my nipples with the right amount of friction.

"Oh, Nathan. Yes!" I moaned, I gasped, I whimpered. You name it, I did it. Nathan's thrusts hit me in the exact spot I needed, and the steady pace perfectly unwound my tension. Nathan touched my face, guiding my lips back to his and kissed me.

I learned he loved slow fucking as much as the fast frenzied way we went at it earlier.

We managed to come together, my pussy grinding at the perfect angle on his cock, my fingers gripping the headboard, his mouth locked on my breast, and his hands digging into my waist.

It was different without a condom. At the party I was able to detach from the situation. Now as Nathan's naked cock twitched inside me with his soft touches and kisses surrounding me, I couldn't imagine walking out of this room.

****

I woke up to a furry caress on my cheek. A small tabby cat, with black-and-white fur, lay in front of me on Nathan's bed pawing my face. "Hi little one," I whispered.

I petted the little cutie and it immediately purred and pushed its pretty face into my palm. I didn't recall Nathan saying he had a cat. *Maybe it was Clark's?* The door to Nathan's room was slightly ajar letting in the morning light. Ah. The kitty must have worked its way in.

A warm arm held me prisoner on my side. Nathan's body was pretty much a furnace against me. Luckily, I put Nathan's shirt back on to sleep in.

I extracted myself slowly from Nathan's embrace. His arm flopped dead to the mattress, startling the curious kitty. Nathan's face was scrunched up in the pillow. He looked like he could sleep for days that way. I'd always heard great sex will do that to you. I laughed quietly at Lucy's words in my head.

I tiptoed out of the room to look for my phone. My purse wasn't where I left it on the table. Someone moved it to the couch. The sunlight glared back from the living room windows. I had to squint. It was so sunny out and the white snow covering the ground heightened the brightness. It only looked like a few inches had fallen.

A door opened down the hallway. Aftershave and soap wafted out.

“Good Morning.” It wasn’t Nathan’s voice.

I whipped around. Clark stood in the kitchen with only a towel wrapped around his waist. Where Nathan was smooth and hairless, Clark was absolutely not. His chest was dusted with light hair; a spiral design tattoo decorated his chest above his heart. I couldn’t stop staring at him. There were more tattoos on his arms, overloading me with the hot untouchable sight of him.

“Remember to breathe, okay?” Clark said interrupting my thoughts. I let out the breath he knew I held.

“Sorry. I haven’t had coffee yet. Good Morning, Clark.”

“Morning.” Clark strolled casually into the kitchen and opened up the oven. He bent down out of sight and then closed the oven pushing at a few buttons on the top. He turned back to me looking normal as ever half-naked. “Breakfast is almost ready.”

“Um.” It was all I managed. Even in my satisfied sexual fuzzy state, seeing him like this stopped me in my tracks. Droplets of water clung to his chest hair and his stomach and there were dark wet spots on his towel right over the outline of his long cock. *Jesus Christ…*

“Um?” Clark said, tilting his head to the side.

“Thank you?” I couldn’t even remember what I was thanking him for. My brain was instant mush.

“You’re welcome.” He walked toward the hall and stopped. He stared me straight in the eye, and asked,

"Did you guys fuck last night?"

"Um, yeah."

"Good. I don't mean to be rude, but I have to go. You can memorize my naked body longer some other time."

*Well, Nathan said he was blunt.* My mouth gaped open. Clark smiled an impish smirk and disappeared down the hall. I still stood in the same spot several minutes after his door closed. So that was Nathan's boyfriend, the musician, in the daylight, in a towel?

*Crap, I'm so fucking screwed.*

# Chapter Eleven

Eventually I moved from my stupor and ran back to Nathan's room. The small cat snuggled up to Nathan and meowed at my intrusion. "Yeah, kitty, I don't know why I'm here either."

I got back under the covers and listened to Clark move around the apartment. How fucking awkward was that? I fucked his boyfriend, and then I ogled him in a towel. Maybe he won't tell Nathan.

The front door shut at exactly nine fifteen a.m. Nathan snored away. I waited another ten minutes before I woke him up. My anxiety simmered to a dull ache.

"Clark said he made breakfast," I said.

Nathan got up and did ten pushups like nothing. *If he clapped every time he ascended, I was going to run for the hills.*

"Sorry, I do that every morning. Are you okay?"

"Yeah, I've never seen someone do pushups so effortlessly."

He shrugged. "What did Betty Crocker make?" Nathan slipped on a shirt and pajama pants over his boxers. It was just as sexy to watch him put clothes on as take them off. "Bri?"

"He didn't say."

"You talked to him?"

"Only for a moment. I was getting my phone. I

hope you don't mind."

"Bri, you can talk to him. Clark isn't off limits. You might like him a lot."

"Okay," I said and looked up at Nathan. I guess the look on my face wasn't exactly reassuring.

"You're totally freaking out, aren't you? The Clark thing is bothering you." Nathan bit his bottom lip and grabbed the outside of his arm.

"I'm trying not to. I'm sorry. This seems so real now. It's been a while for me since I've been in a relationship. I think my ex broke me."

Nathan leaned back onto the bed and kissed me on the lips, not caring about morning breath. He pulled back and said, "You're not broken, baby. We'll figure it all out."

Oddly enough, I nodded and was content with his answer. Even though I wanted to desperately think this to death, I pushed it aside and joined Nathan in the kitchen. Clark made croissants with tiny chocolate pieces in them, shocking Nathan.

"So here's the thing with Clark. He doesn't really cook, and his idea of breakfast is a Hot Pocket that he may or may not nuke in the microwave."

"Ew? Isn't that disgusting if you don't heat it up?"

"I'm being metaphorical. He must like you." Nathan picked up the croissant, took a bite, and rolled his eyes back into his head. "Oh shit, this is yummy."

It was yummy, buttery, chocolaty goodness. So Clark was fine with Nathan having sex with me last night and baked us an amazing breakfast, fully aware he wasn't eating with us. *Who the fuck is this Clark guy?*

"Can I ask you a question and I apologize if comes out the wrong way?" I said.

"Shoot," Nathan said finishing his third mini croissant.

"Are you bisexual or gay with straight curiosity?"

Nathan answered without a hint of hesitation. "I guess you could say I'm bisexual if you have to label it. I've mostly dated women, but I did have a relationship with this guy Brandon in college. Long story short, he thought we were more in a relationship than I did. The few weeks we were together we didn't go very far physically so I guess that's how I missed that he thought it was more serious."

"Okay…how can someone miss something like that?"

"It was mostly drunken nights with sneaky hands under the covers if you know what I mean. It was college and you know what kids say these days, 'YOLO.' " He laughed at himself and continued, "Clark and I are more physical yet less serious."

"So how did it happen between you and Clark? Did you guys live together before you hooked up?"

"We lived together several months before we realized we were attracted to each other. It's actually a funny story."

"Do you want to share it? I've been wondering," I confessed. I tucked my legs under me on the couch and turned to face him.

Nathan brushed his hands down his sweatpants and shook his head. "Clark is going to kill me. It started one drunken night after his show. His last band got Clark to wear skinny jeans. He reluctantly bought a pair and couldn't get them off. He's lead guitar so he was a sweaty mess and asked for my help.

"We were both drunk, so we took a cab home. I

missed a lot of signs that he was hitting on me. In the cab, he put his head on my shoulder. He ran his fingers up my leg, bitching about the skinny jeans. Later he told me he was testing me to see if I was reacting to him.

"When we got back to the apartment, we went straight to his bedroom. He took his shirt off, and I chubbed up watching him. Then, he asked if I could help him take off his pants. He dragged his zipper down and his dick was hard already. I didn't think much of it until I got his jeans off.

"He stroked his dick, watching me fiddle with the end of his pants. I should have looked away, but I wanted to watch. Then he kissed me. It wasn't like kissing my ex-girlfriend or my ex-kind of boyfriend. I didn't want to stop.

"He put my hand on his dick and he was so hard. All I wanted to do was make him moan. The next thing I knew his dick was in my mouth.

"It wasn't my first time sucking cock, but I shocked myself. I remember him moaning, 'Please don't stop' and I snapped. I needed to make him come."

I didn't realize I was panting until Nathan stopped talking. My short intakes of breath filled the room. I felt wet from Nathan's X-rated story telling. "And then?" I urged.

"I sucked him off and it felt so fucking good to see him have his guard down. I stroked him until he finished then I licked his cum off his chest. Let's just say he had his answer if I was attracted to him.

"We didn't fuck, but he took it further. While he sucked my dick, he fingered my ass. I came so fast. I was so worked up; I couldn't stop it.

"It continued on from there. When we were both home, we'd hook up. There is something very natural between him and me, but I know I'm not one hundred percent gay. I had a great time last night with you and appreciate your body, especially your womanly parts."

"I'm glad you appreciate a woman."

"I didn't mean it like that." Nathan leaned into my ear. "I meant I like fucking your pussy, I love your boobs, and there is nothing like having you ride my dick. There are things you can only do with a woman that I don't think I could give up. Especially a beautiful woman like you."

"But you like sucking cock too?"

"Clark is more a fan of licking. What's up with the questions, Bri?

"Honest curiosity."

"I can respect that. Are you in a rush to go home?"

I looked out the window. Most of the snow was melted and the parking lot was completely clear.

"Not really. It looks like a lot of the snow melted already. I can leave now."

"You're going to run out of here, aren't you?" Nathan said. I turned back to him. His arm was thrown over the back of the couch and his mouth morphed into a hard line.

"Not unless you want me to go."

"Of course not. I have tons of embarrassing private stories you can pry out of me first." He kidded, grabbing another croissant.

I sat back down and flicked the odd line in his right ear. "What happened here?"

"A cork gone wrong. I did it for a girl who wanted to do it together. A year later she dumped me, and it had stretched too much to naturally bounce back."

"Ouch."

"You have no idea."

## Chapter Twelve

I went home a few hours later. On my way home I cranked up the radio and happiness curled through me.

But then on Sunday I didn't hear from Nathan. I panicked around seven p.m. on Sunday night. We hadn't exactly discussed if last night was just a one-time thing or if we were going to see each other again. *Fuck, I hope he doesn't think I'm the office slut or easy?* We had sex before last night. Does that discount the skipping over dinner first logic? *Fuck.*

I barely slept on Sunday night fretting about it. I resolved a plan to act like a normal sexually active woman who had casual sex on Friday night with a co-worker. Thinking about it like that wasn't any better. I ran to my desk and threw myself into work.

By ten a.m., Nathan's office light still wasn't on. There was a meeting scheduled for ten-thirty. Where the fuck was he? Sure as hell, the second time I looked up the light was on. No hello, nothing. *Fuckity fuck. This can't be good.*

I stormed away from my desk. The coffee machine and pods got the brunt of my anger.

Back at my desk, I had one email from Nathan..

*Nathan Richards: 10:15 a.m.:*

*I'm an asshole and forgot to get your number. Dinner tonight?*

I laughed so hard I cried. I had his because I put it

in there when we started the project. I cursed myself for immediately thinking the worst of Nathan. It never dawned on me that he wouldn't have my number.

"Are you laughing at me?" I looked up and there was Nathan coming into my cubicle and leaning against the file cabinet.

"At myself. Hey, you're late."

"I know. The train was on a different schedule for Veteran's day. It's not a good day when you fuck up multiple times before eight a.m."

"Oh great you're both here!" Paul stopped mid-stride around the bend. I jumped at the surprise intrusion. "I need to cancel our meeting."

Nathan and I both agreed it was fine, especially with Nathan just getting into work.

"Nathan, I have to apologize for our lack of hospitality. You switched here and we didn't even take you to dinner. I promise we usually do things a lot more formal and professional. Are you available tonight? We can go to Mr. Grant's restaurant."

"Paul, don't worry about it. I don't need any special treatment." Nathan said, touching Paul's shoulder.

"It's our pleasure. Bri, are you free tonight too? If you join us we can go over the topics I wanted to discuss this morning."

"I'm free. Nathan?" I said.

"I'm free too," Nathan said.

"Great. Does six o'clock work?" Paul asked.

"Perfect," Nathan said.

Paul nodded and scurried off. Nathan glanced back behind my wall at Paul's path.

"Did you read my email?" Nathan said.

"Give me your phone?" I asked. Nathan smiled and handed me his phone unlocked. I added my contact information.

"You can't say no to dinner now," Nathan said.

"I wouldn't miss it, Nathan."

****

Dinner with Paul was stats and numbers as expected. I listened to them discuss Nathan's other accounts and our joint client. I wished Nathan and I were here alone.

"How do you feel about that, Bri?" Paul asked, looping me back in.

"Honestly Paul, I think the client will be very happy."

Paul smiled. He started again about demos and Nathan rolled his eyes. "Paul, I'm living, breathing, and dreaming about this project. We got this, man."

Nathan lifted up his drink and both Paul and I did the same. We cheered to the hopeful success of the project.

"Now Paul, tell me about yourself. I realized we've emailed for months, but I know very little about you." Nathan steered the conversation away from work.

"Sorry guys. This project has me so nervous. Mr. Grant has been lurking around my office asking questions. My promotion also came at the worst time. The training is tedious."

"We have a good handle on it, Paul. It's nothing we haven't seen before. We're giving it one hundred and ten percent! Let's order you another drink. You're too tense," I said.

"My girlfriend said the same thing."

"What? You have a girlfriend?" *What the fuck?* I

was shocked.

"I know, right? I practically live at the office. Her name is Sandra. She's a nurse so we pretty much have breakfast together and see each other for a few hours on Sundays. Actually, will you guys excuse me a minute? I need to give her a call."

"Of course, buddy. Take your time," Nathan said waving him off.

When Paul was far enough away, Nathan whispered, "Let's never double date with them please. This guy is fucking high strung."

"Ha-ha. No problem." I chuckled.

I took another sip of my drink and noticed Nathan staring at me. "What?"

"Hi," he said looking cute and sexy.

I returned the "Hi" and he leaned over to kiss me.

"I should apologize. I didn't plan on Paul coming on our first date," Nathan said.

"It's okay."

"Are you doing anything later?"

"After this? Not that I'm aware."

"How about hopping over to Jersey and taking a stranded, sex-starved man home?"

"Sex-starved? Aren't you the one with a live-in boyfriend?"

"He's on the last leg of his tour."

"But he was home on Friday?"

"Only for the night. He went straight to his gig after he finished at the recording studio. He makes a shit ton of money per song he finishes. It's worth coming back home," Nathan explained.

"Gotcha. When does the tour end?"

"I think the last show is tonight. They're in

Connecticut so he should be home later."

"He's playing on a Monday night?" I asked.

"You'd be surprised. He has one crazy ass schedule."

"Is it the diehard fans who see every show?"

"They do have a following. The girl in the band always brings people too. I wonder what music Paul likes?"

"Hip hop." He played the radio in his office all the time.

"Figures. Just so I'm clear on my chances, did you and Paul ever date?" Nathan inquired.

I almost choked on my cocktail. "Hell no. If he accidentally looked at my cleavage, I swear he'd march himself down to HR to confess."

"I had to ask. HR is going to be after me pretty soon. There is something about you in a white button down that turns me on." Nathan gave me another kiss. "Hmm…Paul better come back soon. I can't be held accountable for my actions once I've had a drink or two." Nathan smirked and swiveled the giant ice cube in his drink.

"Oh, you can't?" I played along.

Nathan grabbed my hand and brought it under the table. He pushed my hand onto the front of his pants. He was hard, and I couldn't do a thing about it. I wanted to get down on my knees and suck his cock down my throat.

"Shit, he's coming back," I muttered.

Nathan held onto my hand for almost too long. Paul fumbled with his phone when he sat back down. Finally, Nathan released my hand and adjusted himself in the seat.

“Is it hot in here or is it just me?” Nathan said, pulling at his collar.

“I’m definitely warm. Where were we?” Paul ignorantly answered a rhetorical question.

The waitress came over with our entrees. Three filet mignons cooked to perfection. We resumed a lengthy discussion about the project. I tried hard to focus on Paul, but my mind wandered to more pleasantly dirty things, especially Nathan’s hard cock under the table.

My text message alert chimed. It was Nathan. —*Come home with me.*—

The sides of my mouth curled. I didn’t respond and placed my phone back on the table. I looked over and he pouted back at me.

“This project is making me wish I took the pay-by-the-hour rate instead of salary. We might need to work overtime,” Paul said.

“The trains run late, but I can always drive into the city if necessary,” Nathan said. He picked up his phone again.

“Great. It would be a big help. You two seem to be getting along better than the first few weeks?”

Nathan froze, and then finished his text. I was ready for Paul’s remark and barely hesitated. “We found out we have mutual friends. I swear everyone knows everybody!” Technically true, but I was trying to steer the topic off our relationship.

“Good! You had me worried for a little while.”

I peered at my phone and saw -*Please?*- I gave Nathan a smile and nodded. He reached under the table and squeezed my knee.

“Paul, you have nothing to worry about here. We

play nice when both our names will be on the final paper," I resolved.

"Yeah, what she said. Can we get the check?" Nathan said.

## Chapter Thirteen

By the time we finished dinner, it was later than I thought, but I already said yes to Nathan's invitation. His apartment wasn't that far away when it wasn't snowing.

Nathan bent me over the desk in his living room, bringing my ass up to meet his waist. I gasped when he spread warming lube over my whole pussy. "I want you to enjoy this as much as me."

His fingers felt wonderful, but I yearned for more. His fingers stretched my pussy wide and dipped inside.

"Nathan, please."

He didn't have to be told twice. I looked back at him, spreading the lube over his cock and driving it straight inside me. We both moaned. He pulled out slowly, prolonging the sweet agony, and thrust back fast and hard. I grabbed the edge of the desk as he picked up a frenzied pace.

I pinched my clit the way I liked it and grazed my nails against Nathan's balls. He groaned and stopped his thrusts.

"Oh fuck, Bri. Yes!" he said, gripping my waist harder.

I jerked back against him when the front door opened. Clark stood in the doorway with his hand on the doorknob; his shocked gaze glued to the porno in his living room. His guitar almost fell off his shoulders, but he pulled it back up.

"Shit, Clark," Nathan said. He started to pull out of me, but a second later thrust back into me, hiding our embrace with his body.

I didn't know what to do. Nathan held me prisoner and Clark stared us down. Clark said he was okay with me, right? Everything was all right. But he still caught his boyfriend in the act.

"Don't stop on my behalf," Clark said casually, shutting the door and flipping the lock behind him.

"What?" Nathan said. His long fingers stroked against my hip, soothing my sudden tension.

"You heard me. Don't stop fucking her," Clark declared.

On cue, Nathan's cock slowly moved in and out me again. He was still deep; his cock barely left my pussy. The sucking sounds of my wetness being pushed through resumed.

Clark would be able to see everything now. He had to be watching Nathan fuck me. I didn't turn back to look, not yet. The sensations washed over me, granting me the courage to continue on.

"Bri?" Nathan said. He only said my name, but I knew what he wanted. He wanted an okay, the yes from me. The time to hesitate was gone. I wanted him to finish what he started.

"Please don't stop," I grunted out.

I wish I had said more, but Nathan picked up the pace and fucked me against the desk again. I gasped and moaned at the sudden switch of intensity. The pleasure churned inside my body.

I turned my head toward Clark and he suavely assessed the situation, biting his tongue between his teeth. He put down his guitar and removed his jacket. He rubbed the front of the jeans.

*Holy crap, he was going to get off watching us*. It fucking turned him on watching Nathan fuck me into their desk. *This was insane.* I tightened my hands around the desk's edge to hold on to reality. It was slipping from my grasp with each powerful thrust. I shut my eyes. If I caught Clark's gaze, this would be too intense.

"How does her pussy feel, Nathan?" Clark's voice was much closer than before.

"Fucking snug and wet," Nathan whispered.

"Are you going to come inside her snug and wet cunt?"

"Yes." Nathan dragged out the word. He gained gusto in his thrusts. His hands gripped my hips so hard. His tenderness was fleeting. I heard a slap, and Nathan thrust sharply into me. His body seized straight up, and he loosened his hold on my hips.

"Do you like that, Nathan? Do you like feeling my hard cock against your ass while you're deep inside of her?" Clark said.

"Fuck yes."

I was utterly frozen. Nathan lifted me slightly onto my tiptoes to resume fucking me at a deeper angle. I had never had sex like this, never had someone watch me being fucked, and never had a third person in the room participating. I dropped my cheek against the desk and laid my upper body flush against it. I needed an anchor, something to hold onto for the pleasure tugging through me.

I heard a zipper then denim shuffling. *Shit, was Clark going to fuck him while he fucked me?* I couldn't hold still anymore. I needed to move. My pussy felt so slick from the lube and me. I needed more friction, more pressure, more fuck I wish I could see them. The sight would push me right over the edge. I wanted to see Clark rubbing against Nathan's ass.

"Maybe another time I'll fuck you while you fuck her," Clark said.

Nathan groaned loudly. I had to moan too. The thought of it was fucking with my head. I peeked behind me and saw Clark's forearm jerking forward. His hand moved fast over his cock, but damn it I couldn't see it. I whimpered. Draped over the desk, I was missing so much!

All I did was listen. The mix of sounds pierced my ears—Clark jerking his cock off and Nathan fucking my drenched pussy. I didn't know which sound drowned out the other.

"Make her come, Nate. I want to see her lose it."

Nathan moved his hand in front of me to massage my clit. At this point, it didn't matter. I was almost there from his other hand pulling at my waist, the deep angle inside me and, oh yes, our guest of honor.

"Bri, you feel so fucking good. I'm going to come, baby. Come with me."

I swiveled my hips on Nathan's cock, grinding up and heat radiated through me. My orgasm tore a shout from my mouth, and Nathan fucked me faster. I closed my eyes and two male voices followed, moaning their releases.

The only sound in the room was all our breathing. Nathan pulled out of me provoking another roll of pleasure in my groin. He pushed my skirt back over my ass. We had barely got undressed before we started.

I was covered, but I still felt exposed. Nathan had been flush against me, but I'm pretty sure Clark saw everything when he first walked in. *Fuck, I can't believe he watched his boyfriend's cock fuck me senseless.*

I lifted off the desk and turned around. My legs trembled. Nathan pulled up his boxers, his dress shirt flipped down, hiding himself. He fumbled with his suit pants from around his ankles. Clark turned away from us, facing the accent table. His jeans were still on, loosely hanging on his hips. *Did he come? He sounded like he did?* He tossed a tissue into the small wastebasket. Yes, he came along with us.

I broke the silence. "Can I use your bathroom first?"

"Of course, Bri." Nathan said, kissing me. He looked high.

I walked away from the cleanup and entered their bathroom. It stank of a forest. *Why do men always insist on smelling like trees? I'll never understand it.*

I kind of understand why Nathan used lube, but it was everywhere. My upper thighs were wet and it had smeared all over my vagina. Ugh, my whole crotch was soaked. I inched up my skirt and cleaned up the wreckage.

The one thing I forgot was my underwear. Now that Clark was home, how I do casually stroll out there and grab them off the floor? It hit me how intense the whole situation was now. Clark seriously just watched Nathan and I fuck.

I thought I'd be freaking out, but I wasn't. I didn't even feel jealousy when Clark felt up Nathan from behind. A voyeuristic kink peeked out of my mind.

*Maybe listening to Lucy and her escapades secretly opened up my mind more than I thought. Will this happen often now? Did Nathan actually want Clark to fuck him while he fucked me?*

*Fuck, this escalated fast.*

# Chapter Fourteen

I exited the bathroom and Nathan and Clark were talking. Nathan leaned against the kitchen island with his arms crossed over his chest and Clark stood in front of him. Both men glanced my way. Nathan looked nervous and Clark smiled like a cat that ate the canary.

"Ask her yourself, Nate," Clark said.

Nathan sighed and rubbed the back of his neck.

"Ask me what, Nate?" I took the bait.

"Bri, please don't call me Nate. Clark does it when he knows I'm pissed off. He softens when he wants to get his way," Nathan said pointing at Clark.

"I do not. I like calling you Nate!" Clark huffed, standing defiantly with his hands on his hips.

"Ugh, fine. I don't want to argue with you. I really need to shower." Nathan threw up his hands.

Clark stopped him. "Nope. Ask her, Nathan, or I will."

"Fine. Did we freak you out before? If you're not okay with me and Clark's relationship, we can try to keep everyone separate from now on." Nathan barely looked at me when he said it. He blurted out the words so fast, but he looked more bashful than ashamed.

"No, I'm not freaked out. I'm just unsure where we go from here?" *Whew, okay the ball is in their court.*

"See! I told you she wasn't freaked out and running," Clark said.

A wave of guilt hit me. "Nathan, I'm sorry I went to the bathroom so fast. I was soaked in lube. It was everywhere." I smiled and shrugged my shoulders. He seemed to let go of some of the tension in his stance. I liked that I brought him down off a peak. My words meant something to him.

"It's okay. I think I got carried away with it. I really need to get it off me too." His lips curled up halfway and he scratched the side of his hip.

"You do know she's a woman and doesn't need *that* much lube to fuck her?" Clark kidded.

"No shit, Sherlock. You're really not helping right now," Nathan snapped back.

Clark's mischievous smile faded. Nathan crossed his arms again. Even though, I'd known him about three weeks, it was easy to tell he was back to being pissed off.

"Forget about the lube. Can we at least talk about what happened? Is that what we're supposed to do? Talk?" I asked.

"Yes, we should talk about it," Nathan said, looking me in the eye.

"I'm going to throw this out there. Nathan, how about you and I take a break so you can spend some time with Bri," Clark interjected.

"Geez, man. Are you that eager to get rid of me?" Nathan whipped his head back to Clark.

"No, Nathan. All I'm suggesting is that we give each other some space so you two can figure shit out more."

"Is that what you want, Clark?" Nathan asked. He sucked in a breath. He actually looked pretty upset.

"Of course not, but if it would make things easier

for you, I'll let it happen. I might die of blue balls knowing what goes on between the two of you now, but I want you to be happy, Nathan." All kidding aside, he looked serious and genuine.

"I'm such a dick. That's not fair to you, Clark. I don't want to lose you yet." Nathan raked his hands over his face.

"You wouldn't be losing me. I'm right here. I'm not going anywhere."

"Yeah, but that's really fucked up. I'd be in a relationship and where would that leave you? Waiting for the day Bri and I break up?"

I felt terrible. I knew this was too easy. "I feel like I'm fucking up your relationship. Nathan, let's stop. I don't want to break anyone up."

"You'd be breaking us up, Bri! I don't want that either. Is that what you want, Bri? Is this too much for you?" Nathan asked me.

"No." I squirmed under their gaze. I didn't want to walk away yet either. "I don't want this to end." A small smile formed at the edge of Nathan's lips.

I looked at Clark. His expression morphed into one of worry.

"Bri, Nathan, I'm so sorry. This is entirely my fault. I should have gone back outside or straight to my room and gave you guys' privacy. I didn't mean to force you to define your relationship this soon. Let's chill out and not end anything with anybody tonight," Clark said.

I couldn't agree with him more.

"Okay," Nathan agreed. "Is that okay with you, Bri?"

It was too early to walk away from the possibility

of something awesome with Nathan. I really needed to talk to Lucy. I didn't know how to work this, especially because Clark and I were separate. Nathan was the common bond, but that was it.

Oh yeah, and Clark knew what my pussy looked like with Nathan's cock stuck in it.

"It's okay with me," I said.

They both smiled. Nathan kissed me on the lips. My gaze wandered to Clark while Nathan kissed me. He watched us with an intrigued smile on his face. *I hope I don't feel his eyes on me every time I see him.*

"Where's my kiss, Nate?" Clark asked. The jokester was back in place where he belonged.

Nathan kissed him, however his body blocked the view of their quick peck.

"Can I please take a shower now?" Nathan pleaded.

"Yes. Go," Clark said.

"I'll be back out in a few minutes, Bri." Nathan brushed my arm with his hand, and then disappeared into the bathroom.

Well, that's fucking great. Nathan just left me alone with his boyfriend who just fought for Nathan and my relationship to actually happen. Oh yeah, he also jerked off to me having sex with his boyfriend ten minutes ago. *How does one start this casual conversation?*

"Are you staying the night?" Clark asked me from the kitchen. He rustled around the cabinets.

"I can't. It would look really bad for me to be in the same clothes I wore tonight at dinner with our boss when he knew I took Nathan home." I really didn't think this through. *Fuck, where are my panties?*

"That sucks. You live in Westchester right? It's pretty late."

"It's not that bad. There won't be any traffic on the Parkway."

I walked over to the desk and spotted my discarded panties. They were still damp. I'd been wet since Nathan grabbed my hand under the table at dinner. I scrunched them up and put them on the floor behind my purse.

I took a seat at the kitchen table and pulled my phone out of the charger. It was almost eleven thirty. I really needed to head home. Hopefully Nathan takes a fast shower.

A chill ran down my body. The radiator pumped heat into the apartment, but there was a draft from the windows.

"Do you want a hoodie?" Clark asked.

"Excuse me?" I said.

"You look cold. Would you like to borrow a hoodie?"

"Nah, I'm okay. I'm not going to stay long."

He put something down on the counter and opened the closet by the front door. He pulled a red zip-up hoodie off a hanger. I didn't know the band's logo or the name.

"Are you stubborn?" Clark asked me, handing me the hoodie.

"Depends," I said. The fucker knew me better than myself. "Is this your band?"

"Yeah. The Informal Gentlemen is my latest band."

"I like the name."

"Thank you. I hope I didn't freak you out before. I like to watch two hot people fuck sometimes," Clark said up against my neck. I held back a shiver the hoodie wouldn't be able to stop.

He slithered to the seat across from me at the small round table. He had a bag of chips and opened a container of guacamole.

"Oh, don't worry about it. I'm fine. This is a normal Monday for me," I said, faking a blasé attitude.

"Seriously?" He looked sexy when he was confused. Did he have eyeliner on? His blue eyes looked darker with the makeup. Oh right, he was coming back from his show. He also looked sexy just eating chips. The fan girls must crawl all over him at his shows. Or fan boys?

"Of course not! I'm kidding. I'm trying to lighten the mood. I have to admit this is new for me."

"There's a first time for everything."

"I guess. So, you and I keep getting caught in awkward situations every time we see each other." I occupied myself by taking a few chips in front of me.

"It's only awkward if we want it to be. If it makes you feel any better, this is new for me too. Nathan could have yelled at me to leave or he could have punched me in the face."

"Why do I feel like Nathan isn't that type of guy to punch someone in the face?" I said. Nathan barely hesitated when Clark told him to continue fucking me. Maybe he liked to be watched.

"Oh, he's more than capable, Brianna. He throws a nasty punch. One time, he knocked out one of Kelsey's friends at a party because he made a stupid comment about him kissing me. He broke the guy's nose with one direct hit. There was blood everywhere."

I grimaced. "Yikes! Well I'll try not to make him

mad then."

"Fuck, I didn't mean it like that. He would never hit a girl or even me. Nathan is a great guy, caring, and sometimes tender even. He might slap your ass now and again, but I'm sure you'd want it. He's gentle with you from what I saw. I think he really likes you."

"Is he that gentle when he's with you?"

Clark squirmed. "Let's leave that question for another day. This is awkward isn't it?"

"See! I told you!" I said. I had to smile, but Clark's face was stern, turning serious again.

We put our heads down and ate our chips. "Do you have any salsa?" I asked.

"Not a guac girl?" Clark asked walking over to the fridge.

"I like them together. Oh ,by the way, you can call me Bri. I think we're past formalities."

"Are we now?" Clark came back to the table, opened up the salsa with a pop, and emptied some into a bowl for the two of us. "But you didn't buy me dinner first."

"Well, technically you're feeding me so we can count this as a dinner."

"Ha-ha. You're cute. I don't think you're that cheap of a date to get away with only chips and dip. Let's take a rain check on dinner." Clark followed my lead, dunking the chip in the guacamole and then the salsa.

"So why were you at that key party?" Clark prodded.

I straightened up in my chair, preparing for the interrogation. "Getting right down to it, huh?"

"Most people say I'm blunt. I've been curious for a

long time. Nathan and I weren't fooling around, so he told me everything. He talked about you for weeks. Oh, and why did you choose to be tied to a chair?"

"Only one question per inquisition." My interruption made Clark smile.

"All right then. Why were you there?"

"My best friend Lucy had been asking me forever to be in the game, but I was never single when she planned her parties with her poly group. My last break-up was awful, so I thought what the hell. I almost talked myself out of doing it. I was surprised when Nathan came in. He was someone new, and I wanted to give it a try."

"Lucy also works with you guys? She's the redhead, right?" He squinted trying to connect the story dots.

"Now she's blonde, but yeah she's the redhead in the story and Kelsey's ex. She pretty much changes her hair based on her relationship status."

"I do that a lot too. I switch things up for different band tours."

"That's cool."

"Why was your last break-up so awful?"

My God, he was blunt. Nathan hadn't grilled me at all.

"After three years, he couldn't commit. He said we didn't have enough in common and wanted to go after some girl he always wanted from high school. He wasn't good for me anyway. I can't remember one good thing he ever did for me. Bottom line, I think he wanted me to be something I wasn't, and I got lost in the relationship."

"One of the things I really like about Nathan is that

I can be myself around him. I don't have to pretend. I can just be me," Clark admitted.

I smiled at Clark. He seemed to be someone who wore his heart on his sleeve but guarded. I felt like I saw past a few layers people rarely saw. Every smile went up to his eyes, and he had a small dimple in his left cheek.

You wouldn't see that in his band posters.

"Isn't that what we are all searching for?" I stated.

Clark smiled and winked. "Exactly."

"You're very easy to talk to. I'm surprised," I confessed.

"As long as I'm not in a towel right?" He accused, flipping his chin up and crunching his stack of chips extra loudly.

I rolled my eyes. "I walked right into that one. I just mean that you're being super nice."

"Bri, you're a very pretty woman who happens to be fucking my boyfriend. You've allowed me to take part in your blossoming relationship, and I'm not going to lie…I came pretty fucking hard before. I'd definitely be interested in watching again. So, why wouldn't I be nice to you?"

"When you put it that way, it makes so much sense." I flipped my hand in the air. I'd never met anyone this casual about sex before. Even Nathan seemed more reserved and he was at least bisexual. Lucy would like Clark, or is he gay? *Would a gay guy want to watch his boyfriend fuck a girl?*

"Have you ever had a threesome, Bri?" Clark continued.

"No," I quickly answered.

"Not even in college?" Clark cocked his head to

the side.

"I was a business major with a math minor. Threesomes don't exactly come up over differential equations."

"Damn, you're smart. Nathan said that about you. He's really happy you're his second for the project."

"Really?"

"Yes. He talks about you when you're not here. Does he talk about me?"

"Yes. All the time." We both smiled. The awkwardness had faded, but it simmered back to life. I didn't know if we were juggling for position or sharing idle chitchat. I expected the usual flutter in the space above my heart to pound and explode. Not this time.

Nathan strolled out from the hallway with his hair wet, wearing a sleeveless undershirt and pajama pants. He sat down between us on the other side of the table. His gaze drifted to Clark then me. I pushed the salsa toward him and Clark inched the guacamole.

"I take it you both are getting along." Nathan said.

"She's good. You can keep her," Clark announced.

"Oh, I passed?" I taunted Clark.

"The second you didn't balk from the room when I came in, I knew you were a keeper." He flashed his dimple. Clark got up, without pushing his chair in, and disappeared down the hall, shutting a door a few seconds later.

"So, I guess you've officially met Clark," Nathan said.

## Chapter Fifteen

The next morning, my phone buzzed non-stop. An unknown number texted me constantly. There were at least fifteen text messages of music files from various artists. I recognized some of them, others were completely new to me.

"Who the hell is this?" I said to myself.

"Hey, Bri." Nathan entered my cubicle. He smiled and glanced over my body. I had on a purple peplum top, showing way too much shoulder, but hey my boobs were covered, and black wide leg pants. I flipped my earphones off.

I stood up to kiss him forgetting we were already at work surrounded at all sides. His smile dropped, an unmistakable angst replaced it. "Bri, I'm sorry we shouldn't…" I stopped dead in my tracks.

"Oh, shit. Right. No, I'm sorry. That was so automatic." I punched him in the arm for any nosy on-lookers. "Hey you, what's up?" I got back a shimmer of his smile.

"Don't apologize. You look beautiful today. Let's have lunch to figure out certain situations for the time being."

"Great idea."

My phone buzzed again. "Who is this?"

"Probably Clark." He glanced over at the phone. "Yup, it's him. I gave Clark your number. He wanted to send you some music." Even in a suit uncertainty took over.

"Weren't you supposed to do that like two weeks ago?" I said.

"Well, a lot has changed in two weeks. I had to keep up my end of the bargain."

Nathan flipped up on the balls of his feet and then back down.

"Thank you."

"You're welcome. I'm going to get coffee. Do you want to come?" He did the bouncing thing again. At six feet tall in a dark gray suit, he looked silly, but it seemed to be an anxious habit.

I agreed and followed him. When we passed by the printer room, he nudged my back into the small alcove. I turned to him and his lips were on mine. He kissed me and placed his hands on my waist. I smoothed a long line up from his stomach to his chest.

In a minute, we were both flustered. I ended the mini make-out session out of breath.

"I wish we did have that couch in the hidden back part of the office." Nathan said.

"We'd never get anything done if we had that back there."

"True." My back was still up against the wall and his hands remained on my waist. "Are you really okay after everything last night?" he whispered.

"Yeah, I am. In hindsight, it was pretty hot," I admitted.

"Yeah, it was. Okay good. I like you, Bri, I don't want to fuck this up." He kissed me one more time before he backed up.

I opened my mouth to agree, but Marcia waltzed

in.

"Just the person I wanted to see! Bri, I need your signature on this memo please. Good morning, Mr. Richards." Marcia handed me an email. The highlighted date was over a week ago.

"Good Morning, Marcia. Please call me Nathan. You ladies are going to give me a superiority complex." Nathan teased.

"I always stood by the rule that in a job you state someone's full name before you assume you can call them by their first name," Marcia returned, flicking her hips to the side and smiling at Nathan. In her defense, Nathan was the handsomest man in the department and he wasn't married. However, she better back off because she brought me an old memo I signed last week and was hitting on a man I had sex with last night.

"Marcia, I signed this notice last week. There should be four other ones in this batch. What happened to the other ones?"

Her smile vanished. "What?"

"This memo is old. Please give it to Paul. He should have the other four filed already."

"Can you give it to him? I must have had an old print out. Sorry, Bri." At least, she looked shocked at her mishap.

"It's all right," I added.

"Have a great day, guys!" A toothy smile smacked onto her face. *What the hell was this girl's deal lately?* She turned around and left.

"Is she okay?" Nathan asked.

"I have no clue. Lunch? I have to fix another one of her mistakes."

"I'll be waiting." Nathan stayed in the copy room

and headed toward the fax machine.

"Didn't you want coffee?"

He coughed and said, "Nah, it was only an excuse to kiss you."

I smiled shaking my head back forth. I was kicking myself that I almost lost out on this because of my insecurities. I regretted not telling him who I was from day one.

****

My eleven o'clock meeting canceled, so I visited Lucy before lunch. She hadn't exactly answered a lot of my text messages lately. I knocked on the side of the doorframe before peeking into her office.

She looked up from her laptop and smiled meekly. "Hey Bri, what's up?"

"Not much. My meeting got canceled. Got a few minutes for shits and giggles?"

"Sure. I'm sorry I've been flaky lately. How's Operation Avoid Nathan?"

"Crashed and burned." That got her attention.

"Really? He's gay?"

"Nope better. He knows everything."

"No fucking way! When? How?" Lucy said.

"On Friday night, we were talking and I accidentally let it slip. He was mad at first, but a few rounds of sex pushed that out the window."

"Oh my God, close the door! I want to hear more!" Lucy motioned to the door.

I closed the door. Lucy beamed from ear to ear.

"Well, there isn't much to tell at this point," I said.

"Okay, Ms. Analyst whose project proposals are thirty to forty pages long. I want details! So he wasn't kissing that guy at the speakeasy?"

"He did kiss the guy. Clark is his boyfriend."

Lucy cocked her head to the side. "Wait a minute. I thought you said you two had sex?"

"We did. It was so good. I hadn't had sex in so long."

"Since Nathan at the party right?"

"Yeah. His boyfriend gave us the okay."

Lucy shut down. She still looked perfectly put together, along with her curled hair, her manicure, and the designer blazer hugging her curvy frame. But her eyes told it all. They were big and expressive and her shoulders slumped down and her mouth twisted to the side.

"Maybe Clark thought you were just a booty call." Her voice was flat.

"I think Clark realizes this might be more than that." From our conversation last night, I doubt he'd think that little of me.

"So they're poly?"

"Not exactly?"

"There's no black and white definition to these things." Lucy shrugged. "Kelsey and Diane were already together for three years before they invited me into their relationship. Just because it didn't work for me doesn't mean it can't work for you?"

"Maybe?" I felt like an asshole. I came in here to catch up, but she looked gloomier than before. *I'm going to leave out Clark joining in last night.*

"Were we right? Is Nathan a friend of Kelsey's?"

"Yeah, they met in college."

"Are they close enough to go to the wedding?"

"I'm not sure. It hasn't come up."

"You're still going aren't you?" Lucy asked.

"Lucy, I'm so sorry. I can't tell her no. Please don't be mad."

"I know. I'm still pissed, but not so much at Diane. Never trust a guy who says he's not the marrying type. It's a surefire sign he's a liar."

"Kelsey said that?"

"About a year ago, before he proposed to Diane.

I shook my head. "Fucking Kelsey."

"I hate to be the one to say this to you, Bri, but be careful with until you know more about Nathan and Clark. I hope they're not playing games."

"All right, Ms. Gumshoe. Thank you as always for the advice."

"Anytime, Bri. So, is the sex as good as it was the first time?" She turned the conversation back to her specialty.

I nodded and fanned my face. "Better."

Lucy smiled and promised me we'd catch up soon. On my way upstairs, I contemplated her appreciated warning. From what I'd seen so far, Nathan was a good guy and so was Clark. *I don't think this is a game, but I'm definitely going to play the casual card for as long as possible.*

## Chapter Sixteen

"Baby, let's go home. There's not much else we can do tonight," Nathan whispered. We were the only ones left on our floor by at least two hours. He didn't need to whisper, but it worked wonders on me.

I waited all day for a chance to stop acting like strangers and desperately wanted to enjoy his company. I sighed. The tedious busywork of any project always discouraged me. Most of the time someone had to drag me out of the office against my will. Today was no better.

Nathan glided his hand over my back and latched onto my shoulder, rolling my chair closer to him. He brushed my side bangs back and kissed my cheek. I turned my head and kissed him. His full lips were so soft against mine. Our eyes drifted close and our kiss deepened. His tongue breached my lips and I welcomed the delectable intrusion.

A rolling garbage bin crashed the moment. Our eyes popped open and we ended the kiss. I leaned back for another quick kiss, earning a side smile from him.

"This sucks. I really wanted to get this done before tomorrow. Are you taking the train home tonight?" I asked, gathering my stuff together. When I glanced at Nathan, he was staring me down. "What?"

"Sorry, I was thinking." He stopped rearranging his papers. "I wonder if we didn't know each other from before if tonight would have been our first kiss?" Nathan questioned.

"We've kissed several times now," I reminded him.

"I know, but we're alone right now. If I hadn't kissed you by now this would have been the perfect opportunity."

"Would you still have kissed me even though you have Clark?" I inquired.

Nathan winced. "I don't know. Clark and I are complicated." Nathan fumbled his work into his briefcase and grabbed his legal pad. "Yeah, I took the train in."

"Shit, we should go. I don't want you to miss it."

"It's only eight thirty p.m. We have plenty of time. Are you're going home alone?"

"Yes. Why?" *Please come home with me. Please come home with me.*

"Do you want company tonight?" He flicked up on his toes.

"I thought you'd never ask. The next train leaves at nine fifteen p.m. What about Clark?"

"He'll be fine. We don't hang out every night. Most days we don't even sleep in the same bed."

"Is that normal?" I asked.

Nathan shrugged. "It works for us. I'll text him that I'm not coming home in case he's waiting up."

"Okay. I'll go grab my purse. Do you need anything from your office?"

"Yeah, let's go."

Happiness welled up inside me. I always wished I had someone to come home with me. I hated commuting alone. The same lonely ride day after day. Finally, I had someone to join me.

Nathan and I got to Grand Central just in time and made my train to Tarrytown. I sat next to the window, and Nathan filed in next to me, making our legs touch. He draped his right arm over my shoulders, cuddling me close. "What are you going do about clothes for the morning?" I asked.

"I'll go commando and pick up a shirt in the morning," Nathan answered. I didn't pry any further. I was too grateful for the company.

I laid my head on his shoulder as the train exited the station. "Do you like sushi? There is an amazing place by my apartment."

"I love sushi! Let's do it. You smell fucking delicious. What's it called if you have sex on a train?" Nathan whispered in my ear.

I giggled. "Ha-ha, I have no idea and don't want to know thank you very much."

"I had to try. What is it called when you make out on a train?"

"Hmmm…I don't know." Nathan captured my lips in a chaste kiss. I moved my face away from him. "Um let's wait until the lady takes our tickets. Remember I have to see these conductors every day."

He huffed adorably and folded his hands in his lap twiddling his thumbs.

The conductor came, punched holes in our tickets, and notched the stub under the raised metal. As soon as she left our section, Nathan's lips descended upon mine, in no rush for anything.

His hand lifted under my shirt and caressed my breast over my bra. He dipped his hand inside the lacey cup. I kissed him harder, but he pulled back.

"We're always in a rush. I want to enjoy you

baby."

I let him have his way and he drowned me in lust. We didn't care how loud our kisses were or sloppy. We made out like two new lovers learning each other's mouths, memorizing every detail. It was wonderful.

We came up for air because I had lost track of the stops. I was the ninth stop and thankfully I regained some semblance of myself by the time we were three stops away.

"Can we skip the sushi? I want to go back to your place," Nathan asked.

I agreed. We both sat panting for the next two train stops.

When we got off at Tarrytown, we walked to my car. Nathan tucked me under his arm.

"Are you going to Kelsey and Diane's wedding?" Nathan asked me.

"Yeah. Are you invited?" I countered.

"Yup. See, this was meant to be. We would have reconnected then."

"God, I would have died of embarrassment if you remembered me while I was doing the electric slide or the Macarena."

"Or watching you dive head first for the bouquet. It's scary out there."

"I always stay in the back. I value my life and both my eyes."

Nathan laughed. I laughed along with him.

"Are you taking Clark as your date?"

"To a degree. Kelsey knows about us, but he invited us separately. We booked a room at the hotel. Do you want to stay with us?"

"Yeah, that would be perfect."

"Is Lucy going?"

"No. She's going to hate me forever. I feel terrible for going, but I've known Diane too long not to go."

"I thought you knew Kelsey?"

"I've been friends with Diane since high school and we went to the same college."

"Oh, okay and Lucy, Diane, and Kelsey were in a relationship? Kelsey wasn't cheating on Diane." Nathan put all the jagged edged pieces together.

"Correct. Something happened a few weeks ago and they cut ties with her. I've tried asking Lucy for the details, but she's trying hard to move on."

"Can't blame her. She must be heartbroken."

"She's barely talking about it. Hopefully when the wedding is over she'll open up again. I miss her." We got to my car on the other side of the platform. "One last chance to grab something while we're out?"

"I'm good," Nathan said.

By the time we arrived at my apartment, I panicked. My apartment was a fucking mess. Nathan didn't care. We barely got our coats off before he was on me. I unzipped my dress pants and he fumbled with his own as we kissed. We headed toward my bedroom.

Nathan laid me down on the edge of my bed and pulled off my panties. I reached down to pull him onto the bed, but he kneeled on the floor. "I want to taste you, baby."

His kisses traveled down my body. I peeled off my blouse losing sight of him. That was the moment he spread my legs open and swirled his tongue over my clit. There were no teasing kisses to ease me into it, only his lips, nose, and tongue licking every inch of my exposed pussy. My shirt muffled my moan. I clawed it off me and watched his moving mouth. This time, I moaned loud enough I almost lost my breath. I dove my hand into his hair and held his face to me.

He traced his tongue over my entire pussy repeatedly, thrusting his fingers inside at the same time. Nathan alternated between sucking my clit and licking it driving me crazy. He removed his fingers and fucked my pussy with his tongue. I screamed his name. I held onto him and writhed in ecstasy. The pleasure grew deeper with each lick and thrust. His mouth left me, and I jerked my head down. His amber eyes opened, and he blew his breath over my wet flesh. I shuddered as he dove back down to finish the job. The swirling circles he resumed on my clit finished me off.

"Nathan, I'm coming."

Nathan clamped his hand over my stomach, holding me down. My body jerked up to his mouth and he didn't stop.

I caressed his cheek; a silent thank you before I lost my mind. He moved his face into my hand and trailed wet kisses against the inside of my thigh.

"Did that feel good, baby?" Nathan asked above me.

"Yes. Nathan, you're fucking good at that. Thank you. I'll see you tomorrow." I pretended to go to sleep, putting my hands under my cheek, and turning my face onto the bed.

"I don't think so. I've been waiting for this all fucking day," Nathan said.

As I turned onto my side he fingered my bra strap and undid the hooks. I threw it off the bed. Nathan got undressed in record time.

"I've been thinking about you all day. Come here."

Nathan stood at the foot of my bed. I leaned up, but he palmed my breast and pushed me back down. "No, I want to fuck you standing up."

"Oh." Nathan pulled my ass to the edge of my coverlet and I wrapped my legs around his waist. He gripped my thighs and thrust forward.

"Fuck, baby."

I tugged at his ass and ran my hand up his bare stomach. His face was still wet from going down on me, but I wanted to kiss him. He hunched over me.

"Maybe I should get on the bed," he whispered.

"You can do whatever you want, Nathan." I meant it. He could. I'm not flexible, but I was down for anything. Nathan slipped out of my pussy, but we barely made it to the top of the bed before he positioned his cock, covered in my wetness, and fucked back into my pussy. I cried out. I didn't care who heard me. All that mattered was Nathan didn't stop fucking me until I whimpered I was coming and he did the same a few minutes after.

Nathan nuzzled his nose against my cheek. "I can't believe how amazing your pussy feels. Can we fuck again?"

"If chafing and rubbing ourselves raw weren't a thing, I'd be down."

"Good point." Nathan pulled out and lay down next to me. "Where's your bathroom?"

"Oh right. I was pleasantly distracted. Welcome to my apartment, Nathan. Please don't look at anything for too long. I didn't get a chance to clean up."

"It's fine. If our cleaning lady didn't come every two weeks, my apartment would be worse than yours," Nathan confessed.

*Aha!* That's how their apartment was spotless. "My bathroom is the next door to your right."

"I'll be right back." Nathan pulled on his boxers and put back on his dress shirt, hanging open, and yes, I admired his chest on the way out. I realized I probably should have thought this through better so Nathan could have clothes that would fit him and a toothbrush. I was already failing at almost girlfriend status. It was fun while it lasted.

Nathan came back and got back on the bed.

"You don't happen to have anything I can borrow?"

"I know I don't have pants, but maybe I have a shirt." I retrieved my bathrobe from my vanity chair. Nathan followed me around the room like he would get lost in the one bedroom apartment. In my closet, I did find an XL T-shirt from a concert I went to with Lucy a few years ago. Luckily it fit Nathan perfectly.

"See, it fits great. We were meant to be together," Nathan said and kissed me again.

Maybe he was right. This was falling into place so nicely my anxiety didn't torment me. I guess this was what a healthy relationship felt like? Two people going home together, having great sex, and then snuggling up to watch TV eating popcorn half dressed?

*Fucking A. Count me in.*

## Chapter Seventeen

"So what are you doing tonight?" Nathan asked.

"Going home with you?" I said.

"Excellent."

Every night for the rest of the week I found myself at Nathan's apartment. On Thursday night, Clark was home too. He jokingly knocked on the front door and eased it open with his hand over his eyes. We rolled our eyes and Nathan said, "Too soon." I squashed down the embarrassment from the friendly reminder of earlier in the week.

Clark leaned down and kissed my cheek. He caught me by surprise. Technically it was the first time he'd touched me, and it was a kiss. He ruffled Nathan's hair passing him by to sit on the loveseat.

*Is that weird that I got a more intimate hello than his boyfriend? I must be overthinking it.*

"So do you watch it?" Nathan asked me.

"Watch what?" I asked, confused.

"Are you all right, Bri? I asked if you watch *Jeopardy*?"

"Yes, sorry. I think I'm hungry."

"Me too! I'm famished," Clark said.

"Let's order in soon," Nathan offered.

Evidently Nathan records Jeopardy and the three of us watched last night's episode together, throwing popcorn at each other when someone didn't answer in the form of a question. Clark got excited for the music category and aced the entire thing, and I breezed through a movie one. Surprisingly Nathan knew a bunch of the sports questions and some history ones. Clark strummed his acoustic guitar while we watched.

*I could get used to this*, I thought to myself. I sat snuggled up to Nathan, his arm draped over my shoulders, and Clark's cat purred in my lap. I wasn't sure if she had accepted me as a human she liked or just as another piece of furniture. Clark was home so she came out to play. I had to remember, though, not to wear black around her.

"Amora likes you." Clark said. She purred loudly into my hand when I caressed her cheek.

"She's adorable." I smiled at Clark. He smiled back, and his eyes darted to Nathan's arm around me. He caught me watching him. If I was better at this I would have thought of something to say. Did it bother him to see us? Should we cut the PDA? *This was fucking complicated.*

We missed the last question and the DVR stopped. Nathan got up from the couch leaving me alone with Clark. Clark continued to play his guitar not looking up. I busied myself with petting Amora.

"How's the project coming along?" Clark asked, breaking the silence.

"There's good and bad days. It's a shit ton of work." Just talking about work made me yawn.

"I can tell. Nathan seems tired. Can you make sure he stops to eat and actually takes breaks?"

Clark looked concerned. Nathan *was* his boyfriend after all. There was no doubt in my mind that Clark cared about Nathan.

"Ha-ha, I'll try. He takes his work pretty seriously."

"Once he takes his Adderall someone will have to force him to stop." Clark shielded the side of his mouth with his hand. He whispered, "He crashes pretty hard when you're not here."

"Doesn't surprise me."

"Also, watch how many energy drinks he buys. Limit him to one a day please. The crash is worse after three."

"That's insane. He must be sneaking them when I'm not looking. He should just eat sugar packets all day. Same difference."

"Agreed," he said.

Clark tuned his guitar, and Amora left my lap. I lost my little buffer. Clark caught my gaze and pursed his lips together.

"Awkward again, huh?" he remarked.

"Well, now that you mention it, maybe a teeny tiny bit." Somehow a spunky retort came out. He smiled.

"You're cute. Do you play any instruments?"

"I can play the beginning of the Moonlight Sonata on the piano."

"Why only the beginning?"

"My grandmother passed away, and we never finished it," I said. I used to love hearing her play the piano at my aunt's house for hours and hours.

Clark's eyes widened, and he cursed under his breath. "Geez. I'm sorry." He put the guitar down and looked down the hallway. "How do we get rid of this awkwardness between us?"

"Play me something. I love music." I moved toward the other end of the couch closer to him.

"That I can do. What would you like to hear?" Clark offered. He didn't seem like a pop music guy, so I thought of an older song.

"How about something by Johnny Cash?" I got an eyebrow raise from him on that one.

"I think I can manage one or two by him." Clark tuned his guitar, seemingly impressed at my suggestion and grabbed a capo to adjust the string tension. He brightened up when the conversation turned back to music.

I sat back, putting my feet up on the couch and waited for my song. He played "Walk the Line." It was one of my favorites. I was thoroughly impressed. Clark barely looked down at the chords and hummed the melody.

"Am I hired?" he asked.

"I might need to hear a few more before I fully decide," I kidded. He laughed and his dimple showed up again.

Nathan came back from the bathroom and gathered some menus for us. We settled on Mediterranean food. With Nathan in the room, the awkwardness fell away. We put on another episode of Jeopardy and waited for the food.

While we ate, Clark played twenty questions with me, and Nathan followed along answering the same in turn. I found out Nathan was originally from upstate New York, and Clark only moved up here from Southern New Jersey a few years ago. Their favorite concert they'd gone to together was Rancid, and they took a trip out to Chicago this past summer. Clark mentioned his next show was the weekend after Thanksgiving, and Nathan and I agreed to go. Music was definitely Clark's thing. I couldn't pinpoint what Nathan's big hobby was quite yet. Workaholic was still at the top of the list.

After we ate, I crashed. The day caught up to me. Nathan looked like he was fighting the tiredness as well. I gave up around ten p.m., dozing off against Nathan's shoulder.

I woke up when Clark draped a blanket over me.

"I'm sorry. I didn't mean to wake you up," Clark whispered.

"It's okay. Thank you for the blanket." I grabbed the edge of it and sat up. Nathan was still asleep, snoring with his head thrown back.

"Do you want me to wake him up?" Clark asked.

"Yeah. It's been a long day. He should sleep in his own bed."

Clark leaned over Nathan, palmed the right side of his chest, and kissed his cheek. "Nate. Wake up."

Nathan opened his eyes. He yawned into his hand and stretched out his tired limbs. He saw Clark first and leaned up to kiss him. They both closed their eyes even though it was a small kiss. I imagined them alone on the nights when I wasn't here. Clark always waking up tired Nathan and they shared the same kiss night after night, and then they would follow each other to bed. If so, it was fucking sweet.

Their kiss ended, and Nathan turned to me. "Let's all go to bed."

"This is exactly why I told you to get the bigger bed," Clark said, going along with Nathan's choicc of words. My mouth fell open at the implication.

Sleepy-eyed Nathan caught on slower than fuck. "Ha-ha. You know what I meant."

"Yeah, had to try though. Goodnight," Clark said. He picked up Amora and headed down the hall.

"Bri, he was only kidding," Nathan said, taking my hand. I shut my gaping mouth. Again, Clark left me with my mouth open forgetting to breathe. Nathan sat up and dragged me with him.

"I figured." I laughed it off, but the thought didn't exactly leave my mind.

# Chapter Eighteen

I arrived at the hotel at one p.m. The wedding ceremony didn't start until three p.m., leaving a little wiggle room. I called Nathan, and he came outside to help me with my overnight bag.

I officially decided I liked Nathan best in a black suit. The few times that I'd seen him in a suit I was practically drooling. Each one fit his muscular body just right. Especially the black suit he was wearing today. It was painted on by every correct number.

He greeted me with a kiss and a catcall whistle. "Wow, Bri, you look gorgeous." I wore a classic A-line little black dress with a black lace overlay and a cream bodice. The skirt was flouncy and long enough to hide my garter belt straps. I broke out my old lingerie out of retirement.

"Thank you. You look hot as always," I said.

"Nah, you just like me in a suit."

"Guilty." He kissed me again at my confession.

"Are you set to go? I think the shuttle is leaving in about twenty minutes."

"Yeah, I only need to switch shoes. Is Clark here yet?"

"Yup, he's up in the room. He's finishing getting ready."

"The room? We're all sharing a room?"

"Yeah. Is that a problem?" Nathan stopped

walking.

"No. I'm sorry I don't know why that surprised me. You invited me to stay with you guys. Obviously you'd get one room." *Don't panic, Bri.*

"Well, there are two beds. I can banish Clark to the bed in front of the AC if he misbehaves."

I laughed. Before Nathan slid the card through the door, Clark opened the door. He stood in front of us with his tie hanging loose around his neck.

"Nathan, can you fix my tie? I can't fucking get it. Hey, Bri! Damn, you look hot!"

I froze in the door jam. Nathan looked hot in a suit, but Clark…holy fucking shit, he looked sexy as hell in a suit. I was completely taken aback by his appearance. His dark blue shirt made his blue eyes pop and the bleached hair was totally gone. His new hair color was jet black with a tint of blue. He looked completely different, almost conservative, but the blue-black tint and his earring held onto his edginess.

Nathan entered the room and placed my bag on the desk, not a bed. He went to Clark and fixed the stubborn tie.

"See something you like?" Clark asked with a side-glance and matching sinister grin.

Crap, I got caught gawking at the two hottest fucking men in my life. Well, kind of two men. Last Monday night flashed into my head. *Would Clark watch us again if Nathan and I had sex? Did I want him to watch?*

I walked into the room and the door shut behind me.

"Maybe. I can't believe I'm going to have the hottest two men on my arms at my best friend's ex's wedding."

The two peacocks in the room flared up their feathers and brushed imaginary dust off their suits when Nathan finished up Clark's tie.

"I thought you were friends with Diane?" Clark asked, looking at Nathan.

"Yeah, mostly from school. We used to be closer back then. I met Lucy through her, not Kelsey."

"I still can't believe that fucking guy is getting married. You owe me twenty bucks, Nate." Clark stated, shaking his head.

"I really didn't think he'd go through with it, but Diane is a last girlfriend. When you meet a girl like her, you don't let her go." Nathan's eyes flicked to me.

My chest tightened. Did he think that way about me? We were going fast in our almost confirmed unconventional relationship. Was I the last girlfriend type? Did he want to keep me? How could he when his relationship with Clark was still thriving?

Nathan looked down at his phone. "Everyone ready to go? Kelsey just texted me that the shuttle is ready to leave."

I changed my shoes and out the door I went arm in arm with my two dashingly handsome dates.

****

The ceremony was as perfect as a wedding could be. Diane and Kelsey said their own vows about how they met at a street fair and how multiple people got them to where they were today. *Well, they got that part right.*

The cocktail hour had been okay, but the main venue hall made up for its shortcomings. The centerpieces were high, but I didn't know anyone on the other side of the table anyway. I switched seats with an old college friend so I could sit with the guys.

Nathan took my hand sweetly. "Would you like to dance, beautiful?"

"You dance?" I asked.

"When the occasion calls for it, and I have a gorgeous date who looks amazing. I'm going to grab another drink while the line is short. Do you want one?" I waved him off with a no. Nathan kissed my cheek and left me alone with Clark.

My ego celebrated by doing a happy dance of her own. None of my ex boyfriends carried on over me like Nathan. Even Clark's compliments were unexpected. My mother always said I had met the wrong people in my life.

When I downed my third glass of champagne, Clark scooted closer. He leaned over and placed his hand on my back right above my ass.

Instinctively, my back straightened. He whispered toward me, "If I were you I'd make that my last drink."

I turned my face and almost smacked his nose with mine. He invaded my personal space in every way possible. If I puckered my mouth, his lips would be right there for the kiss. "Why is that, Clark?"

"Just a hunch on activities to come…" When he said come, he peered down at my mouth, which had parted naturally. My breath rushed out in a needy pant before I could stop it.

"Should I be prepared or worried?" I tested.

"I'd be wet if I were you," Clark whispered so quickly I thought I misheard him. He planted a small kiss at the corner of my mouth. The tiny gesture and dirty words twisted my insides sharply. I didn't hold back my gasp at the sharpness. Clark stood up and disappeared into the crowd. I stayed frozen to my chair. *What the fuck was that?*

"What was that about?" Nathan swerved back to our table with an early drunken swagger. He placed two beers on the table.

"Are you and Clark planning an ambush behind my back?"

"Why ever would I do that?" His slightly drunk grin gave me enough of a real answer. *We are sharing a room together but why were there two beds? If I weren't here, would they have slept separately?* Their casual relationship confused me.

"Earth to Bri? Stop thinking, it makes your pretty face frown." Nathan brushed my cheek with his fingers.

"If you haven't noticed, I have resting bitch face and anxiety. It gets me in trouble from time to time." I placed my hand on top of Nathan's, and he led me to the dance floor.

He laughed. "That's so spot on. You definitely have resting bitch face."

I let the music take our light moment for a spin. It'd been forever since I danced with someone other than Lucy.

"Nathan, who's sleeping with whom tonight?" I asked.

"Don't worry about technicalities. I'll take turns."

"Really? I get to watch you and Clark together?"

"There's my girl. You'd like that, wouldn't you? Two hunks going at it. Would you touch yourself?" He rested his forehead against mine.

"Two hunks? How much have you drank?"

"Enough. The four of you are dazzling…"

I laughed. Serious Nathan was taking a hike off a beer-slicked plank. Even when he thought I was just a fellow coworker I genuinely thought he was funny. That was something real I liked about him that had nothing to do with sex.

"Baby, I have to pee. Go make Clark dance with you. He's such a music snob. It drives me nuts," Nathan said, kissing my cheek.

"I don't want to force him to dance if he doesn't like the music."

"Trust me, you're a beautiful girl, he won't turn you down. He dances very well and needs to get off his high horse about pop music."

"Okay, fine. I'll go find him."

"Good girl. I'll be back." After copping a quick feel of my ass, he swatted it gently. I shook my head and rolled my eyes. He stuck his tongue out and walked away.

Part of me didn't want to be anywhere near Clark and his confusing quips, yet there I was marching over to the table, following Nathan's instructions. Clark looked oddly comfortable in his suit leaning back against his chair. He must have gone to the same place Nathan did. It fit his broad shoulders in every right place.

Clark listened intently to the other guests, sipping his drink. I smoothed my hand against his back, breaking his concentration. He looked up and relief washed over his face.

"I have explicit instructions to ask you to dance with me. Can I steal you?" I asked.

"You can do whatever you want with me," Clark answered, his mischievous smile returned.

Clark ushered us to the dance floor with a guiding hand on my lower back. His other hand grabbed around my waist pulling me close as we swayed to the slow song. I draped my hands over his tall shoulders.

His body felt different from Nathan's. Clark may not work out like Nathan, but he was in no way overweight, only different. My arms had to extend an inch or two higher to reach his shoulders.

Clark leaned down to be right up against my ear. "Thanks for rescuing me. I had no fucking clue what they were talking about back there."

"Thank Nathan. He sent me over."

"So you didn't want to dance with me? Ouch, Bri. We were getting along so well up until now," Clark joked. His smile traveled to his pretty blue eyes. Yes, they were pretty. It was the only way to describe them.

"Ha-ha, I didn't mean it like that. I suck at dancing. I get dizzy," I confessed.

"You're doing fine," Clark reaffirmed. He took my hands off his shoulders and twirled me.

"Hey now! No advanced tricks here, mister," I chastised.

"Oh, stop. You like it. Follow my lead."

He twirled me again and took my hand out to the side of us to start waltzing across the floor. I grabbed onto him and held on for the ride. After a few clumsy moments, I got the hang of it.

"Shit, you can dance!" I said out of breath.

"I'll let you in on a little secret." He dipped his head close to my face. I held my breath as he inched closer. "I'm good at everything, but not great at anything. Remember to breathe, darling." The term of endearment was my undoing. His voice flittered down my neck and shivers chased it down my arms.

*Damn.* I understood why Nathan liked him. Regardless if you were gay or straight, or other, Clark oozed sex appeal and knew precisely how to use it.

"Hold onto me tighter," he said.

I looped my hand around his neck and gripped his hand hard. I gasped when he dipped and flipped me back up. I giggled. I couldn't help it. This was so much fun.

"Are you done making me look bad, Clark?" Nathan said coming up to us in the middle of the dance floor.

"Never," Clark said quickly.

"Save the next one for me, Bri?" Nathan asked with a meek smile.

"Of course!"

Nathan nodded, kissed my cheek, and walked back to our table. Clark and I were back to square one to finish the song. I was grateful for my heels, but I was eye level with his sensual mouth. He kept licking his lips, drawing my attention back to him and the small kiss he gave me before.

I listened to the song more closely, and I finally recognized the lyrics, but not the cover artist altering the old tune.

"I think I like the Righteous Brothers version better," I said.

"You mean the original version?" Clark affirmed.

"Yeah."

Clark smiled and stepped closer to me. "Agreed. You've managed to impress me once again. Did you like the music I sent you?"

"Oh shit, yes, sorry I forgot. Thank you so much! I

made a Clark playlist on my phone."

"My pleasure. If you want more, I'll send you anything you'd like."

A genuine smile tugged at my mouth. *Ugh, there he goes again being damn likeable.* The dark hair made him extra striking and handsome. His lips were fuller than Nathan's, his cheeks more hollow and pronounced, and his cute dimple in his left cheek showed up when he smirked.

"Where did you learn to dance?" I asked.

"My grandparents taught me a long time ago. My grandfather said it would help me meet girls. We're very close."

"That's really sweet."

"I can be sweet when I want to be." There was his smirk and the dimple again.

"Thank you for the dance."

"You're welcome." He kissed the back of my hand. *Geez, how much did he have to drink to make the gentleman come out this strong?* He wooed me like it mattered.

The DJ picked a fast song next and that cued Clark's dance floor exit. Nathan was right. Clark was a music snob. I let him go reluctantly back to the table.

Like every other wedding, the room got too warm from all the people dancing and the forgotten high heels were in a pile by the tables. I'd tuckered out Nathan about twenty minutes ago. Clark and he were back at the table reminiscing with Nathan's old college buddies.

The music turned to the popular garbage, so I went out the side door for some air. The groom stood alone, smoking a cigar, and sipping a drink.

"Kelsey? What are you doing out here?" I asked.

He peered up from his solo party and smiled big showing his whitening treatments had actually paid off.

"Hey, Bri. I'm just getting some air. I've never been happier in my life. Thank you for coming. It means a lot to us that you came."

I walked up to the railing and gave Kelsey a hug. "Congratulations. I'm glad I'm here, but I doubt Lucy will ever speak to me again," I said defeated.

Kelsey's face fell, and he put out the cigar in the ashtray on the decorative railing.

"I don't know if it matters, but I'm truly sorry for the way we ended it with Lucy. We never wanted to hurt her. I know you don't have a high opinion of me, but please believe me. I will always love Lucy and it genuinely hurt me to let her go."

"It's hard to believe that from her side of the story," I said.

"I can imagine. I had to give my relationship with Diane a chance to live again. We shared each other for so long we forgot how to be us. I needed the time alone to see if I really wanted to get married and if Diane was the one," Kelsey explained.

For too long I'd always hated Kelsey. His humble words shed a different outlook on the second hand facts. He was still a prick, but at least on this occasion I understood the cause.

"Well, when you put it that way I sort of get it. By girl code, I have to hate you for a few more weeks."

"Hey, it's just my side of the story. Lucy is an amazing woman and she will make some people very happy in her life. I know that for a fact. I have great intuition."

"Oh really?"

"Absolutely. I see my other efforts have paid off nicely. You and the guys are finally hitting it off."

"Well, technically, I'm only dating Nathan."

"Come on. Do you know whom you're talking to? I know everything. I'm well aware of the situation between those two and you. I've known Nathan for years and he tells me everything. Even Clark has let me in a few times. Go to his band's shows and he'll tell you his whole life story."

I gulped. "How much have they told you?" The last person I wanted to discuss my current sexual escapades with was Kelsey.

"Some stuff here and there." Kelsey smiled.

"Care to elaborate?" I asked.

"Nathan didn't tell you? I picked Nathan to go into your room at the party. For some dumb reason Lucy wanted Tom for you. I had always thought you hated Tom and all of my friends. I called Nathan to set up some audio stuff from Clark's past gigs and thought you two might like each other. He had just gotten out a bad relationship like you, and I thought magic could happen."

I stared at him dumbfounded. In a matter of minutes, Kelsey's spot as a number one asshole diminished and my anger toward him lessened.

"But I have to warn you. You might have to fight for Nathan now. They make out when they get drunk." Kelsey winked. *Correction, they did more than just make out.*

"Oh, I wasn't aware…" I mockingly put my hand on my chest like I was appalled.

Kelsey chuckled. "You look very pretty. I hope

they know how lucky they are to have you."

"There you are!" Diane shouted over the flood of music the doors let out.

"Duty calls. I hope you hate me a little less now, Bri. I have the most beautiful bride in the world waiting for me."

Diane looked stunning in her off-white gown. She came out on the balcony to join us and ran up to me for a hug. "Congratulations, Diane. You look *amazing*!"

"Thank you, Bri, and thank you so much for coming."

"I couldn't miss your wedding."

Diane smiled, beaming in the moonlight. She grabbed my hand. "I can't believe it all worked out! I'm so happy."

I believed her. She walked up to Kelsey, and he planted a huge kiss on her lips.

I walked back into the ballroom and headed to my table. Nathan was gone, but Clark sat alone on our side of the table eating a plate of French macaroons.

"Bri, you have to try these! They're so fucking good. I left the girlie ones for you." Clark popped a green one into his mouth. He moaned while he chewed. The plate still had a pink, a red, and a purple left for me.

"What flavors are these?" I said, taking a seat and scooted closer to Clark.

"The pink is rose, red is raspberry, and purple is a mystery flavor. I just had a pistachio one I think? It was so good," Clark said pointing out each one.

"You've never had French macaroons before?"

"Not like these. I thought they only had coconut."

"Those are just called macaroons, silly."

"Tomato, tomatoes. Let's eat them before Nathan gets back." Clark picked up the plate urging me on.

"Why? Would he eat them all?" I popped the red one into my mouth. It tasted like heaven. Once upon a nightmare, I attempted making them. I had seven batches of hard flying saucers that didn't rise.

"Have you encountered a drunk Nathan yet?" Clark asked.

"No, is he plastered?"

"Oh, yeah. I cut him off while you were out with Kelsey. And…Drunk Nathan has a killer sweet tooth and cannot be held accountable for his actions."

"That bad, huh?"

"If he's wine drunk he could eat an entire cheesecake and not bat an eye. On beer, it's the opposite. He becomes very touchy feely if you catch my drift," Clark stated with a devilish wink as he brought his own drink up to his mouth.

"Thanks for the warning."

"Anything to help out our little arrangement."

I picked up my glass of champagne, and we clinked our glasses. I downed it in one gulp. It went straight to my head, reigniting my earlier buzz. Clark watched me intently. His gaze peered up my body and finally settled on my eyes.

"Ahem," I scolded.

"Sorry. You look hot. I haven't gotten the pleasure to see you dolled up."

"Thank you. This is out of the norm for me."

"You're beautiful in anything you wear," Clark said with an unsure smile.

This was not the time or the place to be shy, but my head naturally bowed forward hiding myself from his gaze. It was odd to have someone in your life that's seen you at your most intimate moment, but not be able to touch him. Clark remained a mystery, and I couldn't help but wonder if he would stay only a mystery.

# Chapter Nineteen

Nathan swaggered back to the table and knocked over our moment. Nathan stumbled slightly into the chair clutching a Corona. Okay, so he was beer drunk.

"You all right there, Nate?" Clark inquired.

"Couldn't be better. I got a whole bunch of liquid courage now, Clark. Let's do this!" He burped into his hand and chugged his beer. He looked so damn cute. I leaned over and kissed him.

"Nathan, you're drunk," I said.

"A little bit. Are those French macaroons?"

"I didn't try to save you some, but a little minx didn't get her memo," Clark admitted, pushing the plate toward Nathan.

I shrugged at Clark. He smiled up to his eyes. The ease between the three of us appeared once again, throwing me for a loop. We played well together.

Nathan grabbed the purple macaroon and nibbled tiny pieces off it. I pictured him younger searching parties for French macaroons. He finished it with a satisfied grin. He leaned over me toward Clark and kissed him on the mouth. Nathan pulled away so fast Clark's face fell forward.

"Please go get us more of these magical things, Clarky. It would make us both very happy. Wouldn't it, Bri?"

My brain caught up to the last few seconds. This

wasn't the first time I'd seen them kiss, but there was something intoxicating about watching it. The hint of hazy lust drifted into Clark's gaze. I saw it even though it dissipated as quickly as it came.

"Sugar Fiends. Don't yell at me tomorrow!" Clark said, stealing another kiss from Nathan. Clark's fingers grazed my dress right above my knee as he got up from the table.

"Fuck, that worked. See, Bri, Clark's actually my slave, and madly in love with me. He won't admit it, though." Nathan covered his mouth. "Don't tell him I told you."

I laughed. Drunken Nathan with his guard down was fucking fun.

"Yes! Bri, the photo booth line died down. Come on, I want a photo." He tapped my shoulder, and I turned toward his line of sight. The large white tent, which all night had a line wrapped around it, appeared to be vacant. The large TV showing the interior displayed an empty room.

"Okay, Nathan." I followed his jog, walking briskly behind him in my heels. My feet were starting to cramp in the arches. I should have picked up some foldable flats.

Inside the tent flap to the right were two large boxes of props, hats, and wedding-themed messages on sticks set up on a table. Nathan selected a black pinstriped fedora and slipped an oversized red bowtie around his neck. I combed through the silly things and found a pair of cat ears attached to a hairband. I put it on my head and Nathan wrapped a silver feathery boa around my neck.

"Meow," I mimicked.

“Too cute,” Nathan said and grabbed me by the waist, pulling me into the camera’s view. He pushed the start button. The first photo I put my hands up like a cat begging and Nathan dipped the fedora over the side of his face. The second one, he faced me and kissed me jutting his butt away from me.

I turned to grab a word prop for the third picture, but was ambushed by Clark crashing our photo. He herded me into Nathan almost bumping his drunken ass over. We got caught in our genuine laughs when the flash went off.

The last photo was the best. Clark grabbed me a word plank, quickly throwing it at me. He donned some glasses, and Nathan switched hats for a cowboy one. We stared at the camera in our props, and I held a sign saying Trouble with arrows pointing on both sides.

“This is so going on the fridge!” Nathan shouted.

We stripped off the props and went outside for the final printout. These four photos were priceless.

Nathan placed the second printout in the book, but I stopped him. The boys kept the first one, and I took the second. I stuffed my stolen copy into my clutch purse before anyone noticed.

A fresh plate of five macaroons waited in front of Nathan’s spot. He made one disappear immediately. He moaned again at the delectable taste. He offered me another, but I declined. I enjoyed watching him devour them more than eating them.

****

Thankfully I didn’t catch the bouquet. Women I didn’t know scrambled for the fake version of Diane’s elaborate bouquet. I gladly stayed in the back out of harm’s way. The garter toss followed. Nathan and Clark got up for it, rolling their eyes. The garter landed in the chandelier and luckily fell down.

Nathan and Clark returned to the table and Nathan mimicked wiping sweat off his brow. "Missed that bullet," Nathan said.

"Please tell me you don't believe in that stuff?" I said.

"Of course I do. Clark, didn't Katie catch the bouquet at a wedding and you proposed to her a week later?" Nathan loosened his tie.

Clark squinted up at the ceiling. "I almost forgot. It was her sister. Katie and I were already engaged. Her sister caught the bouquet and her husband proposed to her at the after party."

"Yes! Now I remember," Nathan said.

"You were engaged, Clark?" I was getting good at telling Clark's 'this is fucking awkward' face. His expression morphed into a shade darker and sadder. In our little talks, past engagements hadn't come up.

"Married and divorced too. It wasn't pretty," he said, his voice lacked emotion. He took another sip of his drink.

"I'm sorry. I shouldn't have asked."

"It's all right. I was married for four years, been divorced for two. It happened and now it's over."

I hoped he would continue, but Nathan interrupted, raising his empty beer in the air. "To better and naughtier nights."

"You're cheesy, Nate. I'm done with this wedding. Let's get the fuck out of here," Clark announced spinning his empty bottle in a circle on the table.

"Amen. I'm drunk enough. Let's do this!" Nathan shouted, punching the air.

Evidently, Kelsey and Diane didn't account for the groomsmen and bridesmaids returning to the hotel in the shuttle too. There wasn't enough room, so the hotel sent personal cars to retrieve us.

For a mid-November night, it wasn't as cold as it should be, but we could still see our breaths. Clark removed his suit jacket and draped it over my shoulders. "Thank you, Clark."

He rubbed my shoulders and then dove his hands into his pockets. "You're welcome," he said.

"Hey that's my job," Nathan said, coming up to Clark.

"You were too slow," Clark countered.

"Too drunk is more like it." Nathan pecked him on the mouth.

"We'll take turns caring for her." Clark wore another serious face.

"Maybe," Nathan said.

"I'm fine with that, boys," I added before I could regret it.

"Good," Clark answered, staring me down.

When the car finally came, I was sandwiched between Nathan and Clark in the backseat. Nathan was drunk, Clark worked a solid buzz, and I grew more sober by the minute. I barely registered the driver and some girl from our table in the front seat.

Nathan slid his hand up my silky thigh high. He groaned when he reached my garter belt strap.

"Naughty girl. Always full of surprises," he whispered against my ear and sucked my earlobe into his mouth. I gasped. Nathan's effect on me flared to life.

He traced circles on my left inner thigh. I looked

down at his hand. I hadn't realized he worked the hem of my dress high enough to show the whole car my secret.

Clark's rougher hand turned my cheek. "Do you realize anyone can see your indecent choice of lingerie, Bri?" His voice oozed sex and my pussy twitched. His mouth inched closer to mine for a second time tonight. I licked my lips with anticipation. The car was dark, but he did the same.

My hands were frozen at my sides. Nathan moved up my thigh closer to my panties with each teasing circle.

"He feels too good to move," I said quietly, staring at Clark.

"I know the feeling," Clark responded. He leaned into me and I closed my eyes for a kiss that didn't come.

A second set of fingers inched up my other exposed thigh. The sensation of the two hands from two different men made me clench my thighs together as a wave of need flared up my body.

*Fuck, what was I doing?* The girl I didn't know turned around and made a "woo" sound in her drunken state. I flipped the hem of my dress back down.

"Girl, you going to get fucked tonight," the girl said.

At least, the car was dark. Clark removed his fingers from my leg. "Mind your own fucking business, Trish!" Clark shouted. She made an impatient whine and turned back around.

I coughed and Nathan took the hint, removing his hand from my lap.

"My bad, baby." Drunken Nathan pulled my dress

hem down farther than necessary to emphasize his plea. He kissed me. The sloppy sounds filled the car.

"It's okay." I smoothed my hand over his soft hair. His gel he had before was long gone.

I scooted down in the seatbelt and draped my left leg over Nathan's thigh. I didn't spread my legs like before, but Nathan continued his circles on my knee. Normally, I'd be squealing for being ticklish, but his touch turned me on instead.

I leaned my head back on Clark's shoulder. He lifted his arm up for me to snuggle into the crook of his armpit. His fingers traced up my arm. I don't know what made me include Clark too. Something had changed between us since last week, hell, since earlier tonight.

*It felt wrong not to include him.*

Nathan didn't mind or care. It appeared he was okay to share me for the time being. Clark was his boyfriend, but obviously they both enjoyed me in their own ways instead of fighting for position.

We got to the hotel a few minutes later. I unfolded myself from the boys' questing hands. I stumbled out of the dark car. Clark caught me.

"Be careful with those things." He looked down at my heels. I laughed. His hand brushed mine, but he didn't take it. He coughed and joined Nathan walking in front of me into the hotel lobby.

In the lobby bar, wedding guests lined up for last call drinks. It was already past midnight. Someone shouted Nathan's name, but he only waved at the crowd, and we continued toward the elevators.

Nathan and Clark barreled down the hallway ahead of me. I took my time stretching out the inevitable behind the hotel room door.

Clark slid the key card into the door. The room was blanketed in darkness. Clark and Nathan each took a light switch next to the beds. They both looked like choices to me. I didn't want to admit it, but Clark was weaseling into my headspace as a viable choice.

I removed Clark's jacket and hanged it up in the closet. I turned around and faced the music.

"Doesn't he look hot, Bri? I want him to fuck us so bad," Nathan said, leaning in and biting Clark's neck.

Clark moved his hand through Nathan's hair, embracing the touch. I stood frozen on the spot. It was suddenly too warm in this small hotel room.

# Chapter Twenty

Clark steered Nathan toward the bed. "You greedy man. Have you discussed this with your girlfriend? I'm not the interfering type."

Nathan rubbed the back of his neck, looking guilty. He hadn't talked to me about this scenario.

"Tsk-tsk, Nathan. Always thinking too fast." Clark untied his infamous tie and shook his head.

Nathan looked wide-eyed.

"Hey, Bri, you know the conversation I've been meaning to have with you?"

After Clark's and my mini conversation about me drinking too much, I wondered just what could happen. I thought Clark might watch us again, not participate.

Nathan walked over to me with an insecure look stamped on his face. "Brianna, you are one of most amazing people I've met in a long time. I would never ask you to do anything you didn't want to do. But I have to ask. Have you ever had a fantasy of two very eager men making love to you at the same time?"

Nathan fumbled his words, but I made out most of the speech. Ever since Clark walked in on Nathan fucking me in the living room, the idea of the two of them hadn't exactly left my dirty mind. I had come so hard knowing Clark watched us finish.

*How could I even think of saying no?*

Nathan stroked a hand up my side. "Did I break

you? You can say no, and I'd be just as a happy to continue along as we are."

I was dumbstruck. I had barely wrapped it around my head that Nathan, hot businessman extraordinaire was interested in me, and now two men wanted me at the same time.

Clark removed his tie and draped it over the desk chair. He was so different from Nathan. Nathan was serious, focused, and thought everything through. Clark was soft, airy, fun with a dominant side peeking through sometimes. But he was sexy and hot in his own way, and our little talks allowed me to see parts of him he definitely didn't show everybody.

"Bri, why don't you put your purse down and sit on the bed. We're not asking for your hand in marriage here. It's just a fling with two men wanting to have sex with you," Clark interjected.

"I'll be right back." *I was going to chicken out.*

I threw my purse on the bed and ran into the bathroom.

*Holy shit. Can I actually do this?* Lucy popped into my head. She had threesomes all the time. I could do it too. It was only sex with two sexy men, who wanted me. I blew out a couple of breaths and paced the small length of the bathroom.

It felt so good in the car when they both touched me. *Oh God, how intense would it be if they both were fucking me?*

Someone knocked on the door. "Babe, are you okay? There's no window in that room, so we know you're in there," Nathan yelled through the door.

"I'll be out in a second," I said. I washed my hands and made my decision.

There was no escaping my reflection in the large wall of mirrors. My hair held the soft curls I hair sprayed the fuck out of earlier. My eye make-up was smudged and my lipstick long gone. Overall I looked a little disheveled, but I felt pretty and wanted. They made me feel that way.

I took a swig of the complimentary mouthwash. I wished I could shower, but I'd already been in here too long.

I unlocked the door and re-entered the hotel suite. I gasped at the killer make-out session in front of me. Nathan had stripped down to his boxers and was kissing a mostly clothed Clark. Clark stroked Nathan's cock over the front of his boxers pulling and grabbing at him. Nathan whimpered into Clark's mouth. *I didn't know he could make that needy sound.*

It dawned on me I really hadn't seen them interact besides a few kisses. They had a casualness, or I guess a comfort level between them in their everyday lives.

In the bedroom…all bets were off.

I leaned against the dresser and unbuckled my shoe. The dresser pushed against the wall, interrupting the boys. They parted, and both their chests were heaving, catching their breaths, staring at each other. Nathan's erection was clearly visible in his boxers.

"Are you staying, Bri? Can we have you?" Nathan asked, looking dazed.

I finally answered, yes.

Nathan walked toward me, but Clark stopped him. Confusion and unease slipped over Nathan's flushed face.

"Not so fast, Nathan. Bri, you're stunning and beautiful, but I'm sorry. I don't hop into bed with just anyone. You'll have to answer three questions." I glanced at Nathan, who slumped down onto the edge of the bed. His cock wasn't protruding as much as it was a moment ago. He kneaded his thighs, staring up at Clark and me.

"Hit it. Lay them on me." *This was a year of firsts...why not this?*

"Who's your favorite band from the eighties?" Clark asked.

I giggled. *What type of questions were these?* There was jovial Clark I liked. The sultry succubus hid inside of him.

"You're adorable when you're confused. Please answer the question."

I said, "The Cars."

Clark raised his eyebrows. "Perfect answer. Second question. Does your dress have a zipper or does it go over your head?" Clark donned a sexy grin now and walked up to me.

"Zipper. Third question?"

"Are you still able to fall in love?"

The last question surprised me. The other two were trivial, but this one would reveal my innermost struggles. My immediate reaction was to say yes, but was that the truth? I thought I had been love with my ex. I was wrong, but yeah, I could fall in love again.

"Yes." I closed my eyes.

Clark's knuckle brushed the side of my cheek. "Open your eyes, darling. Never be ashamed of your own intuitions."

The side of my mouth twitched up in a tiny smile. I opened my eyes. His confident stare bored a hole right through me and his gaze lingered on my lips.

"Well, Nathan, now you have your boyfriend and girlfriend here at your disposal…what are you going to do with us?" Clark provoked Nathan. Clark gripped my hand and squeezed it.

"I want her naked, now," Nathan declared.

Clark whispered, "Turn around, Bri. Let's get you out of this pretty dress." He kissed underneath my ear bringing forth a round of goose bumps.

"Ticklish?"

"Yes," I said, too breathy. Clark went behind me, and Nathan stood in front of me. I was shorter without my heels and had to look up at Nathan. Nathan kissed me softly at first, then stuck his tongue deep to tangle with mine. Clark slipped the zipper down my dress. I dropped my arms from Nathan's shoulders and the silky fabric slid down my body. Nathan fiddled with my bra hooks. One more hand finished the job.

Clark hooked his fingers under the edges of my black thong and peeled it down. I stepped out of it, not breaking Nathan's kiss. Clark cupped his hands over my ass.

"Very nice ass, Bri," Clark said, kissing my neck and sucking a chunk of skin into his mouth. I moaned into Nathan's kiss. Nathan's hard cock poked me in the stomach. Clark hooked his fingers into the straps of my garter belt and thrust against my ass. He felt just as hard as Nathan against me.

I touched Nathan's smooth face and reached back with my other for Clark's waist. Clark bit my neck and my knees almost buckled. He let go of the garter straps and moved up to my breasts. His hands covered my them completely. I pulled back from Nathan's kiss, and he mumbled a soft protest.

"To the bed?" I asked.

Nathan nodded. With the space between us, Clark stripped off his shirt. I climbed onto the bed and they followed me on either side. Clark crawled to my left and Nathan on my right.

As my back hit the comforter, Clark and Nathan each took one of my nipples into their mouths. I cried out at the exquisite pleasure coursing through my body.

Two mouths kissed my breasts and two hands moved down to play with my pussy. Lust wreaked havoc with my mind. I didn't know where to put my hands except to try to reach out and caress them each too. Nathan was out of luck because he had my right arm pinned above me. My left hand was free to entice Clark.

I moaned as a pair of fingers massaged my clit and another set led down further. I dragged my left hand over the front of Clark's pants. His cock was harder than before, stretched up straight. He groaned around my nipple and nipped it with his bared teeth. He thrust his clothed cock into my hand.

Clark's mouth popped off my nipple and said, "Can I kiss you, Bri?" I looked down at Nathan for his approval, and he nodded yes.

Before I responded, Clark's mouth claimed mine in a devastating kiss. He arched his face to fit mine perfectly and his hand left my pussy to pinch my nipple. From the kiss alone my body pulsed and jerked.

Nathan released my nipple and leaned down to lick my sensitized clit. My hips lifted off the bed, and I reached for something to anchor me. Nathan's right arm attempted to hold me down as his left played with my breast. Clark's mouth on my lips had me frozen and

Nathan's mouth on my pussy drove me mad. I couldn't hold back the orgasm slamming into me from the overload.

"*Oh* fuck, I'm coming; you're both making me come." Clark stole my scream from my mouth and gripped my thigh harder to spread me wide for Nathan's onslaught on my pussy. Nathan added his fingers to my pulsing hole and speared into me.

"Come. We'll catch you if you fall." Clark murmured against my mouth. My orgasm came on too fast and the ride was too brief. I wanted more. Nathan's mouth prolonged the wave, but it wasn't enough.

Clark sat up and took off his pants. A second later, he kissed me again. My lips already felt raw, but I knew this was only the beginning. They were just getting started.

Clark grunted into my mouth as Nathan's mouth stopped licking my pussy. When I looked down Nathan took Clark's cock into his mouth. Clark brought his hand down to my clit to replace the pressure left unattended by Nathan.

Nathan tweaked my breast as he moved his mouth on Clark's cock. I couldn't look away from the sight. I was mesmerized and it hiked up my arousal to see Nathan finally pleasuring Clark. His cock stretched Nathan's mouth and my body clenched hard. I'd seen porn with multiple partners, but that paled in comparison to the real thing.

Clark stopped kissing me and lay on his back to moan loudly. He brushed Nathan's hair off his forehead and pushed his head down onto his cock. Nathan took Clark's entire cock with practiced ease.

"Join him, Bri. I want to feel both of your mouths,"

Clark said.

His voice pulled me out of my delirium. I could have watched Nathan for hours. Nathan winked and slid his mouth up and down the left side of Clark's cock leaving me the right. I sat up on all fours and leaned down to drag my tongue against the right side of his cock.

"Oh yes. Fuck!" Clark hissed. Nathan chuckled against Clark's cock. He was hard yet ever so soft against my tongue. I flicked my tongue under the head and feathered my hands over his tightened balls. Another loud moan greeted our efforts, and Clark lifted his hips up.

Clark's hand returned to my pussy and thrust deep from behind. The sounds of his fingers overshadowed Nathan's humming. Nathan peered up from his work.

"Get her ready for us, Clark," Nathan commanded.

Clark grabbed my legs by the garter belt strap and pulled them over his upper body. I straddled his chest and popped the tip of his cock into my mouth the same time Clark drove his tongue into my pussy. He lapped up my last orgasm and provoked the next one. He licked me from clit to ass in one swipe again and again. I was overcome with the power of the situation. If Clark's cock wasn't in my mouth, I'd be shouting every expletive like crazy.

Clark's fingers spread my pussy open, his tongue focused directly on my clit. My concentration hanged by a thread before; now it was obliterated. I dropped Clark's cock from my mouth and moaned properly. Nathan left Clark's body and rose up on his knees in front of us. "Stroke him, Bri, and suck me. I want to fuck you while he fucks your ass. Make me good and wet."

My mouth welcomed Nathan's familiar cock and without asking he fisted my hair just enough to entice my submissive side. I thrust my mouth fast over the head of his cock just the way he liked it. When he raked his nails down my neck, Clark sucked hard on my clit, igniting my orgasm. I shouted around Nathan's cock and took him to the back of my throat.

"Oh fuck, she's coming again," Clark said and thrust his fingers inside me.

Nathan removed his cock from my mouth. "I don't want to come unless it's inside you, baby," he said.

My mind was cloudy, but I followed along. I couldn't remember the last time I came so fast without a vibrator. I was going to remember this intensity. A splice of fear crept into my mind. It was so easy to fall into their trap. It felt too fucking good.

Nathan stepped off the bed and headed for his suitcase. Clark stopped licking me and gently lifted my body off his chest. I lay backward next to Clark.

Clark didn't lose any contact with me. His hand caressed my hip and laid his body over mine. I caught his gaze and reached for him. "Are you okay, Bri? Are we being too ravenous with you?" he asked.

"You're perfect. He's perfect. I feel like I'm going insane."

"Enjoy it, Bri. I know I am."

Nathan stepped back onto the messy bed. He came up behind Clark and wrapped his lubed hand around Clark's cock. Clark closed his eyes and he took a deep breath through his nose. Nathan's grip wasn't firm, but Clark's cock looked so hard, I thought he could come any second.

“Have you ever had anal sex, Bri?” Clark stammered out.

I was distracted again. Nathan nibbled on Clark’s neck.

“Bri? I can come like this, if you haven’t. Please tell me. I can’t hold out much longer.” He turned to kiss Nathan.

“Yes, I have.”

Nathan broke off from Clark’s kiss. “Excellent,” he said. He stopped teasing Clark and lay down on his back. “Come here.” His hard cock curved toward his stomach. “Fucking ride me, baby.”

I climbed onto Nathan’s body admiring his tight abs. His body was one hard hairless plank, designed to fuck.

Nathan caressed my pussy with his lubed fingers. The same fingers had slinked up Clark’s cock moments before. He added a finger inside and then another pumping more wetness into me. I grabbed his cock and settled down on each long inch of his length. This was always my favorite part. The sharpness of the first thrust always did me in.

Clark’s breath against my neck gave me goose bumps. “If it hurts at any point, just say stop. It’ll kill me, but I will stop. I want you to feel good. Do you understand?”

With Nathan’s cock buried inside me, I turned and said yes to Clark.

Clark lubed up the condom, and then his fingers prodded against my asshole. He smoothed the warming liquid slowly inside me. So many things were different than the last time I had anal sex. My body hadn’t pulsed with anticipation, and there weren’t two men hell bent on my pleasure.

Nathan brought me up and down on his stiff cock. I felt so full already with Nathan's cock and Clark's fingers spreading me. I took a deep breath. *If I say stop, he'll stop.*

"Are you ready, darling?"

"Oh yes, please."

Nathan stopped mid thrust, and Clark entered me. It hurt for a moment, but Clark pulled out and then went further the next time and so on. Clark was kissing my neck, caressing my breasts and oh the feel of his hairy chest against my back was my downfall. I was completely enraptured. I was theirs to do anything they pleased.

"Your ass is so tight. Please let me in, Bri. Let go," Clark said in my ear.

Nathan pushed me almost off his cock, and Clark thrust the last inch of himself into me. Clark retreated and Nathan thrust up again. I didn't want to shut my eyes but had to do it. This was too much. I rolled my head back against Clark's shoulder. He entwined my fingers with his and leaned our joined hands on Nathan's chest. Nathan moaned, and then Clark did. *Somewhere in the mix, I forgot to say anything, only feel.*

"This feels amazing. Oh Bri! Oh Clark! I'm going to come. Please, baby get there. Please come with me," Nathan said.

The pleasure was so intense I didn't understand how I hadn't come yet. Clark shouted yes over and over. He plumped one of my breasts and Nathan the other. I took in my surroundings one last time and let myself go. My orgasm flared out around Nathan's cock.

Thankfully, he resisted the urge to fuck fast into me. I didn't need anything more right now.

"Ohh, she's coming. Come with me, Clark."

I clenched every part of me I could, and it pushed them over.

Nathan and Clark's cocks were both inside me, and they shouted out their releases. I held onto them for dear life. I dug my fingernails into Clark's forearm. There was no up or down, not even sideways. It was just us riding out the storm, feeling the waves overtake our minds and cloud all reasonable thought.

# Chapter Twenty-One

I was completely spent. I didn't know if I wanted to collapse on Nathan or lie back into Clark's embrace. Clark moved first, slowly retreating from my body. I loosened my grip on his arm. He whimpered and moaned in the process. The feeling of my body adjusting back to normal made me squirm against Nathan's softening cock inside me. He lifted up and kissed me with so much feeling I barely reciprocated.

I lifted up off Nathan's cock. Clark was there ready to help me. Clark kissed me, and his tongue gently massaged my used lips. "Lay back, darling," he said.

I did as I was told, lying on my side toward Nathan. Nathan switched to his side and caressed my body.

I wanted to moan, but nothing came. The bed moved behind me. Clark's strong arms pulled me against his body. I exhaled pure contentment. He knew what I needed before I did.

"That was unbelievable, Bri. We are so lucky to have you," Nathan said.

I smiled and sleep tugged at me.

I dreamed of the wedding or rather a wedding. There were flowers everywhere, scattered on the ground, and blowing through the hall with the wind. I danced amongst the petals with one man and then another. Their faces were hidden, but I knew it was the same two men switching back and forth.

"Wake up, darling. I need you." The whisper tore me from the dream. I groaned at the warmth surrounding me. My head rested on Nathan's chest and Clark moved up behind me.

The hotel room was dark, but the bathroom light cascaded the room in a delightful hue of gray.

"Bri," Clark said. I lifted my face and Clark's mouth crashed down onto mine. His hand cupped my cheek and his lower body connected with mine. He was hard and ready against my ass.

I snaked my hand around to cover his cock. His cock felt feverishly hot, begging me to take care of it. He separated us, making it easier for me to move up and down. I twisted my body to face him, but a firm hand on my waist stopped me.

"No. Stay curled up. I want to watch you suck on Nathan's cock at the same time I fuck you. Let him go in and out of your pretty mouth. I want to fuck you while I still have the chance. I want to feel your dripping cunt come all over my cock."

From his words alone, I was panting. I reached down to my pussy and rubbed my clit.

I took the covers off Nathan and fisted his soft cock. The softness didn't last long. He moaned in his sleep. He'd be awake and hard in no time.

I covered his cock with my mouth and Clark entered me slowly. I whimpered at the sensation. Clark lit up every fuse ready to feel again.

It felt odd to have to two cocks going in and out of me this way. I had been so full with Nathan in my pussy and Clark in my ass. This was different and less overwhelming.

"Hmmm…what a wake-up call," Nathan said, groggy. He entwined his hand in my hair and coaxed me up and down his cock. There was no pressure in his grip, only gratification. Neither man was in any rush with their pursuit. Our bodies were sated from before, now we savored the pleasure as much as we wanted.

Nathan's other hand tweaked my nipple and caressed my breast. Clark fucked me slowly using the side of my hip to aid his thrusts. It was tighter this way, having my legs over each other.

"I could fuck you for hours," Clark said.

Clark rubbed Nathan's thigh as if he missed their contact. It amazed me how attentive Clark was in these moments of bliss. It was as if he needed all of us to be connected somehow. It shocked me how easy this felt. A connection sparked between us.

"Bri, are you almost there? Come with me, darling."

I almost said yes, but my body was sated long before. The different position felt good, but my orgasm was not coming soon. Clark increased his speed, riding out his orgasm. He kissed me and eased out of my pussy.

"Let me, baby." Nathan took Clark's place. He kneeled over me and kept his upper body off me. His hand lightly caressed my breast and I watched his cock move in and out of my pussy.

Clark kneeled next to us and put his fingers into Nathan's mouth. Our sex was on full display once more for Clark's viewing pleasure. Clark removed his fingers from Nathan's mouth and brought them down to my clit. His fingers stroked Nathan's cock and my clit at the same time. The sight bowed my back and enticed my orgasm. Nathan increased his thrusting and it was exactly what I needed.

"Oh Nathan, oh Clark. Fuck! *Ohhhh!*" I shouted.

Nathan leaned forward, and I screamed my release into his mouth. Clark quickened his fingers' movements and I spun out of control, feeling Nathan spurt inside me.

With Clark's help, we were finally done. Nathan collapsed to my right. Clark lay back down on my left side. I wanted to stay in the middle, but I got up. I inched off the bed to the bathroom.

*What a difference a few hours and a "yes" can do for a girl.* I smiled at my reflection. I still saw my imperfections, but it didn't matter to them. I looked royally and officially fucked. Two very willing men made love to me and made me feel like I was the only woman in the world. They stayed true to their promise. *This is going to be a hard smile to scrub off my face.*

I came back to bed. The guys had moved into the space I left behind giving each other tired kisses.

"Come here, baby," Nathan said, when they stopped.

I crawled onto the middle of the bed. My space between them was back, open for the taking. Clark grabbed the covers and pulled them over us. It was hot between them, but I didn't care. I needed the sensation of them once again.

****

When I woke up again, Clark had left our bed. He was sprawled out on his back with only the sheet covering him, snoring on the other bed. I wanted to be upset that he left us, but Nathan curled his arm around my waist tugging me against him.

The alarm woke me up a few hours later. I checked the other bed, but it was empty.

Nathan stopped his buzzing phone. “Baby, it’s nine o’clock. We have to leave by ten thirty.” He kissed me on my forehead.

“I don’t want to go. I want to stay here with you two.”

Nathan smiled and laid down over me. His morning erection also greeted me against my stomach. “I think Clark left. He had to be at the studio by eleven. You’re stuck with just me.”

“You won’t hear me complaining. I’ll be right back.” My weak attempt to pry myself from under Nathan was quickly averted.

“No, don’t go. I want you one more time,” Nathan said.

“Yeah, but you won’t want to smell my morning breath. Give me a sec.”

Reluctantly, I scooted out from under him. I ran into the bathroom. Clark’s toiletries were gone. He had definitely left us. An unexpected pang of rejection fluttered in my chest.

I brushed my teeth and went back out to the room. The air conditioning filtered into the room, but there was no mistaking the musk of sex in the air. The bed Nathan and I slept on was wrecked. Even the bottom sheet was scrunched up, exposing the light blue mattress.

Nathan’s hand busied itself under the covers.

I joined him on the bed and we made love until we had to leave. A persistent hotel maid knocked three times, but we didn’t care at all.

# Chapter Twenty-Two

"Wait a minute. Hold on! Are you fucking kidding me? How the hell are you in a relationship with two men while I'm the poly one? Nope, I don't believe it. I know how to play this game, you don't. I'm sorry. I'm not buying it," Lucy blurted out enraged.

"Seriously? You think I'm lying?" Her words fucking stung. She was my only hope of help.

"Yup. You're a bad liar. I can see right through this shit. You're trying to one up me, aren't you?"

"Lucy, I would never do that! I need your help right now!"

"My help? I'm not helping you! I'm still pissed that you went to their perfect, cliché wedding. I hope they rot in fucking bliss. Do you have any idea how he made me feel? How cheap? It fucking hurts regardless of what crap he fed you. I'm better than Diane will ever be. Fuck her." Lucy's face grew redder by the minute and she was cutting an apple dangerously slamming the knife down on the counter.

"Lucy! Please calm down. I didn't think you'd react this way. I'm sorry."

"Well, neither did I. I know tons of open relationship couples that are married. They just cast me out. And now you're in a relationship with two fucking gorgeous men who fell into your fucking lap. *Ughhh!*"

I stared at Lucy. This wasn't her. In the five years

I'd known her she had never spoken to me this way. She was hurt, and it had nothing to do with me.

"Lucy, please give me the knife. Stop slicing the fucking apple. You're going to hurt yourself." On the last down stroke, I put my hand over hers. Her hair had fallen over her face, and her body hiccupped back tears.

"Oh, Lucy. I'm so sorry." I turned her into a hug. Lucy wore flats so she was shorter than me today. I gripped her shoulders tightly and rubbed her back. She sobbed like she hadn't cried in the longest time.

Luckily, I wasn't wearing white. My blue shirt was smeared with her mascara when she pulled back.

"I'm sorry, Bri. I didn't mean to snap at you. I'm still upset about Kelsey and Diane. I need more time to get over it."

"It's okay. We're okay. Take all the time you need."

Lucy smiled and pulled herself together. She took several deep breaths, exhaling slowly.

After a few moments of self-soothing, she looked up at me. Curiosity beamed in her eyes. "So, let me get this straight. You had sex with Nathan and Clark at the same time? Did they DP you?" I nodded. "Doesn't it feel amazing?" Lucy's mischievous smile reappeared. There she was; the girl I needed. Meanwhile, I can barely say the words.

"Keep it down. Different is more like it."

"I fully recommend it at least once in your life." Lucy sat down at one of the kitchen tables, the murdered apple abandoned. She brushed her hair out of her face and rubbed at her teary eyes. "Did you guys talk about your sexcapades?"

I sat next to her and handed her a tissue. "Not

really. The whole thing is already messed up. Clark left before Nathan and I woke up."

"So you're not in a relationship with the both of them now?"

"I have no idea. The three of us haven't sat down and talked about it, and now we've all fucked each other."

"Uhh, that makes me nervous. You guys really need to talk about it."

"Nathan and I are having lunch today. I was going to bring it up."

"Don't forget to talk about it. Don't let them take advantage of you."

"Thank you, Mom! You're being overprotective," I said.

"Sorry, I'm not trying to tell you what to do. It's just that if they're running this charade blindly, someone is going to get hurt. I'm confused about Clark. How did he get involved?"

I took out my phone and showed her the table photo someone posted online.

"Holy shit, that's Clark? He's hot. Was he the guy at the speakeasy?" Lucy scrunched up her face.

"Yeah, that was him. The photo didn't do him justice. His eyes are gorgeous, and he's got this sexy rocker vibe thing. His voice is…"

"Panty dropping?"

"Ha-ha. Yup."

"I didn't know you liked Clark?"

"Yeah, I do."

"Is Clark gay or bi?"

"I would say a strong bi at least."

"Is that a thing?"

"I have no idea. I thought Clark might watch Nathan and I again, but yeah, it went a lot further."

"Watch again? What have you not told me, Bri?" Lucy leaned closer to me.

In the perfect nick of time, two ladies from accounting walked into the kitchen. I motioned to Lucy to zip it, and she stuck her tongue out.

Lucy continued, "Evidently I need to live vicariously through your sex life now so give me all the details. I want to know who watched who!" The nosy ladies' ears perked up and silence fell at the mention of sex.

"Can we talk about this later? *Much* later?" I said.

"Absolutely. That was a curve ball I didn't expect."

****

My Monday morning was swamped with my daily tasks. I barely left my cubicle.

Before I knew it noon arrived. I turned on my lunch out of office message and walked toward Nathan's office.

Nathan held his cheek, clicking his mouse repeatedly, looking bored out of his mind. I knocked and walked inside. "Hey. Are you ready to go?"

"Shit! It's noon, already?" Nathan looked up. "I'm sorry, Bri. I need to send these demos. Do you mind waiting?"

"Sure. Can I help?"

"Nope. I'm good. As soon as I get the map, I can send it. You did a phenomenal job with the preliminaries."

"Thank you."

"No, really, Bri. I'm happy we work well together."

Nathan's cell phone rang. He picked it up. "Bro, can I call you back? Cool. Later." He ended the call. "Please don't be mad. I'm going to stay upstate longer than just Thanksgiving. I'm going to try and get back early on Saturday night."

"Are you going to miss Clark's show?"

"I think so. My brother and his fiancée are moving and they need my help. Did I mention that my soon-to-be sister-in-law is seven months pregnant?"

"Actually, no you didn't. Aww you're going to be an uncle."

"It's crazy. It hasn't exactly hit me yet. They hired moving trucks for Saturday and I offered to help. I completely forgot about it until he called earlier."

"It's okay. Are you and your brother close?"

"More when we were younger, but he'll always be my little brother."

Nathan scrolled through his social media. He showed me a picture of them from a wedding. Nathan and his brother shared the same megawatt smile and were similar heights. Both of them were attractive.

"He never asks me for anything. I couldn't say no."

"I get it, it's all good," I said.

"Are you still going to Clark's gig?"

"Maybe, I don't know. I'll see if Lucy wants to go with me."

"You should go. He always puts on a great show. The Brewery has great beer and awesome barbecue too."

"I went there a while ago. I'll think about it."

"Bri, trust me, you'll know all the music and there's a girl in his band. It's hard not to like Cleo. Also, it might be good for you and Clark to get to know each other better."

Saturday night in the hotel room flashed through my mind. Every time I thought about that night it was like I stood at the foot of the bed watching someone else writhe in ecstasy. I couldn't believe I did that, actually, that we all did that together.

"Clark is a good guy. I swear I'm not trying to force anything, but I think you should go to his gig. Spend some time with him. I promise you'll like him once you get to know him better." Nathan paused. It was easy to see why Nathan and Clark were friends, then lovers. But adding me into the mix? It would solve a lot of our future problems if Clark and I were together too.

"I think I like him already," I confessed.

"You do?" His eyes lit up. "He's liked you since the night he walked in on us."

"Obviously. Little was left to the imagination for him." I looked away. Of course, he liked me after he saw everything.

"Actually, he barely mentioned that part. He said he liked you after your talk while I showered. Also he said you stopped breathing when you saw him in a towel?" Nathan playfully arched his right eyebrow up.

"Fuck! He told you?" Embarrassment flared up in my mind.

"I don't think you understand exactly how blunt and honest he can be. Shut the door." Nathan said. I closed it softly trying not to draw any more attention to us. He rounded his desk to stand in front of me. He was so close I had to look up to see him clearly.

"Bri, I really enjoyed our time together and I would love to do Saturday night again. If you don't want to, just say the word." Nathan dropped his voice down low.

"Nathan, this is a lot to think about right now. My mind is still overloaded." I backed up against the closed door. "Is it stupid to keep that night as a one-time thing between three drunk people?"

"I know Clark and I want to do it again," he said.

Nathan closed the space between us and pinned me against the door. His lips found mine and his kiss sparked my yearning for him. His tongue twisted into my mouth while his hands caressed down my body. He lifted up my flared skirt and his hand disappeared underneath before I could stop him.

Nathan's hand headed straight for my pussy. He barely hesitated at my panties. He moved the fabric over and rubbed my clit. I moaned into his mouth.

He tore his lips from mine and whispered in my ear, "We want to fuck you again." Nathan's fingers quickly made their way down to my wet pussy, thrusting inside me with one finger first, and then two. I bit my lip so I wouldn't cry out. *We were still in his office for fuck's sake.*

"It must have felt good to ride our dicks. I know it did. I felt you come, baby. You squeezed my dick so hard. I want to do it again. I want to feel Clark fucking you again," Nathan said while he fingered me. His fingers moved in and out of me and his thumb grazed my clit.

My thoughts raced around my head, grasping for some reasonable grip. If I said no, everything would stop. It would be an experience I had and that was it. I couldn't walk away from this chance. I liked both of them.

"We wouldn't have you with us on Saturday?" A

rational blip slipped out of my mouth. His fingers adjusted right where I needed them. My pussy responded to Nathan's hand and clenched my insides sharply.

"I'll be there before the night ends. Fuck, you're wet right now. This turns you on doesn't it? I want to fuck you so bad right now."

I lifted my hand to the front of Nathan's pants, but he inched away. "This is your turn, baby. Say it. Can we have you?"

"Yes, fuck, yes. I want you both." Nathan smiled and latched onto my neck. He sucked my skin into his mouth and grabbed my breast in his other hand.

"Come, Bri. Let go."

I looked up into his eyes and saw nothing but acceptance and the virile man I desperately craved. His hard cock brushed against my hip and I whimpered. Even though, he was only touching me, we were in this together. He wasn't leading me on or playing games. We genuinely turned each other on and wanted to see where this would go.

My orgasm spilled over onto his fingers. Nathan stole my shout with his kiss. My chest heaved, and my eyes rolled back in my head. The orgasm already faded a moment after it flared to life. Nathan kissed me softer as he extracted his hand from my body. I looked down and the front of his pants were tented.

"What about you?"

"I think I'm going to stay right here." Nathan winked and closed his suit jacket over his noticeable erection. "Rain check on lunch?"

## Chapter Twenty-Three

*—Are you doing anything Saturday night?—* I texted Lucy.

*—This Saturday? What time?—* She responded ten minutes later.

*—Eight to ten-ish?—*

*—Sorry Bri. I'm going to my meetup. I already bought the dinner tickets. What's up?—*

*—Clark's band is playing and Nathan can't go.—*

*—So?—*

*—I don't want to go alone.—*

*—Scaredy Cat. What gives? You've fucked him already. Stop being anxious.—*

*—I know. I'm nervous to go alone.—*

*—You'll be fine. Go play with the hottie.—*

I could do this. We'd probably talk a lot. Nathan might join me later.

****

On Tuesday night, I went home with Nathan. We picked up takeout and entered his cold empty apartment. Amora lifted up her head when we entered, but ignored us when she realized Clark didn't trail behind us.

"Clark's not home yet?" I asked.

"I guess not." Nathan flipped on the kitchen light and checked down the hall. He came back into the main living room in a Sublime T-shirt. "He's not home.

When we spoke earlier he wasn't sure when he'd be leaving the studio. There's a timing issue with the drums and bass for an album he's working on."

"That sucks. Can he fix it?"

"Hell if I know. There's a lot riding on this recording. He can't fuck it up."

"I bet." I took off my coat and draped it on the third hook next to Nathan's.

"I got you something," Nathan said. He handed me a gift bag.

"Aww, you didn't have to get me anything."

"I wanted to. Open it, baby."

I undid the red bow, ornately tied around the handles. Buried in half a box of tissue paper was a large pink coffee mug.

"I know you love coffee, so I thought you'd like your own mug to keep here when you sleep over," Nathan said, flipping up on his toes.

It was just a simple pink coffee mug, but it meant so much to me I almost cried. My exes never bought me anything to keep at their homes. This was big.

"I love it Nathan. Thank you!" I jumped up and kissed him.

"You're welcome."

I picked the movie and we sat and ate our takeout. Every now and again, he flipped back to a basketball game. I was shocked. New little bits and pieces about Nathan popped up.

"Some of the guys in accounting have a fantasy league. You should join it!"

"No way, I'm horrible at those things. I never get good players."

"At least do March Madness. Paul won last year

and he knows shit about sports."

"I won't be there in March, but thanks babe," Nathan reminded, fixated on the game momentarily.

Nathan's reminder hit me hard. I almost forgot his time in the city was temporary.

"Ah shucks. Don't be sad, Bri. We'll make it work. I promise. I'm going to figure it out," Nathan assured, cupping my cheek.

"I hope so."

Around ten thirty p.m., I fell asleep against him. Nathan gently woke me up and we got ready for bed. I changed into the clothes I discreetly put in my gym bag and brushed our teeth together.

I shooed him out of the bathroom, so I could finish getting ready. My time of the month came on Monday night. I told Nathan, but he wasn't mad. I volunteered to return the hand job from Monday, but he declined.

"I just want to hold you baby. I'm okay."

At some point in the night, another set of hands grabbed my waist, pulling me away from Nathan. Warm lips cascaded over my neck and shoulders.

"I'm sorry I missed you tonight," Clark whispered.

"Hmmm. It's okay. Did you fix the problems?"

"Yes, finally. Are you coming to my show on Saturday night? Please say yes."

"I'll be there."

Clark hugged me from behind. I reached back and palmed his cheek while he resumed his soft kisses. He moved back slightly.

"It's late. We can spend time together at my show," Clark said.

I nodded and excitement flared up my body. He wanted me to be there and I'd have Clark all to myself.

My earlier panic left me alone and I enjoyed his lips on my body.

"Sweet dreams." Clark kissed me and attempted to leave Nathan's bed. I stopped him before I registered what I was doing.

"Stay, Clark," I said louder than I should in the current situation. Nathan groaned and rolled to his side away from us. Both Clark and I froze. Luckily Nathan's snoring started up again.

"Shhh…don't wake him up. I'll be right back," Clark whispered and left the room.

Before I fell back asleep, Clark came back to bed. There wasn't a ton of space left in Nathan's queen sized bed and after a few ticklish quiet squeals on my part, Clark and I managed to fit under the blanket on our sides. Clark's hand lifted my shirt up and captured my right breast. My nipple grew taut under his fingers.

"Is this okay?" Clark asked.

I pushed forward, filling his hand more. "Yes."

"I could get used to this. Good night, darling," Clark said, kissing my neck again.

*So could I…*

## Chapter Twenty-Four

The old warehouse was no longer a small bar top with a few stools cluttered around barrels of hops, reeking of yesterday's barbecue, but a large open area bursting with patrons. The entire place looked brand new from the last time I'd been here and a whole warehouse size bigger.

There were tons of tables scattered throughout the brewery. Beer and smoked meat wafted to my nostrils. It smelled like heaven.

I looked for a stage or an amp set up because I honestly didn't think I would find Clark. The brewery was packed with people home for the holidays.

"Hey, Bri! Hey!" Clark shouted behind me. When I turned to him, he smiled. "You made it!"

The Clark I'd known up to this point was not the man who stood in front of me. His black hair had more blue at the tip, and it was coiffed up in a pseudo Mohawk. He wore all black. His jeans were basically painted on him. He shrugged off his jacket, revealing a vest and a tank top underneath so his arms were bare. The tattoos blurred in my memory were showcased for my viewing pleasure.

Oh and his guitar had light up tubing outlining the whole thing. My fan girl hormones skyrocketed.

"Breathe, darling?"

I swallowed my anxious spit and then did it again.

Behind him was a short punk girl with green and pink hair, holes in her stockings, and attitude for days. She scrunched up her lips in the fakest smile I'd ever seen. *Who the fuck is this chick?*

"Bri, meet Cleo. She's our bassist." Cleo did the once over glance and rolled her eyes as she extended her hand.

"Hey," she spoke.

"Hi, nice to meet you. I'm Bri." I reached out my hand and she took it softly. Either she sucked at handshakes or she didn't like me already. I couldn't tell.

"I know. Clark with a crush said your name like fifty times in the past few days. Fuck, now I want cheese. I got to tune up." With that, Cleo walked through the space between Clark and me, never looking back.

"What's her problem?" I asked.

Clark shrugged. "Don't mind her. She's still mad the Twilight fad is over." He laughed.

I smirked. "Clark with a crush, aye?"

He kissed my cheek. Lifting up my face by my chin he said, "I'm so happy you're here. Come with me."

"You didn't answer my question."

"That's a topic for another night…or later tonight."

I rolled my eyes. He stopped and looked me up and down. I wore a flared red pleated skirt and a V-neck black sweater deep enough to show a peek of cleavage and Converse sneakers with thigh high stockings. The corset top underneath the sweater did a nice job of thrusting up my boobs.

"You look damn cute in Converse. You are now

only allowed to wear those sneakers in my home."

"I shouldn't tell you I have two other pairs."

"You're the girl of my dreams…Come on. My set starts soon."

He took my hand in his, and my heart leapt.

In the other section, there was a whole other room with two huge Christmas trees, and a large stage against the back wall. A marching band could fit up there it was that big. There wasn't a lot room for a mosh pit, but I'm sure the die-hard fans made it happen.

"Wow, look at this place!" I said.

"Have you been here since they added this on?" Clark asked.

"Nope. This is fucking awesome! It was such a dive bar before. There are so many people here!"

"The headliner is a big local band. They're new—Blue Horse Knight—but each member has a following."

"They're not all here to see you play?" I batted my eyes at him.

"You're cute and amazing for my ego. No, we go on before them and fluff up the crowd. Ergo, cover songs everyone knows."

"Makes sense. Do you ever do originals?"

"Not really. I can do the music part, but I'm horrible at lyrics." Clark brought me to a table to the right side of the Christmas trees. Ms. Happy-Go-Lucky Cleo was sitting with another guy chugging their beers while another punk girl chanted, "Go go go".

Cleo slammed her empty stein down and broke out into a huge smile. "Suck it, Henry! You're going first!"

"Signing our lives away, Cleo?" Clark kidded throwing her a napkin.

"Nah, Clark, just sweetening the pot! We're going second!"

"You heard the lady. Let's tune up lady and gents! Bri, what would you like? I get unlimited free beer here," Clark asked.

"I like that perk! Um, I think there is a lemony IPA I like. I forget the name."

"I'll ask Sean. He'll know. Stay here, I'll be right back," Clark said touching the side of my shoulder. I wanted to follow him, but I didn't want to appear clingy. The view of him walking away was enough to keep me grounded. Nathan's story about Clark and his infamous tight jeans seemed more plausible than ever.

"I think it's called Bikini Release," Cleo said.

Cleo walked up to me, tuning her guitar. "Huh?"

"The lemon one is called Bikini Release or Beach Babe something. It's their summer brew, but they keep a cask of it on tap."

"Nice. I can't believe what they've done with the place."

"The expansion happened about a year ago. It's pretty much Clark's home away from home." Cleo sat on top of the table with her phone out to a tuning app and her fingers turned the end knobs. Her bass guitar was sick. Dorothy's magical ruby red slippers came to mind.

"I love your bass."

"Thank you. She's my best girl." Cleo looked up and inspected my body again. I knew that look. Judgment? Competition? Did Clark have her on the side?

"Am I trying too hard?" I threw out the bait.

"No. You look hot as fuck. Don't worry. He likes

you. You're in." Cleo's voice held a serious genuine tone that made me think I'd been wrong about her intentions.

Before I could overanalyze and suck at more small talk, Clark relieved me from Cleo. He brought me a small stein of my favorite beer called Bikini Sunrise and he took a swig of his own dark brown beer. "A Porter Man?"

Clark almost spit out his beer. "A beer girl too?

"I'm a lot like you. I pretty much know a little bit about everything. Surprised?"

"Every time," Clark said. "How the fuck did Nathan find you?"

"Pure luck I guess." I shrugged and took a sip of my beer. This was definitely the beer I liked!

"Well, I better play the lottery soon," Clark said.

****

Out of all the times Clark played his guitar in the apartment I couldn't remember hearing him sing. He hummed a lot, but no actual singing. The real thing held my gaze, my ears, and my body completely and utterly captive.

*Fuck. Watching him play was making me wet.*

He fucked the mic with his mouth, crushing his lips intimately against the netted metal. His eyes were shut, veins pulsed in his neck, and his throat worked out the song lyrics. He thrust his body against his guitar, feeling the music. When he opened his eyes, they headed straight for me.

I clenched my thighs together, squeezing my pussy tight. If I pulsed my legs repeatedly I knew I'd be coming, watching him sing, staring me down. *God, I had to get a grip.*

Clark stood front and center and Cleo jammed away to his left. The lead guitarist, who also played with the first band and lost the chugging contest, stayed behind Clark and Cleo almost up against the drum set. The drummer Dillon came late and basically walked from his car right onto the stage. The band fucking worked. Nathan had said they were good, but damn. I was fucking impressed.

They breezed through a Weezer song, then Metallica, a punked out Sugar Ray oldie and finished it off with a Chevelle song without skipping a beat. Clark's voice morphed to each song and he added his own flare.

He waved his hand to someone behind me and lifted up two fingers. "You fuckers are lucky tonight! We get two more…usually I let you pick, but tonight is lady's choice."

Clark looked over at Cleo and she curtsied at him. "You know what I want," she said with downcast eyes and a pouty lip.

"All right. It's too hard to find a chick bassist. I'll play it."

Cleo jumped up with glee and flipped him the middle finger when his back was turned.

I recognized the song instantly. He played Celebrity Skin by Hole with practiced ease. It wasn't a song I thought he'd play, but Cleo blissed out. Her body was planted in her rocker stance, head banging away.

After a few notes, Clark looked like he was giving into it too. He cruised around the stage sharing the mic with Cleo. It was fun watching him let loose in his environment. This was where he belonged.

"The last song will be my choice. Sorry everyone!"

Clark said.

The other cover songs were upbeat and punked out with Clark's unique twist. The last song surprised me. It took me a few notes to recognize the song, but this one he played like the original.

The song was about a guy begging a girl to be his. He would be her everything and he'd tell her he loved her every day. He'd put a coat in a puddle for her, he'd rip out his heart for her and Clark sang it directly to me.

The wedding night surged back into my mind. I loved how he never stopped touching Nathan and me during it all. He wanted to be a part of everything.

*Fuck, I'm not supposed to be mooning over Clark.* The tremble of anxiety sparked inside my chest. I was in way over my head.

I had to get the fuck out of here.

# Chapter Twenty-Five

I exited the brewery and fought the urge to run. It was getting too hard to ignore my growing feelings for Clark. But my feelings for Nathan aren't fading? Fuck, how did Lucy do it? I sat at the furthest table from the door next to the smokers. I needed distance. I had to think. I pulled out my phone to call Nathan but decided against it.

I stared at the train tracks, returning to my misery. The three of us were to blame, not just me. *Why the fuck did I have to go that key party?* I acted like a slut for one night in my conservative life and now I'm stuck between two men I can't imagine walking away from. They're still in a relationship with each other so the only one who could get hurt was me.

Clark rushed out the door.

"Hey, Bri, you okay? The Brewery gets warm, but it's fucking cold out here," Clark said. He was bound to find me eventually. He blew into his hands and pulled his jacket closed.

My nerves must have been getting the best of me. The sting of the cold air barely bothered me.

Clark looked fucking hot with his deflated Mohawk and smudged eyeliner.

"I'm fine. You sounded incredible up there! I loved the songs you chose! I love your spin on them!"

"Thank you! I'm glad you liked it! It's a lot of fun

playing at home. I had really missed it."

"You looked like you were having a blast! Even Cleo looked happy."

"Ha! I knew it. She likes to stand behind me so I don't catch her!"

We both laughed. "So what happens next?" I said.

"I'm good to go. Dillon used the last band's drum set, so I don't have to help him dismantle it. Cleo usually hangs around after the show because she likes one of the bartenders. Dillon can drive her home.

"Hey, want to see my recording studio? It's not far from here. I can change there. I'm a sweaty mess." Clark pawed at his shirt sticking to his chest.

"Um sure. That'd be cool."

"I have my own office too. Hop in my car. We'll come back for yours."

"Okay." He reached out his hand and I took it. I stood up and he yanked me close. We stood close enough that his visible breath warmed my face. He peeked down at my mouth and bit his lip. "I promised myself I would hold out on you. Darling, you are making this torture."

I waved my hands up in the air and stepped back. "Sorry, Clark. I don't know my own vixen tendencies yet."

Clark pulled me back into his arms. "No, Bri, you don't." Then he kissed me. Our lips smashed together so tightly my mouth barely opened. The flutter of lust climbed its shameless way up my body.

Clark let up and when his tongue searched for mine I fell further into his embrace. His arms encircled me, and I angled my head to deepen the connection.

The catcalls behind us broke the spell. We

separated, and I glimpsed Clark's drowning expression. His eyes were closed, his mouth slack. Like a switch, his face morphed back into a smile and a sarcastic laugh followed. Cleo and Dillon whistled from the doorway.

Clark fidgeted to close my jacket shut, but it was already buttoned up. A flash of nervousness skated across his face.

"I was right. Clark with a crush my ass!" Cleo drunkenly accused.

"Oh shush up. I played your song. I get at least an hour of civil conversation."

"Blah. You weren't born civil," Cleo shouted, swaying a little. Dillon placed his hand over her shoulder. Were they together? Her hand rested on his chest.

"Guilty," Clark retorted.

"Are you guys hanging out for a bit?" Dillon asked. He was the quiet one of the group. The makeup and the act appeared to be for the show. He was the straight-laced guy hiding out amongst the punk Goth kids.

"Sorry, man. I'm going to show Bri the studio while Nathan's out of town."

"Cool. Nice meeting you, Bri. I'm going to jet home. I'm fucking exhausted. Practice on Thursday?"

They each nodded. Clark wrapped his hand around my shoulder and pulled me close. I simply fit right under his arm. The little nook made just for me. Our height difference matched.

I looked up at Clark, and he kissed me lightly again. "Great set guys. See you on Thursday."

Clark dropped his hand and clasped mine. I waved at his band. They returned the gesture, even Cleo. Her gaze lingered a few seconds longer before she turned away.

Clark led me down the opposite side of the parking lot to his car. He opened the passenger door for me, then reached over me to turn on his car. He smelled so fucking good. His boy smell mingled with sweat was more intoxicating than the beer I had before.

"Stay here, darling. Warm up. I just need to get my guitar and amp. Be right back," Clark said and stole another kiss.

I was dumbstruck. His smell, his kisses, holding my hand, was making me swoon. I was on a date, a real date between Clark and me. *What the fuck was I doing?*

He shut the door and ran back inside. I moved the vent starting to blow warm air toward me to the other direction. I was already warm enough.

Should I use the philosophy I did last week? What if this is it? It didn't seem likely. Nathan was actually turned on by the fact that Clark had fucked both of us. Could I date both Nathan and Clark? God, how complicated can one relationship get?

Clark returned a few minutes later with his gear. "Sorry I got caught up for a second. The owner just offered me the house band job." Clark didn't seem happy.

"Oh wow! Awesome! Is that a good thing?" I asked skeptical.

"It depends on how you look at it. It's a guaranteed paycheck but it's a lot of work. You can't play the same set every time. There are too many regulars. I'd be contracted to play the open mic nights on Sundays. Fuck."

"Do you know a lot of songs?"

"Meh." Clark got into the driver seat. "I'll think about it tomorrow."

He stared at me. "I can't believe how cute you look tonight. Did you dress up for me or is this you?"

"A little bit of both. I used to go to a lot of concerts."

"I dig it."

"If I blushed I would be red as fuck right now."

"You do blush," Clark accused. His focus switched to pulling out of the tight parking spot.

"Oh really? When have you seen me blush?" I called out his bluff. The heat would creep up, but I never saw pink in my cheeks.

"After you come." I stared at him perplexed.

"You blushed after you came on my face. Your cheeks were fucking rosy. You looked like the most beautiful woman I'd ever seen." All his jokes brushed aside, I could tell he was dead serious.

I leaned over and kissed him. "Thank you."

"You never have to thank me for making you come."

I giggled. "I meant thank you for making me feel beautiful."

"Always my pleasure, Bri."

He pulled out the brewery parking lot and we headed off to the studio.

# Chapter Twenty-Six

*How could I possibly think he would behave?* We weren't in the car five minutes and his hand inched up my leg, fumbling with my skirt. I made a pitiful attempt to stop him. His hand swatted mine away.

"Let me in, darling. You know you want me." I looked at him and the darkness I witnessed at the wedding was almost there. I pulled up the skirt.

Clark reached my panties and massaged me through the lace. "Seriously? You're actually wearing panties? You're a cruel, devil woman."

I straightened up in the seat, widening my legs for him.

"I'm sorry. I should have known better. I can take them off?" My response came out breathy…soon enough it wouldn't matter if I had panties on. His fingers were doing fine without bare skin.

"No, don't. I like a challenge. Please don't apologize. You did nothing wrong."

I smiled in the dark. Their words were slowly building up my bruised self-esteem.

Clark stroked me for the few minutes of the drive. He only touched me through the fabric, teasing me, making me ache for his real touch on my heated skin. "Your panties are soaked."

I didn't respond. I was lost to the feeling and watching his fingers.

He drove up to a small office building with metal musical notes etched into the siding. Clark's car was the only one in the small lot. He removed his hand from my crotch and my pussy twitched, yearning for release. I moaned my disappointment.

Clark pushed the gearshift into park, undid his seat belt, and lunged for me. His lips crashed onto mine. His tongue entered my mouth and I gasped for breath. He pulled back from my lips and brought two fingers up to his mouth, wetting them with his spit. He dove passed my panties to touch my aching flesh as I moaned into his face.

"I want it all. Give me everything, Bri," Clark ordered.

His hand blurred in my lap. *There was a benefit to be hand fucked by a guitar player…they're experts with their hands.* He dipped his spit-slicked fingers down from my clit into my empty, drenched pussy. Clark bit the side of my neck and pushed me over. I convulsed around his fingers, squeezing my thighs together. The heat radiated out of my pussy and my orgasm dragged on. I cried out.

Clark licked the side of my neck gently, easing up on his intensity. My body calmed down and Clark extracted his fingers from my pussy. His finger swirled around my engorged clit, and I jerked in the seat.

"I love watching you come." He kissed me with the barest touch of his lips. "Come on, darling. I want to show you my world."

Clark got out of the car and went around to my side. He opened my door and held out his hand.

"My lady?"

Oh, now he's being chivalrous. I shook my head as

I got out the car.

"What?"

"You're surprising, Clark. Every time I see you, you show me a different side of you."

"Do you like the side you see now?" Clark asked, pulling me in for another kiss. He grabbed my ass under my skirt. His cock was hard against my stomach. "Seriously? Why are you still wearing panties? Please take them off. I won't kiss you again until you strip."

I was taken aback by his bluntness, but when I opened my eyes he was grinning at me. He took his hands off me and clasped them in front of his chest. "No more until you do as I say. I mean it, missy."

I worked the damp cloth down my legs and placed my panties on the car seat. "Better?"

"Perfect. Come on." Clark took my hand, and we headed toward the dark building. Evidently, he was really into handholding. He took my hand three times since the night started. Nathan never held my hand. No, wait, once when it was icy, but other times he doesn't. *I wonder why?*

Clark unlocked the main door and led me through a long corridor that ended with a wall sign filled with band stickers. We took the door to the left, and I was shocked to see so many different instruments in one open space. There were a few workstations and the entire place was lined with guitars hanging on the walls. It was a band boy's paradise.

"Here it is!" Clark said, switching on the lights. The lights hummed on and I saw more of the space. There were rooms with numbers lining the left wall and offices with see through glass on the right.

"Wow, this is incredible!"

"Yeah, we got some studios with sound proofing over here and the audio engineers sit over there and master the recordings. The managers are in those peep show offices. I love it here." Clark beamed from ear to ear showing me around the studio.

"Stay here a sec." Clark instructed before heading to the bathroom. There was a faceless man with a guitar holding up the metal sign on the door.

I wandered through the space. I stopped looking around when I came across a sea foam green six string bass guitar hanging on the wall. If I ever was going to play bass I wanted that one.

Clark came out of the bathroom and joined me. His hair was slightly wet and his Mohawk was gone. The eyeliner he wore looked more smudged.

"Anything catch your eye?"

"This bad baby up here! I love the color!"

"Darling, you're adorable. This is the hardest instrument to play in the worst color. That's not a normal bass."

"Yeah, I know. Can Cleo play a six string bass?"

"Not really. It came up once and Dillon's balls got pretty tightly gripped if you know what I mean."

"Note taken." I needed to get on that girl's good side.

"Let me show you my office. It's down here." He grabbed my hand again and brought me to a room at the end right corner. He flicked on the light and I was surrounded by pure Clark fandom.

There were shadow boxes similar to the one in their apartment on the walls. They each had a band photo with ticket stubs and stickers from the venues.

"Welcome to my little haven in the madness.

People see me in here for multiple services."

"Very cool. I always wanted my own office," I said. I walked up to the biggest shadow box. "Do you make one for every gig?"

"I wish. My sister makes me one for every tour. She tries to come to as many shows when I'm up by her. She lives outside of Chicago."

"You have a sister?"

"Yup. I'm a very open book guy. I got nothing to hide."

"Like you said, you're blunt. I appreciate that in a man."

He rolled out his desk chair and sat down. "Poor Nathan. He's not as direct as I am. I feel like he's still trying to figure it all out," Clark said.

At the mention of Nathan's name tightness formed in my chest. Clark and I had been flirting and messing around all night. *How does either of them not have a problem with this? I can ask myself the same damn question.*

"Did I lose you?"

"Sorry. I can't help feeling guilty spending this quality time with you."

Clark took in a long breath and scrolled away from his desk. His flirty, light attitude was fleeting from his face.

"Look, Bri. I like you. It's not a secret. Nathan knows, and we've talked about it. I had a lot of fun with you tonight and I don't regret anything we've done or what I hope we're going to do."

"You and Nathan talked about me?"

"Yeah, we had to talk. He told me about your missed lunch date too. Come on, Bri. We're three adults messing around with only each other. Let's have a little fun?" Clark's lips curled up, and he partially shrugged.

"You make it sound simple. I think I'm a lot like Nathan. I'm still trying to figure it all out."

"I'm here for you if you need me," Clark said, leaning back in his chair, lacing his arms behind his head. "Now onto more important matters. Since you've come all this way, what can I do to service you tonight? I offer a variety of enticing pleasures only after hour guests can reserve." The flirt was back.

"Enticing pleasures? What catalog did you read that out of? Sexy Guitar Weekly?"

"Stop being so fucking cute. You have no idea what I can whip up for you."

"How about I give you a service you can't refuse?"

Clark stood up, approaching my awkward stance. His eyes shined in the fluorescent lighting. They were stunning blue pools of want.

"I'd never refuse you," Clark said.

Clark moved in to kiss me, but I leaned out of reach. I got down on my knees in one swift motion. His hands met mine at his belt. He undid his buckle and ripped his zipper down. I looked up at him and his eyes blazed with desire. It reminded me of Nathan that first time.

"I'm all sweaty," Clark said, breathless.

"I don't care."

He shucked down his pants, and I was face to face with his covered cock. I licked the outline of his hard cock with one long stroke.

Clark gasped and pulled his briefs down. I sucked his cock into my mouth, fisting my hand around him. I took him into the back of my throat, swallowing around the head, and he moaned loudly.

"Oh fuck, darling. Lick me good and clean."

I made a ring with my fingers, found a rhythm, and licked every inch of him. Clark's hand grasped my hair, but he didn't pull or push, just tangled his fingers in the loose strands. I lightly traced his balls with my other hand and got another loud groan.

"Ohhh I love it when you do that, Bri!"

I hummed, and he jerked forward. I tasted his precum that leaked from his slit. He was liking this, enjoying everything I did to him. The thought provoked me further

"Give me your hand," Clark murmured.

Clark took my hand and sucked on my right pointer finger. I never had my fingers sucked and it did a nasty twist to my insides. I watched him intently, a devilish smile never left his lips, while his hips thrust slowly into my mouth.

I didn't dare close my eyes. I needed to watch him.

He released my hair and anchored his hand on my shoulder. I desperately wanted him to touch me more.

"I wish I could lick your pussy while you suck me. That was so hot in the hotel. I want to do it again. Fuck your cunt for me. Use the fingers I got wet for you."

I spread my legs and pumped inside myself with my fingers Clark lubed up. It was doing the trick.

"Next time I want to watch those fingers fuck your pussy. Are you wet, Bri? Does sucking my cock turn you on?"

I nodded and slowed down. I took Clark's cock as far it could go into my mouth before I gagged and heard a new type of groan from him.

"Please do that again. Fuck."

I did it again, and he was coming in my mouth. He jerked and spurted, and I swallowed. I remembered Nathan saying Clark liked to have the head of his cock licked. I removed him from my mouth and only used my tongue to lap up his cum.

"Oh fuck; he told you," Clark moaned.

I smiled to myself. Clark's body shook, and he moaned louder than before. I knew his juicy little secret.

Clark's eyes were shut, and his hand gripped my shoulder pretty fucking hard. His forehead furrowed like he was in pain, but his mouth froze in a big O, gasping for breath. "Bri…"

I took everything he gave me. I licked him good and clean just like he wanted.

"You're addicting, you know?" Clark commented, pulling up his briefs and jeans.

I shrugged. My mouth tingled from being stretched. Clark definitely had more girth than Nathan.

Clark kissed me lightly. "Can you do that to me after every show? That was fucking good. My brain is fuzzy. I want to do something special to you when we get home."

"Special?"

"Good girls who wait will be handsomely rewarded…"

I shook my head at his cheese. He was like me. The cheesy comments naturally flowed.

We didn't say much while he showed me around the rest of the studio, holding my hand the entire time. Twenty minutes later, we headed back to the Brewery.

"Please come home with me, Bri. Nathan might be back tonight. I'd love to spend more time with you."

"Okay, Clark. See you in a little bit."

"Can't wait, darling."

When I got back into my car I pulled out my phone. I had a missed call from Nathan and a text.

*—I hope you enjoyed Clark's show, baby. I should be home in about 2 hours. Miss you! <3.—*

I felt terrible for missing his call, but I didn't have the heart to call him back while Clark's cum coated my throat. This made my brain hurt. I kept telling myself, *It's okay. This is okay.*

I texted him back.*—It rocked! Heading back to your place to meet Clark. Miss you too!—*

*Okay, baby steps.*

## Chapter Twenty-Seven

Even though I had been here a dozen times now, something was off. Their apartment was eerily quiet. Nathan's tablet lay unused on the kitchen counter. Nathan's leather jacket was thrown over the couch. Intense guilt skated up my spine.

I stood stuck in the entryway. I couldn't will myself to move. *Could I do this with Clark? Just Clark? We both made each other come already once tonight and if I stayed what more would we do?*

Clark bumped up against my back, almost knocking me over. His hands kept me from falling.

"Shit, what's the matter? Did we have a break-in? Amora!" Clark asked. He scanned the room as he dropped his keys into the bowl next to Nathan's second set.

"No, it's not that. I'm sorry I'm having second thoughts about tonight. I feel like I'm cheating on Nathan. But he and I aren't in a confirmed relationship. Don't you feel like you're cheating on your boyfriend with me?"

I ranted. I expected Clark to roll his eyes or get mad with my good girl intentions, but no. I didn't recognize the emotion plastered on his face.

Clark pulled off my coat. "Bri, I told you at the wedding that I don't interfere in people's relationships. I also told you I'm not a cheater. Before you came into the picture, Nathan and I didn't talk about our relationship. It just happened, and we were in it. But we both know deep down we're not enough for each other. Come here."

Clark hung my coat on the third hook like it was meant for me. He took my hand and led me over to the couch. I took the right side, and he sat down stretching his legs out on the coffee table.

"If you want to leave, there's the door. I would really like it if you stayed. Even if I don't get to touch you again tonight, please don't leave."

"Well, when you put it that way I should move in!"

Clark frowned. "This isn't a game for me, Bri. I had a great night with you. Music is my passion and sex stuff aside, I enjoyed your company. You get me. Nathan listens to me talk about music, but you're like interactive with me. You understand the passion and the love I feel for it."

My sanity ripped at the seams. There was no sexy pull to his voice, just a bare soul. I wanted to cradle it and let it feel warmth.

"Clark, it's easy to see you love what you do. Watching you up on stage was amazing. You belong up there."

"And?" He was going to make me say it.

"And I did enjoy my time with you too. I do like you. You and Nathan are so different in the best ways. I've been loving my time with both of you."

"Good. I was hoping you'd say that." Clark visibly relaxed. He draped his arm over the back of the couch. His fingers touched my shoulder.

"Can I ask you a question?" I prompted.

"Yes, I'd like you to not wear panties from now

on." Clark lifted my skirt up with his finger. I swatted his hand, and he stopped, flashing me his pretty dark blue eyes.

"I'll think about it. But I'd like to know something. How did it start for you and Nathan? Nathan told me his side of the story, but I'd love to know your side."

"There isn't much to tell…I took a chance on someone who made me happy again. I have a terrible ex-wife who drained me, mentally and financially. Um, I had a few confusing relationships after my marriage ended with a couple people who made me think, love and hate. I learned loneliness in the first degree. It drove a stake into my heart.

"I threw my angst into music, but that's a messier road than any sexual relationship. There's no trust, no commitment, absolutely no integrity, and literally no consistency with people anymore. I never wanted to be a front man, but it was the only way to get some fucking control. It's helped me get back a piece of myself from the trenches.

"But being in a band doesn't always pay the bills. I ran out of the money I had left after the divorce and needed a roommate. Then entered Nathan. A cute businessman with a wandering curious eye."

"Wandering curious eye?" I asked.

"For me, darling. He was dating some girl when he moved in, but it didn't last. After their dates, he would come home, and jerk himself off. I used to hear him watching porn through the walls. In the beginning, I didn't know him that well, but a moan is a moan. Something wasn't right in their relationship."

"Geez, that's awful." *Now I know why Nathan never talked about his ex-girlfriend. That's terrible.*

"Oh, yeah. After they broke up, I would catch him staring at me. Not in a creepy way, just looking me up and down. I don't even know if he was aware that he was doing it. He used to be addicted to the gym so I thought he was doing some alpha male thing sizing me up, but then he would rub his dick.

"Then one night I went for it. He had talked about some guy in college, and I wondered if any of those urges were left. I flirted with him any chance I got. He took the plunge with me.

"We fumbled through the beginning together. It was fun figuring out what we liked with each other. I like him a lot and regardless of where we wind up I've learned a lot from him and our time together."

"Do you love him?"

"Ah, one question per session."

"After all that you're not going to tell me?"

He looked me sternly in the eyes. There was no hiding his response. I saw everything.

"That's never an easy question for me. Love fucked me up this way from Tuesday and back. I care for him and if our relationship ended tomorrow it would fucking hurt and I'd probably eat my weight in burritos." He chuckled, flipping the seriousness back to humor.

"Okay, I understand. Do you find yourself more attracted to Nathan or to me?"

"You know what? I'm done with questions. Right now, I'm more attracted to the sexy woman who has been poking and prodding me to death. If she continues to do so I might have to bind her to my bed and put something in her mouth I'm sure she'd love to play with again." Clark slid down the couch closer to me and leaned in for a kiss. "Does that idea bother you or turn you on?"

"Being tied to a bed?"

"Correction; being tied to my bed."

"Are you a Dom?"

"No, darling. If that's what you want, then we have bigger problems. You might like being at my mercy. Come to my room."

Clark took my hand and led me to his bedroom. It was painted a dark gray and it pretty much had a bed, a dresser and four bookcases of CDs.

"Are you secretly running a radio station in here? That is a lot of fucking CDs!"

"I used to work at one. When they went belly up they let me take things…um a lot of things. I'll be right back. Here, make a playlist," Clark said handing me his tablet. My mind wandered to older songs I thought Clark would like.

Clark returned, sitting next to me on the bed. He reviewed my musical handiwork. His eyes went wide and then a Cheshire cat smile slithered onto his lips.

"Very nice, Bri. I knew I liked you. You have only one more warning. Don't make me fall for you. You're pushing my restraint here. Come on. Let me play with you."

I took off my sweater leaving my corset on. My boobs had been large my whole life. The shape made little moons over the low scoop. I unzipped the skirt's zipper, but Clark stopped me.

"You've been hiding that fucking corset under your sweater all night? Does Nathan know you can dress like this?"

"The opportunity hasn't come up yet."

"He's going to freak when he sees you. Corsets are one of his weaknesses. Leave it on, but take off your skirt."

I took off the skirt forgetting my panties were long gone. Out of pure reflex, I put my hands in front, shielding myself. I'd always been modest. Clark was pushing me far outside my comfort zone.

"Come here, Bri. Nathan told me you have a fantasy of being tied up during sex. I find it's easier to start off with tying someone up off the bed to ease them into it."

His king sized bed was an old four-poster bed with a dark blue bedspread. The edges at the bottom had small nubs with loops on the end. He was prepared for tonight. I was definitely not.

"Are you going to tie me to the bottom of your bed?" I asked.

"Absolutely. Is that okay with you? I'm terrible at mind reading. Your body can be telling me one thing, but if you're uncomfortable you have to speak up," Clark sternly stated.

"Okay. I'll tell you if I want to stop."

"That's my girl. I love your playlist, and I want to listen to it, but right now I need more edge. Stand in the middle and stretch your arms out."

I followed his directions, barely hesitating. My chest heaved up and down, my breathing came out fast, and he hadn't even touched me yet.

*Did he tie up Nathan when they were together? Is that why Nathan choose my fantasy key?*

"Clark, have you ever tied up Nathan during sex?"

"Sometimes. He wanted to try."

"Oh."

Stone temple pilots streamed out of the speakers. Yes, I was going to do a sex type thing. I smiled. He picked a perfect song.

"You're making me very confused here, Bri."

"Why? What did I do?"

"I always thought I was a boob guy. With your tits and ass, I'm at a loss. I can't figure out what I like better." I turned around to peek at him and he caught my eyes at once. "Turn around. Do you want me to blindfold you? And I mean a real blindfold, not one with eyeholes."

"No. I want to watch."

His body brushed up against mine. I whimpered when he cupped my ass. I arched down and nudged my ass against his groin. He thrust forward almost knocking me face first on the bed. His hands captured my hips, steadying my ass against him.

"Let me lead, darling."

One hand stayed on my hip and the other went in front of me to my play with my clit. I hope he felt how wet he made me. His fingers dug right in.

"You naughty girl. You're so wet. Does this excite you, Bri? Do you like it a little rough?" His teeth nipped my ear lobe. I shuddered.

"Yes, please, Clark." I found my words.

"There is something about seeing you laced up from behind that is making me so fucking hard. You're going to make me come so fast." Clark backed away. "Lean forward and put your arms up."

I brought my arms up and stayed bent over the bed. He tied a loose knot around my left hand and then my right. I lifted up. There was some give, but when the seemingly soft loops tightened, I gasped.

"Are you okay?" Clark smoothed his hands over my body. He touched me everywhere that wasn't my pussy or asshole. If he didn't fuck me soon I'd be practically begging for relief.

"Yes. It just dawned on me that I'm fucking tied to your bed," I said. The lyrics of the song spurred me on.

"Good." Clark gave me a simple answer.

With my hands strapped to the bottom posts of the four-poster bed, I was officially stuck. The only option of movement was kneeling or sticking my ass out further behind me. Clark traced the contours of my body with the warm massage oil. The heat permeated through my skin.

Then he slapped my ass hard. I jerked forward from the sting. His hand was back massaging my cheek. He slapped the other one as hard as the first. I yelped.

"Let me hear you, darling," Clark whispered.

Once he hit the same spot twice, I straightened up and drew in a startled breath at the resistance. My flesh stung, but his hand was softer again after.

"Your ass is blushing a pretty pink. Does it sting?" Clark asked.

"Yes. It does. Do you have to hit the same spot twice?"

"Your ass isn't that big, darling. Feel what you've done to me." Clark humped his hard cock against my burning cheeks. "I'll make the pain go away," he reassured.

Clark dragged his oily hands through the exposed shaved lips of my pussy and plunged inside me. His tongue caressed the middle of my back between the laced up parts while he pushed inside me with his fingers. His other hand slathered the oil over my lower back, along the crease of my dimples. He kissed each dip.

"Better, Bri?" Clark said.

I moaned. I had never been bound to a bed or anything except the chair during the party. I was relieved when Nathan had untied me. Tonight, I welcomed the restraint. I trusted Clark to make me feel good and blow my mind.

"I have to have you now," Clark said.

Clark pushed his cock up and down my folds, making me squirm. He knew where to go, but his prolonging actions drove me crazy.

"Do you want it, Bri?"

"Uh-huh"

"Can I fuck you bare?" He dipped his cock inside me and pulled out.

"Yes, Clark."

"Tell me you want it."

"Yes, I want you. Please fuck me."

"Oh yeah."

He eased into me gently and during the crescendo of the song rammed inside tearing a grunt from my mouth. He anchored his hands at my hips and fucked me. He hit every part of me. He was so thick he rubbed against the hood of my clit. An erotic friction grew and rose between us.

My arms tingled yet welcomed the hold. With the energy of the room, the smell of the sex oil, and of us…fuck, I couldn't stay still and just let him fuck me. I widened my stance for balance and thrust back onto his cock.

"Fuck, yeah. Push back, darling. Use my cock. It's yours. Oh, Shit. Your cunt doesn't want to let me go.

It's so pink hugging me, fucking me. Ahhhh..."

His dirty talk was like a drug. He goaded my body into response. *I can't believe he was watching me fuck my pussy onto his cock.*

"Oh Clark, oh yes!" I screamed.

Clark gripped my shoulder with one hand, and he grabbed at the lace of the corset with the other. The corset tightened against my body pulling at my breasts; the sharpness tightened my insides.

Clark cursed again and again, claiming me. When my body was about to push over, he bit against my neck and licked the fleshy part of my ear lobe. My pelvis jerked, and my orgasm exploded; I clenched the innermost part of me, squeezing Clark's cock. He sped up, fucking me through his orgasm.

He shouted in my ear. He slapped my ass again and held tight to my body. His cock jerked inside me. "Oh Bri, oh fuck. I'm coming." He made a high-pitched moan and draped his body over mine. His heated face rested on the exposed skin between my shoulder blades, and his lips planted kisses on my flesh.

"Are you okay? Please say something," Clark asked, nuzzling against my neck.

I moaned. It's all I could muster. I swallowed my spit and tried again.

"Clark." I turned and saw his sated face. His lips curved up in a half smile and he kissed me. Slowly he left my body and caressed his hands over my ass. He hadn't slapped me hard enough to leave a mark, only heat the skin. The pressure felt so good, now.

"Can I do that again to you one day?" he said, every word after a slight pause.

"Yes, definitely."

"Awesome. I'll be right back."

"What?" I jerked up, but my arms wouldn't let me go far. Clark left his bedroom.

"Hold on."

Clark returned from the bathroom with a new pair of boxers on and a washcloth in his hands. "Hold on one more minute and I'll untie you."

He picked up a small remote and my playlist came through the speakers.

Clark wiped the oil from my back with the damp washcloth. Each place he cleaned, he kissed and caressed with his other hand.

"You did so well, darling. Did it feel good or make you feel uneasy to be at my mercy?" Clark asked.

"Uneasy? No. I feel wiped out."

He freed my left hand first and kissed the inside of my palm. "I'm glad. I did the same thing to my ex-wife and she used the word 'uneasy.' "

"I'm not her, Clark. I knew you weren't going to hurt me. You made me feel good." I caressed the stubble on his cheek with my freed hand.

He undid my right hand, repeating the kiss on my palm. I stood up too fast and stumbled back into his chest.

"Be careful, especially because it's your first time doing any bondage play. Even if it's simple like we did." Clark cooed in my ear. He rubbed up and down my arms.

He kissed my hair and rested his cheek against the top of my head. I melted into his soothing gestures.

Clark cradled me further against him. *I couldn't believe his cock was already hard against my ass.* I arched my back, undulating against him.

"Hmmm…you're insatiable."

"Guilty as charged." Clark pulled me back up to him so our bodies were flush, my back against his front. He loosened the strings of my corset.

He peeled the garment off me. *I loved seeing the lines on my stomach from its tightness.*

My body felt so satisfied from the intense orgasm and being stretched out. I shook my arms out. Clark cradled my breasts. "I love your boobs. There're so soft."

"Why thank you." I leaned forward to fit his hand more.

"Are you tired? We can stop if you want…"

"I don't want to stop," I admitted.

Clark pushed me lightly against the bed. He pulled off his boxers and crawled to me, caging me in. I broke through and headed toward his pillows. Clark dipped his tongue into the dimples above my ass. He caught up to me and pulled me quickly underneath his body. His mouth latched onto my perked up nipple when my back hit the mattress.

I practically whimpered when front of his thighs pushed up the backs of mine. His skin was hot to the touch and his thighs were dusty with fine hair. *Ah, yes, I could touch him now. I could see what he was seeing.*

I always liked to watch men when they made love to me. The visual never failed to make me wet. I felt soaked watching Clark prep me for another round. He watched himself toy with my pussy. It was a sight not to be missed.

"Do you like when I play with your pussy?" Clark asked.

I moaned yes. Clark's gaze blazed with desire

directed only at me.

"What do you want, Bri? What can I give you?" Clark asked, holding his cock in front of him, waiting to strike.

"I want everything," I said breathlessly.

"You got it. I'm all yours."

Clark pulled my hips closer. His cock slid through the top crease of my pussy, enhancing the friction. I writhed with want. I needed him to fuck me again.

"Clark, fuck me please."

"My thoughts exactly."

He pushed at my opening and my skin yielded to the welcomed intrusion. I was slick and wet from his cum. He slid further in with each tentative thrust. His thrusts were slow, but there was no need. I hadn't lied when I said I wasn't tired from the experience before. My body was ready to be fucked again.

"Please Clark…"

"Please?"

"I need more…"

"I'll give you whatever you need, dream girl."

He fucked me harder. His hands caressed me so tenderly while his cock pounded me into the mattress. Our lips melted together, slipping inside each other's core. His room could have gone up in flames and we'd still be locked in this decadent embrace.

My body trembled at the difference from one lovemaking session to other. It was one thing to feel the excitement strapped to the foot of the bed, but this was so much more intimate. My orgasm was far from crashing over, hovering out of reach letting me experience the pleasure full on without taking it away.

Clark smoothed his hand down my left thigh and

arched my bent knee over his shoulder. I gasped at the how deep his cock reached inside me. He felt too fucking good.

"I needed to feel you again," he said. He kissed me deep and my mouth gave in.

When he ended the kiss, his cheeks were black from my eyeliner. He kissed me that hard. I cried out at the image. *He wanted me that bad?*

Clark's phone rang. Without stopping he swished his hand over it and moaned,

"Nathan, come home. You're missing something wonderful."

"Are you fucking her?" Nathan's first words came loud and clear.

Clark chose that moment to drag his cock almost out of me and then thrust hard into me. I pretty much screamed into the phone's direction.

"Fuck. You are. I'll be there in a minute. Hold on, wait for me."

Clark stopped fucking me and massaged my clit while he was still nestled inside. His cock twitched inside me.

"Shit, I can't stop. I want you too much." He began his shallow fucking once more. His sweaty body covered mine completely. He smelled of Clark and only Clark. I caught drifts of his cologne long gone from before. I held onto him with one hand over his back and he clasped my other over my head. I turned my head to lick his neck or nibble his ear, but he was too close. He tore himself away and locked his lips against mine.

My orgasm started. It burst through rolling me under. My insides clamped down on Clark's cock and pushed him over his own edge. He hit even deeper inside me and his cock spurted into me and twitched all the way. He moaned into my mouth, screaming his orgasm into my body. I felt it all.

Our breathing slowed as we both came back down. Clark placed tiny kisses all over my skin. He kissed along my clavicle bones, my neck, the tops of my breasts, and finally back up to my mouth. My mouth felt dry, but it didn't matter. It wasn't long kisses, just loving ones.

Clark rested his cheek on my shoulder, nuzzling his lips into the side of my neck, collapsing his full weight on me. I traced my hands up the planes of his moist back and settled them down along his waist.

Nathan entered the room.

"I'm sorry. I wasn't fast enough," Nathan said with a sad look on his face.

Clark slipped his hands under my body and hugged me tight. *If I wasn't mistaken it felt like a goodbye.*

Clark and Bri's fantasy night was over. Our boyfriend just walked through the door.

# Chapter Twenty-Eight

"I'm sorry, Nathan. We were almost there when you called," I said. The awkwardness of the situation blasted through me. Clark wasn't getting off me or looking up from the crook of my neck. He was breathing hard against my neck and his cock still pulsed inside me.

"Clark, are you all right?" I combed my hand through his damp hair. He nodded, kissing my neck beneath my ear and pushed off me.

"Fuck, man. You look hot. I wish you were here a few minutes sooner," Clark said, staring Nathan up and down. Clark gently pulled out of me and a small moan escaped my lips. It felt just as good feeling him pull out.

"I said I was sorry." Nathan tilted his head down and looked up at me then Clark.

"Not good enough. You'll have to make it up to us," Clark said kneeling in front of Nathan.

Nathan placed his hand over Clark's wet cock and stroked. "Can I lick her off your dick?"

Clark's mouth curved into his mischievous smile. Nathan got down on his knees and stripped off his shirt.

"Should I let him, Bri? He was a bad boy leaving us alone. We missed you terribly."

Before I could answer, Nathan said, "Let me make it up to you."

"Ladies first," Clark declared.

Nathan got up from the floor and moved toward me. He captured my mouth in the hungriest kiss he had ever given me. I lifted up, but he pushed me back down. I placed my hand affectionately against the side of his scruffy face. I wasn't used to seeing Nathan rugged and laid back. It suited him perfectly.

"Did he make you feel good, baby?" Nathan asked, parting from the kiss.

"Hmmm…Yes."

"Do you feel up for one more?"

My body was literally done. Every body part, even the ones I couldn't touch yelled at me. *We're good, we've been used enough.* Clark awoke every nerve, every crease; every bit of me I didn't know was there. But I still wanted more. If this was the last time for all three of us, I had to enjoy it.

Clark still sat on the side of the bed, catching his breath. He was still gasping, coming down from his high. His hand lingered on my calf, not losing contact.

Nathan took off his jeans and boxers, releasing his hardened cock. I think he said please, but I was lost in my head. I scooted over to the edge of bed. I wrapped my hand around his cock and pulled him toward my mouth. I danced my tongue along the slit and licked repeatedly around the tip. This was what Clark liked best, but no guy is going to deny the feeling of his cock being licked wouldn't turn him on, urging him to fuck.

Nathan leaned over me, his fingers probing inside my pussy pushing through Clark's cum. I could smell the musky smell of it and Nathan's sweat colliding. It invaded my nostrils and twisted me inside out.

I sucked Nathan's cock into my mouth and he

moaned loudly.

"The two of you are truly something. I could watch all night," Clark said. His hand stroked up and down my leg.

"I want to fuck you, baby," Nathan whispered.

He got onto the bed and draped my legs over the tops of his thighs. We didn't need anything extra. We were both ready to fuck.

He slid right in, my pussy molding around his length. His thrusts were long and drawn out, building a steady pressure. I kneaded my fingers over my clit. It was still swollen from coming. It almost felt like too much, but I pushed at it more.

Clark crawled onto the bed, a tube of lube and a condom in his hand. I didn't know if I could take him in my ass tonight. My body was too used, my mind scrambled to the max. But I'd give it to him if he wanted. Every response switched to automatic with them. No doubt clouded my judgment.

*Fuck, how did I get here? How did I get so lucky?*

I expected Clark to lie down next to me, but he stayed behind Nathan. My eyes widened and I cried out. *Are they going to do it?*

"I love watching you fuck our girl. Doesn't her pussy feel like heaven?" Clark murmured into Nathan's ear. He sucked on his earlobe, waiting for an answer.

Nathan's eyes closed, and his mouth gaped open. Clark kneeled behind him, blocking himself from my view. "Uh-huh. Clark, don't tease me."

"Breathe, Nate. I'll make you feel so fucking good." Clark had one hand fisting Nathan's hair and he sucked on his neck. His other hand was lost behind Nathan. Nathan moaned louder than before and his whole body tensed.

"What is Clark doing to you?" I asked. Bliss was plastered on his face. Nathan's brow furrowed and his face went utterly slack.

"His fingers are fucking my ass. Clark is going to fuck me while I fuck you, baby." Nathan's eyes slammed shut. His right hand smoothed over my breast and gripped me hard. His thumb feathered over my clit, pushing my hand away. Pleasure slithered up my pussy around his cock.

"Fuck me, Clark. Fuck me while I fuck…Oh God," Nathan muttered.

Nathan squeezed my left breast and he winced slightly when Clark breached him with his cock. Nathan stopped thrusting inside me. Clark laid his cheek on top of Nathan's shoulder. "Oh fuck, I missed you," Clark moaned.

I shifted over, so I could watch. Clark grabbed hold of my legs and thrust inside Nathan's ass guiding Nathan's cock inside me. We were connected again. I touched Clark's hand on my thigh. His fingernails dug into me. I embraced the pain, already morphing it into pleasure.

Clark's thrusts were slow at first, but only at first. Nathan's head fell forward. He had stopped fucking me, only letting Clark's thrusts dictate how deep and fast he'd move inside me.

"Nate, your ass is so tight. Tight like Bri's pussy. Let's both make her come," Clark stammered out.

Nathan barely moaned in response. Clark's hand left Nathan's chest and trailed down his body to mine. He palmed my clit, then rubbed it back and forth.

The pressure built climbing up inside me, but I had

come already tonight too many times. I needed more to coax out my release. My body had no time to crank up the intensity. I was too satisfied, too done.

"Nathan, do you hear me? Fuck your girlfriend. Make her scream." Clark pulled back, slapped Nathan hard on his ass, and thrust back inside him.

Nathan gasped and almost snapped out his delirium. "Fuck…" He drew out the word. His eyes shot open and he came back to us. I couldn't imagine how intimate and over the top this must have felt for him. *Your brain can't handle the overload of sensation and emotion clawing its way out of you.*

"Bri…" Nathan's head remained low, his chin hitting his chest. He was still drowning, his gaze roamed over me, but he wasn't seeing anything.

I leaned up, caressed his cheek, and kissed him. His lips were slack against mine, his body still absorbing the pleasure, stealing him from Clark and me. I sucked on his bottom lip and dug my teeth into it.

Nathan's lips strengthened over mine. He groaned deep in his throat and kissed me back. His gripped the back of my neck, strengthening the connection, and screaming into my mouth. I opened my eyes and he stared back at me. "Sorry, I…I…This feels…" Nathan attempted to whisper into my mouth.

I lay back down on the bed and he grabbed my hips thrusting into me. I lifted my hand up to his lips, shushing him. I didn't need to hear what I already knew.

"Nate, are you okay? Was I…" Clark stopped, tensing up. His fingers on my thighs softened.

Nathan shook his head no, "Please don't stop." Nathan and Clark kissed. Their tongues tangled and they panted into each other's mouths. "I'm okay." Clark rested his forehead on Nathan's as much as he could at the angle. There it was, their connection. It lived and breathed amongst the sheets and darkened rooms. "Don't stop, Clark."

Clark kissed him again, thrusting forward back into Nathan, who in turn, fucked back into me. Their kiss ended, and Clark's gaze zeroed in on me.

"Bri, darling, grab those pretty tits for us. I want to see them pressed together." I obeyed Clark's command. I cupped their generous weight and pinched at my nipples, giving them a show. The distraction fueled Nathan to take Clark's thrusts and hit them deeper into me. This was what I needed. I wanted to feel both their thrusts fuck me.

Nathan smoothed his hand up my stomach and clenched around my breast. Clark's hand wrapped around Nathan's chest and hammered into him. Nathan grunted with each thrust.

"Oh fuck, Clark. Bri…I…Fuck!" Nathan grunted out. A scream growl choked out of Nathan's throat, and he grabbed Clark's arm on his stomach. Nathan slid from his knees, pulling Clark down with him. Clark followed his change in position. Nathan's body covered mine and he smashed our lips together. He devoured my mouth, all teeth and tongue. He was back in the moment, twisting it into something rougher.

He pinched my nipple, and then yanked my leg over his forearm to fuck me deep. I felt bottomless until Clark's tempo tipped Nathan to hit against my womb, pumping my cervix with his cock. My orgasm burst as Nathan grinded his hips against me, spinning me into my own oblivion. I thought it would be a rolling wave, but I was wrong. It punched into my pussy and numbed my entire body.

Nathan stopped kissing me and moved his head to the side of my face. He smashed his cheek against mine and grunted into my ear. He whispered things I barely registered. Clark kissed me over Nathan's shoulder.

We were so close to each other; our bodies entwined in the rapture. I gripped Nathan's shoulder and pulled at Clark's forearm on my waist. Clark shouted against my mouth, "I'm coming."

Nathan shook his head against my cheek. "Me too."

Clark thrust hard into Nathan, and Nathan stayed tucked up inside me. Nathan's body fell slack over mine, and Clark draped himself fully on Nathan. My chest constricted, and their weight crushed me.

For the few seconds they needed, they stayed until Clark pushed off first. Nathan moaned against my neck when Clark pulled out his ass. Clark rubbed his hand up Nathan's back like he did to me when I was tied up.

"I'll be right back," Clark said.

"Hurry back," Nathan mumbled from my shoulder. I took Clark's cue and traced my fingertips up Nathan's arm and around his back, kissing his shoulder. "That felt amazing."

"Indeed it did."

"Did you come, baby?" Nathan pried himself off my body and pulled his cock out of me.

"Yes. I don't think I can move, but yes I came."

Nathan laughed. "Sorry."

"Don't be. I'm in a sex coma."

"Ha-ha."

Clark came back wearing his glasses, and I

managed to get up to go to the bathroom. My legs shook from all the sex. *Fuck, they're intense*. Each time was crazier than the next. I brushed my teeth with the brush that was now dubbed mine. When I came back, Nathan left.

The music was off, and Clark put on the second pair of boxers he wore tonight. He took the left side of the bed and pulled me into the middle. "I like to sleep on my right side if that's okay."

"As long as I'm with you it doesn't matter."

"Good night, dream girl." He kissed me and pulled me close. Nathan came back and got into bed on the right side. Clark's bed had to be a king because somehow we fit comfortably. "Good night, Nate." Clark kissed him.

"Good night, Clark."

"Good night, baby." Nathan kissed me a few times, but I was already nodding off. Nothing could have kept me awake this time.

# Chapter Twenty-Nine

I woke up to an empty bed. I was still in Clark's room. His guitars were waiting for him on small pedestals and shadowboxes decorated the walls. It was pretty awesome, now that I had time to appreciate his room and not just the bed in the middle.

I found my sweater and skirt from last night. I left the corset off. Once I dressed, I braced myself and opened the door.

Clark and Nathan were both sitting at the kitchen table eating breakfast.

"Morning, Bri," Nathan said. "Is that what you wore last night?"

Clark's gaze wandered over my body. He knew exactly what I wore last night and underneath it.

"Yeah, can I borrow a shirt?"

"Of course." Nathan got up and kissed me on the cheek.

"You look cute. Please wear it again for me?"

"I will."

Nathan smiled and disappeared down the hall.

"I think your panties are still in my car." Clark winked and flashed me a cocky grin.

"Some boxers too, Nathan!" I shouted.

"Have a seat. I got you breakfast too. Nathan said you like egg whites with turkey bacon and Swiss. The deli put it on a bagel for you. I hope that's okay?"

"I will never say no to complimentary breakfast. Thank you!" I kissed Clark's cheek. He smiled, but it didn't go up to his eyes. "Are you all right?"

"Yeah, I'm really tired. Last night was awesome, but I can't remember the last time I had sex that many times. My brain hurts. How do you feel?"

"Ha-ha, yeah. My ass hurts. I wonder why?"

"You asked for it." He shrugged adorably.

The smell of hot coffee permeated my senses. I desperately needed a cup. I opened the cabinet and took out my pink mug.

"Here you go!" Nathan returned with a T-shirt and boxers.

"Thank you." I stretched up and kissed his cheek.

I went into the bathroom to change. It seemed silly to do. These two men had seen all of me, and I was covering up. But this was the morning. It was a new day and did last night change things? I *really need to figure this out*.

I came back out in Nathan's clothes and joined them at the table.

"I made you a cup. I got the creamer." Nathan informed. My pink cup had wonderful steam wafting out of it.

It was so simple. I felt like I belonged. We were complete. *Is this what Lucy craved? This harmonious trio?*

"This is delicious. Thanks, Clark."

"You're welcome, curly," Clark said. My hair had been pin straight, but my unruly curls made their way back.

"How did the moving go, Nathan?" I asked killing the silence.

"Good. They actually didn't have a lot left. It was mostly a few car rides of clothes and baby stuff from the shower."

"How's Lee? Is she feeling any better?" Clark chimed in.

"Lee's doing great. She popped since you last saw her. How did your gig go last night?"

"Oh yeah, I almost forgot I played last night. It was fine. The acoustics still suck in there."

"Did you get a good turn out?" Nathan continued.

"Maybe, I don't know. I was very preoccupied with my number one fan over here." Clark took my hand and kissed it.

"You must say that to all the girls." I kidded. I spied a few Clark worshippers out in the crowd.

"No, he doesn't," Nathan interjected. His response sounded curt, but he looked interested. "How was the rest of the night before I got home?"

I waited for Clark to talk, but he concentrated extra hard on chewing his breakfast. With every second he remained silent, my guilt about last night intensified. Nathan stopped eating.

"Come on guys. I know you guys had sex without me. It's not a secret," Nathan stated. *Why did I still feel so bad about how we did it? Should I tell him everything? How I got down on my knees in Clark's office and sucked him off? Do I tell him how hard he made me come in the car with only his fingers? Should I confess my conflicting thoughts while I was tied to Clark's bed?*

"I think Clark and I took it too far," I said it. I told the truth. We went further than fucking each other silly. Something tangible appeared far beyond our bodies rubbing against each other over and over.

My gaze flicked up to Clark and immediately, I wanted to take it back. Clark stared back at me visibly pondering what I just said. His brow furrowed and licked his lips.

"I guess I got carried away. I'm sorry," Clark said quietly. He blinked rapidly and crumbled the wrapping from his sandwich.

"No, you didn't," I said. I touched Clark's arm. "I enjoyed every part of last night. I will never listen to the Stone Temple Pilots the same way again."

"But you seem upset?" Clark asked, skeptical.

"I am. Fuck, I don't know. I'm struggling here. Clark, I loved our night together, and I had a lot fun with you, but now what? I'm confused what's happening here."

Nathan cut in, "Bri, I'm okay with what you did with Clark, and I think it's awesome. You two should be happy that you like each other too!" Even though I was relieved that Nathan looked happy, something still bothered me.

"Do you like me, Clark?" I felt like a teenager asking the cute punk boy out in school. *Circle yes or no.*

"I told you, I do. I wouldn't have tied you to my bed if I didn't." Clark stood up, flashing me a dirty grin.

"So you did do it? How much did you guys do last night?" Nathan asked, gripping Clark's arm, stopping him from walking away. His gaze flipped back and forth between Clark and me.

Clark sat back down and exhaled a big sigh. "Um, I took Bri to the studio. We fooled around. We came back here, we fooled around again and again, and then you came home. That sums it up. Right, Bri?"

"Yeah, that sounds about right." I giggled. Clark was playing with Nathan now.

"You've never been a stickler for detail." Nathan accused, his expression slightly annoyed.

"Look, Nathan, you gave me permission to give Bri her fantasy and I did. Did we go outside those bounds and fuck around it? Yeah. Do I regret it? No. Bri, you're like my fucking dream girl, and I would like us all to try being together. At least for a little while."

This was it. The make or break it moment. I couldn't leave if I tried. I'd be an absolute wreck now. "I'd like that very much. I'm sorry for getting overwhelmed. This is hard. I'm afraid of doing the wrong thing."

"Baby, we're going to fuck up here and there. I want to try this out." Nathan soothed, slipping my hand into his. Clark's eyes darted toward our comforting embrace.

"I agree. So we're doing this?" Clark added, reaching for my other hand over the top of the table. I took it and he grabbed Nathan's other hand.

We all said yes, and as cheesy as it sounds a rush came over me bringing forth a breath of fresh air and made me excited for new beginnings.

"All right, fun's over. We look like we're having a freaking séance right now. Let's break it up, people." Clark joked, making us laugh for a second, easing the pent up tension. "Can we also promise to be exclusive to only each other?" Clark added.

"I'm not with anyone else. Who else are you with?" Nathan snapped at Clark.

"Nobody, Nate. I'm only with you and now Bri."

There was a pause, and an emotion flashed over Nathan's face. It looked like Clark rubbed salt in an old wound.

"I'm sorry. I didn't mean to jump down your throat. Are you seeing anybody else, Bri?"

They drew their attention to me. "No, absolutely not."

I must have looked shocked because Nathan asked me, "What is it?"

"You two barely argue."

"We occasionally snap at each other. Even though our relationship isn't conventional, we aren't immune to bickering."

"I feel like it's not a real relationship until you have that first authentic showdown. You have to fight to grow. If you're a dirty fighter, the truth will always come out." Clark interjected, glaring at Nathan.

"Makes sense," I said.

We went back to eating our sandwiches. I'd spent so much time with them apart from each other. Being together, not in bed, or off an orgasm high was proving to be a real eye opener.

"So how was everyone's Thanksgiving?" I took a bite and glanced up at the microwave clock. "Wait, is that the real time on the microwave?"

"Twenty minutes fast," Nathan said.

"Shit. I have to go."

"Why? It's Sunday?"

"I would love to spend the day with you boys, but I promised I would meet my mom for lunch."

"It's only nine thirty a.m. It's early."

"Yeah, but I have to run home and shower and change and yada yada."

"All right. We'll let you go," Clark said. I looked down at his dreamy blue eyes, shining in the natural light filtering into their apartment. He was a striking man, who was now my second boyfriend. *How the fuck did this happen? What did I do right?*

"Can I tell Lucy that we're together now?" I asked.

"I don't see why not?" Clark answered.

"Sure? As long as she keeps it quiet at work, tell away."

"Okay. Thank you so much for the sandwich. I got to go."

"Go, before we keep you," Clark added. He grabbed my coat for me.

"Thank you, Clark." I kissed my boyfriends goodbye and headed home.

****

Every month my mom and I meet for our bottomless mimosa brunch. We started this tradition when I was back in college and even though we only live a town apart life gets crazy. Sometimes my dad joins us, but this was ultimately mother and daughter time to bitch about our lives after the mimosas kick in.

"You look great, hunny! You look so happy!" my mom shouted as we hugged.

"Thanks, Mom. I just saw you on Thursday." I retorted.

"I know, but Thanksgiving is always crazy. I feel like I barely saw you."

"Well, you know. Same shit. Different day."

"Oh, I know. You look rested. How's work? How was the wedding? You've been a busy bee lately!"

I always told my mother everything. It was one of the benefits of being an only child. But now I hesitated.

I could try to explain Nathan, but Clark? I'd have to leave him out. I felt bad not mentioning him, but she didn't need every detail.

"The wedding was fun! I saw a lot of old friends."

"Great! I ran into Diane's mother in the mall and she said everything was great except the DJ played the wrong song when they were coming out. I would have been so pissed!"

"Really? I completely missed that part." Of course I missed it. That's when Clark told me not to get too drunk because they were going to fuck me later.

"I'm not surprised. She told me about the two handsome men following you around the whole night. Is there something you want to tell me, dear?" Fuck, I thought I'd least get away not mentioning the boys today and then think about a plan later. Normally, she wasn't involved in my relationships, but ever since I turned thirty, the clock had been ticking.

"Mom, I would tell you if it was serious."

"I know, but give me something here! Are you seeing one of them?"

Try both? I need a PG rating here.

"Yeah, but it's very early, Mom. We had met at a party a few months ago, he's one of Kelsey's friends from college, and he works for my company."

"Your father would say 'Don't shit where you eat' but how is a girl even supposed to meet a guy these days? Are you two dating now?"

"Yeah, I was already going to the wedding and we decided to go with each other."

"I see. What's his name?

"Nathan."

"All right, so what about the other guy?

"The other guy, Clark, is Nathan's roommate, who also knows Kelsey. We sat at the same table. Kelsey was trying hard to get me with one of them." *Okay, I'll set part of it up.*

"Isn't that always the way, Bri? When one guy comes knocking they all start coming out of the woodwork!" My mom laughed at her own cheesiness. I didn't exactly lie, but I had to stretch the truth. My mother seemed to understand to a degree.

"You can say that again!" We cheered our mimosas and I successfully maneuvered the conversation away from my love life. God knows I was all over the place after last night. This was going to be a long Sunday drowning in my head.

# Chapter Thirty

"This project is going to going to kill me. I'm not going to hit forty," Paul said, sitting down across from me.

"Good morning, what happened now?" I inquired.

"Traill Associates cut the budget for the marketing campaign by twenty-five thousand dollars."

"What the fuck? How can they do that in the last stage?" I shouted. It was only Monday morning, and this project would not crumble under my watch.

After a long exhausted sigh, Paul explained. "We got the email last night. We will have to change the whole presentation. I'm sorry, Bri. It might be better to start from scratch."

My mind scrambled for a solution that wouldn't keep me here all night redoing every single thing we'd done since June.

"Where's Nathan?" Paul asked.

"Sorry, I'm late. My original transfer didn't come." Nathan took in our exasperated expressions. "What did I miss?"

"Paul is overreacting and having a meltdown," Marcia said. I was taken aback by her abrupt bitchiness. She drummed her fake nails on the table. I had barely noticed she was in the room.

"Thanks, Marcia, for throwing me under the bus," Paul said and walked out of the conference room.

She smiled showing too much teeth and got up for some coffee.

Nathan walked over to me and placed his hand on my back. “Okay, that explained nothing. Bri, what the hell is going on?”

“Traill cut our funding by twenty-five thousand. We might have to start over.”

Nathan looked shocked. He took off his tie and sat down in the swivel chair. Marcia pushed him a strawberry donut on a paper plate. “You might need this.” Nathan flipped his chin up and looked at me puzzled.

“Traill, we can handle. What’s up with Paul?” Nathan asked.

“Paul is being Paul. He takes everything as an attack on his character. He’ll puff into a paper bag and be fine. I’m going on break. Be back in ten.” Marcia’s heels pounded on the linoleum floor and out the door she went. She still didn’t look pregnant and God only knew what the fuck was up with her.

“So we should drive in everyday this week, right?” Nathan asked.

****

We wound up driving in for the entire week. Nathan and I worked twelve to fourteen hours a day to get the project back on track. He practically overdosed on energy drinks, and I gained ten pounds from the absent-minded eating. If we were scared people would think we were a couple, this week abolished it from anyone’s minds. We’d meet in the conference room with everyone else and go back to our desks.

Even in Clark’s life, this week sucked. I only got to speak to him on the phone once the entire week. He was stuck with clients every hour of the week. He even slept at the studio two nights because one of his regulars was only available in the middle of the night.

Eventually, the boys rang my doorbell around eight o'clock on Friday night. Nathan worked at the New Jersey office today, so we didn't do our daily routine. Seeing his tired face made my heart skip.

He smiled and kissed me on the cheek. I felt his two-day scruff of a beard. I hadn't seen Nathan with much facial hair except an occasional five o'clock shadow. It made him slightly more rugged and less of the angel between the two of them.

He handed me the roses from behind his back. Clark came up the stairs behind him with his own bouquet. He kissed me on the lips and handed his beautiful flowers over too.

"Aww, you guys. This is so sweet."

"I also brought a growler of the lemony beer you like from the brewery," Clark added.

"Yay! Thank you, Clark!" The boys came inside and took off their jackets while I put the flowers on the table.

"I have to apologize that we never hang out here. I should've invited you both over long ago. Welcome to my apartment."

"It looks different than last time," Nathan said.

"I cleaned up this time," I said.

Through someone else's eyes my apartment might not seem like much, but it had been my home for eight years. It was a small one-bedroom condo on the main street in Tarrytown. Once upon a time, it was my grandmother's and she kindly passed it on to me when she moved into assisted living. I updated the kitchen and replaced a few pieces of furniture, but I didn't change everything.

There was still a ceramic cupcake here and there, and I couldn't throw out her old, sea foam green couch. It made this place feel like home in just the right way.

"I'll go put these in water. Dinner should be ready in twenty minutes."

"Ah shucks. We'll have to ravish you afterward," Clark said pinching my side.

Nathan's face turned a bright shade of pink. I'd be blushing too if I could. According to Clark, I needed to orgasm first. I'd have to settle for chicken parmesan first.

I went into the kitchen and let them roam around. This week was utterly crazy, but I did remove all incriminating pictures from my dance recitals and every elementary school year. Adult me scattered the living room for the most part.

I opened my kitchen cabinet and lifted out three plates and three glasses. Clark rounded the corner into my kitchen and leaned up against the wall. "Aww, look at you, Susie Homemaker."

"Ha-ha, yeah right. I'm ten minutes away from burning everything." I handed him the plates. "Make yourself useful, go put these on the table."

"Yes, Mom." He scurried back into the main room. I ignored his lighthearted scoff.

This part of cooking always made me anxious. Everything could go wrong if I didn't time it right, and I just realized I forgot to make an extra pot of sauce. I quickly retrieved a small saucepot and poured in marinara sauce setting the flame to simmer.

Clark came back and took the glasses from the

counter, and then he disappeared again. I opened the oven, the cloud of steam fogged up my glasses, and checked on the skillet holding my favorite thing to make. The sauce inside of the pan was boiling but the cheese wasn't melting fast enough. I groaned, closed the door to the oven, and increased the temperature of the oven.

"Ugh, that sucks," I said to myself. I grabbed a few basil leaves off the mini plant I bought from the store. I sprinkled them over the almost boiling pot of sauce and stirred them in.

"You take cooking very seriously, huh?" Clark asked, making me jump. I hadn't heard him come back into the kitchen.

"Yes, I do. Cooking is one of my favorite things and I bake too."

"Really? I didn't know that."

"Yeah, I made some cupcakes. I, *shit!*" I touched the metal spoon resting in the saucepan and it was hot as hell. I jerked my hand back. I knew I hadn't burned myself, but it stung like a bitch.

"Be careful! Why are you so skittish?" Clark asked, lightly grazing my arm with his fingers.

"She's nervous. You don't see her every day. This is daily Bri," Nathan added, sauntering into the kitchen.

"Thanks for outing my anxiety." I blamed. My comment didn't faze him. He was already grabbing some napkins and opening drawers, looking for silverware.

"I get anxious too sometimes. What can I do to help?" Clark asked, rubbing my lower back. His questing hand veered toward my ass and he kissed my neck. Instant goosebumps covered my arm, making me squirm out of reach.

"Distracting me is not helping, Clark!" I rubbed my arm to make the goosebumps go away.

"All right, I'll behave, for now."

I pushed at his hips, urging him out of the kitchen. He bumped into Nathan, who dropped a knife on the floor.

"Ha, you got in trouble." Nathan mocked, bending down to pick up the knife. My sauce boiled and splattered red all over my stove. I grabbed the dirty utensil in Nathan's hand and chucked it into the sink.

"That's it. Everyone out of the kitchen, now! Dinner will be ready in about five minutes! Go, shoo!" This time I pushed them both out of the kitchen.

A few minutes later, the cheese had melted, and I served the boys their first home cooked meal in a while they said. I loved hearing their moaning at my cooking. "Oh my God, this is so good!" Nathan said. Clark savored every bite barely talking. They devoured their first helping and I offered seconds.

"Do you guys realize this is the first time we've actually planned a real date between all of us?" I said.

"If you moved in with us we wouldn't have this problem," Clark said it like it would solve all our issues. *I wasn't exactly sure if he was kidding or not.*

"Let's be real, Clark. She's right. We failed as a couple this week. If this is going to work, we have to put our relationship somewhere into the mix. Work killed us this week. We barely saw each other and we live together." Nathan gestured between him and Clark.

"Ugh, can we not mention work. My week long migraine is finally gone." I touched Nathan's shoulder.

"Sorry, baby." Nathan rubbed at his temples.

"The band tour is officially over and the new one doesn't start until January. I have time to put toward us." Serious Clark finally came to the party.

"Great. Maybe we can plan at least one night a week where we all hang out?" Nathan suggested.

"I would really like that." I consented.

"One night? I vote for at least three, but only if you cook. This is fucking delicious." Clark chimed in raising one hand in the air and pushing a fork full of food into his mouth.

"I second that! Sorry, Bri, you're outnumbered. We win," Nathan added.

I laughed at their ridiculousness. They hadn't tried my cupcakes yet.

"Can you guys seriously not cook?"

Both men became super interested in the meager remnants of their dinner with their heads hanging down almost into their plates.

"Fine. You guys have to do the grocery shopping." I gave in.

"*Deal!*"

# Chapter Thirty-One

We sat down on my sea foam colored couch to watch one of the latest superhero movies and within twenty minutes I grew restless. Nathan sat to my left and Clark to my right. They gave me a brief refresher of the last ten films, but my mind had moved onto other things.

*How am I supposed to just sit between the hottest two men I'd ever been with and not be fucking horny?* My legs were crossed so tightly, my heartbeat pulsed in my pussy. The tension was worse than ever.

I tested the waters by smoothing my hands up their legs. Both men spread their knees farther apart. They turned to me, but I pretended to watch the movie more intently. I was already lost in the plot. There were too many characters lumped together.

Each time I rubbed their thighs, I inched a little higher and moved up to their jean covered cocks.

Nathan reached for my breast, but I swatted his hand away. They chose to watch the movie over fucking, and I was going to make it as difficult as possible. Their cocks were both fucking hard under my palms. I pushed firmer to dig the zipper ridge deeper into them.

"Darling," my vocal lover remarked.

Clark unbuttoned his jeans and shucked them down his legs. His hand grabbed mine and I rubbed him through his boxers.

Nathan unbuttoned his collared shirt, leaving on his undershirt. He had been watching us intently. Nathan's cock twitched underneath my palm when Clark pulled down his boxers, freeing his cock, and enticing me to stroke it for real.

I did one better and licked across the head of his cock. He groaned and put his hand on my back. He was a quick study at my bra under the tank top. The hooks were undone in seconds. I pulled my bra off without dropping Clark's cock from my mouth. Clark's hand caressed my nipples through my shirt. Without looking I poked at Nathan's top jean button and he took the hint and helped me. He finished removing his jeans too, and I had both their warm cocks in my grip.

I loved feeling two long, hard cocks at my disposal to do whatever I pleased. Nathan guided me up and down his cock. I was impressed with myself. I jerked him off with my left hand. It felt wrong, but with Nathan's guidance, he was gasping soon enough.

Nathan whispered, "Take off your clothes, baby."

I popped my mouth off Clark and reached for my leggings. Clark yanked down my tank top and took my nipple into his mouth. He used his teeth first, his tongue second. I was instantly distracted and gasped at the momentary pain. Nathan finished removing my leggings along with my panties.

I ran my hand through Clark's hair, gripping the root, and he popped off my nipple. He looked up at me, his eyes dazed. Clark sat back on the couch and watched Nathan and I get ready.

I was up on my knees watching Clark stroke my saliva up and down his cock, waiting for me to come back. Nathan looped his hand in front of me, thrusting his fingers inside me. He trailed my wetness up to my clit, flicking his fingers back and forth. My exposed breast heaved up and down. I peeled off the thin straps of my tank top and was about to pull the garment off my body, when Clark stopped me. He pulled my top low enough to expose both my breasts.

"Don't take it off. You look hot this way," Clark said. He resumed his personal hand job.

Nathan extracted his fingers from my pussy. He finished taking off his jeans. Clark's wandering hands caressed over my ass and up my back. There was his connection thing. "Ahem, wait your turn." I flashed Clark a wicked smile and he did the same back. He stopped his touches. His hand moved over his cock slower than a moment ago.

Nathan's jeans and boxers were off, his cock hard and ready to fuck. Lust grabbed hold of his face. Clark had looked like he was a drowning man, but Nathan's face was fucking determined and eager. I palmed his cheek and kissed him. I sucked on his lower lip and tongued it. He moaned into my mouth, and I tugged on his cock, but Clark had beaten me to it. Clark's hand stroked Nathan's rigid cock already. I broke our heated kiss and glanced down at the naughty sight.

It was still wild to me whenever they touched. I wanted to watch, to see their relationship before me. I knew they both behaved differently with me, softer, cautious of their every move but they didn't have to be. I could take both of them. I caught glimpses of their greedy sexual natures, and I wanted to see it longer.

I leaned down, purposely pushing my pussy near Clark's face, to take Nathan's cock into my mouth. I didn't tease him; I simply took him into my mouth, dragging my tongue over the underside of his cock.

"Fuck, baby," Nathan shouted.

Each time my mouth met Clark's fist I went back up. Clark kissed my hip and pulled my waist over to his mouth. His tongue licked up my pussy and I jerked forward hard. *It was exactly what I wanted him to do.* Clark licking my pussy and Nathan's cock in my mouth destroyed all reasonable thought.

I moaned long and hard. My arms threatened to buckle from my angle. I needed one of them to stop. It wasn't going to be me. I didn't have the self-control left.

Clark hummed against my pussy, almost making me come. He started sucking and stabbing his tongue inside of me. Nathan's fingers combed through my hair, grabbing a tight hold. He pumped his cock through Clark's grip into my mouth. His salty precum greeted my tongue.

After a few reckless moments, Nathan drew his cock out of my mouth, shifting back on the couch. "I have to fuck you now, Bri. Clark, please. I'll lose it," Nathan whispered.

Clark let go of Nathan's cock and kissed my pussy goodbye. One night I wanted Clark to simply kiss my pussy all over. No licks, no dabbing, just sloppy wet kisses over me. He did wonders with that mouth.

Nathan turned my body toward Clark. Clark wiped his mouth on his sleeve and kissed me before I dropped to his lap. His kiss on my mouth felt like the kiss he just left on my pussy; only lips stinging with passion.

"Lick him, baby. Let me in. Fuck," Nathan said breathlessly.

I did as Nathan asked and licked the head of Clark's cock. Nathan's cock prodded my wet pussy and entered me in a single hard thrust. I sighed with relief. My men gave me exactly what I needed.

"Clark, you made her pussy so wet. Oh, Bri," Nathan stammered, rutting into me.

"We both did, Nate. Yeah, darling. Fuck me with your mouth." Clark whimpered. I licked repeatedly under the head of his cock, letting my teeth graze his cockhead's ridge.

Nathan burrowed his way into my pussy. My insides opened up for him. They both caressed my body all over. Nathan's hands stroked my hips, my back, and grabbed at my breasts. Clark's fingers brushed against Nathan's on my breasts and extended down to my clit.

*This was my new favorite position.* Nathan fucked me mercilessly while I kept my mouth tight around Clark. I was helpless to them. I'd given myself over. I was theirs.

"Yeah, Bri. Keep going. Don't stop. I want to come in your fucking mouth," Clark shouted. His hand moved fast over my clit. They were going to make me come. With their moans, their questing fingers, their intoxicating smell, and fuck…all that was them.

"Fuck her hard, Nathan. She's sucking my cock so good. Our good little hostess deserves a reward," Clark continued his dirty talk.

"I want you to come on my dick, Bri. Clark, fuck, keep doing that," Nathan shouted.

Nathan shifted behind me and lifted up his right leg against my hip. He thrust deeper, almost getting me right there. Clark's fast rhythm faltered. I needed more. Clark's cock muffled my moans each time. I screamed "more"…but we were beyond comprehension now.

I used my teeth against Clark's shaft along a throbbing vein and that was it, exactly what he needed. Clark's head thumped against the back of the couch and he pumped his release into my mouth. I kept my head down, my mouth full to the brim with Clark's thick cock, swallowing fast, not wanting to miss a drop.

His cum was sweet then salty as it coated my throat. He spasmed and fisted my clit hard and I was done. My orgasm spurred up, dragging me down. I pushed back on Nathan, forcing him to fuck me even harder, and he shouted his release as well. He shouted yes every time my ass hit his pelvis.

I popped off Clark's cock and moaned. I still pumped his hot hard cock and watched his cum flow out. I licked him over and over.

Nathan gripped my hip sharply and grinded up inside me. It peaked my orgasm, which radiated throughout my body. My pussy throbbed around Nathan's cock, and shivers raked over my body.

Each of us stayed still after those crushing moments. Clark flipped his head back up and locked eyes with me. I was panting, desperately attempting to come back down and catch my breath. With his cum still on my tongue and my lips swollen from his cock, he kissed me. It wasn't light like before. His kiss tugged at me, making me feel him.

*His kiss made me want to love him.*

I gasped, and he stopped kissing me. I didn't want to ruin any part of this moment by thinking too hard. The three of us were in this now. It was okay. *It's going to be okay.*

I turned my head back toward Nathan. His head

dangled forward; his breath came out fast like mine. He watched his cock slide in and out of me. He gripped his cock and traced my pussy with it. The tip of his cock was slippery over me, marking me with our meshed up releases.

When the sensitivity overtook Nathan he stopped. I lifted up off Clark's lap almost tumbling over. Clark grabbed my forearm, bringing me back centered on the couch. I plopped down, sitting in the middle and Nathan joined us in our breathless blank stares at the movie we forgot was playing.

"Wow," we said together.

****

We were back to square one. They sat with their cocks spent and my pussy sated. We breathed out one huge exhale.

"Hey…where's Thor?" Clark asked.

"What?" Nathan asked leaning sideways, glaring at Clark.

"I just realized he's not in this movie."

Nathan punched him in the arm. "Asshole."

"I'm kidding. I only realized it a second ago. You could pay me a billion dollars and I couldn't tell you one fucking thing that's happened in the damn movie. How could I pay attention when I had her mouth on my junk?"

"I know you're kidding. I'll be right back," I said to Clark. I hesitated before reaching down to retrieve my leggings and panties. I resisted the urge to cover up and got up from the couch. Clark swatted me on the butt playfully as I walked by.

In the bathroom I spit out the remnants of Clark's orgasm and used some toilet paper to clean up Nathan's cum from my pussy.

A knock on the bathroom door caused me to jump. I threw on my robe and opened the door. Clark stood in only his T-shirt and boxers, holding a hanger with a red and black teddy I swore was buried in no man's land in my closet.

"Where the fuck?"

"Doesn't matter. Put it on for us. Hurry." Clark kissed me, swiping his tongue once across my lips, sealing the deal.

I peed as fast as I could and abandoned my redressing plan. The teddy had red lace see through cups and a black mesh skirt. It was the softest and the most naughty thing I owned. The skirt ended right below where my pussy began. If I bent over, game over, everything would be revealed.

I redid my hair half up and half down with an elastic tie. In the mirror, I caught sight of the flush Clark mentioned. My cheeks were red, my eyeliner smudged. *I guess I do blush.*

I opened the bathroom door and walked back into the living room. Nathan's head was thrown back resting on the back of the couch. The movie was a blur in the background. My glasses were on the coffee table. I barely remembered when I took them off.

With each step closer to the couch, I heard a little bit more. One of them was humming, but I couldn't tell whom just yet. *Where was Clark?*

I peeked over the couch and found my other lover servicing Nathan's cock with his mouth. Clark's wicked mouth went up and down on Nathan's glistening cock. This was new. I'd seen Nathan take Clark into his mouth, but Clark doing it to Nathan was practically obscene. He did it rougher than I'd ever done. He made loud slurping noises and hummed.

"Fuck, Clark! Fuck!" Nathan shouted. Nathan's face contorted like he was in pain, but he was far from it.

Clark looked up past Nathan and smiled a devilish grin around the head of Nathan's cock. "Red's your color darling. Come sit next to Nathan."

Clark spread Nathan's legs wider and tugged on Nathan's balls. Nathan murmured something incoherent, but Clark understood him. "Uh-huh," Clark said. Nathan entwined his right hand into Clark's hair and pulled his head in time with Clark's movements against him.

I walked around the coffee table to the other side of the couch and kneeled next to Nathan's shuddering body. The focused workaholic was gone. A lovesick, drowning man stared back at me. His eyes looked black like the first time I went down on him.

"Bri, kiss me?" Nathan asked, grabbing the back of my neck.

I kissed him, and Nathan ravished my mouth. He screamed his moan into my mouth. I touched Nathan's flushed face and felt him trembling. I broke the kiss. I needed to watch.

Nathan's cock disappeared into Clark's mouth. He was all the way in, laying deep in Clark's throat. Clark's eyes were closed, his mouth tight against Nathan, breathing through his nose. I saw Clark's Adam's apple go up and down, swallowing up Nathan's cock, constricting his throat on him.

Nathan whimpered, reaching up to pinch my nipple through the mesh. His hand traveled down my body and thrust two fingers inside me. "Does watching us turn you on?"

"Yes. Is Clark going to make you come?" I cooed against Nathan's lips. I kept my gaze on Clark. His mouth worked hard on Nathan's body. He smoothed his hand on my thigh connecting the three of us once again.

Every time his mouth had been on my pussy, licking me, sucking me until I was coming over his lips, it'd been from behind. Next time, I wanted to watch him, watch his tongue lap at my pussy. I'd been missing out on another one of his many talents.

"Yes, baby. Oh Clark, don't stop," Nathan ordered, sliding down further onto the couch. His fingers stopped moving up inside me and held still.

Nathan's body shook, and he came inside Clark's mouth. "I'm coming, Clark. You're making me come." He thrust into Clark's mouth riding out his release.

Nathan stopped humping Clark's face, sighed, and moved Clark's hair from his forehead. Clark continued to bob his head on Nathan's cock, cleaning up the remnants of Nathan's cum. He stopped when Nathan's breath came out in a hiss.

Clark removed his mouth from Nathan's lap and opened his eyes. His gaze was out of focus, and he pulled Nathan's hand from his hair and kissed his open palm. "His cock smelled like your pussy. I couldn't resist," Clark stated almost in an apology. His own cock tented his boxers, peeking out of the hole.

Clark stripped his boxers off and dove for me on the couch, pushing my back against the throw pillows on the other side. He hovered over me, his gaze roaming over the nightie he picked for me. "New rule, you can only wear this when we come over." Clark purred over the skin of my neck. He nipped me, bringing forth a gasp.

He moved to his knees letting me straighten out my legs outside of his hips. Nathan's hands helped me, grabbing my calves, lifting my legs up.

Clark didn't hesitate. The change in our position put him right where he needed to be. He kissed me with absolute abandon. He tasted like Nathan's cum, his lips holding onto his scent. I moaned into his mouth and his cock found my wet pussy, ready and waiting for him. He held himself steady and entered me in one powerful thrust.

He fucked me deep and determined. Nathan grabbed my hands over my head off Clark's back. I hadn't even noticed he moved. My eyes had been shut so tight. I opened them, but I saw only Clark's face. One of his hands latched onto my breast, the other held up my leg, keeping me spread open for his cock.

An abrupt spasm, a delectable twist in my sensitive nerve endings, moved through the front walls of my pussy on Clark's cock, dragging out a grunt from his lips. Clark gasped for breath. "Bri. Fuck." The tightness remained though, building, undulating through me. Clark barely retracted his cock from my pussy; he fucked fast and used short thrusts inside me. I knew I'd come any second. Just a little bit more.

My hands were mine again as Nathan let me go. I roamed them over every inch of Clark I could get. I dug my nails into his ass, gripping hard onto his warm flesh. Clark elicited a loud groan. In the distance I heard Nathan walk away. My peripheral vision saw him walk toward the bathroom and shut the door.

I pushed my fingers across Clark's back and

through his hair. I kissed him again, but he tore his lips away. "Aahh, I can't breathe. I want you too much, my love." Clark said quietly against my mouth. My breath caught. Did he just say my love? No, he couldn't have. I'm "darling" and sometimes "babe" for him. I must have misheard. *Oh my God.*

*Does that mean he loves me?*

Clark lifted off me, ripping his shirt up over his head, stilling his fucking. I was almost there. He stopped just when I needed him. "Hunny, why did you stop?" I touched his chest, feeling his soft chest hair against my palms. His heart pounded in his chest.

"I'm sorry, darling. You steal my breath away," Clark said. His brow was furrowed, his restraint showing. His gaze dropped down to where our bodies were intimately connected. I traced the v along his hips with my fingers and then brought them down to my clit. I circled around my clit earning a guttural groan from Clark. "Yeah, Bri. Your pussy looks so fucking good around my cock." He thrust again, resuming his hard fucking. His hesitation was gone.

Clark moved up the skirt of my teddy daring to obstruct his view of our lovemaking. Movement to the side caught my eye. Nathan got on his knees next to us. He kissed me, thrusting his tongue into my mouth. I palmed his cheek. Nathan's hand replaced mine against my throbbing clit.

Clark laid back down over me and latched his mouth onto my neck. I came a second later. My two lovers mouths fused to my body, holding me down. My hips jerked up pushing at Clark's taut stomach. He placed his whole weight down on me, trapping Nathan's working hand, and found his own release moaning against my neck.

I pulled back from Nathan's mouth. Like Clark, my breath escaped me. Even Nathan's breath came faster. We fucked each other until exhaustion stole our souls, replacing it with nervous bliss.

"I need a minute, darling. Fuck, I need ten." He nuzzled into my neck, dragging his nose up my neck. His cock twitched inside me. I squeezed my internal muscles around him. "You naughty vixen," Clark whispered.

"Sorry." I giggled.

Clark pulled out of me and sat back down on the couch. I pulled my teddy down and sat up. Nathan returned to my left.

"I'll be right back. If I don't come back in five send a search party," Clark joked. His hand glided down my thigh and he used my knee to push off. He picked up his boxers and trotted off to the bathroom.

I leaned over and rested my head against Nathan's shoulder. He fiddled with the remote and brought the movie back on, rewinding to a part he remembered. He'd been oddly quiet for the past few minutes. Fuck, did he hear Clark say my love? Is that why he walked away? No wait, Nathan was out of the room. Shit, we didn't include him enough.

"Nathan, are you all right?" I asked, looping my hand under his. His fingers grasped mine.

"Yeah, baby. I'm just tired."

"I'm sorry, we didn't include you that last time."

"Bri, you don't have to apologize. I don't think I can even get it up right now. I'm so tired. Come here."

I curled up against Nathan's side and he tucked me under his arm. He kissed the top of my head and nuzzled my hair. I should've felt relaxed, I did kind of, but something irked me.

"If there was something wrong, you'd tell me right?" I prodded.

I peered up at Nathan. He did look tired. He rubbed his left eye with his hand.

"I'm fine." He kissed me lightly on the mouth.

Clark came back to the living room. He lifted my legs onto his lap. He moved my hair off my face and kissed my cheek, and then he grabbed Nathan for a kiss on his mouth.

"Darling, can we stay the night?" Clark asked.

"I'd be offended if you left," I answered. I stretched out between them.

"I have to go back to the office in the morning. I'm sorry. We'll have to leave early," Nathan admitted.

"That's okay. I don't want to sleep alone."

"Yet another reason why you should move in with us, Bri," Clark added. His hands caressed my legs, kneading the skin of my thigh.

I rolled my eyes. "Maybe one day."

We attempted to watch the movie again. I lasted another five minutes before I fell asleep.

# Chapter Thirty-Two

"Darling, wake up! Bri?" Someone said near my ear. Sleep tugged hard at me. My eyes didn't want to open yet.

"Brianna! Your mother is on her way over here." The voice belonged to Clark, and he screamed the perfect thing to wake my ass up.

"*What?*" I jolted up in bed.

"I'm sorry. She called like five times over the past ten minutes. I panicked when your house phone rang, so I answered it."

"You talked to my mom? Is she okay? Is my dad okay?" I shouted.

"Yeah, she's fine, he's fine. She needs a table for this jewelry thing she's doing at ten o'clock," Clark confirmed.

I sighed and gripped my heaving chest. "Jesus, Clark. Next time, start with that little tidbit."

"I'm sorry. Shit, you went straight to panic mode."

"You just startled me. When is she coming?" I sat up and rested my back against the headboard. Bits and pieces of last night floated to the top of my memory.

"She said about fifteen minutes. You're not mad that I talked to your mom, right?" Clark stood looking uncertain. He was shirtless, but he had his jeans back on.

"Nah. She's cool. Trust me she will never be mad

at me for having a man in my apartment. In fact she might miss her fair because she'll be too happy and ask you a shit ton of questions."

"Gotcha. So I pretty much walked right into her trap?" he said rolling his hand through the air.

"Sorta kind of," I responded.

"Great. So would she expect a Nathan type or a 'me' type?" Clark sat on the side of the bed, slouching his shoulders over his body.

"What do you mean?"

"Does she want to meet the guy you fake her out with that's perfect or the other guy waiting for you in the car once the front door closes?" Only the side of his mouth lifted in a smile.

"Is that how you see yourself and Nathan?"

"Sometimes."

In the few weeks I had known Clark we had so many heart-to-heart conversations I lost track. I saw him in all his glory up on the stage, tangled in the throes of his kinky passion, and being the most attentive person to his partners' every move. The man sitting on my bed, his insecurities crippling him over his knees, and tiredness thickening his gaze was someone I hadn't met yet.

Unfortunately, my mother had to be the catalyst to bring the other side forth.

"I'm not going to lie and say you're not the bad boy, but you can only be who you are. I want to introduce you to my mother. Please don't change, Clark. You're an amazing man, and I'm proud to be in this with you. You are the exact opposite of Nathan, and that's why I like you, and the difference between you two makes it all worthwhile."

I crawled toward him, still wearing my lingerie from last night. I climbed into his lap, opening my legs over his thighs so we were face to face. He wrapped his hands around my ass and pulled me closer to him.

I kissed him. The swoon returned, the lack of rationality when it came to him. I poured my feelings into the kiss. The connection was strong between us. It was powerful enough to punch a hole into Nathan's and my relationship. There was no turning back with Clark. We were in this together.

"I thought I warned you not to make me fall for you," Clark said against my mouth.

"Then don't. Hold out a little longer. But first, come meet my mother, Clark."

I lifted off him, but Clark's hands gripped my ass harder to keep me in place. He buried his face in my exposed cleavage and kissed the bare skin presented to him. I combed my hands through his hair. Blond hair peeked out at the roots.

"What's your real hair color?" I asked.

"I'm a dirty blond. I have to re-dye it soon." He resumed his kisses. "Is your mom a punctual woman?"

"Unfortunately. She only lives ten minutes away."

"Damn." Clark released me. I surveyed the damage. My bed was trashed, but I could keep my mom in the living room. I hoped the sweaty sex smell wore off.

"Did Nathan leave?" I asked.

"Yeah, I hope you don't mind I stayed. You felt too good in my arms. I didn't want to go."

"I'll never be mad about you staying with me." I cupped his cheek and kissed him again.

The doorbell rang throwing both of us into sheer

panic mode. I ripped off the teddy, put on my leggings from last night, and rummaged for a bra. Clark handed me a pink bra from the other day. He cupped my naked breast. I swatted his hand away. "Control yourself, man! Best behavior now!"

I threw on the bra and a shirt and Clark followed me grabbing his own shirt off the floor. We opened the door to the living room and scurried around as fast as we could. Clark headed to the couch and picked up the discarded pillows off the floor. I pushed the chairs in on the table and lit a candle.

My mom knocked this time. "Hunny. It's okay if your place is a mess!" She said through the door.

Clark looked fucking pale. He cracked his knuckles, blew out a big breath, and mouthed to me, "Ready?" I shook my head no and smiled back.

I unlocked the door and let my mom in. She looked happier than a dog going to their forever home. She grinned from ear to ear, searching for her target.

"Hello, dear! I'm so sorry to bother you this early, but I really need your card table for Frannie's bazaar. Will I get to meet your boyfriend?" My mom scanned the room for poor Clark biting his fingernails in the corner.

"Mom, this is…"

"You must be Nathan. I've heard so much about you!" She did the once-over and outstretched her hand. Clark's smile dwindled, but he held out his hand.

"Actually, I'm Clark, Nathan's roommate. Nice to meet you, Mrs. Owens." Clark shook her hand.

"Shoot, where are my manners? I'm sorry, I just assumed you were the boyfriend when I talked to you. Nice to meet you, Clark."

"Yup, that's me too. I'm the other boyfriend."

*If there was any way to smack myself in the face really fucking hard without my mother and Clark knowing, sign me up*. My mom practically cringed, and stared at me in disbelief. Alas, another person shocked two men like me. But this was my mother. Not exactly a saint, however not one hundred percent up with the times.

"I don't understand. Bri?"

"Mom, it's a long story and it's new. Um, very new. We're still trying to work out the kinks."

"Kinks?"

*In addition to the slap, an earthquake would be great right about now.* A big gaping hole to swallow everything up.

Luckily, Clark took over the explanation. "Look, Mrs. Owens, it's complicated, I know. Simply put, I like your daughter very much. Nathan does too. We're trying to figure it out with minimal collateral damage. Bri makes me happy, and I want to see where this goes with us."

I stopped breathing. My right eye twitched, and I leaned against the table for the final blow where my mom flipped the fuck out. Clark handled this like a champ. I did not.

No one spoke; it was a stare down to the finish.

My mom broke the ice, squinting. "You're the music guy, right? Not the analyst one." My mom had to dig deep for that one. Did I even mention that at brunch? I knew Diane's mom talked to her about the boys, but God knew what else she said.

"Yes, ma'am." Clark straightened up to his full height, towering over my mother, and braced himself for more questions.

"Do you have a job?"

"Yes, I'm in a band and I work at a recording studio," Clark said.

"Do you do drugs?"

"Nope. I stopped smoking pot years ago." Smooth sailing so far.

"How old are you?"

"Thirty-five." Wow, I thought he was younger.

"Can you help an old lady out to her car with a thousand-pound card table and not break a sweat?"

"I'm always up for a challenge."

"You pass. Now hop to, boy. I have to be in Somers by ten!" Somehow he got lucky with only five questions.

Clark and my mom turned to me for direction. I didn't know how to get my mouth to shut. Everything was out in the open…no more secrets and half-truths. Clark passed the interview with flying colors.

I must have a guardian angel. Somehow, I dodged that bullet.

"Darling, where's the card table?" Clark asked. I pointed at my walk-in closet. He walked up to me and said softly, "Hey, remember to breathe, okay? I got this!" He kissed me on the cheek.

He had the table out in seconds, and my mom handed him her keys.

"By the way, you can call me Judy. My car is the gray one parked illegally on the sidewalk," my mom said, touching his shoulder.

"I will, Judy. Trunk or backseat?"

"Backseat, please. Thank you so much, Clark."

"Anytime."

Clark held the table under his arm and was out the door. I spun around to my mom. I didn't expect her to be smiling. She interlocked my arm with hers. "So, he is the first boyfriend. He's adorable. I can't wait to meet the other guy!"

"Mom, I'm sorry. I should have said something."

"Bri, I trust you. You're a smart girl, and I know you'll make the best decision."

"Thanks, Mom."

"Anytime, baby. Should I expect you at the bazaar or are you and Clark going to stay in this morning?"

"Um, Nathan took his car, so I'll probably have to take Clark home at some point. He lives in New Jersey. How long is the fair?"

"Don't worry about it. Let's do dinner next week, okay? I want to know everything about Clark and Nathan."

"Okay."

My mom kissed me on the cheek and hugged me tight. "Everything will be all right, Bri. I'm happy you found someone."

Clark returned a second later. "You're all set. Good luck today!"

My mom let me go and turned toward Clark. "Thank you, Clark! Don't be a stranger now. I want to know about you too! Call me later, Bri!" my mom called out as she left.

"I guess I passed the mom test?" Clark asked.

As soon as I willed myself to stop staring at the door I mumbled, "That went better than I expected. I told you she'd like you."

"Is your dad easy going?"

"My dad? Um, he might clean his shotgun in front

of you, but only if he likes you."

"What?"

"Did I mention it's his souvenir shotgun?

"You purposely left out that detail, you little minx."

"Guilty." I exhaled.

"Can I ask you a question?" Clark said.

"Yeah."

"Why didn't you tell your mom about me?" I saw the blatant hurt in his eyes. Boy, I fucked up that one.

"I'm sorry, Clark. I should have told her about you and Nathan, but I didn't know how to say it. The only time I talked to her was at brunch, and she caught me off guard. You and I just had that crazy night together and I panicked. I had mentioned Nathan before." I paused.

I should have fessed up to my life now. It's pretty fucking awesome and there was no reason to hide it. "It's not exactly easy to tell your mother about the threesome you had the night before."

"I get it. My mother has no idea Nathan and me are more than roommates. But if you're ashamed or embarrassed, we need to talk about it."

"I swear I'm not. I thought about this a lot. I want to be with you and Nathan."

I guess that was a good enough answer for him. Clark picked me up and threw me over his shoulder. "Put me down!"

"Never."

Clark strolled through my apartment back toward my bedroom. The room was stuffy and smelled like sweat. I grabbed the ceiling fan string when we passed it by.

Clark laid me down on the messy bed. I moved to kiss him, but he leaned off me. I reached for his arm and again he didn't let me touch him. He gripped his shirt and pulled it off.

"Keep your hands to yourself, Bri. This is my time."

I folded my hands on my stomach in an over-exaggerated motion. "Fine by me. What are you going to do with your time?"

"You have a couple choices for this morning's showcase." He crawled up my body and pulled my shirt over my head. He bit at the exposed skin at my waist right above my leggings. "What happened to you, here?"

I looked down. He touched the little white lines from my gall bladder surgery. "Surgery. I had my gall bladder removed."

"It looks like you lost a bad cat fight," Clark said. There were only three little lines, but it still made me self-conscious. "I have a bad scar from a hernia operation and having my appendix out. We match, darling." He tucked down his boxers to show me the smallest scars by his groin I never noticed.

"You're still hot," I confessed.

"Thank you. Now where were we? Ah yes, where would you like me to kiss you?"

"My neck." I declared. He proceeded to kiss my neck, skimming my breasts with his fingertips. His mouth latched onto my neck and sucked the sensitive skin into his mouth.

"How about suck? Hmmm…And fuck?" Clark whispered and pressed his fingers against my pussy through the thin cloth of my leggings. I neglected to put on underwear before. I had secretly hoped I wouldn't need them the rest of the morning.

I peeled my leggings down and Clark helped me the rest of way. "I want you to suck my…"

Before I could finish, Clark chimed in, "Oh wait, do you have a vibrator?" His eyes lit up from his mischievous smile.

"Um…Yeah." I lifted up onto my elbows.

"Can I see it?"

"Fuck, no." Your battery-operated boyfriend does not meet current real life boyfriend.

"Come on, Bri. Don't be shy." Clark smoothed his hands up my thighs, resuming his soft touches. His distractions were not going to work this time.

"I'm not being shy. It's personal." I lay back down and crossed my arms over my chest.

"Bri, I've been inside every natural orifice of your body. We are beyond awkward now. Let me see your vibrator."

I side glanced at my end table drawer. *What's the worst that can happen if he sees it?*

"Please? I promise you'll get off." Persistent Clark kissed up my legs next.

"I know I will, but not today, mister."

"All right, one last plea. Scouts honor, I promise I won't judge you. Please, Bri…" Clark lingered on the please. He worked his way up to my aroused nipples. He squeezed my breasts together and dragged his tongue across them. When he bit my nipple, I gave in.

*Who needs a comfort zone anyway?* Mine was obliterated weeks ago.

"Fine." I tore myself away from Clark, reached over to the bottom drawer of my nightstand, and grabbed my battery-operated companion I relied on way too fucking often. I took it out of its stealthy velvet bag.

Clark got comfortable against my headboard and sat up with his legs stretched out in front of him. He screwed up his nose and cocked his head to the side.

"That's a toothbrush not a vibrator."

I rolled my eyes. "This is exactly why I didn't want to show you." I tucked the silly thing back into its bag.

"Wait…I'm sorry. I expected a huge pink one with a bow and cat ears or something. Let me see it." I handed him the non-dildo shaped pink and white vibrator. It had a slender base with an extended metal rod and a hard pink nub the size of your thumb, purposely designed to entice your clit and ignite your g-spot. Clark inspected it way too fucking hard.

"Can you even feel it if you stick it inside?" He asked, holding it limp with two fingers.

"No, it's a clit stimulator."

"Please don't stick that thing up my ass. I'll be scarred for life." He smirked.

"Oh shut up, Clark." I had to grin.

Clark flipped me onto my back and took the toy from my grip. "Does it have to be pink?"

"I won it at a sex toy bingo!"

"Sex toy bingo?" He scratched the side of his head.

"Dive-bar ladies-night extravaganza." I smiled at my victory.

I batted my eyes, attempting to look innocent. I failed. Clark swooped down for a kiss twisting my smile to horny yearning.

Clark's end game was fucking me into my soft bed and ordering me to use the vibrator on my clit at the same time. The intense feeling stroked up my body and poured out my mouth with moans and whimpers. The combination of being fucked and stimulated sucked me down into the depths. My entire pussy rumbled from the toy and his fucking. Clark cried out with me, "Oh fuck, I can feel it. It's buzzing against my cock too. Ahhhh, uhhh, fuck, Bri."

After we came, we abandoned the toy to the abyss of tangled bed sheets. Clark slid out of me and lay down next to me. Sleep tugged at me even though I desperately needed to get up. Clark's tongue swirled around my nipple, and his finger plucked at the other one.

Soon, the bad boy was sated, and he lay back against the pillows.

"Holy shit, that was fun. We have to do that again soon."

"Hmmm…" I mustered a few sounds. A peaceful bliss invaded my body. Clark pulled the hot covers over us, and we drifted back to sleep. I never wanted to leave my bed again.

# Chapter Thirty-Three

When I woke up it was already three o'clock. Clark's arm held me captive against his body. He snored softly into my hair. His cock was hard up against my back, but even as tempting as he was I had to show some restraint. We had to eventually leave my apartment and return to the outside world.

I attempted to slip out from under his grip, but Clark woke up before I made my getaway. He nuzzled my neck with his nose. "Not yet. Little bit more," Clark muttered. His fingers caressed the side of my naked breast.

"Now you're being too ravenous with me, Clark." It sounded harsher than I meant it. He wasn't smiling back.

"Sorry, I'll stop. What time is it?" Clark swung his legs over the side of the bed.

"It's three o'clock. I'm sorry, Clark. I was only kidding. I like when you ravish…"

Clark cut me off, "It's three o'clock? Shit, I have to go. I have practice at four thirty p.m. We have to leave." Clark got up and grabbed his boxers from the floor putting them on in one yank.

"I didn't know. I would have set an alarm."

"No, it's fine. It's not your fault. I'm relieved you woke up! Your bed is too fucking comfortable." He found my discarded vibrator lost in the covers. "You might want to put that away if your mom comes back to return the table."

I snatched it from him and put it back in the drawer. When I peered back at him he shrugged.

"Sorry, not sorry. Go put some clothes on before I teach you what ravishing actually means," Clark remarked.

I threw on jeans and a T-shirt, and Clark found his shirt and jeans where he had kicked them off the second time.

Within ten minutes, we were in my car heading over the bridge back to Rockland County. Unfortunately it was Sunday afternoon and the traffic was murder this time of year.

Clark impatiently called Cleo and Dillon telling them he'd be late to the studio. He let out a defeated sigh. We were in bumper-to-bumper traffic on the most direct route I knew back to New Jersey.

"We should have taken the GW Bridge," Clark mumbled. He sat low in his seat with his hands folded over his chest.

"The app says this is the fastest way. I think there's a marathon this weekend."

"Figures. The universe is battling against me once again."

"How about I just bring you to the studio? We can definitely get there before four thirty p.m. Can you use one of the guitars off the wall?" I suggested.

"That might be a good idea." Clark pinched his sweater over his chest and smelled it. He shrugged. "I keep saying we need a spare instrument room." He checked the GPS app and then picked up his phone. "Yeah, that'll definitely work. Cleo can take me home.

She owes me. I won't have my pedals, but I'll be there. Thanks, darling." He placed his left hand on my knee while he texted the band.

"You're welcome."

"One crisis averted." He yawned. "Last night was pretty crazy, huh?"

"Yeah. I'm a little sore. I need to go back to the gym."

"Seriously, me too. I get a lot of arm exercise playing, but my back hurts." He rubbed his shoulders.

"We should crash Nathan's gym." I giggled.

"I don't know if he has a membership anymore. He stopped going a while back. I'll ask him later."

I flipped on the alternative rock radio station. The middle lane inched forward, but quickly returned to a standstill. Clark opened the granola bar I gave him and broke me off a piece. We had skipped breakfast and lunch for more important matters.

He shifted toward me in the seatbelt. "Hey, are you okay with everything that's going on between us?"

"Yeah. I'm glad you guys came over last night. I feel bad Nathan had to leave."

"Nathan and I didn't plan it out good. We should've driven separately. But I didn't mean the three of us. Can we talk about us?"

I closed my eyes and saw the perpetual shoe falling. The space above my heart stirred the panic button and the first wave of anxiety flashed over me. This was too good to be true. Fucking classic move to wait until we were alone to let me know this wasn't working.

"What do you want to talk about?"

"Jesus. You look like I just broke up with you."

Clark touched my shoulder.

"Then where is this heading?" I stared straight ahead at the stalled cars.

"I need to know you're in this because you want to be with me too," Clark said.

"Of course, I want to be with you. Clark, I like you so much." I touched his face and he half smiled into my hand.

"So you aren't with me because of Nathan? Be honest, Bri. I can take it."

Clark's jaw locked, and he clenched his teeth. I turned back to him so fast, I was grateful we weren't moving. I would've probably crashed the fucking car I was so surprised by his accusation.

"Please tell me that isn't what you think is going on between you and me."

"No, but I've been wrong before," Clark admitted. He looked down at his hands and picked a dry cuticle.

"Clark, I would never do that to you. How cruel? Where the hell did you get that from?"

He brushed his hand through his hair. "I don't know. I want to be sure I'm not forcing you to be with me too." He looked out the window avoiding eye contact.

"You can't be serious? What did I do wrong?" I couldn't keep the escalated panic out of my voice. I analyzed every fucking thing Clark and I had said to each other in the past day.

"You didn't do anything wrong. I'm sorry. I shouldn't have said anything."

"Is this because my mom thought you were Nathan? Honestly, Clark, I've barely spoken to my mother in the last few weeks. I swear I want to be with you so much." Tears ran down my face by the time I finished my rant.

Clark grabbed me into a hug. "Fuck, I'm sorry. I didn't mean to make you upset. I'm an insecure idiot. This has nothing to do with your mom. I'm happy I got to meet her!" He rubbed my back and kissed me through the tears. I pulled back from him.

"Yeah, but that didn't come out of nowhere. If I'm doing something wrong or not paying enough attention to you, please tell me."

"This has nothing to do with you. I got too deep into my head. I care about you and before this goes any further I needed to know where I stand."

"Clark, I care about you, too. I want everything that's happening between all three of us and you and me separate from Nathan. I want to be closer to you if that's even possible."

"Me too. I'm sorry, darling." Clark cupped both sides of my face and kissed me. I meant what I said. I'm in this for both of them.

The traffic moved forward a little bit. My foot eased up on the brake going the few feet. I gripped the stirring wheel. The discussion was over, but I was still shaken up.

"Can I rephrase one of my questions I asked you at the wedding?" Clark asked, kissing my knuckles.

"Are you seriously asking me about more eighties bands now?"

Clark's lightness came back. He chuckled. *Yes, I remembered everything he ever said to me.*

"You got me. I do have more than one favorite eighties band." I played along with my own diversion to salvage the mood of this awful car ride.

"I knew it! No one can have just one!" Clark pointed a finger toward me smiling. "I didn't mean that question." He paused. "Could you find it in your heart to love two people?" Clark asked.

"Who says I don't already."

A small smile danced across Clark's lips before he looked out the window again. There was no contest. I loved them both.

# Chapter Thirty-Four

Even though, I hadn't planned on seeing the boys on Sunday, something was off. I distracted myself by cleaning the house. As soon as it was done, I cycled through everything that had happened since Friday night.

*Fucking anxiety.*

I texted Clark about his practice and he sent back a selfie of Cleo, Dillon, and him in the studio. He said I saved the day. Everything seemed fine. Our tense conversation was in the past.

However, my unease carried throughout Monday. I was a step behind for everything.

I missed part of a meeting I personally scheduled because my reminder didn't go off. Nathan waited to start until I joined them. The discussion topic didn't help matters either. If our bid was accepted, I'd have to make several checkpoints with the client after the first six months. Nathan wouldn't be in this office anymore, so it would have to be me.

Will this relationship work when we don't see each other every day? We sucked last week as a couple. With distance would it suffer more?

I quickly scribbled down the dates Nathan and Paul flipped through fast.

"You missed one. June sixth," Marcia informed me, glancing at my notepad.

I had to be distracted if fucking Marcia was telling me I missed something. Nathan passed his notebook to me, not skipping a beat of conversation. He seemed completely fine riding his focus train.

"You okay?" Nathan mouthed while Paul talked.

I nodded. He pulled out his phone. His text came over a few moments later. *—You're pale, baby. Are you coming down with something?—*

I gave him boyfriend points for noticing my off kilter day. I texted back, *—Nah, just tired. Mondays fucking suck.—*

Nathan chuckled and flicked his gaze up to me. I smiled and turned back to Paul. He stared right at me, and then switched back and forth between Nathan and me. He squinted and went back to his part of the updates.

*Shit, he knows Nathan texted me.* I coughed and sipped my tea. Maybe I was coming down with something. I was super sensitive to everything.

After the meeting, Nathan and I grabbed lunch with a few people minus Paul. They talked about the Christmas party this weekend. I tried my hardest not to show my anger toward the whole thing. Thankfully, Nathan diverted the conversation off topic.

Later on, Nathan asked if I wanted him to come home with me. I declined and told him I just needed some sleep. He insisted, but I assured him I was okay. Clark texted later on, checking in, too.

On Tuesday, I felt better, but after sleeping with two men on Friday, my apartment was awfully lonely. I missed Amora too. I'm probably still furniture to her, but her fuzzy body would've been nice.

After the monthly meeting, I noticed a pretty red

envelope perched on my keyboard. *Was it from Nathan?* Wait, no he was in the meeting with me. There wouldn't have been enough time to place it here. It had to be from someone else.

I tore it open gently. Inside the glittery interior was an invitation to the Grant Christmas Party. "What!"

Mr. Grant appeared in my cubicle smiling ear to ear in his quiet loafers. "You earned it, Anna. Enjoy yourself. This is the time of your life."

I couldn't help the tear of joy that escaped. I wanted to hug my showtune singing guardian angel. "Mr. Grant, thank you so much."

"Like I said, you've earned it. It's your hard work making us all look good." He winked and swaggered back to his office singing his usual tune…"Life is but a bowl of cherries…"

I looked at the ticket over and over in awe of the kind gesture. It was just what I needed to pull me out of my funk.

I ran to Nathan's office. His chair was swiveled to the view and he traced circles in the moisture.

"I know, Clark. How about we head up to the lookout tonight? We can spend some time alone." He paused. "Yeah, the trail you almost killed me on. I'll wear my new boots and break them in. See you tonight."

I backed up hoping Nathan didn't hear me. I didn't want to disturb his moment with Clark. It hadn't dawned on me how much I must be affecting their relationship without me. *Did they even have a relationship without me anymore?* Ugh, I cursed myself for tumbling back down the rabbit hole.

"Hey, Bri." Shit, too late.

"Hey…guess what?" I waved the red envelope in front of me.

"No way, really?" Nathan looked surprised.

"Apparently, I have a fairy godfather who wears designer suits and is tone deaf."

"Wow, that's awesome! You belong at this thing more than I do. Let's go together," Nathan said getting up to give me a hug. He smelled pleasantly of his light aftershave. He gave me a small peck on the lips.

"Thank you."

He sat back down. "I've been struggling with the presentation all morning. Power Point is being a bitch today."

"Do you want me to look at it?"

"Yeah, that would be great." Nathan consented.

*I should have left. Instead, I poked.* "So, you and Clark are going for hike?"

"A short hike. There's a cool lookout near the apartment. Do you want to come?"

"No, thank you. I wouldn't want to intrude on your alone time with Clark."

Nathan scratched his forehead. "You wouldn't be intruding. I love when you hang out with us. We can change the plans if you'd like. This can be our big date night for the week."

"No, it's okay. You two should spend time together." I walked up to his desk out of earshot of any passerby. "You and Clark still have a relationship together when I'm not around, right?"

Nathan cocked his head to the side.

"Yeah. Why?"

"Just wondering."

"Are you sure you're not upset about us going

hiking? We were going to do something yesterday, but Clark got stuck at the studio."

I dropped my voice to a whisper. "This has nothing to do with hiking. Don't worry about it."

"You've been acting weird. Are you okay?" Nathan rolled his chair out from under his desk but stayed sitting.

I walked behind his desk and leaned against it. "I'm sorry. When I heard you on the phone I got the feeling I'm messing up what you and he have together."

"That's not it at all. Baby…you've enhanced every part of me since the moment I met you. Clark says the same thing. You've brought us closer together. Let's go to Clark's gig tomorrow. We can all hang out together."

"Tomorrow night? He didn't tell me he had a show?" I'll admit it. I could care less about the hiking, but Clark playing and not knowing about it, fucking stung.

*I knew something was off.*

"It is and isn't a big deal. He's hosting an open mic event in Jersey for the studio, so it's more like work. He plays a few songs, then it's mostly local bands and kids playing."

"Gotcha. Would we be a distraction?"

"Not really. He's always happy when people come to see him play. He does a lot of these side gigs for extra money. I'll drive in tomorrow and take us."

"Okay."

Nathan peeked at the door and then kissed me with the loudest smack possible. He wasn't the best at discretion.

"I'll send you the pivot table back in a few," I said.

"Thanks, babe."

****

As I left Nathan's office, pain pulsed above my left eyebrow. The reasons for me to be torn about the boys grew from two to five things. This relationship was suddenly more serious and precious to me than any I'd had in the past.

I cleared the hallway, but didn't turn back to the aisle to my cubicle. Tears from out of nowhere threatened to fall. I rushed to the other side of the block and headed for the ladies' room.

"Hey, Bri, do you have a second?" Paul called out from his office as I stepped past. I jumped and hiccupped back my tears.

"Are you crying?" Paul asked sternly. He barely moved behind his desk.

"It's nothing. Is there a problem?" I asked.

"We have to talk about something. Come in and shut the door, please." His tone was too serious for him, especially toward me. Also, I had never been in Paul's office with the door closed.

"Here." He handed me a tissue. "Have a seat."

I sat down tentatively. I hoped there wasn't anything wrong with the project. I waited for another preverbal shoe to plummet down.

"How is the project coming along with Nathan?" *Here we go.* Fuck, this was work related.

"We're almost done. Even with the setbacks we're on par with the projected end date."

"Good to hear. How are you working together?"

"He's brought a nice fresh approach to the analysis. We've been reviewing the demos and making necessary changes. Mr. Grant will be very happy with the outcome."

Paul face remained indifferent. "How is your blossoming relationship with Nathan going?"

"Blossoming? Um, I don't know. We have a lot of mutual friends in common and we knew each other briefly."

"You said that before. In the beginning you didn't seem to like him. Ever since we went to dinner together you two are inseparable."

"Things change, you know."

"Apparently." Paul never used this condescending tone with me. His hands were folded on his desk and he picked at a curled edge of his plotter.

I raced through the times Nathan and I had interacted in the office and almost every time we had been purely professional. We batted ideas back and forth, helped each other out, and well…he did finger fuck me in his office and kissed me in the conference room.

*Would it take someone this long to complain? No one was around that late. This had to be something else.*

"Do you have a problem with Nathan and me? We haven't done anything wrong and the project is coming along great."

"There isn't a problem now. You're my best employee. I know you won't let a silly fling affect your work ethic. I can't afford to lose you. I just wanted to warn you to keep this out of sight out of mind during work hours. There isn't any documented say on interoffice relationships but please be mindful of others."

"Mindful of others?"

"Just keep it on the down low. Don't give HR any

excuse to intervene. Will you excuse me? I have a meeting I'm late for."

With that, Paul got up from his desk, grabbed a folder from his incoming work bin, and exited his office.

"What the fuck?" I said out loud. *I didn't know what was happening with anyone.*

I texted Lucy. *-Hey, are you free for lunch? I think I'm losing my mind.-*

*-I can't do today. Tomorrow? One p.m.? Or we can grab dinner tonight?-*

*-Dinner would rock. When are you done today?-*

*-Five-ish.-*

*-Pencil me in.-*

*-See you at five.-*

# Chapter Thirty-Five

I clocked out at five fifteen p.m. Nathan still worked away. I knocked on his door.

"Hey, I came to say goodnight," I said.

"Goodnight, baby." He got up and gave me a quick kiss.

"Don't miss your train," I reminded him.

"There's a six thirty local leaving Secaucus. I'll head to Penn by six o'clock to get a connecting train."

"Okay. Have fun with Clark. Be careful tonight."

"We will. Say hi to Lucy for me."

Lucy waited for me in the foyer, plugging away at her phone. She almost had to cancel because the traffic was so bad. During the holidays, five miles took five hours.

She looked perfect, but she still wasn't herself. Even her new shoes and expensive as fuck new purse hadn't elevated her spirits quite yet.

As soon as we got in the cab, she said, "Okay, spill it. I want to know everything."

I took a deep breath and told her the epic saga of Nathan and the fortunate addition of Clark. We got to the restaurant and she demolished a whole plate of nachos, a martini, and half a pasta bowl before she uttered a single peep besides "uh-huh."

"Well, fuck me. That's…fuck…I can't talk. Waiter, another French martini please!" Lucy stammered out. She massaged the side of her forehead.

"So, yeah, now I'm in a relationship with Nathan and Clark together." I ended.

The waiter brought over her second martini and she sipped it nodding her head. She downed about half of it and then shouted, "And you thought the wedding night would be a one-time thing?" She accused. "Clark even met your mom?"

"Yup! He passed inspection."

"I'll be damned. I'm proud of you, Bri. You deserve to be in a relationship with two great men who care about you."

"Thank you. But now I don't know what to do. I'm a bundle of nerves walking on eggshells. I'm afraid of doing the wrong thing."

Lucy leaned in close to me. "You can do whatever you want to do. There is no wrong or right way, Bri. Trust your gut, don't play favorites, and communicate."

"I'm trying not to favor one over the other. But, I think I really messed up with Clark. Last Sunday he asked me if I was only in a relationship with him to appease Nathan."

"You're not right? You like Clark as an individual man without the package deal?"

"Of course I do! It's hard to explain, Lucy. Clark and I fell into this very naturally. It was almost like the second he walked in on Nathan and me he switched to automatic boyfriend mode. I should have said something to my mom."

"Bri, it's all right. When people asked about my love life, I would blend Kelsey and Diane together. I didn't even tell my mom about it. I wasn't trying to hide them, but sometimes this type of relationship is hard. But, this is no one's business other than your own."

"Yeah, but my mother found out. She was so thrilled that I'm dating someone I'm not sure it sunk in what we were saying."

"There will be a time for everything. Your mom will be fine. Clark will be fine. It's early enough to work it out."

The nagging feeling in the back of mind held strong. "I want to believe you. I just feel a distance now. I was hard up for one boyfriend. Two is fucking nuts."

"Have you talked to Clark since?" Patient Lucy continued.

"Not since Sunday. We've texted. He sent me more music and asked how my day was going. Nothing major, but he didn't tell me about his gig tomorrow night. Nathan invited me. Nathan seems oblivious about all of this too. He doesn't even think it's odd that Clark and him are spending less time together alone."

"You're getting hung up on tiny details. All you have is what they're telling you. Clark said he was okay. Nathan said everything is going great. This can work, Bri. Go to Clark's show with Nathan and give them an extra blowjob or something to apologize."

"Is that your answer to everything? Give a guy head?"

"It works doesn't it?" Lucy smiled holding up the empty martini glass. Almost on cue, the waiter came back with another one. "Thank you, sweetie." Lucy smiled and batted her eyes at the waiter before he left the table. "He's hot!"

I barely paid attention. I'd been so focused on

ranting about my love life I cut everyone out. "Sure, go for it."

"Thought about it, but nah. He's a waiter so our work hours wouldn't sync up good. Been there, done that late night booty call shit, moved on."

"You're hilarious."

"I don't have time to fuck around anymore. But honestly, Bri, I wouldn't worry about them too much, especially Clark. He let you into the relationship and from what you said he seems to be the casual one. Play it off to early relationship jitters."

"I thought he was the more laid back one, but now I'm not sure."

"Maybe spend extra time with him and tell him how much you care about him apart from Nathan. He did stay the day with you. This might be scary for him too. It makes sense that he'd want to know where he stands, so let him in. Communication is key. Talk it out and then fuck it out." She ended the last sentence with a big know all smile.

"Thank you, Lucy. I appreciate the help."

"Anytime! Order something else so the sexy waiter comes back."

I rolled my eyes and ordered dessert.

# Chapter Thirty-Six

The traffic getting out the city sucked royally. After fifty twist and turns through local roads, we wound up at Rebel Yell Hall. From the outside it looked like another old warehouse with blacked out windows and graffiti on the side. The interior was a different story.

The guy at the door with huge corks in his ear lobes asked for my ID, but when he saw Nathan behind me, his stern demeanor disappeared. "Hey, Nathan! What up man? Long time no see?"

"Hey, Bruce. Sorry been working in the city. How you been?"

"Same old same old. Clark is in the back. He's schooling the new sound guy at pool. Who is this lovely lady?"

"Meet my girlfriend, Bri," Nathan said. I waved at Bruce.

"Nice to meet you. The more the merrier! Hey, I owe you a beer from last time. Tell Jesse behind the bar."

"Will do! Thanks, dude."

"Anytime." Bruce took out two orange neon paper bracelets from his pack and slipped them around our wrists.

"Is there a cover?" Nathan asked, taking out his wallet.

“Not tonight. Two bands pulled out. It’s only Clark and three others.”

“Awesome.”

Nathan put his arm around my shoulders and led me toward the large oval bar pit. Classic rock played from the speakers decorating the top shelf of the mirrored podium housing the hard liquors. Behind the bar was a large empty standing area leading up to a stage where a group of guys were scattered around connecting wires and moving amps. The stage looked pretty fucking cool, with wall-to-wall mirrors in a nestled alcove. A disco ball dangled in the center of the stage.

I heard the loud crack of someone beginning a game of pool. “Solids, man. Just your luck!” Clark yelled. The bar had another section with three pool tables parallel to each other.

Clark chalked the end of his cue stick, and bent down with perfect form to sink two balls at once. Another guy with more piercings than I’d ever seen on one man’s face looked like he just made the stupidest mistake in the world.

Clark moved around the table with ease, hitting another solid ball into the corner pocket. He wore loose jeans and a baseball jersey with one word, Rude, over the chest.

“Did Clark ever mention he’s really good at pool?” Nathan asked.

“Nope! He’s fucking good,” I praised. Clark hit another ball, which rolled perfectly into the side pocket.

“I don’t even try to win when we play together,” Nathan admitted.

“Do you play?” I asked.

"Barely. I'm more of a darts guy. What do you want to drink?"

I peered at the tap handles and didn't recognize any of them except the usual drafts.

"Stella, please?"

"Coming right up, baby. Go surprise Clark." He nudged my lower back.

"You didn't tell him I was coming?"

"I said we might stop by. Go on." Nathan shooed me away and swatted me on the ass.

Clark fumbled his shot when he saw me standing next to the side pocket. The ball hit the outer rim of the hole knocking the cue ball in.

"Ouch. Scratched!"

Clark completely ignored the piercing guy and walked over to me. "What did I do right to deserve this little present?" He looped his hand around my back and kissed me with a small slip of his tongue. Just like that, my body ignited.

"Hey, Clark. I hope you don't mind I tagged along and messed up your shot."

"I never mind seeing you, darling. Fuck the shot. I beat Dave already," Clark announced, keeping his arm around my back.

"I heard that." Dave scoffed and focused on his first shot. He hit the striped ball making it fly around the table with no luck.

Clark squeezed my side and chuckled. "See?" Clark whispered.

Even though Dave gave Clark a death stare, I giggled behind my hand.

"Kicking Dave's ass again, Clark?" Nathan said, joining us.

"Every time." Nathan handed Clark a beer with a funky label on it and handed me the Stella he had balanced in his other hand. We all clinked the beers and took a swig. Clark's gaze never left me. Even when he proceeded to kick Dave's ass sinking the eight ball in the first try. He must of thought I would disappear if he stopped looking.

*Yes, I was here and enjoying every minute with him and Nathan.*

At eight o'clock the show began. Clark sat on a stool on stage for his small set. He waved at me to get him some water after the second song.

"The fucking lights are hot up here! You could kill a vampire with these things." Clark shielded his eyes and looked over at the pool tables. "Dave, stop trying to play pool and turn the lights down please? I'm sweating blue hair dye."

I passed Dave flipping Clark the finger on my way to the oval bar. The bartender had the water ready for me. Dave disappeared behind a half-raised platform. The glare from the lights lessened and Clark mouthed a thank you to Dave.

"All right, let's get back on track. Welcome everyone to the sixth annual folk night. I got three more songs then I'd like everyone to stick around for Lexi hailing all the way from Albany." Clark announced, lifting his hand to a young girl with two pink tinted buns waving shyly at him.

I handed him the water when he stopped talking. "Thank you, darling! Let's hear it for Bri, my best water girl." He winked back, grinning behind the mic.

I rolled my eyes at the applause and Nathan's overdramatic woos. "Oh great, now she's mad at me. I have the perfect song to get back on her good side."

Clark took his pick off the mic stand holder and strummed a different song than he told us earlier. He played "Just what I needed" by the Cars perfectly.

*Did I tell him it was my favorite song by the Cars?* My heart swooned.

Clark barely looked down at the chords he played. Nathan bumped against me and placed his arm over my shoulders. "He's been practicing this song every night for you," Nathan whispered and kissed my neck from behind.

My fan girl hormones were short-circuiting. *This was so freaking cute!*

In Nathan's arms, I watched Clark's mesmerizing fingers and his voice pulled me under his trance. He sang differently than the last gig. His voice sounded like it did when we fucked. My groin twisted and heat flared in my stomach. *Holy shit. That man up there was mine.*

When he was done, Nathan and I clapped, along with the rest of the bar. He placed his acoustic guitar on the short stand behind him.

"Thank you, everybody. Stick around for Lexi!" The pink haired girl hopped on stage with her ukulele and a few younger kids rushed to the front.

Clark walked down the stairs and headed toward us. He hugged Nathan first and Nathan tried to break away as fast as possible. Clark managed to plant a kiss on his mouth too. "Really, Clark? You're soaked!"

"Ah, it's just sweat. You sweat on me all the time!" Clark joked, rubbing his sweaty forehead against Nathan's cheek. Nathan recoiled, but still laughed.

Clark looked over to me, "How did I do? I'm sorry

I fucked up the Cars song like twice."

"Didn't notice. It was solid," Nathan answered, picking at his shirt, clearly ruffled by Clark's manhandling.

"You have to say that. Bri, how did it sound?"

"It sounded awesome." I tried not to be biased. I couldn't tell him I'd like anything he sang even if it was fucking jingle bells.

"Whew, thanks, darling," Clark said. "I need a drink." I handed him my third Stella and he chugged the rest. "Thanks. I get so nervous up there."

"Seriously? I'd never be able to tell."

"Small shows are harder to play than a room packed with drunken idiots wooing and clapping whenever they think a song is over. Here people listen, get in their zones, and sing along sometimes. It's a lot of pressure."

"Aww, Clark. You did a really great job." I hugged him.

"Thanks, darling."

Nathan excused himself to go to the bathroom, leaving me alone with Clark. He sat down on the empty barstool on the other side of me.

"You know, you're my best water girl. You had some serious skills there." He motioned toward the stage.

"Should I add it to my resume?"

"I would! You're a natural."

I laughed it off.

"Hey, can I ask you something?" Clark said.

"I don't know. Last time you asked me something I cried." I meant it as a joke, but Clark's face fell, and his shoulders went slack.

"I said I was sorry. Fuck. I made it awkward again didn't I?"

I hopped off my bar stool and placed both of my hands on his thighs. We were eye level now. His glossy blue eyes met my reddish brown ones. I kissed him and poured all my love into the kiss.

"Clark, stop, it's not your fault. You had every right to ask me and I'm telling you the truth. I want to be with you too. I'm your girlfriend and I'm here for you. I should have told my mother about you and if I can, I'll make it to every one of your shows, big and small. Please let me know when you play."

"You're seriously my dream girl," Clark admitted, letting out his held breath.

"What did I miss?" Nathan came back from the bathroom.

"Not much. Bri just promised to come to all my shows which means you have no excuse not to show your pretty face!" Clark snickered.

"I left you alone for two minutes and you gave my life away? What the fuck, Bri?" Nathan kidded.

"Oops?"

Nathan tickled me under my ribs. I burst out laughing.

We sat and watched the pink haired girl with the ukulele, and then a trio of older gentlemen covering some oldies. I bopped my head along to the music. Clark sipped a few beers, teasing me every now and again. He left to check the sound with Dave.

Their set ended and Clark asked, "Are you coming home with us later? Please say yes."

"Yeah, I brought clothes for the morning."

"Fucking A! Are you guys in a rush to get home?

I'm done playing, but I hate leaving while other people are performing. I try to stay to the end."

"It's okay with me? Nathan?"

"I'm good too."

"Awesome!" I shouted with glee.

At eleven p.m., the folk night was a wrap. Clark thanked the audience one more time for coming and encouraged people to come two weeks later. After he shut everything down with Dave, Clark joined Nathan and me with his guitar bag on his back. "Let's go home," Clark said.

Clark took an Uber to the bar, so we piled into Nathan's car. Sober Nathan drove and his hand never left the top of my thigh. Clark sat up as much as the middle seatbelt would let him and played with the curls returning under the rest of my hair. It had stayed straight for a good part of the day. But along my hairline the errant curls always came back.

When we got back to their apartment, I reached back for my overnight bag, but Clark already snatched it up along with his guitar.

Inside their apartment, Nathan had my sweater over my head before Clark closed the door. Nathan's mouth collided with mine and his tongue demanded I part my lips and let him in. He caressed my boobs through my bra and Clark unbuckled my belt. Clark glued himself to my back, tearing my jeans down my body. He left my thong on, groping my pussy from the front, his cock grinding into my ass. His fingers rubbed tiny circles on my clit, making me shout into Nathan's mouth. They both were already hard. I palmed both their cocks through their jeans.

Someone's hand undid my bra and threw it away

from between us. I wrenched my mouth from Nathan and turned around to kiss Clark. Clark was there ready for me to include him, patiently waiting his turn.

Nathan moved down to take my nipple between his teeth. He bit me, and I moaned, breaking Clark's kiss. Clark looked down over my shoulder and gripped Nathan's hair. Nathan's eyes opened, letting go of my wet nipple and peered up at Clark.

"Your bedroom or mine?" Nathan asked.

"Yours. I'll be there in a minute." Clark left my back and I resisted the urge to reach out to him. I needed both of them tonight. All the flirting, the kissing, the teasing; I grew impatient, aching for one of them to fuck me. Clark headed toward the bathroom and slammed the door.

Nathan and I kissed our way to his bedroom. "Lie down, baby," he said.

I lay down in the middle of the bed. Nathan stripped out of his button-down from work and his jeans, and peeled down his boxers. I took off my panties and played with myself.

"I love this view," Nathan said.

My fingers trailed down to my wet slit, and I fingered myself. It felt good, but nothing like Nathan's cock or Clark's. Nathan crawled onto the bed. I widened my legs and planted my feet on the mattress opening myself for Nathan. He pushed the unmade covers off his bed and kneeled between my legs.

He stroked himself until precum leaked from the head of his cock. "Come up here, Nathan," I commanded.

His gaze darted over my body. He leaned down and licked the soft skin between my breasts. He swallowed and did it again.

I squeezed my breasts together and Nathan slid his cock through the wet space. When his cock came near my mouth, I flicked my tongue against the tip. He moaned each time I licked.

"Suck me, baby." He inched up, and I opened my mouth for this cock. I sucked him into my mouth and licked fast around the head. He spread his legs wider and clenched the muscles of his thighs when I touched his balls. They grew harder in my hand, drawn up tight to his body. He was close.

Nathan fisted my hair with one hand and slapped the wall with the other. He glanced down at me. "I'm sorry, baby. I need to come."

I nodded and moved my mouth over his cock faster. I wanted to give him what he needed. I closed my eyes and thought after thought ran through my head. *I suppose Clark and him didn't fuck yesterday? Are they still intimate with each other when I'm not around anymore?* This was the fastest he'd ever come whenever we'd been together. *Fuck, we're leaving him out too much yet I see him more?*

My thoughts distracted me, and I missed every clue he was coming. I coughed around his cock, but forced myself to swallow. His cum leaked down the side of my mouth, down to my chest. I needed to breathe. I opened my eyes and stared up into his frantic ones. He pulled his cock from my mouth and I jerked the last bit of cum from him.

"Shit, Bri, I'm sorry. I didn't want to choke you." He stuttered as I finished him off. It wasn't coherent sentences; he rutted the words out of his mouth with each jerky thrust of his hips.

"No, sorry. That was my fault." I took my hand off his cock and caught my breath. He looked upset. I coughed and wiped my mouth with the back of my hand. "I was thinking that I don't get to spend as much alone time with you, and I lost focus."

Nathan leaned off me and laid down facing me. "This project fucking sucks. I can't wait for it to be done. I still don't want to do that again with you lying down."

"Okay, Nathan," I agreed.

Nathan took a few deep breaths. I did the same. This was not how I wanted this to pan out tonight. My heaving chest was splattered with cum and spit. I grabbed a tissue from the nightstand and dabbed at my chest.

"Maybe I can book a hotel room for after the party? We can be alone for a night?"

"I'd like that very much."

"Sorry for making a mess. Let me make it up to you," Nathan offered.

Nathan crawled to the bottom of the bed and pushed the back of my thighs up. I waxed everything off my pussy earlier in the week, only leaving a small triangle on top of my mound. Everything else was smooth. Nathan licked my pussy and then sucked hard on my clit. My legs shook, and my hips lifted up to his mouth. He didn't need to be sorry about before, but I appreciated the tender attention.

Clark opened the door with a towel wrapped around his waist. He was such a strikingly sexy man. His naked body and tattooed arms were a sight. He dropped the towel and smoothed his hand up his long hard cock.

"How does his mouth feel, Bri?" Clark asked pausing his hand.

"So fucking good." I groaned when Nathan added his fingers into my pussy. "How's your hand?"

"Not as good as your cunt." His words and Nathan's fingers twisted my insides and piqued my lust. I let out a shaky moan.

Clark walked over to the bed, and Nathan stopped licking me. Nathan sat up, and Clark kissed him as he climbed onto the bed. Nathan's fingers lingered inside of me pushing in time to Clark's tongue fucking Nathan's mouth. The sound of their groans pierced the silence in the room.

I held my breath, hoping this wasn't a dream I concocted in my head. I was here, watching and waiting. Clark stroked Nathan's cock with one hand and caressed my thigh with the other.

"Let's fuck her together." Nathan nodded at Clark's instructions. Clark kissed him again, taking the lead. "Lie down, Nate. Turn on your side, darling. Face him."

We got into Clark's positioning. Nathan prodded my pussy with his searching cock. He wrenched a moan out of my mouth, and Clark's mouth absorbed it. He gripped my chin pulling my head toward him. He let me go and kissed Nathan. "Fuck her pussy."

Clark lay down behind me. I faced Nathan fully, and he slammed his lips on mine. I curled my leg over his hip, and his cock finally entered me. Nathan grabbed my right ass cheek and pulled me against him with each thrust of his cock.

Clark fingered the lube inside my ass. My breath caught when he inserted two fingers.

Attentive Clark noticed my reaction immediately. Nathan stopped his slow fucking.

"Are you okay? I can stop, Bri," Clark said halting his actions.

"I'm okay. I just got nervous." I confessed. I didn't want to tell him no. I needed to feel him close again.

"I'll go slowly like last time. If you want me to stop at any point, I will."

"I know. I trust you." I smiled back at him and watched him slide the condom onto his cock. He smeared more lube over the latex.

Nathan brushed his knuckles against my cheek and kissed me, stealing my attention away. Clark brought the head of his cock against my lubed asshole. My body let him in, inch by inch, and I squirmed when he pushed in past where the lube had gone. I breathed deep into Nathan's kisses. The sensation of Clark in my ass and Nathan's short thrusts drew endless moans from my mouth, captured by Nathan's lips.

Clark gripped my right breast and suckled my neck. He grunted loud as he found a slow, maddening rhythm inside me. I dug my nails into his ass. His cheeks hollowed and puffed back out each time he bottomed out in me. *Oh fuck, I was going to come. This was even better than the last time.*

"Baby, I'm going to go faster. If it's too much, let me know," Nathan whispered. I pushed my fingers through his hair.

"Okay. Oh, yes!" Nathan did as he said, while Clark remained the same. Each time Nathan's pelvis ground upon mine and Clark pulled out, pleasure peaked and retreated driving me higher.

"Give me your mouth, darling?" Clark asked. He

pillaged my mouth with his tongue. I had barely moved up until now, but I managed a few jerky movements while Nathan and Clark's hands held me in place.

Both of them cranked up their speed, and I fell into my release. The pleasure was everywhere, the tips of my nipples, the hood of my clit, the opening to my ass, and my pussy hugging Nathan's cock. I moaned and shouted, the pleasure sharp and intense.

"Oh, baby. Clark, she's coming. Come with us," Nathan stammered out, fucking faster again. Clark reached down and palmed Nathan's balls. Nathan shouted, throwing his head back.

"Yes, fuck yes. Bri. Nate." Clark moaned in my ear. He said something else, but Nathan's mouth stole Clark's words. They shouted into each other's mouths, both of them coming.

We all stopped moving and remained entwined, twitching in the afterglow. Clark entangled his fingers into my right hand and pushed against my stomach. Nathan kissed my forehead, and I lifted up my head to kiss him softly.

"Did we make you feel good, baby?" Nathan asked.

I smiled and nestled into the crook of his shoulder. Clark kissed my shoulder and forearm over and over. "Please say yes. I never want to hurt you," Clark said.

"Yes, Clark. You both made me feel amazing."

"Good." Clark placed his hand on my hip and eased out of my ass. Nathan winced and slipped out of me. He leaned back on his bed, and pulled me over his right side.

"What time do you guys need to wake up in the morning?" Clark asked, snapping off the condom and throwing it out.

“Six a.m. the latest. We need to catch the seven thirty train,” Nathan said, tiredness coated his answer. He lazily stroked his hand over my flushed skin.

“That’s fucking insane. As much as I’d love to sleep with you both, I’m going back to my room,” Clark declared.

I found myself wide-awake.

## Chapter Thirty-Seven

"Clark, stay?" I asked.

"You make it hard to go. Thank you, darling, for coming to my show. I need some sleep. I'll see you tomorrow." Clark kneeled back on the bed and kissed me. He stood by his decision. He kissed Nathan goodnight, grabbed his towel, and walked out of the room.

"Goodnight, baby," Nathan said. He nuzzled his nose into my hair. I said goodnight, even though my body tingled, and adrenaline rushed through my veins. It was already one a.m., but I wanted Clark.

"Can't sleep?" Nathan grumbled.

"Not really. I'm going to take a shower," I admitted partially. I wanted Clark to be here. I knew he wasn't rejecting us by going to his room, but I still felt anxious about it, especially after the last few days.

"Do it in the morning. We'll have time."

"Go to sleep, hun. I'll be back before you know it."

Nathan lost the fight. By the time I got up, he already snored.

I wrapped a throw around my naked body and left Nathan's bedroom. I heard Clark playing his guitar before I saw him sitting on the couch. His back was to me, lost in his own musical world.

"You're still awake?" I asked, walking up to the couch. Amora brushed against my leg. I leaned down and petted the little cutie. She moved her face into my hand.

"I'm too hyped up," Clark answered. He looked exhausted behind his glasses.

"Me too. Do you have any clean towels? I need to take a shower."

"Yeah. Go on. I'll bring you one."

I walked down the hall to their bathroom. I dropped the blanket into the hamper and turned on the shower. The hot water felt absolutely amazing against my tired skin. I dunked my head under the spray, closing my eyes. The door opened, and Clark came in holding a towel for me.

"Here's a towel," he shouted. I pulled the curtain aside and watched him put the toilet seat down, placing the towel on top.

"Thanks," I said.

Clark pulled off his shirt. "Is there room for one more?" he asked.

"I thought you took one before?"

"Not one with you."

Clark finished undressing standing beautifully naked before me. He removed his glasses, placing them gently on the vanity. *How did he know exactly what I needed?* Another time I'd freak out about it. Now, I wanted everything he had to give me.

Clark stepped under the spray and kissed me. His hands kneaded my breasts before I locked my hands around his neck drawing us closer together. He wasn't hard yet, but that changed rather quickly. I moaned as his hands traveled down my body caressing every inch of me.

My back hit the tiled wall. I loved how he switched

from gentle to rough in seconds. He stopped kissing me and gripped my chin.

"I'm sorry for doubting you. I was wrong," Clark said.

"It's okay. We're here together now."

"Relationships are hard for me. Can you forgive me?" He cradled my face; his thumbs stroked my flushed skin. His blue eyes scanned mine for whatever he needed to finally put this past us.

"Yes, I forgive you." *I'd tell him anything he wanted to hear. I'll admit everything, baring the truth over and over again.*

He smiled and kissed me until I panted for breath, desperate to fuck.

Clark pulled me from the wall, shifting his weight off me. "Turn around," he said. I turned toward the spray. He grabbed the bar of soap from the holder. His hands slipped around my stomach and washed the delicate parts of my body.

He slipped his hands between my legs and moved the soap way too slowly against my pussy. He didn't spend too much time there, working his way over more of me. I wanted him to bend me over and sink his cock inside me, but he actually wanted to wash me.

I was speechless. Sensations took over. As he put me back and forth underneath the spray, he kneaded his hands over my tight muscles. Every time I turned around he placed a hand on my back stopping me. I gave up after three tries. This wasn't for him, it was for me.

He grabbed the nozzle off the shower holster and cascaded the direct spray stream over my body. He kissed each part of my body after the water washed away the soap.

"Do you feel better now?" Clark asked.

"Mmmhmm, yes. Thank you."

I kissed him and smoothed my hand over his cock. My fingers skimmed over the soft skin of his slit smearing the liquid I knew wasn't water. He moaned, watching me stroke his cock.

With a shaky breath he murmured, "You should get some sleep."

"I'm not tired yet," I countered, moving my other hand along his balls.

"You will be tomorrow," Clark added, squeezing his eyes shut and moaning again. His hands clenched into fists, until one strong hand gripped the back of my neck.

"Let me worry about it," I taunted.

I tried to look innocent, staring up at Clark's face, his brow still furrowed, his whole body struggling with restraint. "Don't you want to come, Clark?" I lowered myself down to bathtub floor, but he stopped me.

"Not here," he said.

He shut off the water and backed away from my touch. He pulled back the shower curtain and got out. I stayed a second longer admiring his delectable body from behind. Oddly, he had no tattoos on his back; only his arms and I hadn't noticed that he had dimples over his ass. I wanted to kiss each one.

"What?" he asked, dragging my attention back up his body.

"I didn't know you had dimples over your ass."

Clark half smiled, flashing me the other dimple in his face.

He helped me out of the shower and handed me the

towel from the toilet. He used one off the towel rack on the door.

"Come back to bed," I urged. Clark picked up his glasses from the vanity.

"Not tonight. Nathan gives off heat like a fucking furnace. I also don't have anywhere to be until four p.m. No offense, but I really need some sleep."

"All right. Next time." I opened the bathroom door, but I didn't get far.

"No wait. Come to my room," Clark added. "I love when I get you alone."

"Do you now?"

"You know I do."

I ignored the tired woman screaming in my head. I looped my hands over Clark's shoulders and kissed him. *Fuck sleep. I needed him again.*

The towel fell off me. Clark looked down at my semi dry body. "Don't be mad at me tomorrow."

I smiled and nodded. Clark dipped down and grabbed the back of my thighs against his body. I yelped when he lifted me off the floor and my back hit the bathroom wall.

"Hold onto me."

I latched onto him and wrapped my legs around his waist. I sucked the droplets of water off his neck while he carried me to his bedroom.

He didn't let me go until we were on his bed. He laid me down and shooed Amora off his comforter. Clark scooted us to the center of the bed.

"Keep your hands above your head," he said.

"Are you going to tie me up again?" I asked.

"Next time, darling."

He bit the underside of my bicep making me

writhe. I brought my hands down, but he pushed them abruptly above my head. He kissed me softly, a direct contrast to the pressure of his hands on my wrists. I arched my head to get more of his mouth, but he held himself out of reach.

"Clark?" I murmured against his lips.

"Shhh."

His left hand caressed the side of my body and he looped my thigh over his arm. He was done playing. Clark slipped his cock inside me and buried his head in my damp hair, groaning when I arched my back changing his angle. He cried out, grinding into my pussy.

He fucked me slowly and eventually let go of my hands. His teeth tugged on my lower lip, and I jerked my hips up, matching his rhythm. Our bodies clashed together, but it wasn't what he wanted. His hands spread my ass apart, holding me still for his fucking.

His silence worried me that part of us still wasn't okay, but I pushed my insecurities away. His eyes were open, taking in the sight of my body undulating underneath him. We were in this together, feeling and sharing the moment.

The slow burn of my orgasm steadily crept up my body and I lifted up my hips again.

He said, "Kiss me, darling." I grabbed the sides of his face. We moaned our releases into the kiss. Even after our bodies stopped moving, our mouths continued teasing each other. He pulled his cock out of me and kissed me one last time before he climbed off me.

I didn't want to leave the warmth of Clark's bed. He cuddled up against my back and pulled me against him. His hand found my breast and he softly moved his fingers back and forth over the soft flesh.

"You should go back to Nathan's room," he said, giving me tiny kisses.

"I don't want to leave you," I said.

"I'll be okay."

"I won't be."

Clark chuckled and squeezed me tighter. I traced a wilted rose, a flying sparrow, a musical note, and other randomness in his tattoos, each one more colorful and beautiful than the other. I wish I knew the story behind each one.

"Did you fall asleep?" he asked, nudging his nose against my cheek.

"No. I'm awake." I twisted back around, his arms lightening up around me. When we were face to face, he brushed my unruly bangs out of my face. "One day will you tell me about your tattoos?"

"You're so fucking cute. I'll tell you everything."

I smiled excited for the future. Clark yawned into the crook of his shoulder. "One last chance to go back to Nathan's room."

"Okay. I'll let you sleep in."

"Are you coming over before the Christmas party?"

"Yeah, we're leaving from here."

"Good. I'll steal you again then. Goodnight, darling."

"Goodnight, Clark."

It was so hard to pry myself away. I liked him so much. There was a difference between him and Nathan that pulled me deeper toward Clark. Everything seemed so natural and flowing. His full attention fixated on only you.

I flipped my legs over the side of the bed and Clark put a hoodie over me. He kissed me one more time before I got off the bed. Amora glanced up from her plush bed near the door, but laid her little head back down. I know, I didn't want to leave Clark either.

Nathan's room was hot. I hadn't really noticed how warm he got, but it made sense. His hands were always sweaty and that must have been why they requested two beds for the wedding. I figured out their secrets one by one.

I lay down next to Nathan and his eyes fluttered open.

"You okay, baby?" Nathan said.

"Yup. Go back to sleep, hun."

He puckered his lips and I followed suit. He smiled with his eyes closed. I curled up next to him and drifted off to sleep.

## Chapter Thirty-Eight

Around eleven thirty a.m. the next day my phone vibrated.

—*What floor do you guys work on?*—Clark texted.

—*15th floor.*—

—*What's the code for the elevator?*—

—*Why?*—

—*You ask too many questions. What's the code?*—

—*It's 1521. Wait, are you here?*—

I saw the three little dots that he was typing and then it stopped.

—*Clark?*—I texted again.

—*Who the fuck plays rap music in an elevator?*— He responded.

*He's here. What the hell?*

My desk phone rang. "This is Brianna."

"Clark Peterson here for you. Can I buzz him in?"

"Yes please." I squealed into the phone. I ended the call and dialed Nathan's extension.

"Hey, Bri."

"We have a visitor."

"Who may that be?"

"Tall, dark, and brooding about the music playing in the elevator?"

"Ha-ha, yup, that's Clark. I'll be there in a sec," Nathan said, a notable excitement to his voice. I hung up the phone and ran to the front desk.

Clark wore black jeans and a dark blue button down. For him, he was dressed up. He had even slicked back his hair so the blue was barely visible, only the remaining black. His eyes shined when he saw me.

"I'll be back to talk to you about the elevator," Clark said pointing at Linda, the receptionist.

"Sir, I have no say on the music they play in there. Here's a number to call."

"I will call them, thank you very much." He took the card and put it in his breast pocket with a cocky smirk.

"Clark, are you causing trouble?" I asked.

"Always, darling." He kissed me right in front of Linda. He had the nerve to dip me too. She coughed in the background, and he flipped me back up, letting me come up for air.

I scurried out of his embrace and headed down the hallway, not making eye contact with Linda.

"Seriously?" I said when we were out of earshot. I laughed when we were in the hallway away from the receptionist.

"Hey, it made you laugh, so definitely worth it!"

I shook my head and urged him down the hall toward my side of the floor. "You're ridiculous. What did we do to earn this surprise visit?"

"I was lonely." Clark took my hand. "My meeting is downtown, so I thought I'd pop in for a second."

"Aww. I could use a Clark break today," I said.

"Restless?"

"Yeah. I'd never wanted a project to be over as much as this one."

"Is it almost done?"

"Yes, thank God. Here's my home away from

home." We walked up to my cubicle.

"Very nice, Bri. I like your little dancers."

"Thank you. They keep me company."

Nathan rounded the corner and popped his head over my wall. "They didn't throw out your complaining ass yet?"

"I got good connections here." Clark wrapped his hand around my shoulders.

"Ha-ha, give it another ten minutes. She might turn on you too. What's up?" Nathan asked.

"I had a stroke of genius and wanted to give Bri her Christmas present early." Clark perked up showing off his coordinated outfit and tie.

I swatted him playfully in the arm. "You didn't have to do that! I was going to see you tomorrow."

"I needed to give it to you today," Clark said, stealing a kiss on my cheek. He handed me a black and red business card in the shape of a corset. "Be at that address by two thirty p.m. tomorrow. I've arranged for you to get the ultimate beauty treatment experience."

"Cleo's Hair Magic? No way, she's a hairdresser?" That explains her hair at the show a few weeks ago and Clark's changing hair.

"She prefers the term, Mistress Beautician," Clark said, flowing his hands in front of him.

"That's cute. I thought she didn't like me."

"Cleo secretly loves everybody. She just sucks at first impressions," Nathan said.

"I hope so."

Clark pointed at the card. "Seriously, go see her tomorrow. Cleo is super excited to do this for you. I want you have to an amazing time tomorrow night."

The heartfelt and supportive gift melted my

freaking heart. “This is totally super sweet.” I hugged him, and his loving arms squeezed me around my waist. He pulled back and kissed me again on the mouth. “Thank you, Clark. This is above and beyond.” His thumbs caressed the sensitive skin of my hips just under my sweater.

“You’re welcome.”

Nathan coughed, but I didn’t move fast enough.

“Hey, Bri, can I borrow you for a second?” Paul appeared out of nowhere and I yelped in Clark’s arms. “Shit, sorry. I didn’t mean to interrupt.” Paul’s eyes went wide, and he grimaced.

I let go of Clark immediately and pulled down my sweater. Nathan buttoned his suit jacket, fixing himself too.

“It’s all right. What do you need?” I cleared my throat, squashing my embarrassment.

“I’m sorry. I shouldn’t have bothered you. I’ll ask Marcia to do this for me. It’s nothing.” Paul’s gaze darted back and forth between Clark, Nathan, and me. After he stuttered an apology, he walked away. *Fuck.* He outed me for being close to Nathan and then he saw me in Clark’s arms.

“Was that the boss?” Clark asked.

“One of them,” Nathan said.

“Shit, was that bad?”

“No, it’s fine. I’ll tell him you’re her cousin.”

“Um eww?” I said.

“This place is making me anxious. Don’t lose Cleo’s card. I have to get going anyway.” Clark said.

“I won’t lose it. Thank you again, Clark.”

“Anytime. Bye, darling.” He kissed me fast and peeked around then kissed Nathan.

# Chapter Thirty-Nine

Cleo's hair boutique was only fifteen minutes from the boy's apartment. The traffic exiting the city was the worst. Luckily, once I hit New Jersey it was smooth sailing.

I arrived shortly after two thirty p.m. The office closed at one to give the select few an opportunity to get fancy for the extravagant event. For the life of me I can't really wrap my head around the closed-door policy of this event.

I pulled up to a purple house with a big bay window. It wasn't a retail storefront but someone's house with a visible salon in the main room. A cute wooden sign hung on the door with calligraphy edged in. "Cleo's Hair Magic."

I did a double take when a short blonde answered the door in a black button down shirt and black pants. "No fucking way. You actually came!" Cleo bounced my way for a big hug.

I was even more confused. She let me go and smiled from ear to ear. Looking at her closely I noticed her signature dramatic cat eye liner, her bottom lip ring and her septum piercing in her nose. It was really her. Wow.

"Cleo?"

"You got it, baby. I'm so happy you're here! Come in. I'll be done with Mrs. Watson in a few minutes.

Help yourself to anything in the kitchen. Cleo beckoned me into her lair.

When I walked inside, I gasped. There were so many colors in the room and fan girl amazingness. I wanted to drool over every inch for the next five hours of my life.

She had a mannequin with a Mohawk wearing a black and red renaissance wench costume, there was a wall to wall mural of CDs from every album I ever loved, and a Buffy poster. *She was my friend soul mate all along.*

The huge living room was set up with three salon stations, a sink for shampooing, and three old-fashioned hair dryers. There was a woman at one of the hair stations. Half of her head was blown out and the other part was held up by the biggest monster clip with rhinestones I had ever seen. Everything had a touch of Cleo to it. Even the bobby pins were striped.

"Welcome to my salon, Bri! We'll be done in no time. Go on and help yourself."

"I made my dearest Cleopatra some brownies. There in the purple container. I left the pot out this time." The elderly lady winked at me.

"Ha-ha, ah shucks. Thank you, I'll be in the kitchen," I said.

"Feel free to snoop around. I saw your lady boner before. I have tons of fun stuff to play with," Cleo said, picking up her hair dryer.

I backed into the kitchen. It was hard to pry my eyes away from the twilight zone episode happening. I made a cup of coffee, grabbed a brownie, and went back into the salon. There were empty chairs on the right of the room, bathed in the perfect amount of natural light. The magazines on the end table would put any corporate chain to shame.

Even with the hair dryer blasting, Cleo and Mrs. Watson chatted away like they'd been friends for years. The angry misfit millennial vision I had of Cleo was long gone. The boys knew I'd like her, once I got past her outer shell. They were right.

The older woman was finally finished and ready to go to her grandson's wedding rehearsal dinner. "Thank you Cleo! Here's a little something extra." Mrs. Watson placed a twenty on Cleo's hairbrush caddy.

"Next blowout is on me!" They kissed on the cheek and she waved to me as Cleo led her out the door.

"So sorry she took longer than I expected! Do we still have time, Bri?"

"Yeah. I have four hours before I have to be at the boys' apartment."

"Excellent. Hop onto Roxy. She only vibrates if you're extra nice to her," Cleo inferred, motioning over to the shampooing station.

"Ha-ha. I think we can work out something." I got into the magical chair and it vibrated right away.

Cleo turned the water on and massaged my scalp.

"Hey, Bri, I want to apologize for being so bitchy at the gig the other week. I was mad at Clark, and I didn't mean to put my foot in my mouth or anything. I was so fucking beat from the tour and le sigh, I wanted to curl up here and not do anything for like a month."

"I get it. My ex is a musician. It was always hard for him to turn off and return to normalcy after tours. It has to be crazy draining performing every night."

"It is. Trust me. Especially when it's day two of your period!"

"Ouch, that sucks."

"Yeah, but I love it. I love this job too. I'm happiest with a bass or a hair dryer in my hand."

Cleo flipped me back up, and the chair unfortunately stopped vibrating.

"I hope I didn't out Clark's feelings for you. He said you guys were complicated, but he hasn't seemed too mad at me or anything."

She was headed right for the throat with these questions.

"Um…" I said.

"Look, Bri, I swear I'm not trying to snoop into your relationship or snitch anything. It's just that I've known Clark for a long time. I haven't seen him this happy since him and Nathan started fooling around. He likes you, like really likes you. He's super bad at communicating emotion to the people he cares for. If you like him, tell him. Tell Nathan. I am one hundred percent supportive of you guys trying to make this work."

Wet hair and all I hugged Cleo.

"Thank you, Cleo. That's exactly what I needed to hear."

"Anytime, babes. Now let's get you ready for the ball."

# Chapter Forty

I unzipped my garment bag and stared at the most gorgeous dress I had ever seen. It was an off the shoulder little black dress and I had the perfect kitten heels to match. I zipped it up as much as I could from behind. I stared at myself in the mirror and genuinely smiled.

Tonight meant more than just getting dressed up. I earned this spot and Cleo made sure I looked damn good for it. She even did my makeup.

"Hot damn, you look stunning," Clark said from the doorway.

"Why thank you! It's rented." I fluttered my eyelashes at him in the mirror and partially curtsied.

"Not the dress, Bri. You look beautiful." He walked into Nathan's bedroom and up to my back. He zipped up the last part of my dress and hooked the eyelet clasp on top. Cleo had swept my hair to the side and a courageous silver studded clip held it together. Clark kissed the hollow of my exposed throat. It went straight down to my toes.

"Hey there, don't start something you can't finish, buddy." I teased as I put on my charm bracelet I wore for special occasions. When I glanced back up, Clark wasn't smiling anymore. "Clark, I was kidding." I playfully slapped his chest.

"I know." He smiled, but it didn't go up to his

eyes.

“Is something wrong?”

“Everything’s fine. Are you ready? Nathan went to warm up the car.”

I couldn’t help but notice sadness in his voice. Maybe the dress was too much. Fuck, anxiety started to creep up my chest.

“Shit, I don’t know. Did I overdo it?” I asked.

“You’re crazy. You are the prettiest woman I will ever see right here and right now. Nathan is the luckiest man alive to have you as his date. Don’t let anything get in the way of you having a wonderful night.” He leaned down and kissed my cheek, but the sad look was still written on his face.

“Then why do you look so sad? Please tell me.”

“It’s nothing. I’m just tired.”

“Clark?” I’d known him long enough to know something was up.

“All right. I wish I were taking to you to the party. That’s all. Now, go have fun and I’ll be here when you guys get back in the morning.”

“Does your studio have any parties?

“Yeah, in the spring.”

“I promise I will go with you to them.”

“Okay, darling. Now go on, Nathan’s waiting.”

I grabbed my bolero jacket and coat. Clark sat on the bed hunched over his knees. I grabbed his chin and tilted his face up to me. The spike of jealousy was a first on his part. His poker face was unreadable. I kissed him lightly. He kissed me back, but definitely something was off.

“I’ll see you tomorrow, Clark.”

“Bye, Bri.”

****

The hotel hosting the Christmas party was decorated to the nines. The lobby signs directed us to the main ballroom. The low hum of music penetrated the closed doors.

Nathan cocked out his elbow and said, “My lady?”

I gladly interlaced my hand through his arm. I loved his chivalry tonight.

We walked into the main ballroom. Red and gold streamers decorated the walls and gorgeous birds of paradise centerpieces adorned each of table. For an invitation-only event, the room was occupied to the max. I recognized some clients and our office executives from various departments. *My thoughts screamed, network, network, and network.*

I spotted Paul sitting with a gorgeous blonde woman I had never seen before. Nathan’s gaze followed mine and we both gawked at them. “Is that Paul’s girlfriend?” Nathan whispered in my ear.

“I guess so? Holy shit!” I responded.

“He must have a great bedside manner?” Nathan added. I fake gagged and playfully slapped his shoulder. Paul looked our way and waved.

“Hey, Bri! You look lovely. Nathan, good to see you.” Paul got up and gave me the first hug of our four-year acquaintance. He shook Nathan’s hand. “I would like you guys to meet my girlfriend Sandra. Sandra, this is Bri and Nathan, two of the most important members of our analyst team.”

Sandra stood up and shook both of our hands. “I’ve heard so much about you two. It’s such a pleasure to meet you both!”

“Us too! Is there room at the table for two more?” I

inquired.

"Yes, we saved you seats. Bri, I hope you don't mind sitting next to me. Paul said you'd save me from the boredom." Sandra scrunched up her face, looking hopeful.

"Ah, so he described the company perfectly. Awesome. Did your hospital give you the night off?"

"Yeah, I switched shifts with someone. I wanted to be here for Paul. It's been a rough few weeks."

"Tell me about it," I said, sitting down next to her. When I first started at Grant, it took a long while for Paul and me to be friendly with each other and let our guards down. With Sandra it was no time and all. I already liked her.

Nathan sat next to me. "When you're stuck behind a desk all day, it's hard to realize how many clients this company has now."

"I know! This isn't even half of them," Paul added.

"Is anyone from Traill going to be here tonight?" I asked.

"Unfortunately not. Tonight is their holiday party too. Nathan's here so they're not worried about it."

"Good. I was hoping they wouldn't want any peeks at the proposal."

"I spoke to the media director yesterday. They're okay waiting two more weeks," Nathan added.

"Whew."

Sandra leaned over to me. "I love your dress and your makeup!" Sandra said, still no cracks in the perfection.

"Thank you. My punk fairy godmother helped me. She has a salon in Jersey."

Sandra giggled. "You'll have to give me her

contact info. I've been looking for a salon for ages," Sandra whispered into my ear. "Would it be inappropriate if Paul and I danced?"

"Um, good question." I spotted a few supervisors and sales reps dancing along with the clients. "I think it'll be fine. I'll go fetch Nathan. We'll meet you out there."

Nathan and I joined Paul and Sandra on the dance floor. For once, Paul looked relaxed and surprised me by twirling Sandra around much like Clark did to me at Diane and Kelsey's wedding. "Dancing and bedside manner? She's a lucky girl." Nathan kidded.

I shook my head and laughed. "I'm the lucky girl. I have you."

Nathan smiled and leaned in near my ear. "I can't wait to get the fuck out of here."

"Me too, Nathan."

Our entrees came at the perfect time because my feet were killing me. I was ready to move along with the night.

"Anna hunny, you look absolutely stunning! I'm so glad you're here." Mr. Grant waltzed up to the table. We were the next stop on his rounds.

"Thank you, Mr. Grant for the invitation."

"Anytime. Nate, my boy! We're going to miss you when you're gone! You've been such a valuable asset to the company," Mr. Grant shouted to the table.

"Please, Mr. Grant, stop flattering me so much! I couldn't have done it without Bri and Paul and the other team members," Nathan responded, blushing from the praise.

"Best proposal shot in months! Thank you everyone!" The entire table clapped.

Mr. Grant put his hand on Nathan's shoulder. "Come see me if you need any letters of recommendation. I'll wrap it up in a couple of Bens too!" Mr. Grant laughed at his own joke.

"Gee thanks for bringing me back down to earth." Nathan straightened his perfectly centered tie and picked at his buttons.

"I'm only joking. You're such a good kid. We will miss you down here." Mr. Grant patted Nathan on the back and waved to the table. "Please excuse me. I have to check on my wife. She can't resist those cheese raspberry thingies."

"I wish you could stay longer, Nathan. At least remain on hand for the first few weeks?" Paul inquired.

"We'll work it out, Paul."

I'd been so wrapped up with work, I kept blocking out that Nathan was going back to his own office once the proposal was over. *This was really going to suck.*

"Don't be sad. We'll work it out, Bri," Nathan said, rubbing my lower back.

"You just said that."

"I know. I'm sorry. That's all I got for now. It'll be fine."

After the speeches, I grew restless. This never was about the dressing up and listening to the speeches, or even customary good job pat on the back. The acknowledgement that I belonged here made this so special to me. The possibility of a future here was so damn addicting.

"When is this going to end?" Nathan cut into my racing thoughts. "I'm ready for some catching up I have to do." Nathan said against my ear. His hand drifted to the inside of my knee.

Guilt seized me. I snapped my head to him, ready to apologize. “I’m sorry, Nathan. I’m fucking this up.”

He pulled back from my neck and didn’t look angry. “Bri, I’m not mad at you or Clark. It’s hard not to see the connection you two have together. I’ve noticed it for a while now.” Nathan knocked back his cocktail and stretched out his legs underneath the table. “As soon as the project is done, fun Nathan will be back. I promise.” He caressed my cheek.

I forgot where we were and kissed him on the mouth. When we parted he had a small understanding smile.

“Is there anyone else you have to talk to?” I asked.

Nathan lit back up. “No. You?”

“No. I wasn’t supposed to be here remember?”

“Fucking politics. Come on. Let’s go, baby.”

Everyone else was looking for an exit strategy too. I said goodbye to Paul and Sandra and made her promise not be a stranger.

Nathan and I entered the lobby, and he went to front desk to check in.

“Hey, Bri, hold up a second.” Paul ran up to me.

“Is everything okay?” I inquired.

“Not really. I wanted to apologize for the other day. I sounded like a complete asshole telling you to watch yourself with Nathan. HR was buzzing around me, and I took it out on you.”

“Wait, what?”

“I shouldn’t have said anything.”

“Why was HR bothering you?”

“Marcia. I’m the reason she’s messing up so much lately. We dated for about a year. We kept it under wraps, but when I met my new girlfriend, Marcia had a fit even though we were done long before I met Sandra. She squealed to HR to make me mad."

*Well, that's a shock.* "What a bitch!"

"Nah, she was only hurt. I assured HR it was a consensual relationship, which ran its course. I meant my warning to be friendly advice, but I was too mad and upset. You and I have worked so well together. I don't want to ruin the friendship we have."

"Paul. It's okay. I really appreciate you looking out for me."

"I know Nathan won't be here much longer, but I didn't want them buzzing around you too."

"Hey, Paul. Is everything okay?" Nathan asked hiding the room keys in his pocket.

"I hope it is. I'm sorry again, Bri. You two have such great chemistry. Don't let an idiot make you think twice."

Nathan curled his arm around my shoulder and brought me into his side. "Thanks, Paul. Um, is someone going to explain this to me?"

# Chapter Forty-One

Nathan closed the hotel door behind him. I stepped out of my heels and shrugged off my bolero.

"That makes so much sense now. Marcia's been trying to sink her claws in me for weeks," he said.

"She better keep those claws off you." *Seriously.*

"Baby, you have nothing to worry about there." Nathan unhooked my top button of my dress and unzipped me. "You looked gorgeous tonight. It's a shame I'm going to have to mess you up." Nathan cooed into my ear, kissing a line from my ear down to my neck. I shivered at his sweet touches. "I'm so happy you were able to come with me tonight."

"I'm so awkward at these things," I said, moving my hand up to his face. He leaned into the caress.

"Fuck it. Don't bring yourself down like that, Bri, not on my watch."

"My self-esteem loves you, you know that?" I brought the straps of my dress down, but Nathan stopped me.

"Anytime, baby. I want to unwrap my present while I have you to myself." Nathan finished undoing my zipper down my back and fingered the black bow at the top of my thong.

"Fuck, you're wearing a garter belt too? You're going to kill me tonight." Nathan glided his hand up my back. I moaned when my ass met his already hard erection. I reached around toward him, but he backed away.

“Nope. I’ve missed just having you. I want to lead,” Nathan said. He slapped my ass, my dress muffling the impact.

“I’ve missed you too.”

“Really, baby?”

“Yes, Nathan. Please touch me. Don’t stop touching me.”

His hair was still perfectly styled, and his tie still tied. I grabbed his tie and yanked him forward in a kiss while my dress fell to the floor. I peeked at the mirror and saw our embrace. I didn’t see any of the insecurities that plagued my every thought. I saw a woman longing to be loved and fucked and dressed perfect for the right occasion. The black lace strapless bralette made me feel extra sexy, especially when Nathan played with my nipples through the lace.

“I love your body, baby.”

Nathan’s fingers hooked into my lace panties and dragged them down my legs. I placed my hands on his shoulders and he finished taking them off.

“I feel like I’m unwrapping the best present in the world.”

“Cheesy.”

“I don’t care…”

Nathan stayed down on his knees and placed his face against my pussy. His adoring gaze up my body made me eager for his next move. His tongue darted out licking the top cleft of my pussy. I didn’t hide the intensity of my moan. I wanted to let go tonight. I wanted to feel it all.

His tongue explored deeper, hitting my clit,

wiggling his tongue in just the right spot. His fingers dug into my waist, gripping the straps connected to my stockings. I held onto his hands. He gripped my waist harder and licked me faster. He felt so fucking good, but I wanted to be fucked. I needed his cock inside me.

I pushed Nathan's shoulders slightly and he stopped. He nudged me toward the bed. I went to take off my heels, but he stopped me. "Leave them on."

I sat on the bed and tugged at his waist. I opened his belt and undid his zipper. His cock was there waiting and perked up hard. I sucked on the head of his cock through his cotton boxers. He cried out and pulled his boxers down when I let him go. He grabbed hold of himself and stroked.

I lapped my tongue over his tip and took him all the way inside my throat. I hummed as I pulled back. Nathan's body shuddered, and he exhaled slowly. He took the clip out of my hair and threw it on the table.

"I'll tell Cleo you fucked with her expertise," I said.

"I'll take my chances." Nathan grabbed my hair tight enough to elicit a tiny gasp from my lips and put his cock back in my mouth. I loved when he fucking took what he wanted from me. I wasn't going to break. I opened my mouth wide and drank him down. Nathan unbuttoned his dress shirt and stripped while I sucked him deep. I snaked my hand up his soft skin. I took his hand and placed it on my breast.

"Fuck, Bri. I love your mouth, but you have to stop. I want something else." His thumb caressed my cheek.

I extracted his cock from my mouth slowly, staring up at him and dragging my tongue back and forth on the underside. "Tease. Get on the bed."

I scooted onto the large bed. Nathan followed me, gazing at my body like he hadn't seen me naked in forever. Nathan crashed his lips onto mine and my body fell back onto the bed. His tongue probed my mouth rubbing his with mine.

Nathan laid his weight over me. His skin was scorching hot. He gripped my breasts together, and I screamed into his mouth. His lips left mine to drag his tongue over my nipples. He moved back and forth and sucked my left one inside his mouth.

"Please use your teeth." He obeyed at once. He bit at my nipple and the skin around it. A wave of pleasure racked my body. I panted for more.

He latched onto my left nipple and slipped his fingers inside my pussy. He groaned and closed his eyes. I was wet, so wet for him. His thumb grazed my clit. I bit my lip instead of crying out. He was trying so hard to please me. My orgasm already churned.

"Please, Nathan, fuck me. I want your cock inside me," I muttered breathless.

"Who do you want to fuck you?"

"You, Nathan. I want you."

"Are you thinking of him? He's rough with you like this…Is this what you want?"

His question caught me off guard. I honestly wasn't thinking about Clark. *How do I tell him so he'd believe me?*

"I was thinking about only you, Nathan. I missed being with just you, too. You don't have to be gentle with me. Show me what's in you." I gripped his cock in my hand and urged him toward my pussy. "It was your mouth on my clit that made me wet. It's your cock I want to fuck me right now. I need your lips to kiss me," I truthfully declared.

"Yes, baby."

Nathan kissed me, coaxing my lips to open. He entered me and brought my legs, high heels and all, around his waist. My body gave him no resistance. His long cock pushed right in. We both moaned at the impact.

After a few smooth glides inside of me, he picked up the pace and fucked me exactly how I wanted. His hands were on either side of my head and his face hovering above kissing range. We stared each other down, feeling our bodies talk for themselves.

I grabbed his ass and urged him on. He swiveled his hips inside me instead of just going in and out.

"Nathan, fuck!" I threw my head back against the pillows, closing my eyes. Nathan's body shifted on top of me, his stomach laying on mine. His fingers gripped the sides of my face.

"Baby, look at me," Nathan demanded.

I opened my eyes and stared into his face. "Nathan," I breathed.

"I love you," Nathan said. He swallowed down a lump in his throat, while his cock pounded me into the bed.

I didn't hesitate. I knew my answer. It had been on the tip of my tongue for quite some time. *Once they said it first, I would have nothing left to hide.*

"I love you too, Nathan," I confessed, stroking my hand up his cheek. I lifted my lips up to his as much as I could.

"Baby, I love you. Fuck, squeeze down like that again. I love you so much." He kissed me fast and hard with a huge smile on his lips. He raised his chest off mine and dipped his head down to tease my nipple with his tongue. It plumped up wanting more of his wicked mouth.

Nathan sucked my nipple and part of my breast into his mouth. He looked up at me, with his lips still curved up. I admired the erotic view of his mouth on my breast and his cock ramming my pussy.

“I want to come, Nathan. You feel too good.”

“I’ll make you come. Turn around, baby,” Nathan instructed.

Nathan pulled his cock out of me and slapped my hip to urge me to move quickly. I got up on my hands and knees, and Nathan pressed his lips against my neck.

“Put your cheek against the bed and lift up your pussy…yes, like that, baby.” My cheek found the satin edge of the comforter, and I thrust my groin up to Nathan’s waist, knocking his cock up against my ass. He used my wetness to glide back and forth over my ass cheeks.

The head of his cock brushed against my asshole. In all the times we had sex, Nathan hadn’t fucked my ass yet. I was stuck in limbo; waiting for his decision.

“I want to fuck your ass one day.”

I exhaled. A random thought seized my mind that I didn’t want him to fuck my ass. Only Clark had done it. I only wanted him to do it from now on while Nathan fucked my pussy. Shit, why didn’t we invite Clark to stay here until the party was over and we all could have fucked around? God was that why he was so upset? We left him out? But Nathan needed tonight. He needed to know I was still with him too.

Nathan slid inside me and hauled me out of my

thoughts. He pulled my hips back so hard our bodies grunted with each thrust. The sound of my wetness sucking Nathan's cock deeper inside and his balls slapping against my clit filled the room. I lifted my hand back and groped my hand over Nathan's balls and my clit. *I needed to come.*

"Fuck, baby." Nathan groaned. He feathered his thumb over my asshole. When he dipped his fingertip in I came.

My orgasm radiated out from the front of my pussy and pulled the pleasure deep inside me. I stopped thrusting back and allowed myself just the feel his cock sliding firmly into my body. He shouted and muttered that he was coming too.

Nathan draped his body over mine, his hands cupping my heaving breasts. He pulled out and lay down next to me. I curled up on my side facing him.

"I love you, Bri. I'm so happy we're here together."

"I love you too, Nathan. I don't want to move."

"Me either, but I'll be right back. I promise. Get under the covers."

He pulled back the comforter, and I got under it. Nathan walked to the front of the bed and grabbed his boxers to put them on. He jogged to the bathroom.

My body felt pleasantly used. I leaned over to the nightstand to check my phone, but Nathan's phone started to ring. A Ryan C-EX number flashed on his screen. I called out to Nathan. "Hey, Nathan, someone's calling you!" At two a.m., this couldn't be good.

"Who is it?" He called out from the bathroom over the running water.

"Um, Ryan C-EX? What does C-EX mean?"

Nathan's head popped out of the bathroom. "What? Who did you say?"

"Ryan C-EX?

"What the fuck? Why is he calling me?" Nathan came back into the room and only stared at the phone. The ringing stopped. No notification came for a voicemail, but a text message came through.

"Are you fucking kidding me?" Nathan shouted and picked it up to read the full message.

"Nathan, what's going on?"

Nathan looked at me like he forgot I was right in front of him. He looked angrier than I had ever seen him before.

"Ryan C-EX is Clark's ex-fuck buddy. He just texted me that Clark stood him up tonight and asked me to call him."

"Stood him up? What does that mean?"

"Exactly that. Ryan isn't a figurative guy. I can't fucking believe it. Have they've been seeing each other behind our backs?"

Nathan paced the room staring at his phone with a look of betrayal stamped on his flushed face.

"Nathan, come on. I don't think Clark would do this to us. It's only one text message."

"Bri, I can't fucking stand Ryan. He always looked for a way to get a rise out of me every time he came around, busting my balls or whatever macho shit."

"Look, Nathan, if he's calling you at two a.m. maybe something is wrong. Call him back, please. Clark was acting funny before. Maybe Ryan's worried."

"It's two a.m. already?" Nathan's emotional rollercoaster headed straight down to the phone.

"Something's wrong."

He called Ryan back. "Hey, dude. What's going on?"

I couldn't tell much from Nathan's continuous "yup." His anger morphed into another emotion I'd seen too often on Nathan's face.

"I didn't know. Uh-huh."

"Thank you, Ryan. I appreciate you calling me. He's probably at the studio. Reception blows in there."

"Yup! Bye." Nathan ended the call and placed his phone down. He sat down on the edge of the bed.

"Nathan?" I inched up to him and touched his shoulder.

"We have to go home. Get dressed, Bri."

"What? Are you serious? Is Clark okay?"

"Clark's probably fine. Ryan had invited him out tonight, and Clark never showed."

"On a date?"

"Not exactly. I need to talk to Clark. Let's go." Before I could even put my bra on, Nathan had his pants back on and was throwing on his shirt.

## Chapter Forty-Two

The car ride was dead quiet. It was worse than the first time I took Nathan home from the office. We knew each other now. We had weeks under our belt. But he still wasn't talking.

"Nathan, please say something, for fucks sake," I said.

"I can't."

"Why not?"

"I'm afraid of losing you."

"Nathan, come on. What did Ryan say? What spooked you?"

"Do you love Clark, too?"

"I feel like if I say yes, it will hurt you."

"This whole thing is going to rip me in two anyway." He exhaled and continued, "You can say yes, Bri. You're like me. You fall hard when you have feelings for someone."

"Isn't that what we've been hoping for? The three of us loving each other?"

"It's complicated."

"Yeah, when you don't know what the fuck is happening. Talk to me." My frustration level hit a peak.

"Bri, I really don't want to have this conversation in the car."

"Are you going to break up with Clark?" In the back of my mind, I remembered them bickering about

Clark with someone else. Nathan's long pause enhanced my dread.

"If I'm wrong, no. I don't want to end things with him or us." Nathan sounded defeated.

"Nathan, you can't say things like that and keep me in the dark."

"Bri, I have a lot to tell you. Please wait until we get home."

"Can you at least tell me if Clark is physically okay?"

"Yeah, he's home now." Nathan yawned. The windows fogged up from our heated exchange. He switched the blowing heat to defrosters.

"That's good." I only had one text from Clark from hours ago. *-Hope you're having a great time, darling. Take pictures!-* No clue there.

"This is going to be brutal isn't it?" I concluded.

"Which is precisely why I was being quiet."

Nathan's hand had been gripping the stirring wheel so tight it squeaked when he pulled it off. His hand wandered into my lap, and he grabbed mine. It wasn't sweaty like the other times. He was cold as ice.

****

We entered the apartment at three in the morning. Clark sat in the dark watching an old movie. I flipped on the kitchen light.

"I thought you guys were staying in the hotel?" Clark shouted from the couch.

"We were until Ryan called me," Nathan filled in. He wasn't sugarcoating anything. He went right for it.

Clark turned around. He wore his glasses and his usual sleeveless band T-shirt. His eyes looked red as if he had been crying. "You can never trust that fucker," he grunted and joined us in the kitchen.

"Don't you think you should have come to me first if you were having problems with this arrangement?" Nathan said, his calm rushing out the door.

"Why the fuck are you so angry? You have no right to be mad at me!" Clark reprimanded. He glared at Nathan.

"Of course I'm mad, Clark! You went to fucking Ryan before you talked to me!"

"That asshole was supposed to keep his fucking mouth shut, but really who was I supposed to turn to Nathan? Especially after Lee called me. What the hell did you expect me to do?" Clark shouted.

All of Nathan's angst disappeared as he closed the distance between him and Clark. "Lee called you? Oh my God. What happened?" He gripped Clark's shoulder and shouted in his face.

Clark didn't move from his stance. His arms were crossed over his chest tightly. "You just said you talked to Ryan. I called him back after I talked to her. I know everything now!"

"Ryan is even more of a douche than I thought. He didn't mention Lee. Is the baby okay?"

Clark stared at Nathan. He looked up and then slowly nodded. "The baby is fine. She had pains in her side and drove herself to the hospital. She couldn't get anyone on the phone, so she panicked and called me."

"Thank God! Shit, you scared me." His hand drifted away from Clark's shoulder. Nathan took his coat off and draped it over the kitchen island.

"Yup, she's fine and happy her brother-in-law will be living up there with them in his shiny new job and new life."

"Fuck," Nathan said a decibel above a whisper.

My mind blanked as I processed the last few things Clark and Nathan said. Lee was fine, but she and Nathan's brother lived in upstate New York. *What the hell was Clark talking about?*

"What did you just say, Clark?" I asked.

Clark cocked his head in my direction, despair in his eyes. "So, he didn't tell you either. Fucking fantastic. I had hoped he told you." He paused, shook his head, and laughed. "You left us both in the dark? What the fuck were you thinking, Nathan?" Anger laced every word out of Clark's mouth.

Nathan didn't say a word. He stayed turned away, clutching the top of the barstool. "Nathan, please tell me what Clark is talking about? You're leaving?"

Nathan turned around. His face lacked any expression. "I was going to tell you soon."

"Tell me what? Please be very clear on exactly what you were going to tell me soon?" I demanded. The pins and needles climbed up my chest. The space above my heart throbbed with constricting pressure.

"I'm leaving Grant Industries. I accepted a position at Traill Associates. I couldn't talk about it because of the project. I officially start in January after the proposals are done."

"But their main office is upstate?" I cried out.

"I know. I'm going to live with my brother for a while. Baby, I was going to tell you. I almost told you tonight, but I froze up," Nathan confessed.

"You were going to tell me? Anytime you could have told me! How in the world could you keep something this big from us?" I was so fucking angry an odd calm washed over me. My head throbbed above my right eyebrow, but I ignored the pain.

“I messed up,” Nathan muttered.

I waited for more, but that’s all Nathan uttered. I wanted to scream my frustration, but Clark beat me to it.

“That’s it? You messed up? You’re throwing away everything we’ve been trying to build together! How can you just walk away from us, Nathan?” Clark shouted.

“I don’t want to leave you guys. Come on, this isn’t a big deal! So I’ll be a couple hours away during the week. I can come back down on the weekends and we can work it out.” Nathan rationalized.

“Seriously? How is that supposed to work, Nathan? You’ll live your separate life and when you feel like it you’ll come back down here to see us? That’s not a healthy relationship.” Clark slapped his hand on his chest, imitating a heartfelt thought. “I’m glad you thought this through for the three of us.”

“What are the other options then? We scream at each other and walk away with nothing!” Nathan shot back. He clenched his fist and softened his tone. “I’m sorry. I should have said something. Clark, it happened so fast.”

“Fast? I can’t believe anything you’re saying right now. You’ve known for two fucking months! That’s not fast. That’s slow, real fucking slow. What about us? What about Bri?”

Clark tried to rope me back into the shouting match, but I stopped comprehending what just happened. Clark had found out hours ago. This was new for me. A nice and fresh shock wound oozing pus and God knew what else.

I pulled out a chair and sat down. I wanted to shut down everything and crawl up in a corner. I couldn't decide what part hurt more?

Someone said something I missed. My blood rushed around in my head. I looked back up at the angriest I had ever seen Clark.

"If we meant anything to you, you should have told us your master plan. Just fucking saying."

"Will you move past that, Clark? I'm sorry. Yes, I'm fucking leaving! It doesn't change the fact that you're telling Ryan how much you want to be with Bri and leaving me out of this relationship. The only way this can work is if we stay together! You can't fucking steal her away from me!" Nathan spit the words at Clark.

"Nathan, shut up." Nathan tried to continue, but Clark spoke over him. "For God's sake, shut the fuck up," Clark sternly stated. He pinched the bridge of his nose. His breath came out staggered. "Ryan only called about a potential gig and asked me if I wanted to meet up with his band because they were going out for drinks. That's it. I told him a lot of things, and I have no idea what parts he told you. I did tell him I had strong feelings for Bri, and I wasn't sure how to bring the three of us closer together."

"So you aren't snatching up every bit of her free time so she'd love you more? You actually want to still be with me? Ryan made it abundantly clear how you were contemplating continuing your relationship with Bri without me."

"Nathan, I never said I didn't want to be with you. You're messing up everything I told him. This is your grudge against him talking, not you."

“I don’t give a shit about Ryan. Bri was mine first. I invited you into our relationship. You and her were never supposed to be together.”

“Fuck your invitation. You asked me to fuck you both and I did.” Clark paused shaking his head back and forth. “The lines between us have been fucked since day one. We were all over each other without any definition for weeks. How can you stand there and tell me you didn’t want this between all of us?”

“Stop it! You’re just taking jabs at each other. Calm the fuck down so we can talk about this like rational adults.” I got up to stand between them. Both their fists were clenched, and their mouths snarled. They both turned and thankfully their expressions softened.

“I’m sorry, Bri,” Nathan started. “I wanted to be in a relationship with you and Clark together. I still want to be with you.”

“I don’t see how this could actually work. How could you not have told us, Nathan? Every piece of advice people told me was communication. You broke every rule!” Clark added.

“Clark, it won’t be that bad. You two will have each other, and when I come home, we can all be together.”

“You think it’s that fucking easy? You lie to us for two months, and we’re just supposed to trust you again? Crawl out of that thick skull of yours and see the bigger picture, Nathan!”

“Clark, you don’t understand. This is the opportunity of a lifetime. Why are you making this so difficult?”

Clark didn’t answer right away. He gripped his

hips and turned away from us. A low laugh came from Clark's direction.

"What's so funny?" Nathan prodded.

"In the beginning of our relationship, you wanted me to be honest with you. You said that was your one condition, and when we decided to give this a real go, I kept my promise. I even had to push you to be honest with yourself and for what? You dragged me into the best thing that's ever happened to me; meanwhile, you're hiding behind the biggest lie of your life. Now tell me, Nathan, wouldn't you be furious?" Clark managed to say the entire thing without raising his voice or scoffing.

"I didn't want to hurt you." Nathan lifted his hands up in the air and dropped them back down limply to his sides.

"This is worse." Clark let out an uneven breath.

I didn't know where to jump in or even how. This whole scenario went deeper than two men screaming at each other. There was too much to cover, too much to pick at that had gone wrong.

I thought we could do this relationship. We could make this work. But somewhere in the back of my mind I realized, every time we were together, I thought it would be the last. I had squashed my fear, but I knew this would be short term. Something would break us.

*If Nathan left, where did that leave me?*

"Nathan, when do you leave?" I asked timidly.

"January first. If the proposal gets accepted, I might possibly leave after Christmas."

"If we win the bid, you get the job?" I asked. *What?*

"There's a possibility this falls through if Grant

doesn't get it."

"Are you fucking serious? Now you might not go? What kind of fucked up emotional roller coaster is this shit?" Clark added.

"*I don't know!* I don't fucking know! This got so messed up!" Nathan was so disheveled. He yanked off his suit jacket and threw it on the island. He paced back and forth.

Every day in the office replayed in my mind. This was part of his plan. Nathan had been dedicated to this project from day one and pushed everyone to excel and succeed. He knew the whole time. If we won, he'd be gone.

*I helped my own fucking relationship end.*

"Bri, are you okay?" Clark asked. Tentative Clark was always looking out for me.

I must have been pale as a ghost. I was in shock, denial, and every stage of what the fuck crashed into my mind. I closed my gaping mouth, shook my head, and released my rant.

"Nathan. Turn around." He did what I asked. "I've seen you almost every day for two months, and at any time you could have told me. Especially the fact that I'm working my fucking ass off so you can get a better job! I have never felt so betrayed."

"Baby, it's not like that."

"Nathan, I've been here the whole time. There is no way to manipulate a different story, or are we going to go rehash the shame shit?"

Nathan walked up to me and put his hands on my face. "Then come with me. Pack your bags and make the move. You know Traill's capabilities. I can get you a position. Clark, please come with us. Start a new band, and we can be together again. We can get one big apartment." He turned toward Clark and put his hand on his shoulder.

"Do you realize what you're asking?" I said, but my voice cracked beneath my tears. I was getting more upset every moment.

"It could work. We'd be starting over and hopefully it'll bring us back together."

Nathan looked genuine in his plea. We'd be hours from home. It would be a whole new life.

"Nate. I'm sorry. I can't go with you," Clark admitted first. Nathan flinched. Clark took Nathan's hand off his shoulder and walked back toward the kitchen island. He leaned down onto his elbows and placed his hands on his forehead.

"Bri? Will you come with me?"

With Clark answering first, I knew my answer. A part of me wished I could say yes, the part that fell in love with Nathan. A bigger part of me tugged me elsewhere.

Epiphanies are funny. They can happen exactly when you needed them. In this moment, I worried about leaving Clark more. If I went with Nathan, I'd lose Clark and that would be too much to bear. *But Nathan could still stay?*

"I don't know if I can answer you right now. We don't know anything final yet," I said.

Nathan exhaled. "Bri, I'm pretty confident it's a go. We worked too good together." He caressed my cheek. "I'm so sorry, I ruined your night. You're giving me no choice. I feel like the biggest asshole in the world, but I'm sorry. I have to let you go."

"What? Your breaking up with me?" *I don't*

*fucking believe it.*

"The only way I can do this is if I make a clean break. I can do this without you." Nathan crossed his arms over his chest and tightened his muscles. "Yeah, that's how this is going down. I can do it on my own."

"Nathan, come on. You threw a grenade on the floor and expected us to drop everything and move with you? This is so unfair," I accused.

"Life is unfair. I can't back out now."

"Nathan!" I said, but he backed away from us. Clark just stared at him, disbelief in his eyes.

"Who are you right now?" Clark asked. He looked at Nathan like it was the first time ever seeing him. "You're being a selfish prick!

"Well, now I'm out. I'm taking myself out of the equation."

"Seriously? You're not going to fight for us? If you want Bri to go with you, fucking fight for her, Nathan; if you want me, fight for me!" His facial expression screamed.

"Clark, it's over. You won. You get the girl of your dreams. You can take all her time without sharing her with me." Nathan's voice was flat and emotionless. He glanced over at me. "Bri, be with Clark. He won't love you, but he'll make you happy.

"Stop it, Nathan. You're being cruel," I demanded.

"I can't. I need the closure." He pointed at Clark. "Do you know Clark has never told me he loves me? He still holds back. I'm not going to fight for someone who can't love."

"You know I love you." Clark spit the words out.

"Then say it, Clark. Say you love me," Nathan demanded. He leaned toward Clark.

Clark opened his mouth and closed it. "After tonight, I don't know if I can say it to you."

"See. You're still trapped in your own fucking misery. I hope you can manage to say I love you to her. She is the best thing to ever happen to you. Don't fuck it up."

Clark stood there, his eyes burning red. "Fuck you, Nathan. We're done."

Nathan held his stance strong. Clark's anger dissipated when he turned to me. The scowl wasn't meant for me. A slight lift of his brow and twitch of his mouth told me everything I needed to know. This was all directed at Nathan.

I leaned forward to touch him, but he stepped away.

Clark stomped to his bedroom, slamming the door shut. Nathan stared after him.

"Nathan, I love you. I don't want you to leave. If you give us more time, I'm sure we can figure something out."

"We're out of time. It's over," Nathan said quietly. He flicked his eyes toward me once and dragged his gaze back down the hallway.

Nathan's calmness disturbed me. He shook with anger moments ago. Now his chest barely rose with each breath. His arms were slack at his sides.

Eventually he ran his hand through his hair, gripped the root and yanked hard. He shook his head and walked over to the barstool, climbing on, and put his head down onto his folded arms.

The last two months just collapsed into absolute ruin. It would be wrong to console Nathan or Clark.

*No one was left to console me.*

## Chapter Forty-Three

The stab of pain in my foot's insole reminded me I was still standing, waiting for one of them to come to me.

"Nathan…I'm going home," I said to his back. He didn't move, not even a flinch. This happened so fast, I forgot I still had my coat on. I just had to pick up my purse and walk out the door. My pink mug sat in the drain board. If I took it, this would be officially over.

Nathan perked his head up, but didn't turn around. "It's too late to drive home. Take my bed, I'll…"

Clark's door opened. He remerged wearing his jacket and carrying a duffle bag. "We're leaving."

"What?" Nathan asked, whirling around.

Clark paused. "I don't want to say anything else I can't take back. If I stay, I'll regret it."

"No. Stay here. Leave her here," Nathan said meekly.

"Nathan, shut the fuck up. Bri, please come with me."

Clark hoisted his bag higher on his shoulders. He walked toward me and held out his hand. I grabbed it and picked up my purse. He grabbed his keys and tugged me toward the door. Before the door shut shielding Nathan from me, he buried his head in his hands and walked down the hallway.

Clark pulled at my hand faster than I could walk in

my heels. "Clark, stop." He didn't slow down until we were at the elevators.

"I can't let you stay there with him," Clark said.

"Are you okay to drive?" I asked, out of breath.

"Yes. Can I have your keys?"

I handed him my keys. His face was etched in a scowl. In the light of the elevator, the puffiness around his eyes exposed his sadness. He sniffled, fighting off his reaction. The more distance from Nathan dripped tears down my cheeks.

We got to my car, and Clark glanced back at the apartment building doors one last time. He unlocked my doors and got in the driver's seat. The last hope that Nathan followed us abandoned.

Clark turned the heat up full blast and sat there waiting. He laid his forehead on the top of the steering wheel.

We sat in complete silence except for the warm air hissing through the vents. I rubbed his back, and he jerked his head up.

"If you want to go back to him, please do it now." His voice reverberated with his pent up anger.

If I got out of my car, it would be over between Clark and me. I did nothing wrong in this mess, but I'd be an ignorant fool not to read between the lines. If I went back to Nathan right now, I'd be forfeiting Clark.

*Fuck you, Nathan. This is your fault.*

"Drive me home, Clark."

His face remained emotionless and frozen. There was no triumph that he got the girl, no reaction at my choice, nothing at all. My body shivered from the rejection, the cold numbness enveloped me.

He flipped the vents more toward me. It wasn't

going to help this time.

He backed out of the unmarked parking spot and turned out of his apartment complex. He didn't put the radio on. Our uneven breathing filled the space.

At a traffic light Clark murmured, "How could he do that to us? What the fuck is wrong with him?"

"He wasn't thinking."

"Duh, Captain Obvious," Clark snapped back.

"Hey, don't get snippy with me. It's not my fault. I'm mad too!"

"He knew this would end us. That's why he sneaked it around. This is why I can't trust people. The second you let them in, they pull stupid stunts. *Ahhh!*

"I thought I was finally done," Clark muttered.

I couldn't read his blank expression. For someone who'd showed me so much of himself I sat in the dark. "Done with what?" I asked.

"Are you done, Bri?"

"With Nathan?"

"No. I'm asking if you're done searching, fucking scanning through crowds for someone to catch your eye, done with the games? Are you ready to be with someone for the rest of your life?"

This was not the time to blurt out an answer. He was hurt.

"I think so."

"I'm sorry, that's not a good enough answer. I need a yes or no, and please tell me the fucking truth. This is not the right time to lie." Clark looked like he was out on a ledge, begging me to pull him back inside. Anger still loomed in this gaze.

"Clark, you're angry and hurt. Calm down please. I'm telling the truth."

"You're not fully listening either! I can't trust anyone right now!"

"I am listening! You want me to tell you that when I met you and Nathan, I thought I was done for the rest of my life? I can't! No one can that fast. I know I fell in love, but I don't know about the rest! That's the truth!"

"Then what are we fucking doing, Bri? I'm not good for you. I'm a musician who can't pay my rent without some corporate prick to help me out. I have a cat and guitars. That's me. I have nothing to offer you."

Clark's self-deprecating words threw me. Since day one, there had been nothing but the confident, sexy, headstrong Clark who got what he wanted. He had so much to offer me. He had to be spiraling from the pain.

"Clark, why are you poking fucking holes into our relationship for no reason! You're mad at Nathan! I'm mad at Nathan! Why are you trying to ruin us too?"

"The holes were already there. This is why I don't do committed relationships. It's messy and dirty and twists you fucking inside out. I trusted Nathan and look where I am. It's only a matter of time before you leave me too."

"You can trust me."

"Can I really trust you, Bri?" Clark said. His uncertainty fucking pissed me off.

"Of course you can. When have I showed you I'm not trustworthy? Where is this coming from? I thought you and I were good!"

"You came into this relationship on a lie. You lied to Nathan about the party."

"Now, you're using that against me? What the fuck, Clark? I explained why I did it. It was fucking stupid, and I didn't mean for it to go that far. As soon as

Nathan figured it out, I told him everything. I have nothing to lie about now. I want to be with you! How many ways do I have to say it?"

He didn't say anything. He sucked in his cheek, holding back. I said his name and got a no response.

"Clark, why are you pushing me away too?"

"I'm not, I just…fuck. I'm afraid of everything right now. If you have anything to come clean about, you better fucking tell me."

"I have nothing to admit! You know it all!"

"It's impossible for me to know what you're thinking."

"You know what I mean! I've told you more than I've probably told Nathan. Look, I'm here and I chose to go home with you. Isn't that enough?"

"We weren't supposed to be together this way. This is all wrong."

"Then what do you want, Clark? Do you want me to confess my love for you? Do you want me to never see Nathan again?"

"I think I need some space to clear my head."

I was losing this battle. It was a completely unfair fight.

"I'm ready to give you everything, and you want space? Wow, I guess I know where I stand with you."

"You know nothing, Bri. You don't want my love, trust me. It's too much for one person to handle."

"Is that why you wouldn't say it to Nathan? If you said it maybe this would have a chance to be real?"

"This has always been real for me. If I say I love you, that's it. I'll love you more than you could ever think a person could love another person. I'd want every little bit of you for myself. You wouldn't be able to breathe, I'd love you that much. I'm a fucking parasite feeding off my host when I love. I wouldn't wish it on anyone, especially you."

"I want you to love me."

"You say that now. The last three people I loved left me. If I say it, you'll be gone. Nathan doesn't remember, but I said it to him twice and look where we are. I said it to Katie, and she barely left anything behind. I'm still missing something she took from me." Clark nodded his head back and forth, fighting back his own emotions.

*I don't know what to do.* I had my fair share of breakups, but this one would be the ultimate, changing me forever.

"Clark, you are the most attentive and caring person I've ever met. I liked you since the moment I met you. You've accepted me exactly as I am and even brought back parts of me I forgot I liked. My whole world changed when you came into the picture. I don't want to imagine my life without you.

"I can't change your past, but I can give you a better future. I'm mad at Nathan for leaving, but I'm furious that he hurt you. I promise I will never do that to you."

Clark kept driving and staring out at the dark road.

"Bri, please don't make promises you can't keep. I'm sorry for lashing out at you, but this is your chance to end this shit. We can all go our separate ways and pick up the pieces of ourselves before this gets any worse."

My tears scorched my skin. They burned my eyes and held my response captive in my throat.

Clark's voice found its softness once again.

However, his words stung like hell. "I'm giving you an exit, Bri. Take it, darling. You deserve so much more than only me."

"No, Clark. I want to be with you," I said. My gut told me I made the right decision. This path found me, and I wanted to stay on it.

"I'm going to give you until the morning to think about it," Clark said.

"Didn't you hear me? I choose you, Clark. I want to be with you!"

"It's been a long night, Bri. When we get to your place, please get some sleep. We'll talk about it in the morning."

I looked at him in disbelief. He purposely ignored my confessions. Defeat filled my thoughts. I thought I'd be all right if I had him.

*I truly had nothing.*

## Chapter Forty-Four

When we reached my apartment, the sun poked over the horizon. Two heartbroken zombies ascended the flight of stairs toward my door. Tiredness seized my body like a crested wave, attempting to pull me under. I fought it too much tonight.

I handed my keys to Clark, and he opened the door. We both stood in the foyer for a few moments until Clark moved. He headed over to the violated couch I never wanted to look at again. He dropped his bag, took off his shoes, and collapsed onto the couch.

I willed myself to move toward my bedroom. My body screamed at me from every part. I chucked off my shoes and removed my coat. My dress clung to my curves, but I ran out of the energy needed to take it off.

I slumped onto the bed and pulled myself into the tightest ball I could muster. The second my head hit my pillow, I sobbed. My eyes burned from the remnants of my eyeliner. I couldn't stop the hiccups and muffled sounds against my pillow.

*How did this night cause the obliteration of my world?* Nathan and Clark were done. Clark and I were done. *Had I been the glue that had held them together? It didn't seem that way in the beginning or did I not see it?* Erotic moments flashed through my mind. My body had the fucking nerve to react; a surge of pleasure crawled through the base of my stomach. I sobbed harder.

My door creaked opened. *What could he possibly say to make any of this better?* The three of us were broken.

The bed creaked from Clark's weight, and he draped his hands over my waist. I curled tighter into my comfort ball, trying to keep him out.

"Please let me in, Bri. You don't have to cry alone," Clark said, pulling me against his chest. My body relented to him. Tiredness overruled my ability to fight.

He planted small kisses along the back of my neck, my exposed shoulder. I interlocked our hands together and drew our fists into my stomach, hurting myself from the unbearable tightness.

"Turn around, Bri. I want to see you." I flinched. I couldn't help it. My tailspin into despair stole my reasonable actions away. His words weren't strong enough right now to tug me back.

Clark let me go, and I cried louder. He crawled over my body to lie in front of me, brushing my hair away from my face. I turned my head away from him.

"Please look at me. Everything is going to be okay," Clark pleaded, trying to turn my shoulders toward him.

"No. We're broken."

"Shhh. You're okay." Clark wrapped his arms around me and tucked my head under his chin. I grabbed onto his T-shirt, letting him hold me. I drenched his shirt with my tears. His strong hands smoothed over my hair repeatedly, but my body shook relentlessly against his stiff one.

"Darling, please stop crying. You're going to make

yourself sick. Go to sleep, it'll help."

I shook my head. I wrapped my arms around his shoulders falling into his available embrace. His grip tightened around my waist, crushing our bodies together. He smelled like their apartment—his cologne, trees, and fresh ocean soap. He suffocated me, reminding me of what I was losing. A big sob wrenched itself from my throat.

"Bri, stop crying. You still have me." Clark's last admission struck me hard in the chest. I retreated from his haven like he burned me.

*How could he say that after what he said in the car?* He can't love me if he didn't love Nathan. He can't love anyone. He won't fucking let himself get close enough…

A tear escaped his right eye. I wanted to kiss his cheek where it fell, but I stopped myself. Anger from before surged over my body. *I needed to know exactly what he meant by I still had him.*

"I still have you? What the fuck does that mean, Clark? You practically pushed me out of your life in the car! Don't play me too. Either you want to be with me or you don't. Do you love me? Will you finally force yourself to say those stupid words?" I hated that my voice trembled. Doubt clouded my thoughts.

*What if he said no?*

"Bri, I…I don't know," Clark said barely audible in the unchanging silence of the morning.

"You don't know? You don't know if you love me? I don't fucking believe you. What the fuck is this!"

A shudder wreaked havoc on my body. This was not a panic attack, I was unraveling. I should be disgusted by his answer, but instead I pulled him closer.

I acted only on instinct, only the deep burning in my heart. I slammed my mouth against his, forcing my way into his heart like he'd done countless times. His mouth caught my onslaught and matched it kiss for kiss. I thought he had kissed me hard before, compelling me to feel him, to see past his light heartedness to the tormented man below, but no. This kiss was on another level of feelings.

We clawed ourselves into each other, attempting once and for all to not fall apart.

Clark unclasped the top of my dress. In another life, he fastened me up awaiting for my other man, his man, to whisk me away from him. His sad demeanor led up to this startling moment. Now, my body fought for a reaction from him. This had to be love. He had to admit it.

"Please let this be what I think it is! Please!" I said against his mouth.

Clark's answer was silence. His lips returned to mine. I shook my head. I needed to hear those fucking words.

I ripped the dress off me once he pulled down the zipper. I tore my mouth away from his to rid myself of the fabric. Clark captured my breath, my air, my very life force with his crushing lips the second the garment let my mouth be free again. I wish I had the strength to rip his shirt off him. I needed to feel his body against mine, branding me once and for all.

He yanked his shirt off his body and dove down to his pants. I raked my hands over his chest, feeling the soft hair against my palm. I couldn't bear a moment if we weren't touching. It would bring the crying back. I'd crumble down.

Clark's sweat pants and boxers were off, his cock hard. I pushed him down onto his back and straddled his lap. His gaze followed my hand as I wrapped my fingers around his cock. His legs were cold, but his cock was on fire. He could burn my pussy alive if only he said what I needed to hear.

More light shone through my blinds, and I saw his pained expression. It stopped me from sinking down onto him. His breath came out fast, uneven. He held in his emotional spiral. The uncertainty plastered on his face halted my frenzy. His body told me one thing, but his expression killed me.

He nodded, but that wasn't what I wanted. The passion didn't reach his eyes or his mouth this time. He was stripped of his dirty words and his absolute abandon when it came to fucking me alone.

If I had to, I'd rip the words from this throat. I'd beg him to give me everything. "No, Clark! Where are you? I want to hear you!" I screamed in his face.

He wanted me to let him in, fine. I'd let him see how distraught he made me.

Clark winced and shut his eyes. He thrust his head back on my pillows and gripped my waist. I hovered over his body on my knees, holding myself up off his cock. His hands brought me down against him, but I held off.

"No. You wanted Nathan to fight for you; well, I'm fighting for you now. Talk to me. Please! If you're here to be with me, fucking do it! Don't shut down when I'm giving you what you want!" I pleaded. His teeth crunched down on his bottom lip; he said nothing.

I lifted off him, and a barely audible no escaped his lips. His grip on my waist tightened bringing me down onto his thighs. My pussy skidded over his cock. I held back a whimper. I wanted desperately for him to thrust up into me and hear him choke out those three words. *I wouldn't let him show me only in lovemaking. Not this time.*

*He needed to say it or get the fuck out of my bed.*

Clark sat up, sliding into the darkness clinging against my bedframe. I still made out his face, his five o'clock shadow more prominent than earlier. His gaze roamed my body.

"Clark?" I said softer and put my hands on his cheeks. They were warmer now. The coldness subsided. I kissed him while his teeth held strong onto his bottom lip. I stopped. *If he wasn't going to fight for me while we were alone, what the fuck was I doing?*

I sighed and lifted off his body. The tears of rejection fell down my face. His hands scrambled for me, but I broke his grasp.

"No, Bri. Please, don't stop pushing me." Each word grew louder, his voice and nerve growing.

Off his body, my thoughts ran clearer with each tear falling. "No, I'm not going to force you to say something you don't mean. I'm not going to show you love that won't be returned. I need more than just your body telling me you want me." I took a deep breath. "You're not in love with me."

Clark tucked me underneath him, laying his body over mine. He moved to kiss me, but I turned my head. Clark let out a frustrated sigh. I looked him dead in the eye. "You can't kiss me again until you say I love you."

He released his imprisoned lip from his teeth and made his decision.

"I love you, Bri. I'm sorry, you had to force me to

say it out loud. I love you. I love you so fucking much. I loved you the moment your breath caught when you saw me in a towel. I loved you when you let Nathan keep fucking you on that desk so I could watch. I loved you when you hated that cover song at the wedding. I loved you when you got on your knees and brought me some shred of peace at the studio. I loved you when you saw me, the real me. I'm so fucking sorry this turned out this way. Everything is so fucked up."

"I love you too. I…" Clark stopped me by giving me the kiss I always wanted. A kiss empowered by love, fueled by passion, obliterating my doubt. He loved me. I felt guilty I forced it out of him, but I needed to hear it to believe it.

Clark's softness and tenderness fled from his actions after he confessed. His unhinged actions pulled me into his tailspin. He ended the kiss, letting go of my hands, and lifted my hips, burying his face in my pussy. He was ravenous, enveloping my whole cunt, licking me wet. I cried out, driving my freed hands into his hair.

"Say it again, Bri. Say you love me. Say it while I fuck your sweet cunt with my tongue."

"Clark, I love you. Oh God, I love you."

"I've been waiting to hear you say it. I'm a coward for not saying it sooner."

He dove back down into my wet folds, fucking my pussy with his rigid tongue. His hands spread out around my ass. He gasped for breath and lifted up.

He lay down on the bed, beckoning me to come over him. "Use my cock, darling. Push us to the stars. I love you so much."

I gripped his cock in my hand and lowered myself

down onto him. He sat up, his mouth latching onto my nipple. I cradled his head pushing up and down on his cock harder. He pulled back my hands and held them behind me. My breasts thrust forward. As I thrust down he fucked up. *We were together. Finally.*

I was already coming on his cock, fucking him in frenzy above him. He jerked up hard, twisting me onto my back, and growled into my neck. He said I love you over and over and fucked me all over again.

I barely held onto his shoulders and my breath caught against his kisses. Even after we separated, Clark gripped me tightly. "Never stop pushing me, Bri. I need you more than anything." I fell asleep with his breath on my neck and peace only Clark managed to bring forth.

## Chapter Forty-Five

When I woke up, I was cold. The blanket covered me, but someone was missing behind me. I opened my eyes and squinted in the sunlight.

Clark sat fully dressed on the edge of my bed hunched over his knees. Part of me was relieved he hadn't left. The other part dreaded the next few minutes.

"You're leaving?" I asked.

"I have to go. I promise I'll come back. I still love you." Clark stroked up my leg. I sat up and pulled my legs together, hugging them tight, away from his touch.

"Please stay," I pleaded.

"I can't," Clark said.

"I fought for you."

"You did, and I'm forever grateful."

"It's not enough to make you stay?"

"I give you my word I'll be back."

"Tonight?"

"Soon. I love you," Clark said, staring deeply into my eyes. Hurt trapped my answer. He leaned back onto the bed and kissed me.

My lips puckered, even though my mind shut down the usual reaction to Clark. The empty kiss, held nothing in it.

"I have to go. Dillon's here. I'll call you."

Without looking back, he walked out of my

bedroom. By some saving grace unbeknownst to me, I fell back to sleep. I dreaded waking up. In my dream, we were here, smiling, and laughing together.

I woke up to an empty bed. Clark didn't change his mind. He wouldn't be in the bathroom or on the couch. *He's gone.* Sleep gave me no renewed energy, no spike to go on. I pushed myself to check my apartment, but his duffle bag was gone.

Numbness dictated my actions now. I picked up the glass bowl I never put candy in and slammed it on the ground.

My phone buzzed, but I ignored it. It buzzed again and again.

I peeked against my better judgment. An unknown number texted me repeatedly. I crunched over the broken glass with my slippers and picked up my phone.

*-Clark's here. What the fuck happened? Call me as soon as you can. I'll kick him in the nuts if he hurt you.-*

*-Who is this?-* I texted back.

*-Cleo. Call me!-*

I called her. Even though I seized with anger, I needed to know about Clark.

"Cleo?"

"I've been trying to get you forever. He locked himself in my bathroom. What the fuck happened?" She sounded like she ran a marathon before answering the phone. Her raspy voice shrieked into the phone.

"Cleo, leave him alone. He needs time to be alone."

"What the fuck does that mean?"

"We broke up. He told me he loved me and then he couldn't fucking deal with it."

"I'm going to kill him. It'll be easier. I'll get out in

a few years."

"Seriously? You're one scary ass bitch."

"Only when I need to be and I like you, which is why I'm not getting what happened. Where's Nathan? Does he know Clark is hiding over here?"

"Cleo…I…" More sobs wreaked havoc on my body. I crumbled to the floor with my back to the wall.

Cleo let out a loud enough groan to hear over the phone. "*Speaker phone now!*"

I almost hit the end call button, but ultimately hit the speaker phone button.

"I'm here," I said.

"Look, Bri, Clark is like my brother. I have never seen him so upset. Where's Nathan?"

"I don't know. Probably sitting in a dark room sweating to death."

"Um yeah not funny. Help me here, woman! How could three people break up this badly over one night? You posted the cutest picture of Nathan and you less than twelve hours ago. What happened?"

"Nathan's leaving us, Cleo. He got a new job and is moving upstate. He's known for months and didn't tell us. Clark and him are finished. Then I kind of forced Clark into admitting he loved me. He said he needed time to figure shit out because he's afraid I'll be like his ex-wife and Nathan. I told him I could be done looking for someone new, but he didn't believe me."

"Oh," Cleo said. The phone went quiet for the longest time. I peeked at the screen. The duration of the call still climbed.

I heard knocking over the phone, and Cleo screamed something I couldn't understand. *What did Cleo just do?*

"Bri, are you there?" Clark's voice said quietly. I tensed at the sound of his voice. "I'm sorry, darling. I don't want it to be like this between us. I want to be…" I hit the end button.

He took the fucking easy way out, and now I'm left with nothing. I stopped crying and anger took over.

Around three o'clock someone knocked on my door. I stupidly didn't check the peep hole and almost passed out when I saw Nathan standing in my hallway.

"Nathan," I whispered. I'd never seen him look this bad before. He wore a baseball cap, sweats, and a T-shirt under his coat. Not Nathan's style at all.

"Can I come in?" he asked.

"Why?" I quickly retorted.

"I owe you an explanation." He had the decency to look down.

"Now?"

"It's now or never."

"Clark isn't here."

"I know."

I stepped back, and he entered my apartment. He leaned in to kiss me, but I only gave him my cheek.

"I deserve that," Nathan said.

He got points for coming here, but I never started keeping score. I already saw the outcome of this in my mind. The inevitable fucking sucked.

"Have a seat." I walked toward my table. "Do you want a drink?"

"No, baby."

I flinched. I'd been baby since the night we first met. The intimate switch had taken over immediately. The words had urged me on, letting me be bold. Now, it meant nothing.

I sat down, and Nathan sat next to me at the small table. He nudged his chair closer so our knees touched. I inched my leg away.

"Talk. I'll listen," I said.

"Remember the day you found me sitting on the floor outside the office? I lied to you. I didn't lock myself out. I accepted the job with Traill Associates that morning. Mr. Grant orchestrated the whole thing. I interviewed with Traill a week before the big meeting. I was so nervous I would get the job and I did."

"Why didn't you tell Clark then?"

"He was on tour, and I didn't want to ruin it for him. His divorce had just gotten finalized after two years, and he sounded so happy when he called. I couldn't bring myself to tell him."

"I understand. You do realize you made this a thousand times worse."

"I know." Nathan placed his elbows on the table and dragged his fingers over his face.

"Bri, this job is everything I've ever wanted. There's opportunities, benefits, travel, and over one hundred thousand a year. This is the hardest decision I've made in my life. I can't pass it up."

Nathan was like me. A worker ant fighting its way to the top. I'd busted my ass dozens of times to get noticed at work. If I got a chance like this, I'd probably take it too.

"I don't know what to say to make this better. I feel like a selfish prick right now. I think I'm making the right decision."

"Why does it have to be upstate?" I said.

"The main office is up there now. Maybe in a couple of months we can open a Manhattan branch, and

I can come back?" Nathan looked hopeful.

I gave him a doubtful look. He's clutching at straws, scrambling for a way to make this work.

"Nathan, be realistic."

"I don't want to leave you."

"It's too late. You're already leaving."

"Yeah, but it doesn't have to be this way. We can try things. We can Skype during the week, meet up on weekends; we can be in each other's lives. People do it every day. They live apart from their loved ones."

"And then what? It goes strong for a few weeks, then we both get busy, and the calls are fewer, the attempts weak. We barely made time for each other in the last few weeks."

"But you and Clark are strong now, right? He can keep you company while I'm gone."

"Are you serious right now? Did you really think Clark would be a solution to your problem? What the fuck is wrong with you?"

"If you have him, you won't miss me." His voice descended slightly above a whisper.

"Nathan, shut up. Do you want to be with me? Do you want to try to make this work? Please forget every bullshit excuse, and tell me the truth."

Nathan's eyes turned red, tears pooling. I found myself numb. I would sit here for hours waiting for his inevitable answer. I couldn't let myself fight another man to admit he loved me.

*I broke the last one.*

"I want to give myself a chance to make something of the new job. You'd have less of me than you do now. You deserve everything I won't be able to give to you."

Finally, Nathan gave me the truth. It was shitty, but

I understood it. It screamed closure, an end.

"Thank you for your honesty, Nathan."

His tears crested and ran down his cheeks. He sniffled and got up from the table, heading to the kitchen. I hoped he didn't find me heartless. I was not sure if I could cry anymore today. Clark took my tears. *Clark.* My heart had pounded in my chest when he walked out of the apartment. I was devastated.

For Nathan, I didn't quite have the same reaction.

I followed him into my kitchen. Nathan hiccupped over the sink. I wrapped my hands around him and gripped him tight.

The heat off his back suffocated me, but I gave him the comfort he needed. It broke the dam on my tears. I sobbed into the back of his shirt.

I stumbled when he stepped forward and let go of my fingers. He caught me though. Nathan pulled me up onto the counter and kissed me. I opened my legs for him to kiss me deeper and crushed his body against my breasts. His hands cupped my face, and I held onto his forearms. His lips felt so good, calming, soothing. His love felt like a distant promise.

Nathan pulled away, but I held on. He gave me what I wanted. We made out long enough that my lips ached when we parted.

"I'm sorry, Brianna." *No more baby for me*. "Do you want me to stay? I can hold you," he offered.

"No. I'll be all right."

"I'm so sorry."

I hopped off the counter and led him to the door. He apologized again. It helped hearing it over and over. He kissed me once more and left. I lingered at the door and watched him walk down the stairs.

## Chapter Forty-Six

I barely got out of bed until Monday afternoon. I called in sick. Out of some true form of masochism, I kidded myself I was okay. It didn't last long. The emotional whiplash returned, and I cried all over again. It hurt to talk, to move, it…my heart hurt.

Lucy came over that night. "Okay, girlie. We're set. I got cookie dough, horror movies, and eye drops."

"Seriously, I'm fine. I knew it wasn't going to last."

"You're doing some crazy damage control to yourself. You're hurt."

"Of course, I'm crushed, but I knew it. Something told me not to get invested in those boys."

"Let me see your trash can."

"What?"

"I'm not believing this bullshit that you're 'over it.' Your eyes are puffy-ass dumplings right now. When did you stop crying?"

I tried my hardest to put up a strong front. It was too weak to last. The sorrow peeked through. They had gotten into my head, and my heart wouldn't bounce back after hours of crying.

"You know me too well." I laughed. The laugh became more tears. Lucy hugged me, and I cried for who knew how long.

"Nathan asked about you. He looked pale. It's like

his flare is gone. He just looked like a shell."

"What did you tell him?"

"I ignored him until I got sick of him following me. He needs to learn that he fucked up. You can't play around with people like he did with you and Clark."

"I get it. What did you eventually tell him?"

"I told him you're devastated. I'm not sugarcoating shit for him. He's leaving you too, and Clark is a fucking coward for not being here. That upset him more. He didn't try to pawn you off on Clark, did he?"

"He says he didn't do it intentionally, but fuck it. Can you believe a word he says?"

I shrugged. My eyes burned back a fresh wave of tears. I left Lucy in the living room and retrieved more eye drops.

We watched some movies, ate our weight in moo shu and candy. An inexplicable tiredness came over me. Nathan texted me early in the morning and late at night, apologizing again and let me know he would be at his office all week to give me some space. I didn't answer him.

Would the distance help? Probably not. I was mad and upset and fucking defeated. I wanted to finish this project and move on with my life without him. I barely let my mind wander to the dismissal from Clark. At least Nathan texted me…Clark sent absolutely nothing.

# Chapter Forty-Seven

I knew he would come to the office. He had to be here today. He wouldn't forfeit the new job over our mess.

It was four forty-five p.m., and I'd officially bit off every nail. Paul assured me Nathan would be here. I needed him to help me with the presentation; I couldn't lose my job either.

My nerves were shot. My eye twitched as the computer screen blurred. *I can't fuck this up. I can't. We can't.*

I raised my head at the knock on the cubicle. For once, I didn't jump. Paul looked over the top. "Are you ready? The clients will be here in twenty minutes." I swallowed and nodded.

Each step weighed me down as if I walked through a vat of jelly. Thick, slow, and threatening to push me back. I had to do this now and think about the rest later.

Through the glass wall of the conference room, one man with perfect-slicked back hair sat in a chair at the far end. Of course, he'd be early. His future depended on it.

"Hey, Nathan, we've missed you! I can't wait to see their faces with this pitch!" Paul ran toward Nathan with an outreached hand, leaving me out in the open with nowhere to hide. Nathan smiled at Paul and shook his hand. His gaze drifted toward me, and I meekly waved.

Nathan looked sad and tired. His work demeanor looked seamless, but his eyes had lost his light. We were almost in the same spot the second time we met. The anxious man with sweaty palms was frozen for words.

Paul placed his hand on my arm. “Bri? Can you get the spots ready? Nathan play around with the clicker. It can be tricky.”

Paul scurried from between Nathan and me. Our buffer was lost. We had to speak to each other.

“Bri. I’m…It’s nice to see you. I’ve missed…” Nathan leaned toward me and kissed my cheek. *Oh, how I wanted to turn my face for a kiss.* The want was so strong, I gasped. Paul looked up, grimaced, and went back to prepping the room.

“Nathan, let’s get through this meeting. We worked too hard to flake out now. Okay?”

He looked hurt, but the emotion faded into determination. “Okay. Did you read over the final pages I added to the deck?”

“Yes. I like the closing statement. You did a great job.”

“Thank you. So did you.”

Paul placed the bundle of folders with the presentation in my hand. It broke the spell of our awful small talk. Marcia stepped into the conference room and the other team members. I’d been such a space cadet, I forgot to gather everyone else. But this project from Day One had been Nathan and me.

I placed the folders on each of the fifteen spots. Nathan’s eyes burned a hole into my skull. He watched my every move. I looked up and thankfully he looked away. My anxiety fed off the unwanted heat intensifying its grip on me. I had to remind myself that soon it would be over.

*I hope…*

I sat next to Nathan when the room was prepped, and rolled my chair as close as possible to him without being in his lap. He inched his chair the last inch to make the armrests touch and slid his knee against mine.

"Bri, you should start us off. I'll handle the…" Nathan began until Marcia cut him off.

Marcia talked to the room, going over the game like she knew what was supposed to go down. Nathan let her shine for the moment, but redirected the attention back to us.

"Thank you, Marcia. Bri and I will take it from here," Nathan interjected. He started the slideshow and adjusted the lighting on the projector. The past few months looked simple up on the screen. Twenty slides of perfection. Twenty ways to make sure Nathan gets the job he wanted. This will benefit me too in the long run. I'll lose my boyfriend, but I'll gain brownie points with the company.

Technically, Nathan and I forgot to practice our tag team cues, and I wasn't supposed to know about his impending departure. However, when the clients arrived, our chemistry-infused pitch shined with everything we'd worked so hard to do.

And we fucking rocked it.

After Nathan narrated the closing statements, the clients smiled and accepted our proposal without hesitation. This double-edged sword achievement was complete. He had been right. We did our job too fucking well.

A dissatisfying rush washed over me. I sucked in my stomach and held my breath, waiting for the joy to burst out of my mouth. Instead of victory, I heard silence. Everyone cheered and clapped. I only had an annoying monotone buzz filtering out the merriment.

Nathan's hand touched mine, and I snapped back into place. The cacophony of muttering noise pierced my ears. I didn't look up at him. I couldn't do it. His face would tumble me down.

He handed me the tablet and stylus to finalize the deal. I wrote my name under Nathan's and handed the tablet over to the Traill team. I shook Declan Traill's hand, the head of the company. I thanked them for coming and secretly cursed them for the heartache.

When they disappeared down the hallway, Paul shouted, "We did it!" Everybody clapped for us. It was over. Everything would kick off in the New Year and Nathan would move over to them. He just had to walk out to the door and not look back.

His footsteps behind me told me otherwise.

Nathan's large gait caught up to me by the time I got back to my cubicle. I set my laptop down and my own packet.

"Bri, please say something to me."

"Congratulations on your new job."

"Don't be like this. Please, look at me."

I turned toward him. His brow was wet from his anxious sweat, his top dress shirt buttons were undone, his eyes were watery, and his face blotchy red from unshed tears. *At least this wasn't easy for him either.*

"What, Nathan?"

"We have to talk. I can't stand this anymore."

"What's left to talk about?"

"Clark."

Clark hadn't contacted me in the past two weeks. I listened to his music on constant repeat.

"Did he come home?"

Nathan shook his head. "He comes back when I'm not home to feed Amora, and then goes back to Cleo's. Cleo's allergic to cats so um, yeah."

"I see."

Even Cleo hadn't texted me after that Sunday. I'm glad to hear she didn't kill him yet.

"Can we talk in my office?"

"All right."

I walked in front of him, hoping he'd touch me, but he didn't. I opened the door and he went in first. When I was inside, he shut the door behind me.

"Aren't you and Clark now together?"

"Nope."

"What do you mean *no*?" Nathan grabbed my shoulder twisting me toward him.

"He said he needed space to figure his shit out. He hasn't tried to contact me."

"Fucking fool. Did you call him or text him?"

"No."

"But you want to, right?"

"I don't know what I want anymore, Nathan."

"I know what I want right now."

Nathan kissed me, pushing us back toward his desk. His hands gripped my waist hard and ground his hardening groin against me. My hands went everywhere. I held on to his face, his hair, his chest. I thought I could be strong and fight the yearning. I was wrong.

He popped me onto his desk to get closer. I yanked

up my skirt and wrapped my left leg around his waist. I could feel him hot and ready through his suit pants. I needed skin on skin. I had to feel him against me. I ripped at his belt and pants. Nathan pushed at my shirt and alas the top button gave.

"Take your panties off," he said.

I scooted the cotton off, and his fingers were there where I craved them the most. I watched his plunging hand. It glistened with my pent up desire. I was aching for him to fuck me.

Nathan's hands left my body to undo his pants and they fell to the floor. I ripped at the buttons of my shirt. I didn't care. I wanted to feel him everywhere.

"Lie back, baby."

It killed me to hear "baby," but I pushed it aside. Nathan pulled my legs up anchoring my heels on the edge of the desk. I didn't expect him to drop to his knees and crush his mouth on my bared pussy. I cried out. He blew air on my wetness shushing my cries. My legs opened wide, and he licked me fast and hard. He thrust two fingers inside my shuddering body.

"Fuck, I missed your taste."

"Please, Nathan."

Nathan licked my pussy up and down, side to side, and then stabbed deep. His mouth felt utterly amazing lapping up my flesh. He removed his fingers and spread my pussy wide exposing my clit to his tongue.

I was so aroused; I felt it in the back of my throat. I wanted to savor this moment, let my body ride it out, but there was no time. He gave me everything he got and then some; I fell for it all.

"Do you want to come on my mouth, Bri? I wanted to fuck you in this office since day one."

Only moans and gasps escaped my mouth. I nodded, and Nathan went back to fucking my pussy with his mouth. His tenderness fleeted. His sloppy licks and pinching fingers did me in.

My orgasm radiated out from my clit and reached deep inside. I slammed my hand over my mouth to muffle my satisfying groan.

Nathan let go of my lower body and stood up. He yanked his boxers down.

"Do you want me?" Nathan asked.

"I want you so bad."

He pushed his cock into my pussy. He thrust lightly at first, and then fucked me hard. I wanted him inside me every second he could.

I clawed at his hips, wanting him deeper. He gave me exactly what I needed. My legs were spread so wide it hurt, but I didn't care. We kissed and tore our lips away from each other to watch Nathan thrusting inside me.

We panted and begged each other for our releases. I needed to kiss him again. If this was our last time, I wanted to feel everything I could.

He gathered me into his arms and pulled me off the desk. My legs wrapped around him and my back hit the door. His hands flipped to my ass, and he brought me down onto his cock. I felt his full length deep inside. Each thrust was laced with pleasure.

I was coming within a minute. I scrambled for his lips. I grabbed both sides of his face and crushed him to my face. If I kissed him hard enough, we'd become one person and he wouldn't leave.

He tore his mouth from mine and shouted. He thrust one last time and held himself inside me. I didn't feel him come, but I felt the tremors after.

Slowly, Nathan brought us down to the carpeted floor. He didn't leave my body but held me tight against him. He peered at my face. His usual dazed look was one of sorrow.

"Bri, I love you. I'm so sorry. I fucked up so badly." He rested his forehead on mine. "Please forgive me, baby. Please."

My heart beat around pieces of its former self. Forgiveness I could give, but it wouldn't correct the current course.

"I forgive you, but it doesn't change anything."

"I don't want to cut you out of my life," Nathan murmured against my mouth.

"Nathan, you'll be too far away. It isn't going to work."

"Fuck distance. I'll come back when I can. I want to be able to see you."

"We can still know each other."

"But we won't have this," he admitted, looking down where our bodies were joined.

His cock was soft inside me now. I sat up and he fell out of me. Nathan pulled up his boxers. I stood up and grabbed my underwear off the floor. "Bri."

"Nathan, you can't change the inevitable."

"Come with me. We can do this together."

Even now, my mind fixated on every reason not to go. I'd be leaving my entire world behind. My parents, my job, my grandma's apartment; everything that made my world would be so far away. And Clark. *Fucking Clark.*

I wanted to propel myself into Nathan's arms and off into the sunset we'd go. *Not this time around.*

Nathan wrapped his arms around me from behind. "Nathan. I'm sorry."

"It's okay, Bri. I'm sorry too."

He turned me in his arms, and I cried. He kissed the top of my head and sniffled along with me.

We were done. The closure calmed me, though I knew it would take more time to minimize the sting. The distance would help. *An added fucked bonus I guess.*

## Chapter Forty-Eight

The half hour drive to Nathan's apartment wasn't enough to control my nerves. I sat outside a good fifteen minutes until the doorman ratted me out.

Nathan met me at the elevator. "You came?"

"I promised I would. I got you a present." I handed him a case of energy drinks.

"Ha-ha. I'm going to need them."

When I entered the apartment, all of Nathan's things were packed in boxes; only Clark's stuff remained. Amora swished her backside against my leg. I picked up my little buffer and self-soothed, petting her like crazy. She got the hint and jumped down. "Traitor."

A door shut down the hall, and I hoped to see Clark. My fleeting hope vanished when the younger version of Nathan barreled down the hallway. "That's the last of it, bro."

"Awesome. Put it down there." Nathan pointed to the pile by the door.

Nathan's brother followed the instructions and then outstretched his hand to me. "Hey, I'm Will, Nathan's brother. You must be Bri." A duplicate of Nathan's million-dollar smile beamed at me.

"Hi, Will. It's nice to meet you. Congrats on becoming a dad soon!"

"Thank you. One more month to go!" He held up

his crossed fingers.

"That's so cool!"

"Yeah! We are so excited. Hey, Nathan, she got your favorite!" Will turned around and Nathan bounced up on his heels. Will also knew Nathan's impatient signal.

"I'm going to go bring these to the car."

"Thanks, bud," Nathan said patting his brother on the back.

Silently, we watched Will pick up two boxes and head out the door.

"Hi," Nathan said.

"Hi," I responded back.

We both opened our mouths to talk, but I managed to squeak out something first.

"Is Clark coming?"

Nathan pursed his lips and shook his head.

"Have you heard from him?" I continued.

He nodded. "We had to talk. He couldn't avoid me forever."

"And?"

The little lightness I brought Nathan faded. "I wish I could tell you we kissed and made up, but I can't. He has every right to be mad at me. I did the one thing I told him I would never do." Nathan sat down on the floor and leaned against the wall.

My mind couldn't switch him over to a friend. The yearning to soothe him overcame everything. I sat down next him.

We scooted closer together. "You should call him," Nathan said.

"I'm afraid he'll push me away," I admitted.

"He won't this time. Trust me."

I sighed. I wanted to believe him. *If Clark pushes me away again, I don't know what I would do.*

"I don't know."

"Come on, Bri. You love Clark, and he fell in love with you." Nathan sighed. "He's waiting for you."

I leaned my head on Nathan's shoulder. I admired his humility in the situation. He broke us up, and now he tried to save the most unexpected part. He curled his arm around my shoulder, squeezing me into his side. "Please call him, Bri. Promise me."

"I will," I said.

"Good. He needs you. You can do this, baby."

I nodded. It must have been hard to try to convince your ex-girlfriend to call your ex-boyfriend. He did it, though. He made it through.

Will knocked on the door and peeked his head into the room. "Is the coast clear?"

"You told him?" I shouted.

Nathan fake smiled bearing all his teeth. "Maybe? Don't hit me." I playfully elbowed him in stomach and laughed.

Nathan stood up and reached a hand down to me, pulling me up. I helped them pack up a few more things. I picked up my pink mug, but Nathan grabbed it. He shrugged and said, "For when you visit me." I smiled and hugged him.

"I think that's the last of it," Will said.

Nathan winced at his brother's words. I didn't believe him either.

"Clark has practice until six, then he should come home. Are you going to stay?"

"No, not today."

"Bri." Nathan cocked his head to side.

"I'll talk to him. I need a little more time."

"Okay."

"Let me know when you get home."

"I will. Goodbye, Bri."

"Goodbye, Nathan."

We kissed one last time, and he got into his car.

"Hey, Bri. Call me sometime this week after you talk to Paul. I left a surprise for you."

"You did?"

"Merry Christmas."

He waved one more time before he drove onto the road. It was anticlimactic in the worse way.

*Monday was going to fucking suck.*

# Chapter Forty-Nine

Monday fucking sucked, then Tuesday followed. My mind hurt from working so hard. My daily routine was completely wrecked by the absence of Nathan. I flipped flopped between sadness and anger. I went back to doing everything alone. I lost my shadow; my dreamy shadow.

I went to lunch alone and came back. I took the elevator now. There was no need to drag out the time I used to get with Nathan.

My solar dancers danced to a beat I'm sure Clark was playing somewhere, drowning his sorrow in his music. Maybe I should make some cupcakes. Drown my depression in vanilla frosted overindulgence.

The email calendar dinged reminding me of a meeting in ten minutes. Luckily, no surprise guests sneaked in under the radar. I knew every name in the collapsed group of email addresses. No NR's to fuck it up.

I opened my overhead cabinet and grabbed the aspirin bottle. I had skipped breakfast three days in a row and my stomach and head joined forces in bringing me down hard. *The throbbing pain at my temples wouldn't go away.*

I knocked back two aspirins with water, hoping for some relief. I almost welcomed a lovely dose of anxiety to rage through me, but even that abandoned me.

Paul came around my cubicle wall and waved in my peripheral getting my attention. I hadn't been jumpy in what seemed like forever.

"Are you doing okay, kiddo?" Paul asked, looking concerned.

I nodded. My rants begged me for silence. I wouldn't release them again today. The same rumination spilling out over and over again attempting to say it differently, hoping someone heard something I missed.

"That's good to hear. Breakups are always hard. I'm sorry this happened to you."

I smiled at his kind words. He tried as much as he could to pull me out the funk.

"Let's get coffee and go to the meeting," Paul said.

"Okay," I agreed.

He continued talking, reviewing our meeting prep about another new account. I would start the preliminary demographics next week. I thanked him for putting me on the account.

"You won't be a team member for this one. It's yours, Bri. You will be the team leader. It's yours to delegate the responsibilities."

It took me a second to absorb exactly what Paul had said. The senior analysts lead the teams. I wasn't a senior analyst yet.

"I'm sorry, Paul. Did I miss something? I can't lead the project."

"Of course you can. We don't have a senior analyst left in the department, and a certain someone recommended one of the best analysts he knew, and with a little help from me, the right woman will be assigned the job."

"Are you seriously telling me that I'm getting a promotion?"

He smiled and broke every work etiquette rule by hugging me. It was the most awkward hug I'd ever received in my life, but holy shit I got a promotion! I wanted to jump and scream and buy everyone a potted plant I was so fucking happy!

"I can't believe it!"

"Believe it, Bri. You're an amazing part of my team, and without you we never would have landed the Traill Account. I'm so proud of you."

I cried tears I had wanted to cry for years. Finally, I was getting somewhere, and people recognized my hard work.

"No, shoot, please don't cry! This is supposed to good. Please be happy." A panicked Paul thrust napkins into my hands.

"It's okay. These are happy tears! This is so amazing." I dabbed under my eyes. My mascara must be everywhere.

"I wasn't supposed to tell you until the meeting, but I couldn't wait any longer. I thought you might want some good news," Paul said.

"I can't even begin to describe how happy I am. Wow."

"It's a lot more work, maybe some travel. We can move you into Nathan's old office right after the meeting."

*This is why you don't have sex in your office because then you get an amazing promotion and are forced to move into the office you fucking had sex in.* I knew somehow someway it would bite me in the ass. Fuck it. This was too good a day. I'd worry about it later.

"I accept the promotion," I said it loud and proud.

"Shhh…You're not supposed to know for another half hour." Paul laughed and shushed me.

"Ah, you suck. I'll keep quiet. I'm not going to stop smiling though!"

"Good. See you in a little bit." Paul touched the side of my shoulder and smiled.

I tried to hide my excitement in the opening speeches of the meeting. It wasn't working so well. Lucy poked me, mouthing "what's up?" I shrugged and stuck my tongue out at her. She cocked her head to the side. "Did you hear from the boys?" Lucy whispered.

"Nope. Better."

James ended the company overview, and Paul walked up to the podium.

"Thank you, James. We have an important announcement. Grant Industries now has its biggest client, Traill Associates, thanks to our own Brianna Owens and Nathan Richards. Let's have a round of applause for Bri." The room clapped.

"Unfortunately, Mr. Richards could not be with us today because he is now the senior marketing director for Traill Associates. I will let him know we wish him the best and have high hopes to continue our professional relationship with him and the rest of the Traill staff.

"Now on to the most important part. Brianna will be our new in-house senior marketing analyst. Bri, do you accept the promotion?"

"Yes! Absolutely!"

The heat went up to my face, but I held back more tears of joy. Everyone clapped, even Marcia to my right.

"Thank you so much, everyone! This is a shock."

"You deserve it, Bri. Mr. Grant had been eyeing you for a promotion for a while now. With Nathan's position open, you are the logical and perfect fit," Paul explained.

My lip quivered. I never handled these types of events well. My first reaction was always to cry. Then Lucy hugged me. I couldn't hold back the tears any longer.

"That's a wrap, ladies and gentleman. Bri, come with me."

I followed Paul and Lucy back to my new office. It was exactly how Nathan left it. Paul coughed behind me. "It might have been premature to assume you'd say yes to the promotion, but I got you something."

Paul pulled from behind his back a new sign for the door engraved with my name and new title. We never had one made for Nathan. He was always supposed to be temporary. But this wasn't. This was real.

I hugged Paul again and made sure to ruffle his feathers. I was just too happy. Lucy teared up as well when Paul left us to our jumping up and down glory.

"I can't believe it. I just can't."

"Believe it, Bri. This was a long time coming. Drinks on me?"

"Absolutely."

# Chapter Fifty

My aunt's two-story bungalow in the Poconos sprung to life when I flipped on the dormant power grid. Electricity buzzed, welcoming me home. I loved it here. The quiet always rejuvenated my spirit.

Today was different. It was New Year's Eve and I tried desperately to build up my strength in case he didn't come. There were so many devastating ways to crumble the hope into despair or it could turn out exactly how I planned it.

I wheeled my suitcase into the spare room I claimed as my own years ago. The house had three bedrooms, but no one ever picked this one, except me. It was mine.

I put my clothes into the drawer and lay down on the dusty bed.

It was time to wait for him.

A car drove up the pebbled stone driveway. Someone was here. The boys had done wonders for my self-confidence, but it was far from my brain right now.

The car door closed, and someone knocked on the front door.

I knew who it would be, but panic took over. This could be the start of something wonderful, fresh, and new. I just had to make my fucking feet work.

He knocked again and snapped me out of myself. I unlocked the latch and opened the door. Clark stood there with flowers in his hand. His hair was greenish blonde for his new band tour starting next week. He jerked open the screen door beyond its reach and crushed his lips against mine.

I yelped into his mouth. I missed his kiss so much, his all-consuming lips asking for it all.

He pushed me back into the tiny house. Clark's hands roamed over me, grabbing at my face, skimming my breasts, and latched onto my waist.

"Oh, Clark, I missed you!"

"You have no idea how much I missed you. I missed you so much." He trailed kisses down my neck; anywhere there was exposed skin. "Are you mine, darling? I want to be yours. I've never wanted anything this bad."

"Yes, Clark. I'm only yours."

"I love you."

"I love you too."

We somehow made it to the bed. Clark clawed at my clothes, and I tugged off his shirt. We ripped our zippers down and removed our pants first. I didn't care if I was wet or not, I needed him to fuck me, possess me, anything to make me feel him lying here with me, starting our new chapter.

He nipped my bottom lip with his teeth and sucked it into his mouth. I peeled my panties down and rolled the edges of his boxers down his thighs. He tore them from his body, just as desperate as me.

I wrapped my hand around his cock. He moaned into my mouth and pushed my hand away. His hands spread my legs wide, and he entered me.

"I'll never leave you again. I love you so much," he said.

"I love you, Clark!"

****

After Clark made love to me for the second time in the New Year, I found myself wide awake. The blurry clock read three o'clock in the morning. This happened sometimes. When the world was asleep, my day restarted from minute one analyzing all the imperfections. This time I had relief and love to mull over.

I found my smudged glasses on the floor. We must have knocked them off the table during round one. I cleaned the lenses with the mesh from my red and black teddy Clark liked so much.

Clark lay on his stomach facing toward the wall. He's sleeping away, snoring every few moments. I had to smile. He's mine. All mine. I had been so afraid he'd ignore me when I called him two days ago. *I should have known better.*

I tiptoed through the bedroom and the trail of clothes we left behind. I'm shocked we got to the bed.

The lights were still on throughout the main floor. Dillon was curled up on the couch. His feet dangled off the open edge of it. Cleo must be upstairs in my aunt's bedroom. *I still can't believe they kissed at midnight.* I was so happy they could join us tonight.

I shut off the lights throughout the house. My phone buzzed somewhere in the room. The soft sound tinged again. I found my phone on the coffee table next to the three empty champagne bottles.

I had expected a response from my text to Nathan. He made me promise I would text him Happy New Year, but all I had was the read notification at twelve fifteen a.m.

There were tons of likes from the pictures we took before. There even was a like from Nathan on the picture where Clark kissed me to death.

I thought about texting him again, but I decided against it. *Maybe it will be better this way. I hope he's okay. I hope we'll all be okay.*

My bedroom was cold, even with the heat rattling away. We were missing Nathan's heat. I tucked myself back into the nook of Clark's body. His hand found mine, and he pulled me back further into him.

"I can't wait to spend every day of this year with you, darling."

"Me too, Clark. Me too."

## Chapter Fifty-One
*Nathan*

Everything was cold up here. The beer was cold. The fucking bar was cold. My heart was cold.

Her body was always warm. Our kisses and her smile scorched every part of my being. He was always hot. The turbulent boiling he surged in my brain rewrote every step I made since the first time.

"Another beer before the new year?" The bartender asked.

"No, thank you," I answered.

The party raged on. A band without Clark played on stage. My ears hurt to listen.

At their break, the countdown started. The ball dropped down on the big screen. The new year started. My brother kissed his fiancée and got down on his knees to kiss her pregnant belly. *Lucky fucker.*

They walked over to me. I wanted to smile. It was the appropriate reaction. Part of my face cooperated.

"Happy New Year, Nathan!" Lee and Will shouted.

"Happy New Year," I forced myself to say. I leaned down and kissed Lee's cheek. Even her cheek was cold. I removed my suit jacket and draped it over Lee's shoulders. She shouldn't be cold like me.

Couples danced to the heavily distorted music suffocating the party room. A pretty girl waltzed up to me, laying it on strong. I excused myself as politely as I could. She did nothing wrong. She saw what everyone thought they saw looking at me tonight. A single man getting drunk at his brother's party scanning the crowd for the first mistake of the New Year. None of it was true.

I walked through the silver streamers leading toward the main entrance. The bouncer checked my hand for the stupid re-entry stamp. "Yeah, I'll be back," I shouted over the music.

There was a wraparound porch to this old bar and grill. Every floorboard creaked under me. I sat down on a high-top table furthest from the door, away from the drunk, happy people. My phone beeped in my pocket. I already knew whom it was from. She promised me she would text and call.

*-Happy New Year Nathan! We wish you were here. Love Bri.-*

She would see the "Read" notification by now. I scrolled through her social media. I found the picture I should be in. Bri, Clark, Cleo, and Dillon smiled at the camera, saying cheese. The next one hurt more. Clark held up the camera and kissed Bri like his life depended on it. My hand twitched on the screen, and the little red heart lit up.

"Fuck." I hadn't meant to do that.

"Hey, Nathan!" Will walked over to me. "We were looking everywhere for you." I glanced up, but God knew what he saw staring back at him now. "Are you okay? Bro, you're shaking."

My phone slipped out of my hand and hit the metal table leg in the perfect spot to crack the old screen. Before I could pick up the fucking thing, I jumped off the stool and threw up over the edge of the railing until the snow below was stained with my gross yellow bile.

Will tried to console me, rubbing my back, blaming everything under the sun for my sickness except the truth. I sat down and looked up at my sympathetic brother.

"Will, stop. It's none of that shit." My throat burned and I coughed up more stomach acid.

"You sure?"

"I'm positive. I just made the biggest mistake of my fucking life."

*Yeah, I really fucking did.*

## About the Author

I'm a marketing analyst by day, writer by night. I've always wanted to pursue this passion of mine and finally had the guts to do it. I've lived outside of New York City my entire life, and it will be always be home. I live with my husband, two kitties, and our son on the way.

~*~

Visit Melanie at
https://tootsplusdill.blogspot.com

~*~

To chat with Melanie Hoffer and other Wild Rose Press authors of erotic romance, join us at www.groups.yahoo.com/group/thewilderroses.

Also Available
from The Wild Rose Press, Inc.
and major retailers.

# Ella's Triple Pleasure

*Sinfully Hers*

## By Anna Lores

It takes three men to satisfy one woman's needs…

Single mom and massage therapist Ella Winthrop isn't looking for a relationship. She has enough problems without risking a business that barely meets her needs. Then her world is turned upside down by three men, each offering something she isn't prepared for—love so deep it hurts, sex so hot she's afraid she'll melt from the pleasure, and a future beyond her wildest dreams.

Steamy businessman Cade Jackson has it all—money, looks, a giving heart, and a dominant nature—but Ella refuses to date a client even if she's lusted after him for a year. After his brother's death, Garrett Winthrop moves back to town opening old wounds and even darker fantasies. Dr. Derek McGregor gives her balance and understanding that speaks to her soul. All three men force Ella to question the limits of a traditional relationship.

Also Available
from The Wild Rose Press, Inc.
and major retailers.

# Theirs to Protect

## By Melissa Klein

College student Claire Matthews has panty-melting fantasies about her roommates but can’t imagine choosing just one. But when her rapist is released from prison, she knows it’s time to disappear—again. First, she needs a memory of the duo to take with her.

Firefighter Sean Dalton is mind-blown when Claire suggests a threesome. Watching her kiss his friend under the mistletoe is a turn-on. Being asked to share is like gasoline on the spark of desire. He’s shared a woman before, but he’s been crushing on his sexy roomie since she moved in. He’s not about to say no.

Chicago police officer Max Devon isn’t new to the ménage scene, but he knows Sean has a thing for Claire and he won’t be the third wheel again. Been there, done that, has the scars to prove it. Still, he’s not immune to Claire’s charms. He’ll play her game, but only if he’s in charge. Then he'll know when it’s time to withdraw from the relationship.

A night of blazing passion leads to more than one discovery. Sean is caught off guard by his feelings for Max, Max struggles to keep his distance from both his roommates, and Claire must make a choice—flee or stay. Trusting these two strong men with her heart and her life means endangering them and giving in to the belief she is theirs to protect.

Thank you for purchasing
this publication of The Wild Rose Press, Inc.

For questions or more
information contact us at
info@thewildrosepress.com.

The Wild Rose Press, Inc.
www.thewildrosepress.com

To visit with authors of
The Wild Rose Press, Inc.
join our yahoo loop at
http://groups.yahoo.com/group/thewildrosepress/

CPSIA information can be obtained
at www.ICGtesting.com
Printed in the USA
BVHW092013060822
643973BV00008B/735